The

FALSE
FLAT

Melissa R. Collings

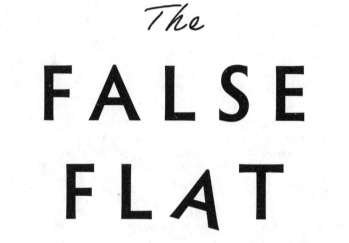

The

FALSE
FLAT

Montlake

Published by Montlake, Seattle

www.apub.com

Amazon, the Amazon logo, and Montlake are trademarks of Amazon.com, Inc., or its affiliates.

ISBN-13: 9781662521201 (paperback)
ISBN-13: 9781662521218 (digital)

Cover design by Ploy Siripant
Cover image: © Rushikanth, © KVASVECTOR, © Carboxylase, © Cosmic_Design / Shutterstock

Printed in the United States of America

To David, with my greatest thanks; this story wouldn't exist without you

The grief that does not speak whispers the
o'erfraught heart and bids it break.
—William Shakespeare, *Macbeth*

False flat (a cycling term):

Noun

1. a road that appears delightfully flat and straightforward but in reality is a low-gradient climb that wears a rider out
2. a hill lying in wait
3. a metaphor for Penelope Auberge's life
4. "Your eyes tell you it's flat. Your heart hopes it's flat. But your legs and lungs feel the truth."
—Grant Miles

5, 4, 3, 2, CHAPTER 1

Life was easier when you pretended people were numbers. I didn't mean it in the typical way people mean this, like a faceless corporation with too many employees. Not a rating system either. I meant literal numbers: hard-edged, perfectly sequenced, constant, definable *números*. People had too many crevices, too many preferences, too many irritating qualities. People couldn't be easily divided, added, or subtracted. Numbers were straightforward, uncomplicated—at least for me—even the decimal points: *especially* the decimal points.

That's why I assigned nearly everyone I met a number. It had nothing to do with how attractive they were, their socioeconomic status, or their age. It was mostly decided based on their personality or the feeling they elicited when I was around them, occasionally their shape. It was a coping mechanism that had started at fifteen, when I saw a little girl conversing with the numbers she'd drawn on a piece of paper in a therapist's office. My robotic mother had ripped me from the waiting room, insisting I didn't need therapy. So, I hadn't had it, but I'd kept the numbers.

I rubbed my hands together to warm them, then secured my bicycle to the rack located in front of the law firm next door to Twin Cities Financial, my office building in downtown Minnesota. Several people used the rack, but I felt particularly entitled because my boyfriend was an aspiring partner at Simon, Crusler, and Bach. I pulled my high heels out of my backpack and clipped down the sidewalk, past the gold-handled front doors where thousands—no, millions—of dollars walked through every single day. More numbers. The best kind of numbers, the kind with decimal points. Money.

I slipped into the elevator and turned in time to see Lynn, a perky number eight from the marketing department in my office, running for the door, way too excited to see me. I eyed the gleaming side panel and contemplated pushing the "Door Close" button, but the smile under her expertly applied lipstick made me feel guilty. She meant well. I jabbed my finger into "Door Open" and forced my lips upward, a maneuver that made me feel plastic.

Smiling was ridiculous. It looked nice on Lynn, the perfect complement to the pencil skirt currently hugging the lower circle of her eight-ness, but a smile always seemed wrong on my face. If the corners of my mouth stretched too far, it was entirely possible my cheeks would crack and fall onto the elevator floor.

"Penelope! Hi!" Lynn cooed, shifting into the elevator, her red coat slung over her arm. Everyone—except my mother, and apparently Lynn—called me Pen. That sweet-as-sugar tone . . . I knew exactly what she'd talk about next—her most recent email. I could feel it. The polite request that would be posed as a question but really was a demand for me to do something utterly outrageous.

I should've pressed "Door Close."

I pulled my wind-resistant trench coat around me like a shield. "Hi, Lynn." This elevator was too slow and too small. I should've called maintenance, had a discussion about how *slow* and small the elevator was, which was surely a code violation.

"How has your week been?" She drew out the words, practically singing them.

Instead of contemplating ways I could hoist myself through the trapdoor at the top of this too-tiny box to avoid the inevitable, I concentrated on her assigned number. Eight. This wasn't human Lynn with ulterior motives to find out more about my personal life. It was a congenial number eight. (Because if the number eight were a human, it would be congenial—a delight—most of the time.)

"It's been great," I said, desperate to think of another word or several more words to keep the eight from detouring to the email.

I watched the electronic number at the top of the wall, changing like molasses as the box moved through space like it was on a sightseeing tour.

This elevator!

I took a breath.

"I haven't heard from you about this weekend. Are you coming to the dinner?" There it was. We'd made it to the fourth floor, our floor, and I'd failed. All I'd had to do was ask her about *her* week or where she'd bought her skirt—the woman knew how to dress—or mention my really good business news. But I'd panicked at the possibility of her asking exactly this, giving her the opportunity to ask . . . exactly this.

The doors finally opened, and I squeezed through them before there was room to exit. Lynn followed me. Why was she following me? Right, she worked here.

This weekend. Not a client dinner, which I never missed, but a company-wide family *gathering* where people would talk about gardening or football or the million other activities they had outside work, which I did not have and could not relate to.

Four weeks ago, when the event had seemed fictional, I'd told Lynn, "Sure! Count me in." I'd even waved my hand like I'd bring the potato salad. But when she'd sent her follow-up email, I'd smelled the burgers on the grill, felt the wind from the passing Frisbee—did people play Frisbee?—and I'd deleted the email. The last thing I needed was for my coworkers, who respected my job acumen, to see my *questionable* performance at interacting with other humans in a nonwork capacity.

I adjusted my bag on my shoulder. "What are you talking about? What email?"

She hadn't mentioned the email, had she?

She crossed her arms and stood in front of me, a demanding marketing professional's stance and stare. She was going to get what she wanted.

"It's just the office and their families," she assured me. "Really casual. Everyone's anxious to get to know the Pen Auberge under all the fancy clothes and spreadsheets."

My face was doing that cracking thing again. "I'll be there," I heard myself say.

Thankfully, she walked down the hall. I turned in to my office and dropped my bag and helmet by my desk.

I needed to forget about Lynn. Today was my day. In about five seconds, I'd walk through Houston McGregor's door and be lavished with congratulations. I smoothed my hair in front of his door. I'd risked helmet hair even after I'd freshly straightened my unruly curls, because riding was my medicine, something I needed a dose of every day.

"Pen," Houston's secretary said.

I turned toward Erin, who was chewing on a pen. I wasn't sure if she was calling my name or talking to the writing implement. She opened her mouth, then shook her head as if I should disregard her sudden outburst.

I turned back to the door. I didn't want whatever had caused her look of concern to ruin this moment.

I knocked, and Houston bellowed, "Come in!" As I stepped into his office, I was hit with the cloying scent that is Houston McGregor, the kind of stench only a man utterly in control and with an obscene income could get away with. His neck fat shook over the top of his collar, part of the overpriced suit that looked like it was trying to eat him. "Good morning, Pen. Good news."

He gestured to the maroon leather chairs opposite his shiny executive desk—complete with a gold-embossed lion's head on the front—and crossed his Italian loafers on said desk. This was why finance people got a bad rap, but I focused on Houston's more charming qualities, namely his "Good news" comment.

"My clients signed," I affirmed, ignoring how my throat wanted to close at the concentrated cologne in this room. How did he function in here? He needed to open a window. He needed a good scrub with unscented soap. I needed to stop. This wasn't about his cologne or how near to passing out I was because of it. My clients had signed.

Six months earlier, I'd decided to go from financial analyst to financial planner. CFA to CFP, a move from behind the scenes to in front of them. Some saw the transition as a step down. I saw it as conditioning. Because, while I exceled in business, I did *not* excel in personal relationships. It's not that I wanted to be cold, but at twelve, I'd lost my brother, my best friend, the *one* person who understood me and my (our) biracial struggles. And when the people I should've been able to turn to weren't there, I built up a shell and latched on to what I was good at, my distraction. Yep, my numbers.

So why the recent job change? Aurora Auberge (my mother) had turned her (well-meaning) attention on me because my dad had died, and she needed someone else's life to hyperfocus on. I quickly saw that *I* needed other people in my life, real social engagements, a.k.a. excuses. So it made good sense to me that if I wanted to start making those personal relationships, and chipping away at that twenty-year-old shell, then I should interact with people in an arena in which I was most comfortable.

When I was talking estate planning or finance, I was completely at ease. Apparently, I was pretty good at interacting with finicky, opinionated people, as long as my precious numbers were there as a buffer. Which was why I was standing in this migraine-inducing office. I'd schmoozed a whopper of a client. Not only were the Fletchers a high net worth catch, but they promised generational wealth. If I played my cards right, I'd not only add the Fletchers to my book, but I'd manage the massive wealth that came with their extended family. Mrs. Fletcher was a fashionista, and, much to her delighted surprise, I'd worn shoes by her favorite designer to a multiclient dinner meeting, which had instantly connected us. Though, secrets revealed, I'd known this tidbit of information thanks to Chad, my observant lawyer boyfriend, who'd dined at the Fletchers' home several days before and had witnessed the shoe delivery.

Life was all about connections. It's who you know.

"Yes," Houston replied. "You did a good job."

I beamed. Actual light was probably coming out of my ears.

I opened my mouth to reply, but he wasn't finished. "A great job indeed, but I'm putting the Fletchers on Tyler's book. You two worked together on this, and he needs the victory more than *you* do." His condescending gaze slid down my face and back up, making me wonder if this was a race thing or a gender thing. But I didn't think Houston even realized I was biracial because he'd made a comment about a Black client that bordered on racist several months back in front of me. He might've been arrogant, but he wasn't the type to make that kind of mistake.

I blinked.

I coughed.

I asked him to repeat himself.

He repeated the same words. *The same words.*

He was giving *my* client to the new guy I'd been training for the past month?

This wasn't happening. This couldn't be happening. Was this happening . . . again? I looked around the room, but for what? A pair of scissors to cut off the tie that must've been restricting the blood flow to his brain?

Weeks ago, I'd worked hard to win a modestly funded client, the Herberts, and when they'd signed, I was informed that Dougan—I know, ridiculous, but that was his name—would be adding the client to *his* book. I was frustrated then, but Houston had assured me it would only be this once and that Dougan had initiated the relationship with the Herberts, so the clients were rightfully his. It didn't seem fair, but I'd let it slide.

The *Fletchers* had been initiated by me, through Chad, who'd made the introduction when he'd heard they were looking to invest their funds.

The Fletchers were *mine*.

"No." My whole body shook.

He smiled, like the word was a fly, irritating but easily eradicated.

"I'm sorry. Decision's been made. You're good at this. Your next one will be worth even more."

"And who will you give that one to, Houston? The janitor?"

"Come on. You know these things are complicated. It has nothing to do with you personally." There it was again, that sweep, almost imperceptible this time, that assured me that it most certainly *was* personal. And he was trying to sweet-talk me. I struggled to control my breathing. My fingernails dug into my palms.

"Pen, Pen, Pen, don't get worked up. You know you're my gal."

His gal? His. So it *was* a gender thing then, confirmed by his unconcealed eye drop to my chest.

I buttoned my blouse all the way up to the collar. It felt ridiculous, but I didn't care; I was proving a point. Then, I splayed my hands on his desk and leaned in, coming close to touching the eggplant posing as a nose in the center of his bulbous face.

"The Fletchers are my clients. Tyler was on the sidelines for this. I was lead. I'm not going to let you do this. Do they know? Did you tell them you're handing them off to an inexperienced new guy?"

"Tyler's not inexperienced. He's been a planner for nearly as long as you have."

Choked disgust flew out of my mouth in a sound that was half scoff and half growl. "I've been an analyst for *years*. He was an adviser."

"Then you agree: he's got more people experience."

"Fuck you." I shouldn't have said it, but, I mean, seriously, how could I not? He deserved it. He deserved a lot more.

"For your sake, I'm going to pretend I didn't hear that." He stood, adjusted the dark-gray flap of his jacket across his gut, and sauntered over to me, then wrapped his arm around my shoulders and leaned in. "Now, suck it up and go grab us another client because, between you and me, you've got something they don't have."

"Breasts?" I jerked away from him and stomped back to my office. From the hallway, I heard Houston call out, "We're team players around here, Pen. You'd be wise to remember that."

I should've been praised for my restraint.

I did not slam my door. I did not run outside and slash his tires.

A soft knock interrupted me midfume.

I said nothing, but the person came in anyway. Erin, Houston's secretary, stepped into my office and closed the door.

"I'm really sorry." She sat in one of the so-purple-it-might-as-well-be-black chairs across from my desk.

"You knew?"

"I heard them talking yesterday. It's not right."

"No, it isn't." My anger was morphing into anxiety.

"When I get back from Nashville, I'm going to do everything I can to find you someone else. I wouldn't go, but I've got to help clean my grandparents' house *in Nashville*. We're selling it because they're moving into an assisted living facility."

As Erin detailed her trip, likely feeling the need to further explain why she wasn't dropping everything to support me—she wanted to climb the corporate ladder—I stared out my crystal clear, single-paned office window. In the parking lot of the building next door, an extremely fit woman in a hot-pink yoga outfit and matching earbuds stood on tiptoe and kissed a tall, brawny man in a suit that screamed "high-priced lawyer."

My chest started to hurt as the anxiety made its way up my body, like a disembodied hand clutching at my windpipe. I didn't want Erin to see me have a panic attack, so I tried hard to focus on what she was saying. Her grandparents' old house, the Nashville market, the boyfriend she'd moved to Minnesota for, how much cleaning she was going to have to do, how many repairs.

But my eyes strayed back to the couple, the woman reaching up to touch the man's clean-shaven face, her finger tracing his jawline.

My phone pinged. I tore my gaze from the window long enough to see who the text was from. My mother. It didn't even matter what the text said. The fact that it existed on my phone, along with everything else now crashing over me, made the thin threads of an idea knit themselves together: *escape.*

I looked back at the couple. "I want it."

Erin paused, confusion scrunching her features. "You want what?"

My eyes remained laser focused on the public display of affection outside my window, something I would never do.

"I want your grandparents' house. You don't have to worry about cleaning it or repairing it."

I was minutes away from putting my head between my legs. I needed the comfort of my bicycle before I broke in front of this woman and ruined my reputation.

"You can't be—"

I held up a hand. "I've never been more serious about anything in my life." It was so much more than her grandparents' house. It was freedom from a life that was suddenly suffocating. A career shift wasn't enough change. I'd been kidding myself, distracting myself from what was really going on with me.

I stood, kicked off my heels, and shoved my feet into my sneakers, my heartbeat whirring in my ears. Then I grabbed my helmet as Erin repeated the word "but" over and over again.

"Listen, Erin." *Whir. Whir. Whir.* "I've got to . . ." *Whir. Whir. Whir.*

Was I still speaking? I swallowed and glanced at the couple one last time, then looked in Erin's direction, avoiding eye contact for fear that would be the last straw. At the sound of another ping from my phone, the whirring turned into a helicopter, and my vision tunneled.

"Gotta go. Want the house. Serious. Make it happen." I think that's what I said, at least, or something to that effect. I ran down the three flights of stairs and into the lobby, then pushed past a three on my way out the door. The three cursed.

My hands shook as I fumbled with the lock on my bicycle. The lock and key fell to the ground. I left them both. I needed to ride, and so I did, right past the PDA couple, past the high ponytail that swung back and forth as the woman teasingly turned her head, past the man who held her in his muscled arms, arms I knew well because they belonged to Chad, my boyfriend.

CHAPTER 2
THROW-DOWN ON AISLE FOUR

Two weeks passed in a blur, and Nashville wasn't at all what I'd expected. But given the whirlwind move, I hadn't had time to expect much. Age and a musty odor clung to every crevice of my new (very expensive) two-story house located in too-trendy-for-you East Nashville. But it was quaint, situated in a tree-lined, bikeable neighborhood with a sizable backyard, and it was five minutes from downtown (why it was so expensive). Its biggest selling point, though, was its distance from my life back in Minnesota. And it was mine.

The sun threatened to set as I stood in the part of the driveway that curved into the backyard and waited for the ancient door on the detached garage to ratchet upward. The cool (yet much warmer than Minnesota) late-March breeze fluttered the new leaves on the overgrown bush beside me. A bee hovered in midair, its hum merging with my stomach growls as we (the bee and I) scanned the property. The lawn was manicured, the wooden house slats freshly painted a midnight blue, and the flower beds around the perimeter of the house had a solid two inches of mulch. I could smell the cedar.

The house was like me, strong and stately on the outside, all but falling apart on the inside.

I maneuvered into the now-open garage, past all the unpacked boxes to my bicycle, my best friend, my *only* friend, and current chauffeur to the grocery store, because I needed Cap'n Crunch, the best cereal, and therefore dinner, on the planet. It made my soul sing. I yanked out my new bike, bumping my elbow against the handlebars in the process. As I rubbed my arm, I felt eyes on me.

When I looked up, sure enough, "The Nose" dropped a section of blinds on an upstairs window of the house next door. That woman watched every move I made without apology. I'd assigned her a number four—the kind that comes to a point on top, most resembling a nose—though we hadn't officially met. Erin had told me her real name was Mrs. Snoe, but until further notice, she'd remain "The Nose" to me, which wasn't the nicest title since I didn't know her, but I didn't like the feeling of being spied on in the only place I could let loose—home, which this wasn't yet.

I threw my long leg over my bicycle, and then my phone buzzed in my armband.

My knuckles blanched white on the handlebars because even without looking at the screen, I guessed it was Aurora. I'd hung up on her five minutes ago because she couldn't believe I'd walked out on my job and my boyfriend and *her*. She wanted me to come back.

"You don't even have a plan, Penelope!" she'd said, her voice stern but not shouting.

"I have a plan." I didn't, at least not a solid one. I was going to start my own business, now that I was out from under Houston's sexist thumb. But the idea was all I had. Her words gnawed at my intestines, made me doubt my ability to do this—without her, in a foreign place.

Aurora Auberge wasn't like other mothers. She didn't meddle in my thoughts and feelings. However, she *was* compelled to make my life sparkle. In Minnesota, she'd picked out my apartment because I'd previously been ready to "settle" for one that had a faulty closet door. Then she'd furnished it with all the "must-haves" for a high-powered woman in finance. That was how we had a relationship. I *let* her run certain aspects of my life. It was easier. And left to my own devices, I'd be a slob, at least in my homelife.

Our relationship, such as it was, came with an unspoken contract:

1. No feelings. Those had stopped after my brother / best friend died, and my mother responded by morphing into a combination of Stepford wife and corporate powerhouse.

2. No problems. Potential problems were polished, shined, put in an Armani suit, and fed a wholesome dinner someone else had cooked. The fact that my physician father had coped by becoming a cheating alcoholic wasn't a *problem*; it was a *task* for my mother to tend to.

3. Appearances mattered. If we looked fine, convinced everyone around us that we were fine, then we *were* fine. I sort of liked this one.

4. ABM. Always be moving. Downtime led to thinking. Thinking might lead to discovering problems, and since problems didn't exist in my mother's world, thinking too long was strictly prohibited.

As a child, I'd harbored resentment. As an adult, I harbored that same resentment, but I'd become accustomed to the unspoken contract. There was an odd comfort to our way of life. "Comfort" wasn't the right word. We were too rigid for that. "Predictability," maybe? That was it. Predictability held appeal. But now that my mother *only* had me to focus on, the attention was stifling.

I shoved my feet onto the pedals and moved like my life depended on it, flying by the overpriced houses along the street on my new Trek bicycle.

I shouldn't have spent the money on it, but my old bicycle was like a human who knew my previous life, so I'd given it away. But I didn't even have furniture. And while I had money because I knew how to multiply funds by a few clicks of my keyboard, that pool had been drained by this house. A bicycle was more important than furniture anyway.

I'd let the bouncy, fit guy at the bicycle store talk me into this one, partly because I didn't want to admit I had no idea what I was doing. People thought you were fit when you rode a bicycle, but I wasn't a typical cyclist. I didn't eat kale or fawn over microgreens.

Cycling was simply how I managed the rising panic, a discovery that had changed my life a few years ago.

My legs started burning as I turned the corner. A little white-haired lady smiled and waved as she walked her curly-haired brown dog down the sidewalk. The wind blew, taking some of my thoughts with it. I was pedaling on, very near able to pretend it was okay again, when a little ping indicated Aurora had left a voicemail. The first flares of a panic attack shot across my stomach, and I screeched to a stop, ripped the phone out of its pocket on my arm, nearly tearing the tiny stitches holding the extra flap of fabric in place, and stared at the screen.

Not my mother.

Chad.

He'd called at exactly the wrong time or exactly the right time, depending on who was asked. Because right then, I didn't want to hear his baritone voice, and I certainly didn't want to admit how the sound of it still slid around my body, settling inside me like a decadent cup of hot chocolate. And I wanted even less to hear what he had to say. I was moving on.

I made a mental note to pick up some packages of hot chocolate.

I deleted the voicemail without listening to it, smiled, and decided that if deleting one voicemail made me feel this good, then blocking his number should be orgasmic. Not that I wanted to have an orgasm on the side of the road in front of the new neighbors. Chad's hot breath cascaded down the side of my neck as he whispered, "Don't do it," and so, I did it. Illogical spite? Maybe. Whatever it was called, it made me feel better.

I found his name, scrolled to the bottom of his contact page, and saw three little delightfully red words: "Block this Caller." I didn't even hesitate to hit the button. Maybe I hesitated when the box warned me that I would no longer be receiving this handsome, cheating bastard's phone calls, messages, or FaceTimes, but the hesitation was brief. I needed him blocked from my life.

The words changed from an angry red "Block this Caller" to a soothing blue "Unblock this Caller." I secured my phone back into my armband, shoved my feet onto my pedals, and took off again as fast as my legs would move. When the wind whipped around me again, I imagined a cape flapping in the spring breeze behind me.

I'd ride away from Chad.

I'd ride away from my mother.

Hell, I'd ride away from all my problems, like usual.

∽

My stomach growled like a vicious animal as I rode into the Publix parking lot, secured my bicycle, and headed straight to the cereal aisle, unconcerned with my sweat-stained T-shirt. Kids' cereal wasn't a glamorous dinner choice for a thirty-two-year-old, successful (?) financial planner, but it kept me functional.

There he was, nestled between a box of bran flakes on one side and little heart-healthy circles on the other: the sexiest Cap'n I'd ever seen. I rolled my eyes at myself as I licked my lips. When had a *cartoon* man with a spoon in his hand incited such lust? I shrugged. Being Mrs. Crunch wasn't the worst thing, but what *was* the worst thing was the perky woman who also appeared to want to be Mrs. Crunch.

Nuh-uh. Not today. Not now. Not when there was only one box of the Crunch Berries kind left—the other options, the peanut butter, the plain pillows, the Oops! All Berries, weren't going to cut it. Not when my mother was annoying me, and Chad was calling, and I'd been looking forward to this treat for hours now. I was leaving on the arm of the Cap'n if I had to throw down on aisle four to make that happen. I towered over her, every inch of my six feet filled with an irritation her happy little face probably hadn't ever experienced.

I could take her.

We reached for the box at the same time, but the woman pulled short and put her hands on her hips. "Okay, how can you eat this and stay so fit?" she asked, a defiant grin on her face.

"You look fine," I said, the sole box of Crunch Berries held in my Momma's-keepin'-her-man death grip. And then I thought she'd be a good number two because she was *second* to arrive at the final box.

This was also the third time since moving to Nashville that I'd been in the store and someone had just started talking to me. A few days ago, I'd been wondering if I'd made a horrible mistake by moving to Nashville, missing my job and, alarmingly, Chad. I'd hopped onto my bicycle without noticing the dark storm clouds. Rain had seized my flattened hair and frizzed every single strand.

I'd been a little worried about moving to the South, but I definitely hadn't expected an older Black woman to come up to me in this very grocery store, touch the untamed animal on my head, and ask me who was Black, my mom or dad? I was so taken aback I couldn't remember what I said. I think I short-circuited at the uninvited touch. I'd gone to the salon the next day for a keratin relaxer, a tear-inducing and semi-permanent antifrizzing treatment.

She'd been nice enough, but it made me want to hide.

This woman, however, didn't appear to want to touch my now stick-straight hair. I tried to picture my icy, northern mother talking to a random stranger next to the line of cereal boxes. *My* mother, nose in the air, would've stalked off, but my mother would've never reached for a box of sweet, crunchy cereal in the first place. A much more digestively sensible Shredded Wheat was her thing.

"Fine?" the two said with a sigh. "One hour on the Peloton, *every day*, and yoga three times a week. And I look 'fine'? Maybe it's best there's only one box."

Great. I'd offended her. "I didn't mean—"

"I'm kidding. Well, not about the Peloton, or the yoga, but I'm a caterer, around food all the time, so if I sample—and I always sample—I have to pay. And you don't even want to know what I was going to do with that cereal."

"'Do' with it? You weren't going to eat it?"

The woman laughed. "I wasn't going to eat it like a civilized person with milk, if that's what you're asking. But *desperate times* . . . someone bought the B and B space I've had my eye on for the past month now. I was going to add it to my ice cream sundae. Comfort food."

I stared at my arm—*my own arm*—as I watched my betraying appendage extend the yellow box toward the woman. "Here." What the hell was I doing?

The woman reached her hand out, then pulled it back, eyeing me, probably also wondering what the hell I was doing.

"What's your story?" she asked. "Because if this is medicine for you, too, then the only fair thing is to figure out who needs it most."

She was giving me the chance to come to my senses and run away with my treat like a ninja in dark leggings. It's what I should've done, but instead, I said, "We could ask customer service if they have any in the back . . ." *She* could ask customer service, because this box was mine.

"We could, but that would require hunting someone down and explaining the situation and me admitting to *another* person I can't cope with life's disappointments. So . . ."

A laugh flew out of my mouth before I could stop it. She was serious. She seriously wanted me to tell her why I wanted—*needed*—this box of cereal.

What the hell? I probably wasn't ever going to see her again.

"My dad died six months ago, my mother now wants to control my life, I quit my job because my boss is a jerk, I don't know if I'm capable of running my own business because I don't have a plan, and, turns out, my boyfriend had a wife." The faces on the cereal boxes cheered, or maybe that was the blood rushing through my ears because I'd opened up to a stranger in the middle of a grocery store.

At least I hadn't said that my dad was a cheating alcoholic, that my mother had always been a control freak, or that my brother had died when I was twelve and I'd never properly coped. This woman *was* a stranger, after all.

But if I was being honest with myself—let's get real, I was never honest with myself—I had to admit it felt good saying those truths.

Was this what it was like having a friend? I hadn't had one since elementary school, and then not even my childhood bestie Chelsea wanted to be friends after . . . I let the thought drop. I might've spilled part of my misery to the woman who shared my love of Cap'n Crunch, but if I let my thoughts go *there*, I'd turn into a babbling puddle, awaiting cleanup by a Publix employee.

Instead of replying, the woman snatched the box out of my hand and opened it. "Wow. I'm inspired by your honesty. We both need this cereal, and after what you just told me, we both need it *right now*." She reached into the bag, pulled out a handful of electric-yellow pillows and medicinal, psychedelic balls, moaned as she crunched them between her teeth, then tilted the box toward me, an invitation to munch alongside her.

What was the proper etiquette here? An old man in a T-shirt and suspenders pushed a cart full of cat food around us. I looked at him with apology.

The woman popped another piece of cereal into her mouth. "You ride? Of course you ride; look at you. Do you ride with a group?"

Oh no. Did she ride? Was this southern etiquette, or was she trying to bond? How did I tell her I would never consider a group ride? I rode to recover *from* people, not be *with* people.

And she was just going to stand here and talk? Right here in the grocery store, after opening another customer's food choice and eating it in said customer's face? Who was this woman? I kind of envied her.

"I ride," I replied, nodding like one of those creepy, slow-moving bobblehead dolls you occasionally see on dashboards.

She shook the box toward me. I glanced down the aisle, then reached in.

"Alone, typically." I finally embraced this bizarre moment as if it were completely natural to eat in the middle of aisle four. "I just moved here, so I don't know anyone." Again, I left out the big picture stuff. I *chose* to ride alone. People complicated life. I was better with numbers and money. Numbers didn't rip your heart out; numbers didn't leave you, or if they did, they usually came back, more numbers with them.

"Great!" The woman dusted off her hands, handed me the box, and then searched in her purse. "My husband's a cyclist. My brother too. They ride in a group. You should totally join them."

Interior hard chuckles. It was more likely that the Cap'n would jump off the box and start breakdancing in his underwear—seriously, you couldn't see his pants behind that bowl—than it was for me to join a group of "cyclists" who actually knew what they were doing.

"What's your number?" the two asked. "I'll text you mine and William's; he's my husband. I can let you know when their next ride is. Better yet, you should come to dinner. I kind of owe you for eating your cereal."

Dinner? I'd just stopped for a pile of sugar to drown my sorrows in. Friends had been a previous goal before my life fell apart. I wasn't sure I wanted a friend anymore, let alone *friends*. Casual acquaintance, maybe. The kind you called when you wanted to go out somewhere but would look too pathetic if you went alone, like a fondue restaurant or an escape room. This woman didn't look like a casual acquaintance; this woman looked like she'd pry my whole life story out of me before I could skewer a piece of meat.

"That's not—"

"Nonsense!" she said, cutting me off. "You're new around here, and you don't have to be alone. We've already bonded. I mean, how often do I meet someone who loves Cap'n Crunch, is a like-minded aspiring entrepreneur, and is so refreshingly honest about life and how hard it sucks sometimes. Please come to dinner. What's your number?" Her phone was poised in her hand, waiting.

Wow. How did I explain to her that my freakish outburst was an anomaly? I held everything in, all the time. Though she was right about the Cap'n and the entrepreneur stuff. Still.

I bit the inside of my cheek and then decided that giving her my number was the easiest thing to do here. It wasn't like I had to go to dinner. It wasn't like I had to answer calls or texts. Once I was out of this store, I wouldn't have to see this woman ever again. And I'd check the cereal aisle before I walked down it the next time I needed a fix, which would likely be soon, given the state of my life.

I peered down the aisle again, like this was some covert operation, and then gave my phone number to the amazingly bold, cereal-scarfing, *second* Mrs. Crunch.

"I'm Deanna, by the way." Which I guessed was my clue to tell Deanna who I was.

"I'm Penelope. I go by Pen." I sounded like a robot, like my mother!

"I love that. I just texted you, Pen. Next Friday? A week from tonight? Me and William, and you and . . . I'm guessing you won't want to bring a date, but so you don't feel like a third wheel, my brother Grant will be there too. His girlfriend is out of town; he was planning to come over for dinner anyway. It works out! I'll be in touch." The woman scampered off, leaving me holding an open box of cereal in one hand and my regret in the other.

The idea of dinner and riding groups made the cereal squirm in my stomach.

I grabbed a box of hot chocolate mix, the kind with the tiny, desiccated marshmallows, shuffled to the self-checkout, past the eager woman in lane five because I'd reached my people limit for the day, scanned, paid, and headed back to my bicycle.

On the way home, I had a flash of me sitting on Deanna's plush sectional—she seemed like a woman who owned a sectional—legs tucked under me, chatting with her over ice cream, like a real friend.

It was such a pleasant thought, but then I remembered who I was. Could I be a real friend?

No. Not now at least. I couldn't entertain the thought of *friends* when I was trying to get a financial practice up and running. Friends would have to wait. I'd continue watching the TV show *Friends* and pick up a few pointers for way, way down the road.

Back at home, I returned my bicycle to the garage, grabbed my sad, brown grocery bag, and sighed when I realized how light it was.

I'd forgotten the milk.

Ten of my well-placed mutual funds said Deanna wouldn't have forgotten the milk.

CHAPTER 3
LIFE REALIZATION #1: BLACK AND BEIGE ARE SUITABLE TREATMENTS FOR PANIC ATTACKS

Mondays are unattractive. But when you're scrambling to start a business on your own from scratch, they're hideous: 1980s-sweatband hideous. On this particular Monday (three days after the grocery store incident), I was sitting at Frothy Monkey on Fifth Avenue, sipping a "hand-brewed" coffee with "house-made caramel" and staring out the window at all the sharply dressed businesspeople who knew what they were doing with their lives. Their long strides were determined, going somewhere. Their chatter was carefree, tipped with smiles and threaded with laughter. I tore my eyes away from the window and stared down at the crisp, bleached legal pad that popped against the lacquered wood in front of me.

The top three items on a financial planner's to-do list are as follows:

1. *Marketing.* At TCF, Lynn and the marketing team found and lumped clients for all the planners. All I'd had to do was walk in and seal the deal. Now, I was flying solo. Scary.

2. *Content creation* (not social media). One of my strengths. I stood out from the crowd by presenting my ability to manage client cash flow but also make recommendations on market investments. A lot of planners excelled in only one area; I could do both.

3. *Client services.* My existing portfolios were pristine. I'd sent personal exit emails to all my clients before Houston could tell me not to. Navigating my noncompete would be tricky, but I hoped at least a few of my clients would stick with me.

This business was all about making financial goals, developing strategies, and reacting to curveballs. But since I had very few clients, portfolios, or *money*, all those goals, strategies, and reactions, along with my fancy experience and colorful charts, meant little.

My eyes shot back up to the window as my pen drummed against the legal pad, keeping time with the blender running somewhere in the background of this coffee shop. The window started to fog, my breath obscuring my view of all the confident, successful people out on the sidewalk. My hand hit my paper cup, nearly knocking it over as I crammed my numbered to-do list into my satchel. The page snagged on the zipper and ripped, and the severed shred peeked out of my bag, a little white flag waving in the nonexistent breeze.

"Laney, we've got to figure out how to declare this on our taxes. Don't you care?" This came from the table next to me; one woman spoke loudly to another, intruding on my self-deprecation. I casually turned. The pair looked like sisters, possibly twins, but were easily distinguished by their clothes and hair. One had black, spiky locks, a nose ring, and a killer black coat that made her look like she was a Guardian of the Galaxy. The other was full-on beige: skin, hair, turtleneck, and slacks, or possibly a jumpsuit because I couldn't tell where the top of her outfit ended and the bottom began. I guessed they were around my age—*bonus*.

"That's ages away," a much calmer voice countered. "We have a whole year."

"Don't you at least want to invest it?"

Taxes.

Invest.

Was I hallucinating? Because this was too good to be true, too perfect, almost like a joke. Or maybe it was fate, and that's why I'd decided to pay $5.19 for a coffee instead of brewing some at home. The ladies of Nashville needed me.

My heart ticked too fast: what I can only assume a predator feels when she spots prey. The sudden shift in my mental state—despair to aggressive hope—made me the slightest bit unsteady on my feet. I gave myself five seconds to get a grip and walked over to the table, where one sister insisted this was about *asset growth* in a tone that said she didn't really understand the term but knew it was important.

It *was* important. It was also music to my ears.

Black Coat tapped a chart she'd likely printed from a Google search.

"Ladies, excuse me for interrupting, but I couldn't help overhearing." I stood tall and spoke with a confidence I only had when I was talking finance. No need to turn them into numbers because they were already potential bank accounts. Nothing personal here. "I'm a financial planner, starting my private business in Nashville, and I think I could help you." I handed them each a card I pulled from my satchel. They were branded with the TCF logo, but I'd crossed out my office number and highlighted my cell. Until I printed new ones, these would help establish credibility.

I slid onto the third chair at their table.

Within five minutes, Black Coat (Lenni) and Beige (Laney) told me that one week ago, they had inherited a large sum of money and a run-down building in East Nashville from their childless uncle.

Within ten minutes, I'd briefly outlined my business model, discussed my investment philosophy, and emailed them worksheets to fill in that would better articulate their goals.

Within fifteen minutes, we were shaking hands, and I was telling them we'd discuss next steps at my office in one week—*if* my office "maintenance" had been completed by then.

We parted ways on the sidewalk, and I headed for my bicycle, mentally mapping out my next destination, the office I didn't have yet. One Nashville Place was a coworking space I'd briefly considered leasing on Fourth Avenue, which would look professional without the heavy investment or commitment. Now that I had clients—these ladies were mine—I could risk my dwindling finances and rent some office space.

My chest rose and fell as I sucked in the aroma of hot dogs and fries and downtown sewer, the smells of possibility.

Within an hour, I'd scarfed two hot dogs, toured the WeWork space, and signed a three-month lease on a private office, all thanks to Black Coat and Beige. By late June, I should know whether or not this whole Nashville business endeavor meant professional freedom or was an impulsive disaster.

CHAPTER 4
LIFE REALIZATION #2: GETTING RID OF A MARRIED MAN IS HARDER THAN YOU THINK

Two days later, I was on my way home from my new, pristine workspace with one hand on my steering wheel and the other in a crinkly Doritos bag on my lap, an appetizer before my frozen pizza dinner. Today, I'd met my new "coworkers": Michelle, a very innovative, easy-to-talk-to graphic designer, a massage therapist, a husband-and-wife talent agency who booked gigs for country music singers, and an eccentric social media star, Lady Mama, who needed an office space because . . .

Michelle hadn't minced words; she'd immediately insisted I needed a brand to go along with my platform, something edgy. Then she'd jumped in to designing a logo wherein my pantsuited silhouette would lead to razor-sharp high heels, which would end in the point of a pen actively writing my name, *Pen Auberge*. I wasn't *exactly* sure what that looked like, but she was excited about it, and her confidence gave me a boost. Her card coupled nicely with my history of advising large corporations and my market hunches, which I strategically called "expertise," and—this might work.

I pulled a perfectly triangular Dorito out of the bag as I turned in to my driveway.

The Nose was sitting on her front porch drinking from a ridged glass that caught the light from the rusty lantern sconce on her house. There was something about that woman that made me curious.

She waved and pointed to my house. I nodded. *Yes, that's where I live.* As I tried to figure out what she was attempting to communicate, a face popped up in my window. I screamed, flailed, and knocked the Doritos into the passenger floorboard.

Once I realized who it was, I closed my eyes, waited for my heart to stop racing, and tried to pretend my ex wasn't standing in my driveway. Maybe I could run him over. How many years would I get for accidental manslaughter? Would it even be accidental manslaughter? No, The Nose would tell the authorities I'd put the car in reverse before "accidentally" gunning it forward.

This was *my* place. My new life. I dusted crumbs from my hands, gripped the handle, and shoved the door directly into Chad's unexpectant legs. He jerked back.

"What are you doing here?" I barked. His expensive sweater and jeans, styled dark-blond hair, and perfectly proportioned face (he had to be of Scandinavian descent) didn't belong in this old, quiet neighborhood.

"Shh. The whole neighborhood's going to hear you." He held his finger to my lips. "Can we please go inside and talk?"

I slammed the car door shut, dropped my bag, and crossed my arms over my chest. "It's cute you think we have something to talk about." I glanced toward my neighbor's house, but The Nose wasn't morbidly fascinated by the near-promise of drama like other people would be. One of her eyebrows rose and her mouth pursed, as if concerned more than interested.

Caring what people thought had been ingrained in me since birth. I didn't want to care, but I did. I needed people to like me, to think I was capable, strong, and worthy of praise. Like Chad, I wanted to go inside so my neighbors wouldn't suspect I had some sort of problem, which I most certainly did. Truth be told, I cared about appearances just as much as Chad did.

"I'm still your client," he said, calmly, logically.

On some level, I'd known I'd have to either let him go as a client or program him back into my phone and establish a purely business relationship. Messy either way, which was why I'd been ignoring this little, gigantic problem.

"You came here to talk about your finances?" I kept my voice low.

"Maybe."

I stared at him, trying to decide which Chad was in my driveway: Client Chad or Cheating Chad. My approach would be wildly different, depending on which one.

"Your mother, she told me to come." The regret on his face was real. "I made a mistake. Please let me explain."

Damn my Chad-adoring mother. She knew I didn't want this man anywhere near me. But what should I expect from a woman who didn't seem to think his wife was a problem? "A little obstacle," she'd said. "People are complicated. In a lot of cases, there's more than meets the eye. Chad isn't a bad person." But that was probably because she'd lived so many years with a cheating husband herself. She was used to it.

This was Cheating Chad. I calmly picked up my backpack and strode to the back of my house.

My house.

He grabbed my arm, but I yanked it away and kept moving forward.

He ran a hand through his a-little-longer-on-top hair, a gesture I used to love, tried not to love right now. "Pen, please."

I missed him. Being alone, starting something new . . . it was scary. I wanted to fall against him, cling to his familiar, clean scent (a bar of soap in a briefcase). Instead of giving in, I let the anger build inside me now. I rode that anger like my bicycle, let it put distance between us.

"If you don't want to talk about your money, then . . ." I looked back over at The Nose, who'd moved closer. Her arms were folded in front of her, and she was actively scowling. My stomach flipped. Was her disapproval because she didn't want a daytime talk show scene in her quiet neighborhood? But then when she looked at me, her eyes softened, and she nodded. And I didn't know how to feel. On one hand, she was inserting herself into my business, but on another, it was almost like she was on my side. I was probably reading too much into it. I aimed for Chad instead. "Just go."

"I don't care about the money." His loafers tapped on the pavement behind me as he jogged to keep pace. "But I'm not leaving until we at least talk."

Did I owe him words?

"You're not—" I whirled around, pressed a finger into his chest, started to shout, remembered Mrs. Snoe, then pulled the front of his sweater toward my door.

"Five minutes," I growled, shoving him into my small, untidy kitchen.

I flicked on the light switch, illuminating a domed pendant lamp with blue-and-yellow flowers painted on it, then slammed my leather satchel down where a table should've been—would've been if I cared enough.

We stood in the mostly empty space, me waiting for him to say what he'd traveled 889 miles to say.

Instead of talking, he walked around my kitchen much like the home inspector who'd turned his nose up and then recommended a bunch of repairs. "You're living lean."

My heart played a game in my chest: *Do I want him here or not?*

He slid his hands in the pockets of his designer jeans, jeans that hugged his butt like he'd had them tailored for the sole purpose of making his backside something people wanted to bite. "I guess I'm stalling."

I reminded myself that his was a cheating backside. "Well, you've already wasted two of your minutes looking around. You have three left. I'd suggest you start talking before time's up and you're leaving with only a tour of my 'lean' kitchen."

He wasn't bothered by my threats, which fueled my anger. Good, I wanted to stay angry. Though I couldn't decide who I was angrier at: him for coming here or me for letting him inside.

"Are you really happy here?" He attempted to shut a cabinet that defiantly popped back open. "This place isn't your usual . . ."

He was used to my—Aurora's—apartment in Minneapolis. In general, I had enough energy to pour into my appearance and job, which left nothing for the interior of my home or body. Since Aurora wasn't in Nashville—thank goodness—my living space reflected me instead of her.

"I'm ecstatic." The words fell flat.

He walked into the living room, past the closet under the stairs that held, like a shrine, a box of my brother's old things. "You've been in Nashville three weeks." Then he looked down at the rumpled blankets splayed out on the brownish carpet and back at me as if I owed him an explanation for having nothing cushy to rest his sculpted ass on. "And there's nothing here."

Three weeks, two days, and twelve hours.

"There's a TV." I pointed to the fifty-inch on the floor opposite the blankets.

I smiled, satisfaction warming me as I noticed the Dorito-dust stain on the front of his shirt. He wouldn't like that when he realized.

"Your five minutes is up. Thanks for coming to insult my first home purchase. Let me show you to my favorite part of the house." I moved to the front door, just off the living room. "You'll notice the paint is peeling here, too, but the blinds are new; be sure to admire those on your way out."

"Come on. Please don't be like this." He stood close enough for me to smell the clean yet rugged notes in his cologne, close enough to see real pain in his eyes.

That look extinguished a few flames of the fire I'd been stoking ever since I'd found him in my driveway. It reminded me of the night we'd met; that animal magnetism had drawn us together and made my body react whether I'd wanted it to or not.

"I'm sorry I didn't tell you about Vicki, but I was afraid of losing you. I never should've married her."

"But you did." An uncomfortable coil tightened in my chest. I had to remember to be angry.

He ran his hand through his hair again, and I was momentarily taken aback by the turmoil brewing on his chiseled face.

He grabbed my hand, led me to the blankets, and pulled me down onto them, taking my hands in his.

I ripped my arms back. I might be foolish enough to give him a chance to say his piece, but there would be no physical contact.

"Fair," he said, nodding and clasping his hands together in front of him. "And you're right. I did marry her. But it was a mistake. And I know that's not an excuse. Can I just . . . can I tell you how we got here?"

"I know how we got here. You pretended you weren't married and started a relationship with me. Then you continued that relationship for six months! For six months you made me and your wife a statistic. *You* did that. No one forced you."

He buried his face in his hands. "I'm so sorry." His words were slightly muffled and edged with emotion. "I made a mistake, a horrible one. But I'm doing everything I can to fix it."

"You can't fix it."

His head snapped up, his storm-coming-over-the-horizon eyes shiny in the dim light. I'd never seen him cry, not that he was crying now, but his regret felt real, not the attorney determined to get his way in a courtroom, but a screwed-up human who was suffering because of his own asinine choices. I knew that feeling, and so I had to close my own eyes and shove away the sympathy that was ridiculously rising on his behalf. Because this was different.

"You know how I am," he said. "I'm competitive, and if someone says I can't have something, I consider it my personal duty to prove them wrong. It's stupid, but that's why I married Vicki. We grew up together. She said our families' lives were too intertwined, and we'd ruin things by dating. And of course, I saw that as a challenge. We were attracted to each other, and we had fun together, but I was blinded by the conquest and didn't see that we had nothing in common until we had rings on our fingers."

He paused and took several deep breaths, his jaw shifting, like admitting this about himself and his life was hard.

I said nothing, torn between feeling sorry for him and feeling delighted that he was suffering, because he deserved all the pain, didn't he?

He swallowed hard, his Adam's apple bobbing, and then turned back toward me. "When I met you, I saw what I was missing with Vicki. You and I are on the same page. We're both career driven, and we have the same sense of humor, and I like that you're unique, and the chemistry . . . that's undeniable."

His gaze was too intense; I had to look away.

"And I know it was wrong," he continued, "but I felt so good when I was with you, so right, that I compartmentalized. I didn't want to admit to everyone that I'd made a mistake, and so I made the biggest mistake of all."

My head whipped back to him, a burning anger rising in my chest. "So what was your plan? I don't understand why you let it go on for so long, how you could be so duplicitous. That takes a special kind of person."

His answer came more quickly than I would've expected. "If I'd told you I was married, what would've happened the night we met? If half-way through our conversation on investing, when I was having more fun talking to you about the stock market than I'd had in months with my wife, what would you have done if you'd found out I was married?"

"I would've left," I whispered, picking at a loose thread at the corner of the blanket we were on.

He nodded, like I'd just answered my own question. "It wasn't right, but letting you walk away didn't feel right either. And then it spiraled, and I didn't know what to do. Every time I thought about coming clean, I'd picture you bolting. Because the more I got to know you, the more I realized that's exactly what you'd do."

"It *is* what I'd do. You wanna know why? Because that's what a decent person would do. And I have a lot of issues, but I am not a cheater. And you made me one. I watched my dad cheat on my mom when I was a teenager, and it didn't matter what his reasons were to me. It was *not* okay."

He pulled back like I'd slapped him. "I didn't know."

"Because I didn't tell you."

And there were so many other things I hadn't told him. Because being with Chad was like being with someone and being alone at the same time. He had his life, and I had mine. He was a well-rounded version of myself. That had been the beauty of it. No commitments. But I'd been so preoccupied with how he didn't require what other men had required of me that, blinded by our chemistry, for six months I missed all the red flags. What made our relationship perfect was that he'd spent half his time with another woman I didn't even know about. And what did that say about me that that was my perfect relationship, half a man?

"I think you should go."

But he didn't move. "I'm getting a divorce. It's what I should've done a long time ago."

Tears stung the backs of my eyes. I hadn't expected him to say that. "Why are you telling me this?"

"Because I want you back. I want this." His hand moved between us. "I want us. I think I love you."

I closed my eyes.

"You don't have to give me an answer now," he went on. "If it makes you feel any better, I'm leaving Vicki whether you take me back or not. It's the right thing to do. But I'm not giving up on us. This feels right to me. You're right for me. And I don't deserve another chance. I know that. But I'm human. I made a stupid, stupid mistake that hurt a lot of people, but I can't lose everything because of it."

My breath pumped in and out of my lungs too fast, and I counted. I counted the little holes in the blinds on my front door, and when that wasn't enough, I counted all the things I didn't have in my house, all the paintings I didn't have on my walls, all the knickknacks on the shelves I hadn't assembled.

"I just moved here. I just bought this house. I'm trying to build my own business." It all sounded hollow in my own ears.

He took my hand, squeezed it slightly. I liked the warmth of his palm; I hated that I liked it. I hated myself too. "You didn't move here for friends or a job or anything." His fingers interlaced with mine, and he pulled me closer.

I *hadn't* moved here for friends or a job. To my shame, Chad was the closest thing I had to a friend, and he knew this about me. I think he liked it about me. I fit into his life without complication. No arguments over who to spend time with. No fuss when he wanted to hang out with his guy pals. He'd lead and I'd follow, because what else did I have?

"I mean *something* to you. I have to," he said. "Why else would you move across states when you found out I was married? That kind of action means something."

Sweat stung my underarms, a sharp pinprick of guilt. He was right. That kind of action *did* mean something, but it didn't mean what he thought it meant.

I hadn't moved across the country because I'd been devastated to find out my boyfriend had been lying during our entire relationship. I'd uprooted my whole life because, looking out my crystal clear office window back in Minnesota, I'd discovered what a truly despicable human being I'd become—I should've known he was married. Like, why hadn't I been at the Fletcher client meeting with him? Because he'd taken his *wife*, and I should've seen it.

But I'd never been with him for love. If you loved, you were vulnerable, and if you were vulnerable, your heart could be sucked out of your chest. If you got too attached to someone and that someone left you—I couldn't go through that again. It was easier to do without it in the first place. Experience had told me that.

All those months ago, I'd slid onto the black short-backed barstool beside Chad the night we'd met, the night of my father's funeral. The clean-cut, muscled bartender placed my father's favorite drink, a scotch and soda, on the shiny, midnight blue bar top, and Chad laughed, told me he was having exactly the same thing. Conversation flowed. He'd had a rough day in the courtroom, and I told him about my job. I didn't even need to turn him into a number. And then later, after we'd slept together and continued to meet, I didn't question the unexplained texts he got, or his sudden need to leave when we were together, or his flimsy excuses. Because that allowed me to keep him at arm's length, companionship without all the depth of real commitment.

But when I saw that pretty, blonde ponytail, those electric-pink earbuds, the earnestness as she stood on tiptoe and looked into Chad's face, her *husband's* face, I realized that my desire to maintain distance had turned me into a *cheater*. I'd done this to myself, to all of us. Because if I'd just been more suspicious or observant or if I'd cared more about him, I could've spared us all this pain.

Shame burned in my belly. I should've known.

Houston undermining me professionally had infuriated me, fueled me to do something rash. But the scene out my office window had been the catalyst for me to pack my bags. I didn't trust myself anymore. When Erin mentioned this house, it seemed like a way out, an escape from everything I'd done wrong. I could start over and build a new life, avoiding people so I wouldn't hurt them as much as I'd been hurt.

Now . . . *divorce*. Had I caused this? Was I the reason some other woman's life would soon be in shambles like my own?

He needed to go home, back to his wife, and leave me to this new life I was creating so I wouldn't have even more guilt.

"Aren't I now exactly what Vicki was to you then? Something you can't have?"

He shook his head violently, a desperate gleam flickering around his cobalt irises. "No. This is different."

He looked like he believed it was different, but I shook my head.

"I'm going to prove it to you," he said, nodding again.

My phone buzzed in my pocket, and for want of something to do with my hands, I pulled it out and looked at the screen. A text from Mrs. Crunch: Deanna, the woman from the grocery store, apologizing for the late reminder and confirming dinner this Friday night, as promised, two nights from now.

I glanced up at Chad. "You're wrong about one thing. I have made friends here." This wasn't strictly true, but, as always, I had appearances to keep up, and he needed to believe there was no place for him in my life.

I quickly replied to Deanna before I could process what I was doing; I asked for her address and told her I'd be there.

"In fact," I told him, "I have plans Friday night."

CHAPTER 5
LIFE REALIZATION #3: MUSTACHES ARE RIDICULOUS

On Friday night, my hand shook as my finger was poised over Deanna's Ring doorbell. I'd written and erased so many texts backing out of tonight that my thumbs had calluses, but I needed a distraction from the haunting conversation with Chad. I also needed to try to get over my fear of social events. So I'd decided to come, a box of Cap'n Crunch stuffed in a purple gift bag with lavender tissue paper that complemented my dress. I pushed the button, hearing the tones announcing my arrival from somewhere behind the opaque oval pane of glass.

When Deanna opened the heavy mahogany door, she waved me inside. "You look amazing! Purple is your color."

My favorite color was purple, the color of royalty, power, and ambition. The color of my dress silently whispered my first impression before I ever uttered a word. The real reason was because of the royal purple Princess Diana Beanie Baby my brother gave me, the last gift I ever received from him.

I handed her the bag. "Thank you."

"You didn't need to bring anything." She peeked inside and squealed. "This is perfect."

Deanna sparkled. From afar, everything about her was medium—her hair color, her skin tone, her height, her weight—but as soon as she opened her mouth, it was like she transformed into a princess who charmed wildlife and conversed with common household items. Just like the other night at the grocery, she was the number two, a swan floating on a glittering pond.

I didn't look half as good as she did, because she had something I didn't: real confidence. I spotted it because I knew what trying looked like.

"Come back to the kitchen with me." Her eyes were alive with excitement behind her black plastic frames. "Dinner's almost ready!" She slapped her forehead. "I'm not thinking. You need to meet William and Grant. They're in the living room, discussing some 'hot article' in *Popular Mechanics.*"

I nodded politely, like I knew what she was talking about, but I think my face gave me away.

"I don't know," she said. "I heard the words 'tiny nuclear reactors' and got the hell out of there."

She grabbed my arm and pulled me to the living room like we were old friends.

What did this woman see in me? Now that I was here, standing in her warm house with brightly colored paint on the walls and monochromatic photographs scattered around like a professional gallery—a far cry from my own place—I wasn't sure why I'd ever agreed to come.

Oh yeah, Chad. And *his wife*. And I liked Deanna. She had a way of making me feel comfortable, even though I knew tonight was about distraction, not about lasting bonds.

Two men turned as we entered the room.

The taller, with skin the rich color only biracial people have, came forward first, his hand extended. "It's nice to meet you . . . Pen, right?" His eyes—I couldn't tell if they were green or blue—hid behind glasses that matched his wife's. I tried not to imagine him on a billboard in an underwear ad, but he'd be perfect for it. I instantly liked him, and as he smiled at me, I relaxed a fraction.

Why do humans act this way? I didn't know William at all, but the fact he was a mix of Black and White, like me, made me feel less alone, like this *hadn't* been a gigantic mistake. And maybe he knew, just a little, how it felt not to belong, to be caught between two groups and not really identify as either one. Maybe I'd met Deanna in the grocery store for a reason.

I focused and turned off the sappy voice inside my head. William, in his orange T-shirt and dark-wash straight-leg jeans, was a nine, the shape of a helium balloon at the circus. No, not the circus—I hated the circus—but maybe a fair, with colorful lights and cotton candy. Yeah, William, with his vivid eyes, was a number nine at the fair.

As the other man moved forward, Deanna said, "And this is my brother, Grant, and his mustache."

Grant extended his hand to me. The polite smile that was affixed to the bottom half of my face faltered as our eyes met. If William was a balloon, Grant was the fork that popped him. All my hopeful positivity was skewered by this Grant, the number four, and turned upside down, hence the balloon-popping thing.

His devastatingly blue gaze shot through me, like he saw past my perfectly positioned facade, and I didn't like it. It wasn't possible, at least I didn't think so, for him to be able to read as much as his eyes seemed to suggest he could, but I swallowed and struggled not to rip my hand out of his.

"Grant," he said, pointing to his dark-blue-button-down-covered chest. "And this is Henry," he continued, gesturing now to the perfectly groomed line of facial hair under his nose. A faint, amused smile bloomed under Henry.

"Grant," Deanna sighed. "You named your mustache?"

"Of course not. You're the one who made it awkward if I didn't provide a formal introduction."

I forced myself to smile. I hated mustaches. They reminded me of overconfident, sleazy Sal, who had referred to his facial hair as "Stache." I'd spent the first fifteen minutes of our one and only date learning about Stache and Sal's morning routine: special stache shampoo and conditioner, followed by application of either stache oil, stache balm, or, if he was feeling frisky, stache wax, all either applied with or activated by a set of stache-grooming tools.

There was nothing more pretentious than a man with a mustache.

Grant, with his solicitous stare and hideous lip fur, was already starting from behind. Though he did look, ironically, like Henry Cavill, during his mustache days of course.

"How do you know your mustache isn't female?" I asked, hoping I'd covered my scrunched-nose disgust.

He cocked his head, considering. "You're right. It's entirely possible I'm sporting a Henrietta."

William threw his arm over Grant's shoulders. "Male, female, non-binary, can we all agree either way it's ridiculous so we can go get some food?"

"I'm going to apologize in advance for the two of them," Deanna said, then clapped her hands together. "I hope you don't mind being my guinea pig tonight. I'm practicing for an event I have coming up."

"Whatever it is, it smells heavenly," I said.

"Everything D makes is heavenly." William winked at his wife.

"Grant, take Pen to the dining room," Deanna instructed. "William and I will serve." William absently ran his hand over Deanna's back as they walked to the kitchen.

I wondered what it would be like to have what they obviously had. I tried to picture Chad rubbing my back. Then I wondered why I was thinking about him at all.

I'd been in this house for less than five minutes, but I felt it already, that closeness, that ease people have with each other when they're family and they belong to each other, that knowledge of *no matter what happens, I got your back*. I braced myself. I'd definitely made a mistake in coming here. I was way out of my league. These people knew how to do family, and maybe William and I shared a racial background, but the three of them shared *history*, pleasant history. I was an outsider.

Was it too early to feign a stomachache and head out the door?

Alone in the dining room with Grant, I felt the warm golds and burgundies curving around my shoulders like a straitjacket. This was one dinner, I told myself, breathing the herbed air into my nostrils and counting the lights in the chandelier. One dinner. I could do this. I needed to do this. Because maybe they could be friends and distract me from the thing I definitely wasn't going to do: date. Growth, right? But *having* friends meant *making* friends, and making friends was hell. I sat straighter, pulled the linen napkin tightly over my lap.

"So, you ride, Penelope?" Grant steepled his hands, elbows on either side of Deanna's creamy, gold-rimmed place mats. Everything matched here.

And why is he calling me Penelope? I mean, that was my name, but my mother was the only one who called me Penelope, and maybe the occasional person, like Marketing Lynn, but Grant only knew me as Pen.

"Sort of. I'm not a professional or anything, but I started about ten years ago. I don't like being stuck in a gym." If I worked out in an enclosed space, all those feelings bounced around the room and came right back to me. I went to the gym anxious and left tired, sweaty, and . . . anxious.

"Once I started, I fell in love with it," I continued, talking to fill the uncomfortable silence. But I seemed to be the only one finding the silence uncomfortable. He leaned back in his chair and crossed his arms. His shirtsleeves were rolled to expose his forearms, and I ignored the muscle definition and the smattering of hair that matched his mustache as he looked at me as if what I was saying was the most fascinating thing in the world. My leg bounced. I manually stopped it, determined to appear as he did—absolutely fine.

Where are Deanna and William?

"Here we are," Deanna said in a singsong voice as she and William entered with loaded plates. *Did I ask that out loud?* "I hope you like it."

I picked up my fork.

"William, would you say grace?" Deanna asked.

I put down my fork.

When it seemed appropriate, I picked up my fork again and filled my mouth with a huge piece of tenderloin, an excuse not to talk. Plus, the faster I ate, the faster dinner would be over. And I couldn't decide whether I wanted to be here or whether I wanted to leave.

"They're always trying to get me to go on a ride," Deanna said. "That's what you and Grant were talking about, right? Cycling?"

I nodded; then my phone buzzed in the pocket of my dress, startling me because I didn't remember the dress had pockets. I peeked at the screen. A number I didn't recognize. The call went to voicemail, and then I immediately got a text from the same number.

> Can we please talk? I miss you so much. And I had a conversation with Vicki, we're on the same page. Did you get my email? I sent it this morning.

I rolled my eyes. Blocking Chad hadn't stopped him. I'd been thinking of unblocking him anyway because he was a client, a client I needed because I had so few. Several of my previous clients had chosen to stay with Houston, who'd convinced them that working with a company was safer than a solo adviser. There was nothing I could do about that. If those clients didn't trust me, then I didn't need them, but I needed who I had.

I hadn't talked to Chad since he'd materialized by my car window, but I had read his email, a well-thought-out list of why we belonged together using lawyer lingo that concluded with a picture of his divorce papers.

"Riding is my adventure," Grant said. When I looked up, he was looking right at me. "The thing I do for myself."

"Don't let him fool you," Deanna said. "Cycling may be number one, but he loves any kind of adventure."

"Like our Quebec trip with Chuck." William pointed at Grant. "Sleeping in an ice hotel was Grant's idea."

Grant nodded, the hairs of his mustache standing out around his grin as he continued to look—at me.

"Aww, Chuck!" Deanna stuck out her lower lip. "Have you talked to him recently, Grant?"

Finally, his gaze shifted. Antsy for the seat of my bicycle, I struggled to keep the smile on my lips as my muscles jumped. How awkward would it be if I hauled my own stationary bike into Deanna's home? It could be my thing. Other people carry a purse; I would roll in exercise equipment. I could set it up beside the cherry dinner table, maybe even attach a rudimentary tray, then feverishly pump my legs and talk about this Chuck with ease as I moved through imaginary space.

"Yeah, yeah. Chuck's great, but we were talking about the Quebec trip!" William turned to me and said in an impressive accent, "We rode P'tit Train du Nord. Have you heard of it?"

I shook my head.

William explained the bike trail, sounding authentic as he pronounced other French names.

I tried to be conversational. "Your accent is amazing." Maybe instead of the bike, because it wouldn't be as freakishly weird, I could start talking to them like clients. I was comfortable explaining the market. What would happen if I started spouting financial terms—"fiduciary," my favorite—or maybe I could explain the difference between traditional and Roth IRAs. No, then I'd be like Sal with his stache, his own eyes alight with glee while the other person thought of creative ways to use the steak knife just to end the conversation.

"Merci beaucoup. Ma mère est française."

"His mother is French," Deanna translated.

"Oh really?" I asked. "I was in Paris for a semester in college." That was the spring of Javier, a no-strings distraction from life and my parents' issues.

"Nice, and yeah." William nodded. "My grandmother, aunt, and cousins still live there, but my mom was traveling in the US when she met my dad here, then never went back. Except to visit, of course."

"His cousin Atticus has been asking us to come." Deanna pushed her chair back, walked to one of the two twin white recessed shelving units in the dining room, and picked up a four-by-six picture frame. "William's French family is a story for another time." She extended the frame to me, the glass glittering in the light of the chandelier. "This is us at the Hôtel de Glace."

A winterized William, Deanna, and Grant stood with a heavily bearded man with flannel peeking out from under his coat in front of glowing translucent pillars while holding shot glasses that appeared to be made of rough-hewn crystal.

"All the structures you see around us are made of ice." I jumped at the voice. Grant was unexpectedly behind me, so close his scent—somehow capturing a crisp spring day—curled around me, intensifying as his arm extended and he pointed to one of the columns, cast in blue light.

I nodded. No big deal that his body heat was warming the side of my arm. No big deal.

He returned to his seat diagonally across the table from me, and I tried to listen to him describe the intricately carved ice sculptures and snow domes, like the architect I'd learned he was, but my mind wouldn't stop picking at the details of this night. The crinkle at the corner of Grant's eye, the uncensored way in which Deanna's head was tossed back in levity, William's hand reaching for his wife's. This was what normal looked like. All little things—all things they likely took for granted but I couldn't stop paying attention to, because I'd never had this.

I'd misjudged Grant, though. He'd morphed from a forky four to a ten. Not a "ten" in the sense that he was hot—a "one" could be a runway model; my numbers had no hierarchy—but he was the kind of "ten" who wore a sophisticated monocle, which I'd heard was making a comeback. Even under the shadow of his mustache, he lit up the room with every story he told, propelling the conversation forward. And he looked at *everyone* with interest, not just me. If someone was talking, his monocled eye was on them, making them feel heard and important, and he didn't look like he was pretending. It filled me with a mix of admiration and jealousy.

Worst of all, being here in this room made me think of family, which meant, despite my best efforts, I thought of my own. What if Brandon and I had had the life Grant and Deanna had? What if *my* brother had lived to see his late thirties? Would I be more like Deanna then?

How many times had I fantasized about a situation like this? But instead of William, Deanna, and Grant, it was always me sitting across from Brandon, laughing with the girl he'd brought home, evaluating her suitability for my big brother, the man I admired most in the world.

Family. A part of me wanted to keep watching, while another part wanted to run because my mind kept circling like a vulture hungry for decaying memories.

I excused myself as dinner transitioned into dessert, asking Deanna to point me to the bathroom.

I pressed my palms into the wooden vanity, around the white bowl sink, and observed myself in a mirror framed by distressed pine. Rosy cheeks, sparkling hazel eyes, not a hair out of place, a deep-purple dress that fit all my curves. That's what I wanted everyone to see. In reality, my cheeks were red because I constantly bit the soft flesh inside, my eyes sparkled because they were always on the brink of tears, my hair was pulled into a bun to keep me from pulling it out, and the dress was there to distract onlookers from the moments I slipped.

I ran my hands under the cold water as it cascaded down from the waterfall sink, then pressed them to my cheeks.

What was I doing here? I didn't belong here. Even William wasn't like me, not really. Our similarities ended at skin tone.

I wanted what these people had, but I was never going to have this. I wasn't equipped for relationships like these. My inhales chased the heels of my exhales as I contemplated the unthinkable: *Chad.* I thought about the divorce papers and what he'd said.

I'm leaving Vicki whether you take me back or not. I want us. I think I love you.

I looked back at my phone, at the last text he'd sent me, and I realized I'd missed another message from him, a wall of words that filled the screen.

Chad: Vicki said she knew we'd made a mistake by getting married. She told me she's had feelings for her best friend for a while, but, unlike me, never acted on them. She's upset, and I don't blame her. But she's also relieved. She's felt trapped for a while and didn't know what to do about it. I thought she was happy, which tells you how wrong we were for each other. We're telling our families tonight. And I told her about you, that I came to Nashville to see you, and she asked me if I loved you.

I do love you. I love you, Pen. And I meant what I said the other night. I want it to be us.

I flicked the screen away and made it go black as my breath struggled in and out of my lungs. It was as if he'd felt my doubts and pounced on them.

I was so tired of being alone. Being in Deanna's warm house tonight was making me realize how lonely I was. No matter how much I tried to convince myself I was better off without the complication of people, the thought of a life completely alone scared me as much as having someone did. But I didn't know how to be with anyone, except I'd had *something* with Chad.

I had the sudden urge to call him, to pick up the phone and hear the voice of the man who'd told me he loved me. Who else was going to love me?

I took several deep breaths. I'd spent too much time in the bathroom. They were going to start thinking I was having an intestinal issue if I didn't get back out there. I blotted my face with a tissue—pulled from a rustic wooden box—took one final deep breath, and opened the door, tripping over thoughts of what to do next.

CHAPTER 6
LIFE REALIZATION #4: FRIENDS ARE OVERRATED

"I'd be even luckier if you hadn't had that third helping of roast," William was saying as I entered the living room. "What will I snack on tonight, Deanna?"

She rolled her eyes.

"Is that how you treat your guests?" Grant feigned offense in a proper English accent.

"You aren't a guest."

"Still angry about that twig, I see." Grant rocked back and forth on his feet beside the wheat-colored sectional in Deanna's living room.

"It was the size of a tree! I could've really done some damage, possibly skinned my knee!" William glanced at me, affronted. "They're one of my best features."

I didn't know what to do, so I stood, rapt with morbid fascination.

"Oh, here we go again," Deanna said. "On their last bike ride, Grant ran into a twig . . . *branch*," she corrected when William cleared his throat. "And it flew into William's wheel. They won't let it go."

"You can't help that you married a weenie, Deanna." Grant gestured grandly with an imaginary sword, then slid it into the invisible scabbard around his waist as if he were the victor.

William sprang to his feet, dislodging a fluffy couch cushion, pulled from his hip, then passed nothing between his hands. "I beg to differ. *In fact*," William said, stressing the two words, "I think it was all part of your elaborate plan. But"—he shifted the sword that only he and Grant seemed to be able to see into his right hand and pointed it at Grant—"my adept skills and catlike reflexes not only—"

"Did you say 'inept'?" Grant interjected.

William lunged forward, stopping a sword's length away from Grant, who inhaled and looked down his nose as if the tip of William's blade were hovering just shy of his skin.

"You. Know. I. Didn't," William replied.

Grant moved sideways, rolled across the couch cushions, and leaped to his feet, drawing his nonexistent weapon once again.

I leaned toward Deanna. "Is this really happening?"

"Oh, it is. Though I'm a little surprised it's happening in front of you this soon."

"I . . ." This was like a Shakespearean flash mob in Deanna's living room . . . with two guys . . . over a serving of pork roast.

"Oh, it'll get worse if we allow it." She turned to the men. "Stop it, children. You're being ridiculous. William, knees are no one's best feature." She tossed her hair and reached toward the coffee table to pick up a small black box with the words OUR MOMENTS written in all caps on the front. "It's time to play our game." She opened the box.

"Game?" I asked. No one had mentioned a game.

"Have you ever played? It's a get-to-know-you card game. I thought the four of us could play."

I had a flash of fifteen-year-old me sitting next to my aunt Tif in a small waiting room as I bit my fingernails and slammed my heels together like that could transport me to a home where Brandon was. Tif had taken me to a therapist because she knew I was depressed, but she'd done it without my mother's approval or knowledge. A little girl on the floor a few feet from our chairs drew numbers with faces and fancy clothes on a sheet of college-ruled notebook paper. She was talking to them; she was soothing herself with them. I was transfixed by that little blonde head as she cheerily conversed with the numbers on the page, except Naughty Nine and Sinister Seven, whom she scolded and threatened with an eraser. It was the first time I'd smiled probably that whole year, but I stopped smiling when the door to the waiting room was flung open and my mother stood, red faced and tight lipped. She'd been running. She walked over to me, grabbed my arm, and lifted me to my feet.

She scowled at her sister. "How could you?"

"Aurora, she needs to talk to someone." One of Tif's hands wrung the other as she stood and followed us toward the door. I looked back at the little girl on the floor, and she smiled and waved at me, then said, "Bye, One."

"Maybe if we'd done this when we were kids, when Mom . . ." Tif paused and then continued in the hallway: "Things might've been different."

Aurora stopped. "You need to mind your own business." She was calm. No one would've guessed she'd just plucked her daughter from a therapist's office or that she would never speak to her sister again. Aurora looked straight into Tif's eyes, and Tif nodded like my mother had said something. And that was it, the last time I saw Aunt Tif, the last time I'd entered a therapist's office. I'd never understood how my mom had let her sister go like that, especially since their parents had been killed by a drunk driver when she was fifteen, and the two sisters were the only family each had.

"I'm . . . I'm afraid I need to go," I stammered. I glanced at Deanna's door. *So very far away.*

"Oh, come on. One question."

That little black box grew until I was shoved up against the wall, trying to breathe against its boxiness. *What kinds of questions are on those cards?* I tried to force these three people back into their crisp number shapes, but they wouldn't go. I'd cope by leaving. This was too much.

"I've played before." Grant's voice held tenderness; his eyes searched mine. "It's a conversation starter. Not a big deal. Deanna, hurry up and read one so we can show her they're harmless."

My face must've given me away, or maybe I was sweating worse than I realized. Damn. I felt it now, the sweat collecting on my scalp, ruining the hard work of my flat iron.

"'What's one dream you have but haven't acted on yet?'" Deanna read.

Was she asking me? Because I could answer that one: *Getting out of this house.*

"I'll go first," Deanna said. "I want to own a bed and breakfast."

"You're serious, D? You never—" William started.

"A restaurant?" Grant interrupted. "Your own business? A restaurant is a lot of work. It's a time suck. You'll work your life away."

Deanna had told me this at the store, but she hadn't told her family. I'd known something they didn't.

"So what, if it's her dream? Maybe she wants to put the work in." I wasn't sure where the words or the near-hostility behind them had come from, and I paused to make sure I was actually the one who'd said them.

Deanna waved her hands in front of her face. "Maybe." Her inhale was long and deep. "Now that it's out there . . . yeah, I'm thinking about it, having a space, a venue, a small restaurant. I think I'd love it. That's one of the reasons I was drawn to Pen. She's going for it. It's inspiring." Her smile was weak, like she'd been afraid to bring this up until now, when *I* was here. Her admiration was so unexpected. That someone so put together could be inspired by someone like me, it made me feel—valuable.

"You're good enough for sure," Grant continued, glossing over most of what Deanna had said, "but I want you to think this through. Life is more than work. I don't want you to turn into one of those people who—"

"One of those people?" I asked, too loud and too abrupt, his words rubbing my skin the wrong way. I forgot about leaving. "Some of *those* people have ambitions, goals. They're motivated. What's wrong with that?"

They all turned toward me. I was overreacting, stepping in where I shouldn't, but I couldn't stop. Anger seemed to be holding back the tears I'd been keeping at bay all evening.

"There's nothing wrong with being motivated," Grant replied slowly, as if approaching a bomb he had to talk out of detonating. "I value the trait. I know my sister, and I know what it takes to own a restaurant, which is what a bed and breakfast would turn into. It's hard work. She's a hardworking woman already, but she values family and free time, and it's hard to do both. I'm not sure she'd be happy with the increased workload."

Deanna opened her mouth to say something, but my mouth was going again before she spoke. "So you think someone who works hard to get to the top professionally couldn't possibly value anything else?" I was shaking. He was essentially telling me I was a fool for trying to start my own business, but I'd avoided the topic through dinner because I didn't want to talk about it. The whole issue was still raw, a walk out onto a limb that might not be strong enough to hold my weight.

Let's go, Grant. I can take you and *your chauvinistic mustache.*

"No. I'm saying I think this is something my sister should *think* about."

Deanna put her arms up. "Whoa. I appreciate you both trying to figure my life out for me, but this is just an idea."

A curious expression curled under Grant's mustache. "Do you love your job, Penelope?"

The question caught me off guard. I was worked up, hackles raised, ready for a fight, and it irritated me that this silly man with his ridiculous mustache remained calm and in control.

"I like my job." My job was what I had, what I was good at, what I'd been doing my whole life. Those numbers had always been there when no one else was. Work *was* my whole life; of course I liked it.

"But you don't love it? Does it make you happy?"

"Grant," Deanna said. "Leave her alone, and stop being intense. Not everyone has your same life philosophy. People love and want different things, and that's okay."

"I'm just asking. And sure, differences should be celebrated. But if something doesn't make you happy, well, you should question why you're still doing it."

Who is this guy? I started to ask him if he loved his job, but he'd already talked about the buildings he'd designed like other people did their children. For him, each room in a house had its own personality like each member of a family. *Blah. Blah. Blah.*

"There's so much that goes into them," he'd said during dinner. "Including pieces of myself. Intellectually and spiritually fulfilling."

Suddenly I hated this evening, this man, and this game.

"People *are* different," I huffed. "And you'd be well served not to be so judgmental and controlling. What if your sister were a man? I bet you'd slap him on the back and break out the damn cigars. If your sister wants to start her own business, then you should support her for her bravery." I turned to Deanna. "I bet your bed and breakfast would be awesome, Deanna."

Grant's eyebrows went up as his jaw went slack. For three solid seconds, the only sound in the room came from eyelids opening and closing. The two, the nine, and the four (he was definitely a four again) merged into one big fifteen and then broke into their respective figures at the sound of clapping. It was William.

"Bravo!" he said.

Deanna nodded. "Thank you, Pen."

Grant was silent.

William steered the conversation back to food and then suggested I come on their Sunday bike ride. *Yeah, right.* But Deanna wouldn't let me leave without agreeing to go or without taking leftovers (she'd made a whole second roast). So I took my pork, packed neatly in a biodegradable to-go container, and promised Deanna I'd go on their ride as I left their home, pretending I wasn't still simmering and that the evening *hadn't* ended in a way that showcased I wasn't friend material.

At the door, Deanna leaned in. "I had a feeling about you. I needed that. Grant is an angel, the greatest man I know, but he's also overprotective of me. No one stands up to him when he goes on his verbal tangents. Because they know his intentions are good, and, most of the time, he's right. But you, you took him down a peg right when he needed it. I think I'll keep you." Her smile held so much humor it crinkled the corners of her eyes.

But the interaction had thrown me off, and I couldn't really respond. I kept a weird, crackly smile on my face until I got into my car, where it dropped onto the floorboard of my Mazda.

I closed my eyes and took a deep breath.

A sharp tapping on my window startled my eyelids open again.

Grant.

I rolled my window halfway down and stared at him.

"I need to apologize," he said. "Deanna told me about your financial business. I didn't mean to insult you or to insinuate anything about someone who works hard. Sometimes I come off as a bulldozing know-it-all. It's just that my sister's been through a lot, and as her older brother, I try to take care of her. Good intentions . . ."

Exactly what Deanna had said. He loved his sister. He cared about his sister. It was sweet.

It was crushing.

"I shouldn't have been so defensive." The words slid through my tight lips, my smile lost in the dark floorboard.

Silence.

More silence.

Was he expecting something else? Because that's all I had.

He nodded and wished me good night, a hesitant wave on the end of his hand.

My head gave a curt nod as I watched him walk to his own car, and then I pushed the gas harder than I meant to, forgetting I was still in park. I jerked the car into drive, my face reddening, and sped off down the road, wishing I'd biked the six miles over.

Hell as it was, this evening had taught me a quick lesson. I had a past. My past had shaped me into an immovable form, and that form didn't belong with these people. Despite what Deanna had said, it would only be a matter of time before they cracked me open and uncovered the scrambled eggs inside.

And that's when Chad settled back into my mind, and even the thought of him made me feel comfortable. He was what I was used to. I didn't even have to pretend he was a freaking number. He was just Chad. He didn't make me feel inferior. I knew that Deanna and her lovely family—minus Grant—hadn't meant to make me feel that way. They'd been delightful. But I couldn't help it; the feelings were there. And I didn't know how to manage them. How could I be surrounded by people but lonelier than ever?

What I'd had with Chad, before the cheating was an issue, wasn't perfect (obviously), but he was driven, successful, sure of himself. A workaholic who didn't want kids. Best of all, he was taller than me, one shallow prerequisite to my personal "fairly" tale.

Maybe committing to him *was* progress. Didn't everyone deserve a second chance? He hadn't been the *complete* jerk I'd thought he'd been. It still wasn't okay, and I wasn't justifying his actions, but he and his wife had both been unhappy. This situation wasn't black or white. It was gray. Like it had been with my mom and dad. Aurora had forgiven my dad because of what they'd been through. We'd lost Brandon, which had led my father to do things he wouldn't have done previously. Aurora understood that, and her words sprang back to my mind. *People are complicated.*

Before I changed my mind, I pulled over, located my cell, and did a quick online search for Vicki Gwinn. I found links to her Instagram and Facebook accounts. Before I did what I was thinking of doing, I needed to see more of Chad's soon-to-be ex-wife, prove to myself that she wasn't devastated, that what he'd said was true—that they both wanted this divorce.

The beach, a cabin in the mountains, painting some guy's toenails, a girls' weekend in Sonoma Valley, a "then and now" family pic with her brothers and sisters. His wife was surrounded, *surrounded*, by people. And just when I started to doubt I had the right woman, I found one picture of her with Chad, and he looked out of place.

If her online profiles accurately told her story and represented what was important to her, then Chad wasn't.

I reread the text he'd sent me earlier in the evening.

He wanted me, was willing to work for us. Maybe, if I worked at us, too, we could have something more.

I typed Let's talk into the reply box before I could overanalyze. Then I pressed send.

Three little dots appeared on my screen and then abruptly stopped. Two seconds passed, and then my phone rang.

CHAPTER 7
LIFE REALIZATION #5: NEVER TRUST A MASSAGE THERAPIST

Monday morning, in my new temporary office, I felt like I was living someone else's life. And I couldn't shake Friday night's dinner, even though I'd ridden my bike all weekend to compensate. Chad was coming in on Friday night to talk, and if things went well, he wanted to spend the weekend. I hoped I'd feel more settled by then. I glanced at my watch. 8:50 a.m. Ten minutes until my meeting with the clients who had fallen into my lap over coffee at Frothy Monkey.

"Black Coat, Beige! Come in, come in!" I said, inviting the twins into my office at 9:00 a.m. sharp. Okay, I didn't call them Black Coat and Beige, and I certainly wasn't that animated when I gestured to the two spartan chairs—dark leather and chrome—opposite my glass desk, but inside I'd done it all.

Black Coat pulled her *black coat* around her as she sat and looked around. "Lovely office." It was crisp, clean lines, with absolutely no color, which suited me fine. I was here to do business.

"Thank you." *I only have it for the next three months, and if you don't sign with me today, I'm likely going back to Minnesota a miserable failure who will never get clients on my own because I'm terrified of marketing myself.*

I think I was smiling. I hoped I was smiling.

"Oh, I love lilies," Beige said.

I looked in the direction of her focus. "Who's that?" I closed my eyes. The plant. Which I hadn't even known was there until Beige started fawning over it.

"Your peace lilies." Beige got up and touched one of the white flowers adoringly.

"My freak sister loves plants. Her whole house is filled with them." I reached for the folder on my desk. "Sounds . . . fresh."

"For our birthday this year"—Black Coat was still talking—"she gave me an aloe plant."

Beige smiled. "The pot read, 'Aloe you vera much.' How cute is that?"

"Okay, that was kinda cute," Black Coat admitted.

Now I knew I wasn't smiling. This was small talk. They were here to talk money, and unless Beige's plants had a trust fund that needed managing, we needed to get down to business.

I opened the folder, and the numbered chart whispered, "It's going to be okay," and I carried on.

Turns out Beige was willing to be much riskier than Black Coat, but we finally settled in a good place for each of them, and at the end of the visit, I had two new names in my finance book.

I gave them firm handshakes and told them to let me know when they sold their property, so we could get those funds squared away.

After they closed the door, I did a quick victory jog around my office, grabbed the plant—too alive to be in my care—and headed to the coffee stand in the lobby, where I was immediately assaulted.

Hands were on my shoulders, a soft voice in my ear. "You must be Pen."

I whipped around.

The woman had long, golden dreadlocks that were pulled away from her face. She wore a flowy white top over a long, multicolored skirt that dragged the floor.

"I'm Piper." I never saw her lips move, but words came from somewhere on her person. Or maybe it was actually all the jangly bracelets up and down her left arm.

She didn't say anything else but stepped back behind me and started digging her thumbs into the muscles at the base of my neck.

I froze. Should I run? Scream? Throw her over my shoulder and press my heel into her jugular?

Michelle walked up, a coffee cup hiding a smirk that said my panic amused her. "Oh, you haven't met Piper, have you?" Her smile grew.

This wasn't funny. This was outrageous. But it felt—oh my goodness—did I *want* this woman to keep touching me? Of course not, but I—ohhh.

I slid to the side, out from under Piper's confusing hands.

"You need sex," Piper said matter-of-factly. "But a full body massage will be almost as good. You also need acupuncture. You're too tense."

"I . . ."

Michelle laughed out loud now. "She's the massage therapist I was telling you about."

She had not told me about *this* massage therapist.

I had no words.

In an attempt to quell my anxiety, I'd tried yoga-light, acupuncture, hot stone therapy, anything that didn't require me to talk about my family. None of it had worked. There were a few days I'd even seen a holistic specialist and had my chakras realigned or cleansed or opened, whatever those were supposed to be. I wasn't entirely clear on what chakras even were. I probably had no business cleaning them or buffing them or . . . bottom line: I would stay away from Piper.

"And I need someone to manage my money. We'll trade." Piper smiled and walked away. "Let me know when you're free. We can talk numbers while I get rid of the rocks in your trapezius."

What the hell did that mean?

Please, please don't let me get so desperate I have to pimp myself out to Piper just to sign another client.

I needed to figure out how to market, or maybe I needed to go back to Frothy Monkey and eavesdrop, or maybe I needed to go back to Minnesota, where I knew what I was doing.

I thought of Black Coat and Beige. Right now, they were pulling me through.

CHAPTER 8
TWELVE OUNCES OF . . . MMMM

Five solid beats, like a fist on loose panes of glass, hammered in my head. My eyelids fluttered as they fought to stay closed against the sun streaming through the blinds over my bedroom window, about as good as a colander at keeping the day out. It was Saturday morning, and Chad, who'd flown in the night before, sprawled, still asleep, on the floor mattress next to me. We'd had a brief discussion about our "relationship." We both agreed to take it slow, and our commitment was loose. Throughout the week, I'd regretted my rash decision to send that "Let's talk" text, but as soon as he'd walked into my new Nashville home and swept me up into his arms, I'd melted into the greeting. He was so sure, sure enough for the both of us. Then, we'd had the sex prescribed by the insane massage therapist I'd managed to avoid all week.

The rattling continued, and I threw back the covers and looked down at my faded Counting Crows T-shirt, the one I'd had for years. As soon as I'd seen the words, already flaking—*I'm not ready for this sort of thing*—at a thrift store, I'd bought it, my homage to the nights I'd lain in bed in my early teens, listening to "A Long December" on repeat, low, so my mother wouldn't hear it as I cried myself to sleep.

With my robe belted around me, I went to the door and peeked out the window, pulling up one blind.

Oh my goodness. Oh my goodness. It was that guy from last weekend. My mind went blank. Greg, Deanna's brother, the number four. No, not Greg, Grant. Grant and his damned mustache.

What is he doing here?

I danced and paced, trying to decide whether to pretend I wasn't home or to open the door and find out why he was on my front porch standing next to Erin's grandparents' plant I'd let die.

"Penelope? Are you okay?" The voice came from the other side of the door. "I can see your outline, and it looks like you're having some sort of fit; do you need help?"

My inhalation sharpened. "Just a minute."

I gripped the belt of my robe and pulled the two sides as tight as I could until my abdomen ached, physically pulling myself together. Ever practical, my mother had taught me this trick: in an uncomfortable situation, give yourself something else to focus on: shoes that pinch, a bra latched too tight, an itchy garment, anything to distract you and keep you on your toes.

I touched my head, making sure my hair was smooth, only to realize I was still wearing my silk bonnet, a nighttime hair-wrapping method I used to keep it from frizzing. I ripped it off and threw it behind the TV. Then I ran my hands through my hair and over my eyebrows and swiped at the corners of my eyes and the edges of my mouth. At least I could count on my overnight makeup, which I'd kept on so Chad would be charmed by my oh-this-is-just-naturally-what-I-wake-up-like morning face.

With my shoulders squared and my chin up, I unlatched the drafty door and pulled it open as if I wasn't surprised at all to see him standing there, the sun hitting his back and making him glow like a mustached Adonis.

And then I saw The Nose, who smiled and waved at me. She pointed at Grant, holding a cup up in her left hand, then gave me a thumbs-up, which instantly made my face glow.

"I'm well aware I'm too early. I'm hoping these help." Grant held out a four-pack of muffins in a brown box with a window on the top of it and a covered paper to-go cup that matched the one The Nose had. "From Deanna."

"She made them? For me?" I took the box and the drink, but my hand stung on contact. Guilt. Over the past eight days—from the night I'd attempted human friendship over dinner—Deanna had texted me four times and tried calling twice. I hadn't returned any of the messages. I was too embarrassed; also, she'd been so complimentary that I'd wanted to leave on a good note. Why ruin things by renewed contact?

He nodded. "She also made me come here."

I wished my hands weren't full so I could belt my robe tighter. I barely knew these people. Why wouldn't they fade into the background?

"Coffee?" I held up the cup. "And did you bring one to my neighbor?"

"Matcha. I didn't know if you drank coffee. Everyone likes green tea. And yes. She was outside when I drove up. We got to talking, and I gave her the one I'd brought for me."

I looked away from him because that was really sweet, and I didn't want to find him charming, so I rolled my eyes and said, "Who prefers green tea over coffee?"

"You don't like it?"

"It's disgusting, and I hate it." If he didn't want brutal honesty, then he should've come with coffee, after I'd ensured my makeup hadn't gone rogue in the night, when I had on proper nonrobe clothes.

"That seems about right." His mouth cocked to the side, amused. "Try it. I made it myself."

"That's supposed to make it better?" I didn't know why I was being snarky. This man brought it out of me. Or maybe it was his mustache. If he'd just shave it, we could be friends, or, at the very least, I could be civil.

"Taste it."

I rolled my eyes again and brought the cup to my lips, taking a tentative sip. The warmth hit my mouth first, followed by a faint hint of cinnamon that was laced with mild sweetness. It was delicious. I'd heard Deanna say describing food as "delicious" was a sure indication of an unsophisticated palate.

It is delicious.

"So?" He waited for my answer.

I shrugged. "It's not really doing anything for me, sorry." How long before I could take another sip?

He nodded and let out a little "Hmm" before asking, "Are you going to invite me in?"

Chad floated through my mind. It was Saturday morning, almost eight a.m. He never slept past eight a.m. And then there was my house, the antithesis of the image I wanted to portray. Had I told them how long I'd been in Nashville? If Grant was judgy now, wait until I fueled him with my empty, crumbling house. He'd have a field day. *See, you're so busy, you can't even keep a proper home!*

Grant must've seen the hesitation in my hesitation because he said, "I promise I won't stay long. I have a job I need to get to anyway."

I moved aside and motioned him in with the glorious drink he'd given me that didn't taste a thing like green tea.

"Whoa!" he exclaimed.

I nearly dropped the drink. Had he caught me? Was he that shocked at the house? Had Chad come down shirtless, showing off his incredible abs?

He ran his hands over the wall with a tenderness that veered toward weird. "Incredible. She's incredible."

"She? What?" Was he having a stroke?

"Your house. Can't you feel it? Well, you bought it. You must feel it."

"Are you talking about the general decay or the musty smell?"

"Every house has energy," he said. "You can feel it as soon as you walk through the door. This one has great energy, but it's going to take some work to get her to her full potential." He turned toward me. "It'll be worth it, though. This is the kind of house where whatever you put into it, you'll get back and then some."

I took another sip of the can't-possibly-be green tea and pondered. When I'd walked into this house, I'd felt none of those things, but it had felt like home. Maybe Grant was the equivalent to a sommelier in the wine world, some sort of house whisperer. I liked him better for it. Slightly.

"Deanna made you come?" I was still holding the muffins and the cup, but I couldn't dare take him into my kitchen. The few dishes I owned were indecent. And he probably expected me to offer him one of the muffins, but I wasn't going to do that either. I needed him to leave.

"Yeah, she said I was the reason you weren't answering her calls or texts and that I needed to fix it. For some reason, she likes you."

His gaze was too intense, like he was looking inside me again. I cleared my throat, then automatically took another sip, forgetting the drink wasn't supposed to do anything for me. "And how long are you staying?"

He chuckled. "I guess you determine how long I stay because I have two objectives here, and if I fail, Deanna will stop returning *my* texts and phone calls."

Why do I matter to this woman? She didn't need my example of wonky entrepreneurialism. So I couldn't fathom why she wanted to be friends with me, wanted it badly enough to send her brother over with fresh baked goods and an amazing drink.

"And what are the two objectives?"

"One, you have to text her that it was actually all your fault and that you've come to your senses and realize what a great guy I am."

"Okay, so she sent you on a suicide mission. I hope you have another sister because—"

"I'm sorry. I come off as a jerk sometimes, and I have no idea how to correct this flaw. Deanna likes you." He stopped, smiled. "Like I said, don't know why, but she does. Please text her. That's the first thing."

"And the second?" I bit the inside of my cheek to keep from smiling.

"Go on at least one bike ride with our group." He winced, then held up a hand to stop the protest poised on my tongue. "Don't use me as a measure for the group. Everyone else is charming. You'll like them."

"I don't know. They associate with you, though, so . . ."

"Do I need to beg? I'll get on my knees."

"I forgive you, and I'll text Deanna. But the bike ride? That's really not necessary."

"You don't know Deanna well enough yet. She gets what she wants, and she follows through on threats. You have to come."

"I don't have to do—"

To my significant alarm, he was getting on his knees.

"Pen, what the hell? Is this guy proposing to you?" The question came from the stairs behind me. Chad was awake. Slightly jealous, slightly possessive, slightly macho-around-male-threats Chad was awake, and Grant was kneeling in front of me.

I closed my eyes.

When I opened them, Chad was standing beside me, a shirtless wonder with loose gray jogging pants around his slim waist, and Grant was extending his hand up to him—his knees still on the floor like this was a completely normal situation.

"Not proposing." Nothing derailed Grant from his business, not even a half-naked man walking into the room. "Convincing Penelope to save my relationship with my sister. I'm Grant, by the way."

Chad took Grant's hand. "Chad, Pen's boyfriend." Well, so much for taking things slow.

"I gathered that." Grant eyed Chad's abdomen. "So, Penelope, will you go on that bike ride? We meet every Sunday. If tomorrow's too soon, you can go next weekend or the weekend after that."

"Bike ride? Like a date?" Chad asked. "So, you're not proposing, but you *are* asking my girlfriend on a date . . . right in front of me?" He looked around the room as if to find someone to sympathize with him.

I opened my mouth, closed it again. I wanted to slowly walk backward, ascend the stairs, and be alone with the treats I was still holding. I'd always kind of liked how Chad got jealous, and it had never seemed too much—until now. Now he looked like a muscled meathead.

Pen Chad's. Grant not take Pen away from Chad. I stifled a giggle.

"Not a date, just a—"

I cut Grant off. "Fine. One bike ride, but please get up." I turned toward Chad's open mouth. "I'll explain when he leaves, which he was about to do, right, Grant?"

Chad's jaw clenched. "I can tell you that."

Oh my goodness.

"I've accomplished what I came to do." Grant was already up and walking toward the door.

Chad started to follow, but the back of my hand on his chest stopped him from moving forward.

At the door, Grant turned, and his right hand came toward me. I saw Chad flinch out of the corner of my eye.

Grant's hand wrapped around the cup in mine. Our fingers touched, and I swallowed the flutter coming up from my stomach. Holding my gaze, his eyes asked *This is what you want?* as his lips said, "I'll save you from my disgusting drink."

How dare his eyes ask if Chad was what I wanted. If circumstances had been different, maybe I'd want something else, someone else. But certainly not Grant. Why had my mind gone there? "Dating" and "Grant" didn't belong in the same sentence. It was the tea. He'd spiked it with something. That's why it'd been so damned delicious. Or maybe I was reading too much into his expression. Ugh! He needed to leave.

He eased the cup out of my hand.

Neither one of us acknowledged that it was empty.

CHAPTER 9
LIFE REALIZATION #6: CHICKENS ARE SURPRISINGLY RESILIENT

Two weeks later, officially in a long-distance relationship with Chad and inching my business forward like a turtle with no legs, I made good on my promise to Grant by going on that freaking group bike ride.

To avoid people watching me, I chose the back of the pack, where I could relax enough to enjoy the gently sloping landscapes of the Tennessee countryside. The green, everything was green. The hills. The trees. The stems on the wildflowers. All contrasting beautifully against the bright-blue sky. The air was filled with a symphony for the nostrils: cut grass, honeysuckle, and unpolluted air.

A short, stocky woman named Dani rode beside me, giving me the details of the group.

Frank was an accountant and full of himself but surprisingly knowledgeable. Sarah, his wife, was a quiet triathlete who crocheted. William was an electrical engineer, kind, but usually boring. Grant was a nonconformist architect whom Dani had a difficult time summing up in one sentence. It was funny getting these one-liners from a stranger, especially about the two I'd already met. There were others, but her rundown was interrupted by an incident ahead.

Everyone stopped, either straddling or standing beside their bikes on the road, next to a white wooden fence, a farmhouse in the distance.

Someone was on the ground, in the middle of the empty street, yelling. Someone else was helping him to his feet.

"I gotta see what's going on," Dani said and then rode away from me.

Before I could figure out what had happened, the crew was once again riding in the direction of Marcy Jo's, our midride lunch destination. Only one person stayed behind, hunched over something I couldn't see in the patch of grass beside the road.

Grant.

I don't know why I stopped, but I did.

"What is it, little gal?" I heard him say as I unlatched my kickstand and got closer. He bent forward; then a bird screeched, leaped up, and smacked him in the face. Grant's arms shot out and grabbed the floundering mass of feathers.

"Is that a chicken?" I asked, wide eyed.

"Look in that pack right there, will you?" Grant nodded toward the folded leather pack in the dry dirt beside him.

I bent to pick it up.

"I'll need an antiseptic pad, the small packet of styptic powder, and gauze."

I dropped the pack, my vision blurring.

"Gauze? Why do you need gauze?" I backed away, holding one hand over my mouth.

"Superficial scratch on her leg. Amazing, since a man-child and his bike ran *into* her." I didn't move. "I'll get the supplies then." He shifted to the pack, keeping his eye on me.

"I don't . . . I don't do blood." My voice was far away, as if it had left my body. It wasn't blood exactly; it was anything medical. The gauze, the injury, the implication of a hospital, all of it triggered an internal storm. Okay, panic. I panicked at all that stuff.

"Why don't you sit down?"

I didn't *want* to need to, but I needed to. I sat and viciously plucked at the clover on either side of me.

"I have to ask," he said to my back. "What did you expect to see here after witnessing that collision?"

"Collision?" My voice cracked on the word.

Damn it. Damn it. Damn it.

Why hadn't I ridden on with everyone else instead of staying with this insane man, tending to a random chicken on the side of the road.

"You didn't see William run right into this bird?"

"What? No! I would've never come over here if . . ." I trailed off, my stomach splashing acid onto the words. "I was in the back. I thought you said you were an architect. Shouldn't a vet be doing this?"

Out of the corner of my eye, I watched his hands move as he spoke. "I came across a dog once, riding on the back roads. She'd had . . . a little accident." He paused. "Now, I'm always prepared."

That would never be me. I couldn't do things like that, which was why I'd never had a pet or a plant and never wanted kids.

Grant did things like that.

He looked down and smiled at the bird. "Good as new."

"You're done?"

"Yep. And everything's covered." He stepped over to me, the animal tucked firmly under his arm. "Just an ornery chicken."

I stood, then stepped closer to Grant and the bird, squinting so I wouldn't accidentally *see* the injury. I calmed at the sight of sweet little beady eyes and ran a shaking hand over soft feathers.

Grant looked down the empty road. "Heartless jerks. At least you stayed. Thanks for your . . . help."

"Does it count if I was wishing the whole time that I'd left with them?"

He laughed. His laugh was nice. "It counts."

He gestured toward the farmhouse and told me he was going to take the bird home.

He blinked. I blinked. The chicken blinked.

"I'll come with you." Why was I drawn to a situation that also repulsed me? The sun reflected off a golden fleck in his eye. "I don't know how to get to our next stop anyway." *That* was why I was following him. Right?

"Marcy Jo's? You keep going straight. Run right into it."

As we moved forward, a teenage boy wearing a white T-shirt and jeans materialized beside us. He took the chicken and, after listening to what had happened, thanked Grant, all while rubbing his face against the bird's feathers and whispering, "You know better, wild Gloria." The boy tipped his head. "We'll get her seen to." He bellowed another "thank you" as he backed away and then ran up the hill.

Disappointment curled in my stomach. I ignored it, passing it off as a side effect from helping the chicken and not from my realization that we weren't going to be walking up to the farmhouse alone together.

Grant put his hand on the fence next to us. "William's a cheat. We had an unofficial bet going on, first to Marcy Jo's."

"Racing?" I needed to be back on my bicycle. There was too much about this man, this ride, that chicken.

"Yeah, William was behind me before—"

He cut himself off as I ran over to my bicycle, hopped on, and took off, a little plume of dust spitting out from the back of my tires as I bumped onto the asphalt.

"I thought you said you didn't know how to get there!" he shouted.

I called out over my shoulder, "You keep going straight. Can't miss it."

❧

The split rail fence at Marcy Jo's Mealhouse supported twelve bicycles. I was the thirteenth. The last. The loser because Grant had caught up to and passed me.

A smiling woman in a lightweight blue sweater and jeans greeted me when I walked through the very red door, said her name was Marcy, and gestured animatedly toward two mismatched tables that were so scratched up they were charming and had been pushed together to accommodate the large cycling party.

Grant was at the other end of the table, and as soon as our eyes met, my stomach twitched for some ridiculous reason, and I stuck out my tongue at him like a child.

He grinned.

I ordered—biscuits and gravy, even though I wasn't hungry—then sat beside Dani, who immediately started talking like I'd been there the whole time. I inhaled, turned everyone into agreeable numbers, and nodded like I was fascinated by the fact that Dani's daughter had perfect pitch.

Despite my effort to ignore the men at the other end of the table, my ears, *and eyes*, had other ideas, damn them.

"I don't know anyone in their forties that can put food away like you can and still look like a beanpole," Grant said.

William pushed a healthy bite into his mouth. "Not forty yet."

Grant dusted his mouth off in an effort to hint at the jam on William's face. "Your table manners are obscene."

"Someone didn't throw a chicken at you."

"You're lucky you didn't kill her."

"He looked fine!" William said around two-thirds of a biscuit. "How did it feel to be left in the dust, though, all by yourself?"

"*She.* The chicken was a lady, Gloria. And I wasn't by myself." Grant looked up, directly into my eyes. Mine ricocheted away, fastened onto a small sign that read **HOMEMADE BUTTERMILK PANCAKES** in the middle of the table as my cheeks burned. *Look at the way they dust that powdered sugar!*

I forced myself to focus on Dani, but all through the meal—I ate two bites—I felt Grant's eyes on me. Those eyes prevented me from demolishing this gravy-smothered amazingness. Too nervous.

Relief flooded me when someone suggested we head back outside, but then Grant stepped up beside me. My pulse giggled like a schoolgirl. Ignorant pulse.

"You've enjoyed the ride?"

"Yeah, thanks for the invite." But it wasn't an invite . . . begging? It was begging.

"Think you'll come again?"

No.

I shrugged. "Sure."

"Good."

I grabbed my helmet and put it on. Why was he standing here?

"Has Deanna talked to you about Wildhorse yet?"

I pinched the skin of my neck in my helmet strap. Ouch! "Who's Wild Horse?"

"Wildhorse Saloon. Downtown."

I shook my head, and Grant smiled.

"You've been downtown, right? Broadway?"

"I have an office downtown."

William came up beside us, threw his arm around Grant's shoulders. "But have you been down Broadway? Honky Tonk Highway? Line dancing? Country music?"

I shook my head.

"If you're going to live in Nashville," William continued, "you've got to go down Broadway at least once."

"But I don't dance, and I don't like country music."

William grabbed his chest as if I'd insulted him personally.

"I don't like country music either," Grant admitted, still smiling. "But a swing group rents out the first floor of Wildhorse once a year. We're going in a couple of weeks. You should come. You can get a taste of downtown Nashville without having to listen to that much country."

"You have to come," William insisted.

Grant looked at me, waited for my answer, that smile still just under that mustache.

"But . . ."

I needed to ride because I had the uncomfortable feeling country music was in my future.

CHAPTER 10
EIGHT CALLS, PENELOPE?

"One card before we go out to meet Deanna and her friends," I said to Chad two weeks later as we sat on my bed, and I held up a small box.

I'd covertly ordered the cards from Amazon, something similar to the ones Deanna had that first disastrous night I'd gone over there. I couldn't remember the exact name of what she'd had, and I certainly wasn't going to ask. I'd found my own, a set with four and a half stars and 5,230 ratings that promised "150 Conversation Starters for Couples to Strengthen Their Relationship." I'd broken out in a cold sweat after I'd ordered them, again when I was alerted they were out for delivery, and my whole body shook when I first took them out of the package.

Who buys this stuff?

But exposure therapy works, mostly. Every day for two weeks, I'd taken them out of the shoebox in the closet and made myself hold them.

Chad, in his slate button-down and crisp black slacks, leaned over and kissed down the side of my neck. "So, what are we doing?"

I hesitated, thinking maybe this was a bad idea, but Deanna had asked me if Chad had siblings. I didn't know, and she couldn't believe I didn't know, and I couldn't believe I didn't know, and—we needed to do this, to get to know each other better.

I also needed to distract myself because tonight, he was not only meeting William, Deanna, and Grant, but I was meeting Deanna's friends.

In the two weeks since Grant had shown up with matcha at my door, I'd gone on another ride with their bike crew. I adored William, who complemented Deanna in every way, and, to my surprise, Grant had also grown on me. He needed to lose the mustache, but he'd been nice enough and had taken the time to show me the benefits of using clips on my bicycle pedals, which I hadn't known were a thing. Best of all, Deanna and I had forged an unexpected relationship, building on what had apparently started that night at her house. We'd lunched multiple times. She randomly texted me. And after she'd seen my house—*she'd insisted on seeing it*—we went shopping, and she helped me decorate. I'd even heard her refer to me as her friend.

I liked the slow progression of incorporating someone into my life. And now, Chad was a part of that; at least I wanted him to be. He seemed especially important since my feelings for Grant were shifting. I *liked* spending time with him, and Grant was absolutely off limits for so many reasons, the chief being his girlfriend, Elaine, whom I'd be meeting tonight. No, the chief being, I wasn't interested, no matter what other parts of my body seemed to suggest. Thank God for Chad was all I was saying.

I opened the box like a live tarantula was inside and yanked out a card, read silently, then aloud like a robot, "'What's one thing you think I could improve on?'"

For the first time, I needed to turn Chad into a number. It was the only way I was going to get through this. *A smooth five.* I hadn't asked him; I'd asked a smooth five. The five rolled his eyes.

"You're serious? You think a box of cards will help us 'get closer'?" He tried to kiss me again, but I shrugged him off.

"Fine," he sighed. "What was the question again?"

I looked back down at the card I'd already memorized, repeated it.

He smirked, took the card out of my hand, slid it back into the box, and tossed the box onto the floor. It made a loud thud and then a swish as the cards fanned out across the hardwood.

"You know what you need to change, Pen Auberge? The fact that you have clothes on." He pulled the tie on the side of my black wrap dress and slid his hand around my bare waist. "I have a better way for us to get to know each other."

I stood, throwing him off balance, and pulled the dress—which matched his outfit—back around me. I didn't know why I was surprised. This was how we worked. We connected in bed. And while it was amazing, we needed more. Didn't we?

"We'll be late if we try to do anything now."

He lifted one eyebrow. "But we have time for a game?"

It wasn't a game, but I didn't argue. I wanted him to be in a good mood when he met everyone.

He bit his lower lip and let a sigh rumble up from deep in his throat. "Now that I'm here and we only have the weekend and you look so sexy, I want to keep you to myself. Why don't you call Deanna and cancel?"

"Because I like Deanna. She's important to me." My tone was firm because I was irritated that he was trying to back out. "And she wants me to meet her friends."

He shifted upward. "More important than me? You've known these people a handful of weeks, tops. Come on, Pen. You can't possibly want to stay in Nashville, and these constant weekend flights are going to bankrupt me."

He could make weekend flights for an entire year and barely touch his significant nest egg. I knew; I managed his money.

"If we're going to be together," he added, "then don't you think it's more important to focus on us?"

I wanted to bring up the cards, but I bit my tongue. I didn't have a good answer for him. But I did know that Deanna had kept close even when I'd tried to push away. It was like she knew what I needed, like she sensed my desire under my reservation. Most people would've called me an ice queen and moved along. To be honest, I was a little giddy at the whole business, which is why I'd finally agreed to this evening. Simultaneously, it felt terrifying and good having a friend, even though under the surface doubt hummed, a constant reminder not to build anything too high, or the inevitable crash would leave scars.

"What if I said I wanted to stay in Nashville?" I ventured.

His jaw sprang shut, clenched. He didn't want to believe me. Long distance was *not* working for him.

His face relaxed as he shifted off the bed and walked the three feet to me, then wrapped both his arms around my lower back and pulled me to him. "I'll change your mind."

His eyes were heavy lidded, and his mouth held a hint of a smile. He was banking on his sex appeal, which he had in spades, to woo me.

I shouldn't have pushed the conversation right before dinner, but I didn't cave in to him, like I usually did when his voice was low and I liked how he wanted me. "I'm serious. Everything is better here."

His arms dropped with a slap on his thighs. "Business is better here?"

I threw too much enthusiasm into my voice. "Yes! My business is thriving." Wow. My business was *not* thriving. I had one new client, a guy who thought two thousand dollars was a ton of money. But in the last couple of weeks, with Michelle's help, I'd developed a website and marketing collateral. And I'd also created an account with BNI, a referral organization. My *materials* were thriving, and that was part of my business. *Part* of my business was thriving!

"You know you're probably only staying afloat right now because you manage my family's money. My dad *was* a little concerned when you left Twin Cities."

Why is he mentioning this?

A week after I'd met Chad, I'd started managing his money. A week after that, he'd talked his family into signing with me, though they knew a good planner when they saw one. And I knew full well that Chad had talked his dad into staying with me when I left TCF, but that was less for my sake and more for theirs. It'd been sticky keeping them all as clients, but I needed them. He knew I needed them.

"Are you threatening to pull your family's money if I don't go back?" My body shook.

If he pulled their business, I'd be crippled, and I might be forced to go back, exactly what he wanted. Because I couldn't grow my own money fast enough, given all my recent expenses, without a lot more smaller clients or at least another large one.

I turned away from him, trying desperately to harness my breathing. I eyed the stationary bike I'd purchased a couple of weeks ago, which was positioned by the window, for the stormy days. A mental necessity.

He sighed again. "Of course not. I'm worried about you. I feel like these people are changing you. You're not the same girl I loved in the Cities."

"You mean I'm not the same girl who goes along with everything you want to do?"

"See, this is what I mean! We're arguing over stupid stuff, like Vicki and I used to."

Vicki. For the past several weeks, I'd cyberstalked her just to confirm to myself that she was happy, but there was no need. She was already engaged to someone else, anxiously awaiting her and Chad's divorce to be final so she and her new guy could wed in Maui—she'd indeed been in love with her best friend. She looked really happy. Ironically, I wanted what she had.

"Well, you don't have to worry, Chad, because I'm not like Vicki."

"I didn't mean that. I'm sorry. I—"

My phone started ringing on the dresser Deanna had helped me pick out, white wood that matched the white sleigh bed I'd also purchased. All the white made the royal purple accent pillows and fleece throw pop; the room was morphing into a livable space, like a real human lived here.

I went to my phone.

"Hello, Mother," I said, and then held up a finger to Chad, not the finger I wanted to either.

His lips curled in satisfaction as he returned to my bed, propping himself up on his arms and crossing his legs at the ankles. He was glad my mother was calling. They both wanted me to return to Minnesota, something they discussed during their weekly lunches without me. Gross.

I turned my back to Chad.

"Eight calls, Penelope?" My mother's tone radiated high and mighty.

"I'm sorry. I've been busy. I was planning to call you tomorrow when I had more time. Chad and I were about to leave for dinner."

"At least you have a good excuse."

Bingo.

"Give Chad my love, will you?" she continued. "Has he convinced you to come to your senses and move back here yet? What's that noise? A saw? Is Chad sawing?"

That had been my teeth grinding, little pieces of enamel shearing straight out of my mouth.

"I'm putting on lipstick," I lied. "It must've been the phone against my cheek."

"Oh, speaking of! I found the most perfect perfume for you. It'll go flawlessly with the summer outfit I found. I can see it now, you on Chad's arm floating into summer garden parties, impressing everyone. I've been keeping in close contact with Houston. TCF still wants you back." Duh, so they could have me work my ass off, then serve said ass with a chilled chianti during a celebratory dinner where they congratulate Dougan or Frenchy or some other equally douchey-named finance sleaze on *his* new client acquisition.

I wanted to scream, but I held it in as my lips twitched and I stared at the wall like a psycho in an asylum.

My mother's mission was to mold my life into *her* perfect vision. I was her Barbie doll. Now, she had a dream house, matching Ken doll, and high-profile career picked out, all in demure shades of beige, black, and white, all made of plastic. And not the good kind of Beige and Black who inherited money. Some part of me still wanted to bend to her will. It was easier when she made all the decisions.

"Mother, can we talk about this later? Chad's waiting, and he looks like he's getting impatient."

Chad sat up and whispered, "Why did you tell her that? I want her to like me."

I covered the mouthpiece. "Oh, stop. You're so far up her ass, I can smell your cologne when she talks."

His mouth dropped open, and he reddened slightly.

Was it wrong to take pleasure in using them against each other?

"Of course," Aurora said. "You two have fun. I can't wait to see you. Make it soon."

"Soon. Yes. We'll talk soon."

"Kiss, kiss."

I ended the call and attempted to inhale. My phone rang again in my hands, and I gripped it so hard the plastic case started to crackle. But when I looked at the screen, it wasn't my mother. An unknown caller from Minnesota.

"Hello?"

"Oh, Pen, thank God I got you." A woman, but whoever it was, was whispering. I couldn't place the voice.

"Excuse me?"

"It's Erin. I need to talk to you."

"Erin?" As in Houston's secretary Erin? I didn't know anyone else by that name.

"Yeah. From Twin Cities. I can't talk now, but there's some shady stuff going on here, and I think you should know about it."

"What?" I pushed the phone harder against my ear, waiting.

"They're in the conference room now. I excused myself to go to the bathroom, but I had to call you, give you a heads-up. Houston's in there with—"

The phone went silent.

Who? Who is in the conference room? Why is she at the office on a Saturday night?

"Shit! They're coming out now. I gotta go. I'll call you later."

Later? No. I needed to know now, or my whole evening would be ruined.

"Erin? Erin?" I frantically tried to make sure she was still there.

But she was gone.

CHAPTER 11
THE DANCE NUMBER

The Wildhorse Saloon was huge, with multiple open levels, a stage, and fancy lighting shaped like rays of the sun. Even though the room was large, it appeared intimate, which was almost enough to take my mind off that phone call.

After Deanna had excitedly shaken Chad's hand, she introduced us to her two best friends, who were already seated at a long, polished wood table.

"This is Meredith; she goes by Mere. And this is Keyondra. Please don't call her Kiki; she stopped responding to that years ago, when she decided she wanted to be taken seriously."

I already knew Mere was married, liked cats and red wine, and taught kickboxing on weekends, and that Keyondra, who incidentally hated cats (or at least was allergic to them), liked fruity cocktails, had an African art collection, and spent her time being followed around by her "skinny-ass White boyfriend." Her words, not mine. That's literally how she'd introduced him, because what self-respecting 180-pound proud-to-be-Black woman fell for a tall, lanky White guy with no ass?

Keyondra (an eighteen) helped Deanna with party organization and decoration, and Mere (a fourteen) did the accounting. I only occasionally envisioned people as double digits past ten, but sometimes it fit. The three women were like a well-oiled machine in business and friendship. They made sense. They all liked the same books, which they discussed in an official book club along with three others, including the elusive Chuck's sister and Grant's girlfriend, Elaine, the newest member of their club. Though she'd been mentioned the least, and what did *that* say about their relationship? Surely that meant . . . of course I didn't care.

I liked these women, but I'd known Deanna for weeks; they'd known her for years. I tried not to let it eat at me.

I ended up wedged between Chad to my left and Elaine to my right, and they were the only people I could hear because of the noise. I wasn't really paying attention anyway. I clutched my phone, sneaked peeks at the screen, and stress-ate "Nashville Hot" chicken dip.

"Everything okay?" Grant asked, leaning over Elaine so I could hear him.

I'd tried calling Erin back three times, but my call had gone straight to voicemail every single time. And I couldn't stop thinking about that call, the equivalent to her accidentally lighting me on fire and then running a few blocks away to get a fire extinguisher after telling me to hang tight.

I didn't tell Grant any of this. Instead, I smiled, nodded, and tucked my phone under my thigh.

"What do you do, Chad?" Grant yelled across me and Elaine (a seven, a perfect, sparkling seven) as caramel apple pie was being delivered to the table. "Are you in finance like Penelope?"

"Attorney," Chad answered. "Criminal law. You build houses, right?"

"Essentially . . ." Grant trailed off, which was odd because Grant could converse with a tree stump and very likely had.

"What do you do, Elaine?" I tried to cover the awkwardness that might or might not be in the air while also trying to distract myself so I wouldn't place a fourth call to Erin.

"Oh, I'm a therapist."

I accidentally frowned. Elaine looked like she was going to say something else, but the lights dimmed, and music started.

"It's go time!" Keyondra's skinny-ass White boyfriend, whose real name was Conner, said as he stood up and put a bowler hat on his head. He stuck his arm out to Keyondra, who latched on and rose.

"You guys coming?" Keyondra asked. Mere and her husband, Devon, stood, followed by Grant and Elaine and William, who went to stand by Deanna, hand outstretched.

Deanna looked back at Chad and me. "What about you guys?"

I shook my head.

"Electro-swing night!" Conner interjected. "You gotta come!" His feet were already moving to the mash of vintage swing and the thumping beat of more modern hip-hop. It made me want to move, too, only . . . out of the saloon.

Keyondra dragged Conner away from the table. Mere shrugged, grabbed her husband's arm, and left too. Grant and Elaine were already on the dance floor. Elaine laughed, touching Grant's arm as he instructed her on how to slide a few feet to her left.

Chad put his hands on the table as if to lift himself up and out onto the dance floor. "You wanna show 'em what we got?"

"What who has? And how do you know about this?"

"Andy's into this." I'd never met Andy. He was one of the lawyers at Chad's firm. "One night me and the guys got drunk, and Andy made us all learn to shuffle. It's easy. Follow my lead." He snapped his head toward the others as I shook my own.

The only way I was getting out on that dance floor was after hundreds of private lessons with a guy on YouTube before I attended an in-person class as a beginner so as to impress my teacher with how quickly I was picking up the dance steps I had supposedly never seen before.

I glanced at the now-crowded dance floor, bodies gyrating together like they were in a blender.

No, I wasn't going out there. And even if I could dance, Erin could call any minute.

Chad's crossed-arm pout suggested I was ruining the only fun event of the evening. To his credit, he'd tried, but after his second drink, it was obvious he didn't want to be here. He joked about the crappy food and the cowboy hats the tourists wore. After the fourth comment, I dug my fingernail into his thigh. He stopped talking, but then he started drinking . . . a lot.

Deanna wouldn't go without us, so the three of us, me, Chad, and Deanna, watched everyone else. My phone rang once, a wrong number. After biting the caller's head off because they weren't Erin, I decided I needed to tuck my phone into my purse and look back at the dance floor. But why wasn't Erin calling?

Keyondra and Conner were actually pretty good.

Grant came back to his seat. "What'd you think?"

He was looking at me when he asked, but Chad answered, "I think we do it better up north."

"You must've missed *me* out there then," William added, so winded he barely got the words out.

"Oh, I think he saw you." Deanna rubbed her husband's back. "Why don't you sit down."

"Good idea." William flopped into the chair and drank from a glass I wasn't sure was his.

"I didn't see *you* out there," Grant said to Chad. If he'd been drinking, too, I couldn't tell.

Chad's eyebrows went up on his forehead. "Oh, I can shuffle. Pen didn't want to get out there."

"I guess we'll never know for sure." Grant winked.

What was he doing? Didn't he know he was provoking Chad? He read people too well not to know.

Chad threw back the rest of his drink and stood up a little too fast, nearly knocking his chair over. "That sounds like a challenge. You wanna see me dance, Mustache?"

Yeah, he'd had too much to drink. I started pulling at Chad's arm, looking around with a smile on my face like *He's kidding, totally kidding. Nothing to see here.*

The half smile on Grant's face along with his sly shrug pushed Chad over the edge.

"Come on then." Chad nodded over and over again. "I'll show you how it's done."

I was clawing at his arm now; any second, I was going to draw blood. "Oh, I don't think that's—"

"No." Chad cut me off, then shrugged out of my grip. "Mustache thinks he can shuffle better than I can."

No. No. No. No. No. NO. This wasn't happening. Where was Lawyer Chad, the one who made good decisions based on well-thought-out arguments and evidence? Good Chad was floating in a hot tub of whiskey, actively being drowned by drunk, jealous Macho Chad, who was suggesting some sort of dance-off.

Who does that? Even drunk, who does that?

William, Mere, Devon, Conner, and Keyondra pounded on the table, shaking the water glasses, and chanting, "Chal-lenge! Chal-lenge!"

Grant rolled up the sleeves of his white oxford, then twirled the edge of his mustache. He was enjoying this, the bastard. They were all enjoying this. They were all nuts. What was in the alcohol here?

My eyes flew to Deanna, pleading with her to do something. Grant was her brother, after all.

"If they want to look like fools, who are we to stop them?" she asked.

I wanted to stop them. I'd wanted a distraction tonight, but this wasn't the one.

Grant bent low as he passed my chair. "I hope you don't mind me taking your fancy boyfriend down a peg." Then he winked at me, grabbed Conner's bowler hat off his head, and turned away before I could beg him to stop.

Elaine covered her eyes. "I can't look." But she was smiling.

"If you're worried about Grant, don't be," Keyondra said. "He got this."

I scooted a little lower in my chair, *a lot lower*. A new song came on, and Conner popped up. "I'll judge!" he said and then ran out to join Chad and Grant.

The crowd parted for the three men. A slow thumping beat with a thin line of brass accompaniment overtook the room as Grant stood to the side and threw his hand out toward Chad, giving him the honors of going first.

Chad's chest expanded; his grin took on a devilish slant. And then he started moving, a frantic heel-to-toe tapping, arms swinging like a machine fueled by too much liquor and pride. But he was doing it, and he didn't look too bad doing it. His turn ended with a stationary running man followed by a scissor kick. Sweaty and breathing heavily, he motioned to Grant, who was already clapping and nodding in appreciation.

Grant tilted his hat on his head and moved slowly, snapping in time with the music. His arms shot out, then his feet swept him to the side with a long hum of the trumpet, like he'd heard the song before and knew exactly when to move to make each note work to his advantage. His arm moved up and down, a casual snap in the air, as his body rocked from side to side, and then he spun and grabbed his hat and let it roll down his arm until it reached his elbow, when he jerked, flicking the hat into the air and back onto his head.

Elaine squealed with delight.

Chad's moves had been capable, something else I didn't know about him. But Grant's moves were effortless. He was lost in the rhythm, his body one with the song.

Just as he appeared to be slowing down, Conner jumped beside Grant, and the two men moved in sync. When Grant's leg kicked left, so did Conner's and vice versa.

"Oh, I gotta get in on this." Keyondra vacated her chair and ran to the dance floor. And then it was the three of them, moving together in a triangular formation, with Conner at the apex, arms and legs moving in tandem like well-practiced, synchronous pendulums.

"They're good," William said.

"They're *really* good." Deanna, elbows on table, was mesmerized like everyone else.

"How come we've never seen them do this?" Mere slapped Deanna's arm, and Deanna shook her head and shrugged.

The song ended, and the four dancers returned to the table, but not before Chad had bowed to the other three.

"The victors," Chad admitted as they returned to the table. "But I didn't have backup dancers, so it wasn't a fair fight."

Conner laughed. "You held your own, man!"

Everyone was laughing, except Chad, who kept the same grin plastered on his face.

He leaned down until his clenched teeth were next to my ear. "Let's go."

I stood, grabbing my jacket without protest. His tone suggested he was barely holding it together, and I couldn't take another scene.

"You guys leaving already?" Grant looked between the two of us. "Had enough, have you?"

I closed my eyes and swallowed, hoping Chad could keep that grin on his face until we made it to the door.

"Of some things." Chad stared at Grant. "But really, I want this girl to myself. I've only got the weekend to convince her to come back to Minnesota with me." He winked. "It's been a pleasure." He started toward the door.

"Are you thinking of moving back, Pen?" Deanna looked like she'd been slapped, which touched me.

"No. At least, I don't think so. Can we talk about it later?"

"Yeah, of course."

I wanted to sit back down, but Chad was already a good distance away from me.

"I'm sorry to cut the evening short. It's been great meeting you all."

"Girl, this is the beginning. You're all right," Keyondra said.

Everyone else said their goodbyes, but Grant wouldn't make eye contact. He held on to Elaine's hand. I tried not to let his snub bother me, or better yet, I wouldn't acknowledge that it was a snub as Chad opened the saloon doors, and the country music swallowed us on the sidewalk of Second Avenue.

CHAPTER 12
THREE WORDS: HOUSTON FREAKING MCGREGOR

Midnight. That's when Erin finally called. I got out of bed so I wouldn't wake Chad, but he'd had so much to drink that starting drum lessons beside his pillow probably wouldn't have roused him.

I was angry with him, but that didn't matter right now. I needed to hear what Erin had to say.

I'd cycled through all kinds of possibilities, from Houston in a sex-trafficking ring, handcuffed, his no-longer-smug face above the newspaper article that said his clients would be transferred to independent financial planner Pen Auberge, all the way to Houston guaranteeing Chad's dad better financial returns, an impossible promise.

"Sorry for the delay," Erin said. "My boyfriend just broke up with me."

Uh. How to respond?

"I'm so sorry. Are you okay?" For me, this wasn't a huge deal. But for normal people, breakups weren't necessarily par for the course.

"Honestly, it's fine. It's going to be a little weird living with him until I get my own place, but . . ." She inhaled. "Don't wanna talk about it. I'll cry if I do." She sighed. "I want to tell you about Houston instead."

I was downstairs now, pacing in my still-empty living room.

"So, you remember the Fletchers. Ugh! Of course you remember them. They're why you left Twin Cities. I'm sorry. I'm tired and angry—so, so angry. And I did something. I could really get into trouble, and I need this job, and . . ."

"Erin." I forced patience into her name. "Take a second and calm down. There's no pressure. No rush." There absolutely was pressure, definitely a rush.

"So, Tyler's been managing the Fletcher account, right? Mrs. Fletcher called the office earlier today—apparently this wasn't the first time, but it *was* the first time *I* talked to her. She asked for you, and when I told her you no longer worked at TCF, she was livid. She demanded I transfer her to Houston immediately. I did."

I hoped the next thing she told me was that the Fletchers had pulled their business. My noncompete prohibited me from going after them, but them dropping Houston was a glorious thought.

"He had them come into the office, and I listened to their conversation," Erin continued. I heard her take a drink of something. "Pen, Houston never told them that Tyler was handling them solo. Mrs. Fletcher said, 'How dare you lie to me,' and Houston tried to smooth things over—you know how he does—but she wasn't buying his back-alley crap. She told him she wanted your information, but he wouldn't give it to her. He suggested she and her husband come to the office so he could explain the *delicate* situation. Totally sus because all you'd done was an awesome job. You're literally my idol, and I've been trying to think of a way to get you justice."

Her last words rocketed into me. I had to sit down on the carpet. Her idol?

I must've misheard. I wasn't anyone's idol.

Her idol.

I cleared my throat.

"I haven't told you the worst part," she continued. "Houston told them you left under shady circumstances."

"What?" I couldn't swallow. All the saliva in my mouth evaporated.

"He told them he was trying to spare your reputation by keeping it quiet because he felt bad about putting their funds into your hands, someone so unworthy of it."

My vision blurred. The room went red, red and too small and lacking the proper amount of oxygen. They were huge clients with a long reach. If they believed Houston . . .

"He told them what?" I spit into the phone.

"I know. I was furious. I didn't know what to do. You should've seen his fat, smug face. He was proud of himself, like lying about you gave him another ball or something. He called me into his office after, but I told him Mrs. Fletcher had dropped her bracelet, and I needed to catch her to give it back. She hadn't, but I couldn't let them leave thinking what Houston had told them about you was true. I caught them in the parking lot."

My head swam. "What did you do?"

"I told them Houston was lying." A dog barked in the background, and she paused again to soothe it. "I told them everything, laid it out right beside their freakin' Mercedes. Mr. Fletcher was skeptical, but there was doubt on Mrs. Fletcher's face. She wanted to believe me. You'd made an impression on her. Stop it, Hulk!" I blinked, wondering if this was what Erin had screamed at Mr. Fletcher, but she was talking to the dog again. "I begged her to call you, gave her your cell, and she promised me she would Monday. Mr. Fletcher wanted to go back up and talk to Houston again, but I told Mrs. Fletcher I'd be fired if he knew I'd told them. She said they wouldn't say anything. I should've been relieved because I think she meant it, but I'm not. I'm sick over this whole thing. Can you believe this?"

I'd had a ton of negative thoughts about Houston over the last several weeks, but I'd never thought anything close to this. He'd screwed me over so badly that day when he'd told me he was giving Tyler the Fletcher account. Tyler, whose parents had money, whose parents' parents had money. My parents had money, too, but apparently not enough. And my dad was a Black doctor who drank too much and cheated on his wife, and my mother was the White control freak who allowed it. The truth was, Houston had a fair amount of ammunition to ruin my reputation if he wanted to, and he appeared to want to.

My eyes were leaking, but not from sadness. These were the tears you curse when you want to be taken seriously but your eyes betray you. They make you look weak, like you're a fumbling, emotional mess who doesn't know how to have a proper argument.

"Please say something," Erin said.

"I don't know what to say."

"Say you're going to skin Houston McGregor alive and use his hide to make me a hideous, faux-human jacket."

I laughed. Despite it all, I laughed, and while I laughed, I came back to myself—a little.

"Thanks for that, Erin. Thanks for all this. Thanks for sticking your neck out there for me. No one else would've done it."

"I'd do it again a thousand times. No one deserves to be lied about, especially not you. And I meant what I said earlier. I wanna be you when I grow up. You're a boss and you slay. Nothing stands in your way. This won't either."

I thanked her again. This woman believed in me. And Deanna did too. For all the pretense in my life, my work was real, and I wasn't going to let either of them down. I may not have had many personal victories, but I sure as hell was going to have some professional ones.

Her idol.

"Well, if I don't get more clients soon, what Houston says about me will be the least of my worries. My book isn't competitive right now."

"What happened to the TCF clients who said they were following you?"

"I have a noncompete. I can't—"

"Yeah, yeah. I know that, but that doesn't count if clients follow you on their own, and at least four have said they planned to. Haven't you heard from them?"

A rock landed in the base of my stomach. My noncompete expressly said I couldn't pursue TCF clients for a period of one year, but that didn't apply if they contacted me first.

"I haven't heard from any of the clients I had at TCF."

"Shit," she whispered.

"That bastard." The Fletchers weren't the first. Of course they weren't.

"I'm so sorry. Is there anything I can do?"

"Let me know if you hear anything else. You've done a lot already."

"I definitely will, but I better start looking for a new job myself," she said. "Because once Houston finds out—"

"I'll make sure Mrs. Fletcher doesn't say anything. You'll be fine." I had no business promising that, especially since this had the potential to get real ugly, but she had faith in me.

We said our good nights, and I told her to get some sleep.

If Houston thought he could get away with this, he had another think coming. I went upstairs, ignoring Chad as I slammed doors and drawers too hard while looking for a pair of leggings. I needed to call my mother, tell her about this and see what she could find out in her social circles, tell her to be careful about what she said to Houston. But before facing my mother, Mrs. Fletcher, Houston, or anyone else, I needed my bicycle, and not the stationary one either. I needed the wind in my face. I needed the open air because this room couldn't contain my fury.

CHAPTER 13
LIFE REALIZATION #7: BEING SOMEONE'S INSPIRATION IS DANGEROUS

It had taken nearly an entire week, but early Friday morning, my phone, resting on an investment portfolio, vibrated with a text: Pen, this is Yolanda Fletcher. In a meeting. Will call later. Please prepare the necessary docs. We're looking for a new planner. 😉

I stared at my phone.

The Fletchers.

The Fletchers.

The freaking Fletchers!

All week, as I'd invested the funds from the twins' property sale and exchanged emails with Erin, explaining my weird shared office space because, for some reason, she was interested, I waited. I was waiting for this moment, sure it wasn't going to come. The Fletchers were worth dozens of smaller clients, and they'd surely bring other, bigger ones with them. And I'd be set, no longer scraping by. I'd go from *trying* to build my own business to having one, a solid one.

I fired off a text that was way too long and way too schmoozy and then danced around my office, too keyed up to remain at my desk.

As usual, I needed my bicycle, and I knew exactly where I was going to go. I grabbed my bag and headed to the bathroom to change.

Twenty-five minutes later, I was on my bike ride in an area someone had told me was a perfect riding spot on the outskirts of the city.

Okay, it was Grant.

Grant had told me about this spot, and he'd also told me he came here every Friday morning for a solo ride. No conversation. Just him, the wind, the trees, and Gaia, which I later realized was the name of his bicycle. Such a Grant thing to do.

I wasn't here for him, though. I wasn't.

I just wanted to experience the magic he'd said this place had after getting the good news about the Fletchers.

I probably wouldn't see him anyway.

And . . . there he was.

I'd been on the trail, riding past moss-covered tree trunks and quaint wrought iron benches, for three minutes. And there he was.

I rode past him, hoping he'd be too preoccupied in his meditation, or whatever he'd said he did here, to notice.

The thing was, we were fading into friendship. At least, we had been until the silly dance-off a week ago. And now I wasn't sure which of us was keeping distance.

Several moments elapsed after I rode past him. Then I heard my name and the sound of approaching tires.

He came up beside me. "What are you doing here?"

"What are *you* doing here?" Beautifully evaded.

"I thought I told you. I come here every Friday morning."

"Oh right. I couldn't remember where I'd heard about this place." No sense in him getting ideas.

He pointed to a clearing. "I usually meditate over there, but today . . . you got five more miles in you?"

"Yeah. I'm just getting started."

"Good. I want to show you something."

Almost exactly five miles later, we pulled off the street and onto a long driveway that led to a—dump.

"Look." He was smiling like I should be excited by this eyesore. "I bought it off a pair of twins who inherited it. They couldn't believe I wanted it, and I couldn't believe they were letting it go."

"Why did you want it?" It was an enormous space, but that was about all it had going for it. The pale-gray paint was chipping, pieces of the house were literally in active free fall, the house equivalent of a person on their deathbed. If it sneezed, the whole structure would simply disintegrate. "Wait. Did you say twins?"

He dismounted his bicycle. "Yes, and this is my new project, thanks to you."

"Thanks to me?"

He smiled again and pulled a bag from a compartment on his bicycle, held it out to me. "Want some trail mix?" We stared ahead like this was a horror movie, and I waited for the zombies to amble out from behind the tall grass as I reached in and grabbed a handful. He had a talent for trail mix, but it was missing something. "Have you ever thought about adding Cap'n Crunch to this?"

He snapped and pointed at me. "That's it! Captain Crunch!"

I nodded, excited he agreed. "It's Cap'n. Would be perfect, wouldn't it?"

"Absolutely not. It would ruin my special blend. Do you know what that stuff's made of? Anyway, I just realized that's what you smell like. Lavender and Captain Crunch. Do they make lavender Captain Crunch?"

My mouth fell open in disbelief. "It's Cap'n, and what is wrong with you?"

"Why do people keep asking me that?"

"Because it's the logical question any sane person asks when they've spent more than five minutes with you."

"I'm strange because I have good taste?"

"You're strange because you don't want to put *Cap'n* Crunch in your silly trail mix. And you buy junk property. Just when I was starting to think we could be friends."

"I haven't told you what I'm going to do with the property."

"Or how I'm responsible. By all means." I extended a hand in invitation.

"This is the future home of Deanna's bed and breakfast."

An almond flew out of my mouth. I looked from him to the heap, back to him. "Has Deanna seen this place?"

He shook his head. "And I'm trusting you not to tell her about it. I want it to be a surprise, her Christmas present, if I can get it done by then, and I'm going to get it done by then."

"But it's . . ."

"Incredible? I know. They start work on this place Monday morning. I'd take you in to show you, but we'd need hard hats." He put his hand on my arm. "Trust me."

My body did this Jell-O-y thing because of his touch, his words, because of what he was doing for his sister. And even though I couldn't envision what he obviously could, I *did* trust him.

"I distinctly remember you discouraging entrepreneurship when I first met you."

I needed his hand off me. Why was he still touching me?

"Me? Never. You must be confusing me with someone else."

"Right. That must've been the *other* arrogant guy with the mustache."

His hand dropped. *Thank you.* We were silent for several minutes as we stood side by side and stared at Deanna's B and B. "You're really building your sister her own space, her own business?"

"Because of you. You inspired me. And you've been good for Deanna. She's a strong woman, but after meeting you, it's like something's lit up in her. Seeing what you're doing made her feel like it was possible. I don't think I took her seriously. You did."

Warmth spiraled down to my belly and then infiltrated the rest of my body, like getting in a hot tub. Hot tub. Grant in a hot tub.

Hot Tub Grant looked at me.

The same silent conversation passed between us that had when he was holding Gloria, the chicken, and I didn't know what to do or how to feel. Except that something felt like it was blooming in my chest.

And since I couldn't process my own feelings, I did what I'd done that day: I got back on my bicycle and rode away from him.

Within seconds, he passed me and gloated as he went by.

My legs moved like pistons as I tried to catch back up. I was going too fast. One second, my wheels were on the ground, my body on my bicycle; the next, I was in the air, and then . . .

CHAPTER 14
SEVEN BOTTLES OF WATER

Through the molten pain, I squinted at the two people across the room. No, after blinking, it was only one.

"Chad?" I sat up, but I immediately had to lie back on my pillow when my head erupted like a volcano.

The light was too bright, searing my retinas and making me feel like I was on a spaceship, about to be probed.

"Why is it so bright in here?" My voice came out scratchy, veiled with a weakness I didn't understand.

What happened? I wanted to ask this out loud, but I couldn't make the words come out. Had I been in an accident, a fight?

"Thank God you're awake." He was beside me in two large strides. "What can I get for you? Do you need water?"

My eyes snapped shut as my breath stuttered to a stop. The man talking to me, the man moving in my bedroom wasn't Chad—it was Grant.

After several seconds, my eyelids slowly slid back open, and my eyes tracked Grant to the bedside table, where three bottles of water poked out from a plastic-lined cardboard box.

I didn't own a table like this. My nightstand was wood, white, part of a suite of furniture I'd picked out with Deanna. This table was plastic, gray, and portable.

My chest went hot, the bad kind of hot. Too hot. My insides charred.

Not only was the man in this room not Chad, but *this wasn't my room*.

"They're chilled," Grant continued. "I wasn't sure what kind you preferred, so I got every kind they had, and if you'd rather room temperature, I have those too." He pivoted to the windowsill, where four other waters stood at attention. "Which can I get you?"

I needed the water. All the fluid had been sucked out of my body, leaving my husk of a self to look around the room, dry eyed and dry throated.

Nightmare. This had to be a nightmare.

I bit the inside of my cheek so hard that were I actually dreaming, the pain should've jolted me awake. I closed my eyes again and let my hands fall to my sides, hoping to feel the line of cording on the edge of my mattress. But the sheets were rough and the mattress unfamiliar.

No. No. No.

My breath caught in my throat, trapped by the decreasing size of my windpipe. Panic seized everything inside me until my body bucked against what I could only guess was a hospital bed.

Definitely a nightmare.

"Penelope?" I was vaguely aware of Grant moving beside me. "Talk to me."

A strangled scratch clawed its way out of my throat.

"What?"

"Out!" The single word tore into the room. My head felt like a shaken bottle of soda pop, waiting for someone to unscrew the cap and release the pressure, but that wouldn't stop me. "I want out!" Clearer this time.

My eyes flew open, my eyeballs wild, skittering orbs barely contained by my eyelids as I looked around the room—the florescent lights, the curve of the chrome sink, the sickly gray countertop, the skinny metal pole beside the bed, the flat screen that swiveled out from the wall, the black keyboard underneath it.

"Let me get the nurse . . . ," he started, but I was already moving the flimsy sheet aside and placing my bare feet onto the speckled ER linoleum. "Nurse!" Grant was in the doorway, but to me in that moment, he wasn't a person, just the obstacle I had to eliminate to get out of here because *I was getting out of here.*

A large woman in scrubs scooted us back as she pushed her way into the room, a man in a white lab coat just behind.

"What's going on?"

I wasn't sure who had asked the question. Their voices melded together, one robotic tone that I didn't want to hear.

The doctor's hands moved to my shoulders. "Ma'am. What's the matter?"

"Out!" I jerked away from him, moving again toward the door.

"Your IV!" the nurse shouted, stumbling forward to prevent the IV pole from crashing to the floor.

I stopped long enough to stare into the crook of my elbow, where I saw a thin tube sucking like a leech at my soft flesh, and then, I was twelve, back in my brother's hospital room, the same vines clinging to him, choking the life right out of him.

My hand clasped the thin plastic tube, and I yanked. Blood followed, but I was free.

My bare feet slapped the hallway as a nurse with a clipboard fell into the wall to get out of my way.

Escape, retreat, bury.

Shouts reverberated down the corridor, echoed in my head. But my body moved on its own, without fear of consequence, toward the exit. I flew through the waiting room—past the stunned-faced patients waiting to claim my now-empty cage—without pausing to wonder how I knew where to go or what I'd do once I got there.

The bright sting of sun landed too harsh on my too-wide eyes. But I wasn't in that place anymore, and the rest didn't matter. The cool air brushed against my face as it entered my lungs, and I breathed for the first time since realizing where I was. The last time I'd been in a place like this, I'd vowed never to step foot in one again.

Small drops of blood landed like spilled paint at my feet. I bent my elbow, holding my arm close to my chest, like a wounded animal, like a chicken.

Arms—firm, comforting, scented with nature and trail mix—circled around my shoulders, the grounded counter to the erratic hum under my skin.

Tears dripped from behind my closed eyes, and we were quiet, until I was steady enough to say, "Take me home."

His silence made me turn, made my belly constrict. But I stared into his blue eyes and willed him not to betray me, to obey my unreasonable demand.

He put a hand to my face, swiped a tear with his thumb.

"You have a concussion," he whispered.

"I'm not going back." Nausea rippled in my upper abdomen. "Nothing you say will change that."

He glanced at the entry to the ER, where a nurse stood, her arms folded tightly in front of her.

"You won't go back?" Grant confirmed, indecision creasing his forehead.

Several beats of silence passed between us while I let my eyes tell him I'd rather die on the pavement than go back through those doors.

Motion pulled my attention to the car beside us, where someone else in a lab coat stood next to a security guard as they waited.

They think I'm unstable.

If they only knew what a hospital had taken from me, they might've understood.

CHAPTER 15
TWO SIPS OF TEA, ONE BAG OF TRAIL MIX, FOUR IBUPROFEN

"Thank you" didn't encompass my gratitude, but I said it anyway as I motioned for Grant to come inside my house.

He'd silently driven me home—no questions—taken my key when my hand shook too hard to get it into the lock, and opened my door.

We hesitated inside the doorway.

"I—"

He held up a hand. "You don't have to explain."

My eyes scanned the carpet as I nodded, thankful for the permission to remain silent.

"I'm going to shower." A medicinal film clung to my skin, along with the dried blood on my arm. I needed to get it all off.

"Good," he said. "I'll make you some tea. You haven't had dinner."

My stomach swayed. "I'm not hungry."

Instead of insisting, he nodded again, and I turned to walk upstairs, leaving Grant alone in my living room without further instruction.

I peeled the clothes from my body, popped four ibuprofens into my mouth, and swallowed them in the shower, where the water scalded my skin and burned away the memory. Though maybe this was more like branding, driving it in until it rode with the blood in my veins, always there, always a part of me.

A wave of embarrassment rose up from the steam in the shower. The morning played through my mind. *What was I thinking?*

I'd gone to that riding spot because I knew he'd be there. I'd wanted to tell him about winning the Fletchers over, about being one signature away from victory.

I gently shampooed my hair. I'd spent an hour straightening it this morning, which felt like a year ago, and now it was ruined. I could straighten it again, but I had a lump on my head that likely wouldn't appreciate the 410-degree heat of the iron. The strands curled under the hot water, and my already pounding head felt like it was coming off my shoulders. I pictured Grant finding me in a heap at the bottom of the bathtub, water pelting my unconscious, naked body. The image was enough to get me out. I placed my feet on the plush rug at the entry to my shower. The white fibers brushed the inside of my toes as I ripped my robe off the hook at the side of the shower, threw it on, belted it too tight, and sank down against the shower door.

My soppy curls dripped onto the rug and my shoulders, soaking the fabrics as my head fell back onto the glass. I ignored the pain that shot through my skull and let the tears fall down my face, unstoppable as the force that had ushered me through the hospital, barefoot, and into the parking lot. I suddenly felt like I couldn't do any of this, not my business, not friendships, not life. And now Grant knew how uncapable I was. Suspicion was so, so different from cold, hard evidence.

Several minutes later, after the tears had stopped, my leaden feet took me to my closet, where I pulled out a T-shirt and leggings. I twisted my wet hair into a loose bun without a mirror because I was unable to face myself.

I pulled open my bedroom door, stopping short when I saw a collection of goodies on the hardwood floor at my feet.

My eyes went to the note first. I picked it up and shoved it into the tiny pocket of my leggings, then grabbed the steaming mug of black tea and the glass of water.

He'd been right at my door. The thought unfurled an ache in my shoulders.

The plate I grabbed next was neatly arranged with cheese, crackers, grapes, and a baggie of Grant's signature trail mix, the one that, ridiculously, didn't contain Cap'n Crunch. It took me two trips to get everything he'd put outside my door. I filled my arms with what was left: granola bars, another bottle of ibuprofen, an ice pack wrapped in a kitchen towel, an energy drink—the kind frequently found on bicycle rides—and the paperwork from the hospital that told me what to do for a concussion. I placed everything on my dresser, all but the papers from the ER; those I crumpled up and tossed into the bathroom wastebasket. How had he even gotten those anyway?

I crossed my legs on the bed, pulled open the baggie of trail mix, and inhaled, then placed the bag on the pillow beside me. The tea was still warm, and I wrapped my hands around it, wishing it was the green tea I'd pretended to hate.

After two sips, I pulled out Grant's note.

> Let me know if you need anything. I'm here if you
> need me. Please don't hesitate. *Please.*
> —Grant

I found my phone and texted him a thank-you. This is what any friend would do. The kind of friend who bought his sister a whole property that he planned to pour countless funds, time, and energy into. Just for her. Because he cared that much. Because *I'd* inspired him.

I winced as my head made contact with the headboard. My eyelids closed, and as I waited for the pain medication to kick in, I felt myself falling asleep.

My neck ached—my head had fallen into an unnatural angle—when I woke up to the sound of a text. The glowing red numbers on the clock next to my bed made my eyeballs quiver as they told me it was eight p.m. The little gray bubble on my phone held a message from

Chad, telling me he'd be getting in late tonight and would Uber over, so I didn't have to pick him up from the airport. He said something cryptic, too, about his gift arriving before he did.

I'd completely forgotten about Chad because it didn't seem like a Friday night. I wished he'd been delayed until tomorrow. I didn't want to talk to anyone. At least I'd have the next two hours alone.

I downed another two ibuprofen and shivered. Lingering tendrils of the day swept over my skin like a spiderweb, making gooseflesh rise up on my arms.

Coffee, I thought. Maybe another cup of tea.

The air-return vent rustled in the hallway outside my bedroom door, but other than that, the house was quiet until I maneuvered down the stairs. Each creaky board moaned under the pressure of my foot. The last one was so loud that it sounded like it said, *Hey there.* But my temporary amusement was replaced with panic when I realized the words hadn't been from a stair tread but had come from the man sitting on a couch I didn't own.

The man and his mustache.

CHAPTER 16
LIFE REALIZATION #8: TALKING TO A MUSTACHE IS STRANGELY THERAPEUTIC

For five solid seconds, I thought the whole scene was a mirage: the man, the couch, the elaborate house of cards on the floor. I needed distance from Grant because now he was in my mirages. Was this a normal side effect of a concussion, seeing people and couches that weren't there?

"I didn't know if you'd be coming back down or not. I told myself I'd leave by ten p.m. if you didn't."

Okay, this was a full-on audio-visual hallucination.

I threw my phone at my mind's projection, hoping to watch the figment fade away, but Grant caught it midair.

"Umm. Did I do something wrong?"

Why couldn't he have been a random intruder holding me at gunpoint?

I patted my hair. "Grant! It's you." Thank God I'd had that keratin treatment; otherwise the relaxed curls would've been unruly spirals, rendering me ridiculous.

"Did you expect someone else? I told you I was staying."

Had he?

Damn, I didn't have on makeup or a bra. I turned around and went back upstairs, hoping he was far enough away not to realize what a mess I was. Likely too late for that. "I'll be right back," I called over my shoulder. "Forgot something."

"No problem. I'll be here."

I needed to think, and I couldn't think with my hair wild, my face naked, and my nipples poking against my shirt like a porn star's. I conditioned my curls, not great, but it would have to do, and fastened my bra much too tight. Then I did my "natural" look with a small handful of products instead of my usual pile.

I came back downstairs after a record-breaking remake of myself, with a concussion, I might add, and instantly asked, "Where did you get that couch?"

"A couple guys delivered it right after you went upstairs. Did I accept delivery of the wrong couch?" He rubbed his facial hair in concern. "They said it was for Chad Gwinn." He added, "You look angry. I probably should've—"

I shook my head, regretted the movement, then took the phone he was extending and tried to sound pleasant. "Must be the gift he was talking about. I think he's sick of sitting on the floor."

"That's nice."

Was it? I found it irritating. He'd picked the piece without consulting me.

I moved to Chad's couch because my muscles were threatening to throw their collective hands up and leave me to flop on the floor. The cushion gave only slightly, which fit. It was like Chad, the perfect mix of good looking yet stiff and professional. I slid to the floor in front of the Chad-couch. Chadouch. Chaouch.

Grant leaped over as if to catch me.

"I'm okay. I want to be on the floor."

He nodded as if my preference for the hard walking surface seemed reasonable.

I stared at his unbelievable house of cards. Had he glued them together? No way they were standing on their own.

He retrieved a blanket and sat on the floor beside me, propping his arm up on the chaouch cushions as he faced me.

"I didn't know your hair was curly. It's nice."

"Yeah. Thanks. I hate it."

He chuckled. "We all want the opposite of what we have."

I hated when people said this, that straight-haired people wanted curly hair and vice versa. I didn't want straight hair. I wanted manageable curls. I did not have manageable curls. I had some sort of defiant nest, where each hair had its own agenda and was hell bent on executing its unique, original style. People were naive when they said they "would give anything for my natural hair." It had been a source of grief my entire life. One time, when my hair had been particularly knotted, my mom gave up and handed the comb to my dad, relenting to his authority because I had "Black people hair" and he was Black. But his solution had included scissors, the wrong choice. The hacked hair had been too short to put in a bun or contain in any way, which had resulted in threats from the Black girls in fifth grade and then being detained after class by a Black male substitute teacher who thought it was appropriate to touch my hair and give me pomade advice while the two of us were alone in the classroom.

Brandon, my equally mixed older brother and best friend, had come to my rescue. He didn't have the hair problems I had or quite the same social issues, but he understood. We were a matching set.

I wanted to cry again, but I couldn't. Grant was right here, and my mother's words, "Hurt in private, heal in silence," bounced inside my damaged head.

He shifted beside me, his hand gently patting my arm.

I inhaled and kept the air in my lungs for as long as I could stand it, then let it all out in one big puff. I didn't think I'd breathed that hard, but the entire house of cards came tumbling down in a flurry of queens, kings, and spades. *An actual house of cards.*

"I'm sorry I just blew your amazing architectural masterpiece down," I said. "I bet it was the best house of cards in the history of card houses. I bet if you'd applied for the Guinness—"

"It wasn't that great, and you didn't blow it down. I accidentally kicked it with my foot when I—"

"When I was twelve, my brother died from leukemia." My head whipped toward Grant as my hand slowly covered my mouth. Had I said those words out loud? But he pulled my hand away from my face and held it in his own.

"I'm here. You can tell me," he invited.

Six words.

My whole life had been packed away for over twenty years, and with six words, he was asking me to unpack it. I hadn't put the memories in neat stacks or organized them in any fashion. I had crumpled them up and thrown them in, stuffed the mental suitcase so full that I had to jump on it to get the lock to fasten.

You can tell me. An open invitation.

I couldn't meet his eyes. I glanced over at the storage closet, the coffin for the box of my brother's things.

When I attempted eye contact with Grant, I shut down again. But some part of me *wanted* to tell him. Earlier, I hadn't used my usual coping mechanisms because I'd been past consolation. Now, I didn't want him to be a four or a ten. I wanted him to be Grant. He made me comfortable in a way I couldn't explain. It didn't make sense. This man didn't make sense. I'd never wanted to talk about this with anyone, hadn't.

I looked down at his mustache, and despite everything I'd said about it, despite how much I'd despised it, I could talk to that damned mustache.

"Brandon, my brother . . . he was everything to me, like you and Deanna." The words fell out of my mouth, simultaneously raw and dust covered. "We didn't have much extended family. It was mainly the four of us. My parents worked a lot. My mom was a corporate boss. My dad was a doctor. Brandon and I . . ." It was coming back, that feeling I'd had, someone being there for me. Someone I cared about so much. That someone being ripped away. I stopped, swallowed. "Brandon was my best friend. Our lives were happy. Our parents weren't always there, but we knew they loved us, and we had each other." I stopped. The mustache wiggled a little, encouragement to keep going. "And then . . ." I swallowed. Even a sideways glance at the memory was proving to be hard. Tears pulsed behind the dam I'd built. My voice thickened, weighed down with the grief that had torn me open. Grant massaged my palm. He didn't ask me to go on. He didn't say anything, but his touch, the contact, the increasing pressure, told me he was there. And he was safe.

I was safe.

I found my voice: "Then he started feeling bad—little things at first. I don't remember the details, but my dad consulted one of his colleagues. From there, life completely changed. As soon as Brandon started going to the doctor, it wasn't long before he was hospitalized."

My breath changed. I saw Brandon in that bed—wires, cords, pale skin, and sunken eyes—and all the little passageways allowing air into my lungs seized, like they disliked the memory as much as I did.

He must've noticed the change, too, because he squeezed my hand again, hard, and then when that wasn't enough, he pulled me to his chest. I hesitated but didn't draw back.

Had I fallen into my mother's arms, she would've stiffened, transformed into the statue she'd become. She would've told me to think of something else. She would've told me to stop being weak. *Be strong . . .* for Brandon.

His grip loosened when I tried to pull away. But when the pressure of his arms was gone, I crumpled. He folded me back into his embrace, and for the first time, I let the arms of another person hold me together, the real me, the one with the problems. My mother's voice told me to support myself, to will my muscles erect. But right then, I needed arms around me. And until they were there, until I no longer felt like

I was shouldering the burden alone, I didn't know how much I needed another human being to . . . be there.

I wasn't sure if he heard any of my babbling through my tears, but I kept talking into his shoulder as he held me. "I had to watch him die, Grant. I was the only one in the room. He was talking one second, and the next, he was gone." *Gone. Final. Permanent.*

His hand ran down my back, slowly, and I closed my eyes, pushing away the feeling that this was wrong somehow.

With one final breath, I'd lost my best friend. I'd lost the one who'd always told me it was going to be okay. I'd lost my mom and dad too. They left with Brandon, both of them fragmenting and rebuilding themselves into people I didn't know.

"I'm so sorry. I'm so sorry."

I'm not sure how long we would've stayed there like that, me curled in his arms, him rubbing my back, if we hadn't been interrupted, but the jangle of keys had me pushing away, looking startled at the door.

Chad.

I tried to leap up, but my body, spent from the accident, from the tearing open of my soul, took too long, and he was already inside the door, staring down at me halfway up and Grant still on the floor by the couch.

Time slowed.

Chad stood, anger unfolding on his face. "What the hell?" His overnight bag hit the floor.

"She had an accident. I brought her home from the hospital," Grant explained.

"You two look like you were pretty cozy next to *my* couch."

Grant stood, his jaw clenched as he faced Chad. "Didn't you hear me say she'd had an accident?"

Chad's gaze flicked to me. The features of his face seemed unsure what to do, where to settle, concern or anger. They landed somewhere in between. He blinked, moved past Grant, and came to stand in front of me.

"You're hurt?" His tone was brusque, but the look in his eyes had softened.

His eyes remained on mine as Grant explained. "She fell off her bike during a ride today. An ambulance took her to the ER. I stayed with her to make sure she was okay. She has a concussion."

"I appreciate you taking care of her." The appreciation didn't sound like appreciation. "But I'll take it from here. You can go."

Grant moved to where I could see him, where Chad wasn't completely between us, and looked at me with the concern of a friend. "Is that what you want, Penelope?"

My eyes, no longer focused on his mustache, looked into his. There was so much more to tell, but I'd never told anyone what I'd told him. I'd never let myself trust anyone enough. And I'd known him for what? *Six* weeks? I didn't know what that meant. Were we friends now? Or was it the concussion talking?

When I didn't answer, Chad answered for me: "Of course that's what she wants. Like I said, we appreciate what you've done."

Chad had no idea what Grant had done, but I didn't say anything. I couldn't tell him how much this meant to me. All my life I'd been told I was fine when I wasn't, by my family, by myself. Tonight, I'd told someone else I wasn't, and Grant hadn't told me to be strong. He'd let me be weak.

"Thank you. Chad's right. You should go. I've taken up too much of your time."

I hated the smugness on Chad's face, the possessiveness, like Grant was ruining a moment between the two of us, when it was really the other way around.

"You'll call if you need anything," Grant confirmed.

I nodded.

"I'll go then."

Chad's arm came around me, but Grant stepped up to my open side. Without a word, he touched my shoulder and gave me a look that conveyed sympathy, telling me without telling me he knew what we'd shared wasn't trivial. I wanted to collapse again at that look, but Chad's body straightened, a lingering bit of self-control that kept him from throwing Grant out.

When Grant left, Chad pulled me into a hug. "Are you okay?"

I remained quiet for several seconds, and then I said, "I don't know."

He pulled back and looked into my face, his brows knit.

"You don't know?"

"I'm in a little pain, but that's not the problem. I'm . . . I had to go to the hospital, and—"

He rolled his eyes. "Right. It's not a big deal. Big people go to the doctor." He pulled me to his chest and sighed. "You've got to get over this phobia."

"It's more than that."

He waited for me to go on. If I was ever going to let him in, tonight was the open door.

"Have I ever told you about my brother?" I knew I hadn't. My mother never would.

He looked pensive for a minute. "Maybe. What was his name again?"

"Brandon."

"Yeah, I think maybe you did, but I don't remember ever meeting him. I'd like to meet him," he assured me. "Unless there's bad blood or something . . ."

"No, no bad blood."

"Then of course I want to meet him." He smiled, moved a strand of hair back away from my face. The gesture was tender. He was trying.

"I like the couch." I surprised us both by changing topics.

His eyes lit up. "Yeah? I'd been holding off, hoping you wouldn't be here that long, but when the time comes, we can sell it. No big deal." He shrugged.

"No big deal," I repeated, ignoring his comment about time.

"I'm going to grab a quick shower; then let's get some rest, put this day out of its misery. I almost lost a case today."

"Why don't you go ahead? I'll check the doors and meet you up there. You can tell me about the case as we fall asleep."

He kissed the top of my head. "You're one tough cookie. That's one of the things I love about you. Nothing ever gets you down."

I let my lips turn upward, the mask I knew how to wear way too well. "Right. I'm fine." I knew it was what he wanted me to say. It's what they all wanted me to say. *Almost all.*

He grabbed his bag and jogged up the stairs.

My legs moved to the door, but my muscles were heavy and awkward. A breeze stirred the trees outside, drawing my attention to the cool air hitting my thigh. The door was still slightly ajar.

I looked back at the stairs, heard the water come on.

And then I closed the door and locked it.

CHAPTER 17
IT'S BEEN EIGHT MONTHS, AND SHE'S AS ICY AS EVER

Every single one of my six-hundred-plus muscles tensed as I sat in an Uber on the way to my mother's house an excruciating *two* weeks later.

I was back in Minnesota to take the Fletchers to dinner because they'd put me off every time I'd tried to make contact. They were busy people, but they had an abundance of money because they made money a priority, so it was time for a physical appearance to let them see I'd do anything for them and their business. Houston could try to spin this as a violation of my noncompete, but Erin's involvement aside, Mrs. Fletcher had contacted *me*. And I was getting worried because, despite my better judgment, I'd put all my eggs in their basket, essentially waiting it out until they were mine.

None of my other previous clients had contacted me, even the ones Erin said were looking for me. I *had* hosted a free webinar on retirement planning, but only four people showed; none of them signed. But it hadn't shaken me because I'd assumed that, any day now, the Fletchers would sweep in and I wouldn't have to worry about huge marketing gestures.

My original plan had been to fly in and fly right back out of my hometown and not even tell Chad or my mother that I'd be in

Minnesota. This trip was purely business, and I didn't want either of them getting the wrong idea about me coming back here.

But if they found out—well, it wasn't worth it, which was why I'd arranged the Uber without my mother's knowledge because I couldn't spend thirty minutes trapped in her car, her hands at ten and two, eyes on the road while she talked at me. I'm not sure when my mother stopped talking *to* me and started talking *at* me, but that's definitely how it was now.

As Arthur the Uber driver drove, the trees and houses sped past my back seat window, and I pretended not to smell feet or think about how horrifying it was that Chad was staying with my mother until he found a new place, one without his soon-to-be ex-wife. *My mother's idea*, but he'd been all too pleased to comply.

I also tried not to think about the last time I'd been to my mother's house, when I'd attended my father's funeral and white calla lilies flanked the entryway. My hand had brushed one of the cup-shaped blooms when I'd left my father's catered wake, heading for a bar, where I unknowingly paid homage to my dad's memory by doing what he'd spent his life doing: drinking too much and picking up someone married.

I certainly hadn't wanted to be that person, but in all fairness, my dad hadn't wanted to be that kind of person either. I think he'd tried to tell me that a few years ago, one afternoon when he'd been drinking heavily. His deep-brown eyes were glassy when he looked at me.

"I do it to forget, you know. Your mother thinks she's responsible, and maybe she is, but maybe I want to believe she is so I can put my blame somewhere."

"What?" My heart raced. What did he mean? My mother responsible? For what? The alcohol? The cheating? Brandon? Was he going to acknowledge how much our family had changed? But my mother had overheard and pulled him into the kitchen for some silly reason that we all knew—but wouldn't acknowledge—was a ploy to shut him up.

And just like that, the sudden burst of emotion was contained, like a fire without oxygen.

I didn't unbuckle when Arthur pulled his green Ford Explorer into my mother's driveway. I opened the car door, closed it again.

"You gonna get out?" he asked, twisting his body toward the back seat.

It was entirely possible I'd walk into my mother's house and get tied to a chair until I agreed to move back to Minnesota.

And Arthur didn't care. "I've got another ride," he said.

To look out at the greenest grass on the block—not even a whisper of a weed—swaying slightly in a late-May breeze, the multicolored, adequately hydrated flowers, the freshly painted porch swing with the plush, navy blue curtains that matched the shutters on the whiter-than-reasonable two-story, you'd think this was where I wanted to be.

Reluctantly, I exited the smelly vehicle, smoothed my blouse, and straightened my jacket, both pieces of clothing my mother would approve of. In fact, I think she'd given them to me, a not-so-subtle reminder that appearances mattered.

I climbed the three steps to my mother's pressure-washed porch, then went back down again. I took a deep breath, climbed the stairs once more, went back down again.

Just as I was about to leap into the holly bushes after my earring—the one I was about to throw into the bushes—Aurora Auberge materialized in her doorway.

Stalling was over.

Framed by the perfectly painted wood with crystal clear side windows, my mother was the picture of stability. Age was even commanded by her hand. Surgery, expertly applied makeup, night creams, and face masks were all tools in her arsenal of deception, melting her sixty years to forty, barely older than me. I knew her routine because that's what she'd passed on to me. Comfort and understanding be damned, but ways to keep crow's-feet at bay? Now we're talkin'.

I let myself be held by my mother. Not a hug. She held my shoulders in her hands while she *inspected* me.

One perfectly plucked eyebrow arched. "You're not drinking enough water. Your skin looks dry."

I gave her a complacent smile. "Then I'd better get a bottle of water."

And after eight months of not seeing each other, there was our hello.

After the first bottle had been downed, compacted, and neatly placed into the green recycling container, I sipped on a second bottle and listened to my mother tell me how great Chad was over a sparkling countertop so shiny I could easily use it to apply a second coat of lipstick.

Chad was working on a high-profile obstruction of justice case and anticipated a late night. I wouldn't get to witness his greatness until tomorrow.

My finger slid down the bottle. Condensation trickled onto the granite.

"He's happy you're here, Penelope."

I nodded. Hearing her say my full name made me think of Grant. My friend Grant. After I'd blubbered about the dark secrets of my past, we'd entered a new relationship phase. Grant was officially my friend: mustache, cereal aversion, and all. I'd continued to hang out with Deanna, and he was frequently there.

"When are you coming back to stay?" A microfiber cloth appeared in Aurora's hand, and she used it to wipe up the water that had pooled underneath my bottle.

The gesture irritated me, and I ignored her question. "Have you talked to Houston, found anything out?"

Her face went red. Not a good sign.

"Chad and I are working on a plan, but Houston is using the fact that you had an affair with a married man to taint your reputation."

I let my head flop onto the counter; the contact jarred my skull, reigniting my concussion from two weeks ago and giving me an instant headache.

"I didn't know." The fact that I should've known, could've known if I'd even halfway *looked* at my relationship with Chad, was beside the point.

"I know that. But he's using your father to further drive the point home because unlike you, Charlie knew what he was doing. Houston's more than suggesting it's a familial pattern."

I raised my head to find her rubbing her neck like the words had caused her throat physical pain, but she, like always, held herself erect, not even a hint of a tear.

"I'm sorry, Mother." And I was. Despite all my mother's shortcomings, she'd loved my dad. She'd always taken care of him, put a cold cloth to his head, cleaned up his vomit. Everything had to be perfect, but their relationship had been the one exception. It hadn't made sense.

She squared her shoulders. "Don't be sorry. I'm not."

For a brief second, I thought about asking her why, but instead I asked, "Do you think that's why the Fletchers have ghosted me?"

"Doesn't matter. They're meeting you for dinner, right?"

I nodded. "They haven't rescheduled . . . yet."

"Go to the meeting. Win them over. You'll need to change, of course."

"Of course," I agreed. "What have you picked out for me to wear?"

"Right this way."

∽

"Just coffee and dessert for us. We ate before we came." Mrs. Fletcher pointed to the tres leches cake and handed her menu back to the waiter.

I wasn't all that hungry, either, but I *was* suddenly craving that table-side bike I'd fantasized about at Deanna's. Perhaps a portable

unicycle, something I could unfold out of my purse and ride around the restaurant because my *dinner* companions weren't planning to eat—
Dinner.

I racked my brain for words, but I was too late. Mr. Fletcher was already speaking.

"I'm afraid we can't put our trust in you."

"Fiduciary!"

Oh crap. Oh flying, I-can't-believe-I-just-shouted-that CRAP.

"Excuse me?"

I thought about looking over at the other table and pretending someone else had yelled out a random financial term. I needed this. I needed them. "Please. Please give me a chance. You know what I can do." I was extremely close to getting on my knees and grabbing their hands.

I opened my satchel in search of the paperwork where I'd laid out investment strategies, retirement income securities, potential risks, potential goals, where they were now, where I could take them. There were even pie charts, colorful ones I'd had printed on glossy paper with a professional logo on it. I'd even calculated all their assets in pairs of shoes, which Mrs. Fletcher loved!

Mrs. Fletcher put her hand on mine to stop me from opening the folder, the one that had taken three attempts to get out of my bag because my hands were shaking.

Shoes! Didn't she want to see how many shoes she'd be able to buy with me managing her money? Thousands, millions of shoes.

"We do know." Mrs. Fletcher's voice was soft. "Which is why this has been such a hard decision for us. However, given your . . . background, we simply can't."

"My background? You know I managed . . ." I stopped, trying to think of a single large company whose finances I'd handled. I couldn't think, and I couldn't say, *You know that mattress place with all the mattresses, or that electronics distributor that makes the tiny little gadgets that go in the bigger machines?* Finally, vaguely, I said, "I've managed large companies."

"We have no doubts regarding your financial expertise," Mr. Fletcher said. "It's your values that fall short."

Values?

This had nothing to do with my professional reputation and everything to do with my personal one.

"I didn't know he was married," I whispered. It shouldn't be about this. This was personal, none of their business, and I hated that I felt compelled to say it.

Mrs. Fletcher's pitying gaze cut deep. "But your father. And now, we hear that you're with the man who . . . it . . . well, I think you can understand the position we're in."

No, I couldn't understand. Reversing our stations, I'd want my money in the most capable hands without considering the person's personal life. I'd want my money in *my* hands.

"If it makes you feel any better," Mrs. Fletcher said into my stunned silence, "we aren't staying with TCF. Houston's behavior was inexcusable, and we won't reward it."

I didn't care about Houston. I cared about my business and how much easier life would be if I had the Fletchers in my book. I opened my mouth to tell them why Chad and I were together. How he and his wife had both been miserable. How it wasn't black and white, how—but none of it mattered. They'd made their mind up about me. And the Fletchers and the Gwinns, Chad's family, knew each other, which probably meant they knew his wife's family. Who knew what had been said, how this narrative had been spun. I only had Chad's perspective, and he'd likely only tell me what was favorable, which made me wonder what he wasn't saying, like how his parents had taken the news about his divorce. And why he was staying with my mother and not his own family. It didn't add up, but I couldn't process those things right now.

"Is there anything I can say to change your mind?" I asked, defeat inching up my spine.

Mrs. Fletcher shook her head. "I'm afraid the decision has been made. I'm sorry. We wish you the best."

They both stood. They weren't even going to eat the cake. I watched Mrs. Fletcher tuck her arm into Mr. Fletcher's, and the handsomely dressed pair—her in her bright-blue shift and him in a black suit with a tie that matched her dress—left the restaurant without a backward glance.

The waiter brought out three pieces of cake, set one in front of me and the other two in front of the empty chairs, still warm from the not-clients who had vacated them.

"My dinner companions left," I told his tie, unable to look him in the face.

"Should I clear these away then?"

"Leave them."

He shrugged as I scooted both plates nearer to my own. After he'd walked away, I dumped both pieces of cake onto my plate, pulled out my phone, and started eating as I crafted a text.

Text: They aren't signing. It's over.

Almost immediately a reply popped up on my screen.

Reply: They're fools, and you don't need them.

As I typed Are they the fools, or am I?, I got cream on my screen.

Reply: They are. No doubt.

Text: I'm the one eating three pieces of cake.

I drew a frowny face with my finger in the icing and took a picture of my plate, sent it.

Reply: Stop eating that right now. I'll make you some real food when you get home.

Home.

Text: I'll be there tomorrow night. Pie?

Reply: Definitely.

Text: Thanks Deanna.

Reply: What are friends for?

CHAPTER 18
LIFE REALIZATION #9: EVERYONE SHOULD OWN A GOLDFISH. JUST. IN. CASE.

True to her word, Deanna made me pie as soon as I got back to Nashville on Saturday night. I told her that Houston was spreading rumors about me, but I couldn't tell her the ultimate reason the Fletchers had decided not to sign with me. Because what if she thought of me differently? I was dating the man I'd cheated with, and it didn't seem to matter that I'd been unaware of his marital status or why I'd made the decision to be with him. And how could I explain that? From the outside, it looked awful. I couldn't risk her looking at me the way the Fletchers had.

So I kept it all to myself, feeling isolated and unsure of what to do next. The thing was, the more I connected with others, the more I wanted to connect. So, four days after my return, when I was banging my head on my desk at the office, still reeling from the loss of what I'd thought had been a sure thing and feeling paralyzed with indecision, I called Deanna to ask her to lunch.

"I'd really, really love to, Pen, but I'm swamped." Deanna's voice was heavy with apology as she turned me down.

"My produce order just came in, and the stinkin' arugula was soggy in the middle! I'm prepping for a fancy fiftieth anniversary party tomorrow, which means a mad dash to Costco . . . right now. And we just got a bachelorette party order, also for this weekend. But I would've had to say no anyway because Grant and I had plans to meet at that horrible little meat 'n' three he's always going to. He's the only almost-forty-year-old I know who willingly eats at the same place the nursing home field-trips to. Which reminds me, I need to call him! He's probably almost there by now. Ugh, I'm such a horrible sister and friend."

I pulled the phone away from my ear to exhale the sharp sting of regret. "You are neither. It's not a big deal on my end." It kind of was a big deal. I'd initiated a nonbusiness, recreational activity. Her refusal, while logical, felt like a kick when I was down.

"I'll make it up to you, I promise. And we need to discuss that event to get you clients. *In* Nashville. Erin's idea was perfect."

Erin had decided I needed to use my WeWork office contacts, coupled with the networking site, to throw a party. She was picturing a concert, arranged by the husband-and-wife country music team, and sample massages from Piper to draw people in. She'd written a long email about it, likely because she felt sorry for me. Deanna loved the idea and swatted my second thoughts away like gnats. I really wanted to believe something like that would work, but I couldn't get excited over it because nothing had panned out so far.

"We're gonna do this. I'd love to chat about it now, but I really should call Grant."

"Of course. We'll catch up soon." I worked the disappointment out of my words and spun in my chair. My knee hit soundly into the side of my desk, but I barely noticed because—Deanna might not be able to meet Grant for lunch, but I could.

My lower lip throbbed with the force of my bite.

Should I?

The last time I'd done something like this, I'd ended up in the hos . . . won't think about that.

Without thinking about anything, I grabbed my purse and headed for the door. The term "meat 'n' three" had come up in conversation several times before I finally realized what they were talking about, but now, I knew the place Deanna was referring to.

I kept my head down in the lobby so I wouldn't accidentally make eye contact with Handsy Piper. In my woe-is-me funk, I'd had one burst of business effort. I'd set up a meeting with Piper to discuss her personal finances the second week of June because it was the first time she'd had a gap in her schedule. Apparently she was good at her job and in high demand. Though I didn't plan on ever personally finding out.

⌒

A glimpse at my reflection in the glass door to the restaurant made me pause and ask myself what I would tell Grant if he *was* in there.

He was my friend, wasn't he? It wasn't like I was trying to date him or anything. We were friends. He had Elaine; I had Chad, whom I I . . . I . . . liked a great deal.

This is innocent. I ripped the door open as if I owned the place.

Grant sat alone at a table in the center of the room, the sleeves of his blue collared shirt rolled up on his forearms. I lost my nerve, making a beeline to the stream of people getting food, as far from Grant as I could get without stepping into the ladies' room.

When it was my turn to order, I pointed, aiming for the fried chicken breast behind the glass, but when the man in a white apron slopped some brownish meat dripping with gelatinous blobs of gravy onto my tray, I didn't say anything. Though I did make sure I clearly pronounced my other choices so I wouldn't end up with the alien greens.

What *did* it say about Grant that this was his favorite place to eat? I scooted my tray off the line and headed for a table, forcing myself not to look at him. It was like his body was giving off heat from across the room.

I slid into one of the red booths that lined the walls, my heart racing under my ribs.

I was repeatedly picking at a dent in the Formica tabletop when a familiar male voice said, "Penelope? What a coincidence."

If by "coincidence" you mean planned, noncommittal stalking . . .

"Grant?" I questioned, as if I was as surprised as he was. I flipped my flat-ironed hair back nervously, hoping he wouldn't pick up on my awkwardness.

"This is great. Deanna had to cancel on me. Some salad emergency. Mind if I join you?"

I gestured to the other side of the booth, then tucked my hand under my thigh because I was shaking, which didn't make sense, except that it did because I'd opened up to him. That was it, the reason for my awkwardness. He knew something about me that other people didn't, which made him a slightly different kind of friend.

I was still working this out in my head as he said, "I'll go grab my tray."

As he walked away, I took a deep breath and turned him into the number ten with a charming monocle. I thought I was growing out of the number thing, but my shaking hands and spastic stomach suggested I might be better off talking to an integer.

If the number ten wanted to think this was a chance meeting, what was the harm in letting him do so?

༄

"Completely naked?" I leaned forward, engrossed in the conversation.

"Completely naked."

My back hit into the taut seat cushions as I raised my eyebrows at Grant. "What did you say?"

"What could I say?" He let his shoulders rise and fall. "I stood there for several seconds, hoping I was having some sort of episode. Then, when they invited me in like everything was normal, I turned around to find the cameras." He forked a piece of baked fish and chewed. Halfway through the bite, he opened one side of his mouth and said, "No cameras."

"You went in?"

"'Shock' is all the explanation I have. They seemed completely normal the first time we met to discuss their project. Delightful couple." He shook his head. "I don't even know what I said the whole time I was there." He put his hands to his face. "At least the woman put a shirt on after their workout."

"Workout? What kind of workout could they possibly . . ."

"Naked yoga." He shrugged again. "Very freeing, I suppose."

I laughed, a little too loud, but it felt good. It felt good to be with Grant. A friend. The conversation was happening without effort, and sometime in the past several minutes, the numeral armor I'd mentally cloaked him in had faded.

"Who thinks it's normal, or even slightly okay, to meet your architect in the nude?"

He stroked his mustache. "They were young and in incredible shape. Who knows, maybe if I'd ever looked that good, I'd have done the same thing." He winked, and I did *not* picture what was under his clothes, but during the rides, his bikewear had highlighted promising features.

I shoved a ginormous bite of macaroni into my mouth. "Well, that tops any story I've got."

He smoothed his napkin over his lap, a smile tugging at the corners of his mouth as he watched me talk through my pasta. "I have a feeling almost any story you tell me will be more interesting than my naked client one."

I swallowed the bite before it was thoroughly chewed. "How can you be sure?"

"Because you're the one telling it."

I was the queen of pretense, so why couldn't I keep the flush out of my cheeks?

"Grant, don't be cheesy."

"Am I being cheesy?"

I nodded. "I'm actually not that interesting. Before moving here, the most exciting decision in my life was which bicycle I was going to purchase."

With his elbows propped on the table, he replied, "Fascinating."

I rolled my eyes. "So how's Deanna's B and B going, and are we getting dessert or what?"

"Oh, we're having dessert." His napkin slapped the table as he jumped up. "Stay right there. Then I'll tell you how great my plans are going."

He jogged to the line, and as I watched him from our table, a warm, fuzzy feeling settled in my chest. I decided it was the kind of affection and admiration a starved dog would have for the first person who gave her a hot meal. Right now, the rest of my life wasn't charming, so my perspective was skewed.

These warm feelings toward Grant would pass, and we'd settle into a normal friendship. Until then, I'd pretend this *was* a normal friendship . . . with a number ten . . . wearing a monocle. Great . . . I was diagnosable. But he wasn't *always* a ten, only when I needed him to be.

He returned with two cups filled with some sort of yellow cream with a frothy, white topping.

I sniffed the one he placed in front of me. "What is this?"

"Taste it. And you should see Deanna's place. They've got it stripped down, and she's a beauty, like I suspected. But I do have one problem. I'm adamant on keeping this a secret. Deanna loves surprises, but I don't know what goes in a B and B. I can find that out easily enough, but what goes in *her* B and B? And how trustworthy do you think Mere and Keyondra are? If I ask them questions, you think they'll keep my secret?"

I loved that he was asking *me* these questions. "Am I the only one who knows?"

"The one and only."

Tehehehe.

Get a grip!

"You haven't said anything, have you?"

I shook my head. *Our* secret. If I kept his secret, maybe he'd keep mine, the fact that I was a mental case.

"I don't really know Mere and Keyondra well enough."

"Eh. I'll probably have to tell them. Mere handles the finances. I think she's the only one who could convince D that she can't afford a place, which she can, but I don't want her going out and buying something else."

I nodded and picked up my spoon as he pointed to the corner of the room. "Do you see that couple over there?"

"The man in the blue shirtsleeves and the woman in the flowered dress?"

He nodded. "Fred and Doris. Excellent names, right?"

"Uhh . . ."

His jaw dropped, like he couldn't believe I didn't get it. "Fred and Doris . . . biking terms."

"How many times do I have to tell you that I ride, but barely? I'm not like you guys. Anything more than yoga pants, a tee, a helmet, and kneepads were foreign to me until recently."

"You're proving my point."

"What point?"

He sighed.

"Are you actually irritated with me because I don't know who Fred and Delores are?"

"Doris. And no. That would be irrational."

"Which you are never."

"Of course not." His mustache twitched. "A Fred is basically an amateur rider. Doris is the female version of that. You're a Doris."

"*You're* a Doris," I countered, shoving my spoon into the wiggly banana pudding.

"I mean—"

"This is amazing," I interrupted him. "I'm listening; I promise. But this is seriously the best banana pudding I've ever had. Right up there with snickerdoodles and chocolate chip cookies, my faves."

"It's why I come here. It's like a tiny cabana boy's massaging my taste buds."

"*That's* your metaphor? A tiny human in your mouth?"

"You got something against cabana boys?"

"I just—never mind. Have you tried the other desserts?"

"When something's this good, why would I need anything else?"

A flush worked its way down my body. He was talking about pudding, but my ridiculous mind was traveling elsewhere.

"I guess that's fair." I turned back to the couple while scraping the bottom of my container, the contents of which I'd already devoured. "So, before I rudely interrupted you about this very fine dessert, what were you going to tell me about . . . Fred and Doris?"

His forehead crinkled with delight. "Worth the interruption. But to address another possible one, I've seen you eyeing my dessert." He lifted the clear glass container toward me. "Want a bite?"

I put a hand to my chest and leaned back in an act of manufactured indignation and ignored the vibration of a text in my pocket. I was taking too long of a lunch, but who was going to notice? It wasn't like the boss was going to care. She was a flake whose talents were wasted because she didn't know how to pull people in.

My spoon dove into his custard like an Olympian. "Tell me about Fred and Doris."

"Every time I come here, they're here. Same spot, same positions at the table. And they're always having an animated discussion, as if no one else is in the room. I think they're half the reason I come here, aside from the pudding of course. They remind me of my parents."

We stared at the couple, and I wondered about Grant and Deanna's parents. Deanna referred to them in the past tense, but neither sibling had elaborated.

As the elderly man leaned over the table toward his wife, she reciprocated. Their faces were only inches apart, their conversation intense and steady. There was also a lightness about it that came with familiarity, a bond between two people who knew each other better than anyone else in the world.

"I wish I knew what they were saying." I shifted. "You know what's odd?"

"Tell me what's odd."

"Usually older couples settle into a companionable silence, don't they?"

He nodded. "You understand my fascination. They've been together for a hundred years, but those two are chatting it up like they've only just discovered they're both marine biologists who specialize in microscopic phytoplankton."

My eyelashes flapped. "Microscopic what?"

"Phytoplankton. Autotrophic single-celled microorganisms and the basis of marine ecosystems."

"Are you still speaking English?"

"How about 'tiny important water creatures that larger things eat.' Better?"

I considered. "Mildly insulting, but better."

Laughter rolled alongside his words. "I'm interested in that sort of thing. Forgive me."

"Sounds like a snoozefest. Interesting! I mean interesting! Sounds interesting."

He kicked me under the table.

"Ow!"

I threw my plastic spoon at Grant's face, but he ducked in time.

"They're going to kick us out of here," he said.

"They'll kick *you* out of here. I'll plead self-defense and then sit in the window, eating the complimentary banana pudding I'll receive for everything I've been through."

"Is that so?"

My nod was exaggerated.

"I'll simply convince them that I barely tapped your leg and then win them over with my good looks and outrageous wit."

"You plan to develop an outrageous wit between now and then, huh?"

He pushed back into his seat as if he'd been shot. "I'll have you know I have a sizable wit."

This time my nod was placating. "You're right. Sizable. Like microscopic phytoplankton."

His snort drew the eyes of several diners.

He pulled the napkin from his lap and dabbed at his eyes. "Enough."

"I wasn't the one who started it."

"And from the sound of things, you won't be the one to end it." He stood and then reached out for my hand. "Shall we?"

I removed the napkin from my own lap and placed my hand in his, trying not to read anything into the literal spark that was jumping between our hands.

At the door, I glanced back at Fred and Doris. The couple had shoved their empty plates aside and were going back and forth as steadily as they had been thirty minutes before.

A pang of longing shot through me. I couldn't picture Chad and me doing that.

"Where did you park?" Grant asked, shaking me back onto the sidewalk and out of Doris and Fred's marital anomaly.

I pointed to the parking garage.

"I'll walk you," he said, and we moved away from the restaurant to my car. "This was fun. I'm glad Deanna's spinach was ruined."

"It was arugula, and that's a horrible thing to wish on your sister."

He shoved his hands into his pockets and shrugged. "Arugula, spinach, watercress, I'm glad you picked today, and I'm glad Deanna couldn't make it."

I wanted to rip the wings off the butterflies in my stomach. I was glad, too, but now, I needed to get away from him because I'd glanced at his lips and felt something happen in my lower regions.

"I . . . I need to go. My . . . goldfish is hungry."

In one seamless movement, I got into my car and closed the door before Grant could wonder how I'd known it was arugula instead of spinach or before he realized I didn't actually have a goldfish.

CHAPTER 19
TWO GIRLS AND A PAIR OF JIMMY CHOOS

My cell phone buzzed right as I entered my house several days later, causing me to drop a binder on my toes, toes that had spent the last twelve hours jammed into low, number-crunching heels. I'd spent the whole of Monday at the office, first making binders and reviewing the portfolios of the few clients I had, then reading over Erin's surprisingly detailed follow-up email asking if I'd arranged that cohosted group networking dinner. *Which of course I haven't, because I have no idea where to begin.*

Then I completely wasted my time with Mark, a potential client who ended up being interested in what I could do for him in the bedroom rather than the office. I was having more days like this. Clients here and there from my online ads, but the effort-to-gain ratio was wicked. I could talk my face off, only to realize in the end that the person didn't want a financial planner; they wanted to open a bank account. I felt like I was an actress who hadn't properly studied her lines but went out onstage anyway, only to be laughed at by an audience who wasn't fooled. If people would just give me a chance to prove myself. But getting them was tough.

My irritation completely faded when I saw that the text was from Deanna.

Deanna: What are you doing right now?

Me: Just getting home from work. What are you doing?

Deanna: Actively thinking of all the ways I can murder this guy King and get away with it.

I threw all my stuff on the kitchen counter and attempted to take off my heels, but they were really wedged onto my feet.

Me: Poison? Who's King anyway, and why are we poisoning him?

I seriously couldn't get these shoes off. I sat on the kitchen floor and promptly stuck my hand in something sticky—what the hell was all over my floor? The floor film gave me enough traction to get the shoe off my red, swollen right foot. The left one appeared to have permanently fused to my skin. I gave up, leaned against the counter, and picked up my phone again.

Deanna: Okay, remind me never to plan murder with you. Poison? Seriously? No one is going to want to eat at a restaurant or stay at a B and B where the owner poisoned one of her husband's acquaintances! 😵 🤢 Now, a nice fall down the stairs . . .

Me: Then you'd have to explain why he was upstairs. And give me a break. It's been a long day and also a long time since I murdered anyone. So . . . King? Is that a nickname?

Deanna: Broken toilet downstairs? He'd have to go upstairs to do his line of cocaine, right? Xavier Octavius Skrunk a.k.a. King because he looks like Jack the Pumpkin King from The Nightmare Before Christmas. 🎃 He went to school with William, and somehow, they've STAYED friends. He's obnoxious.

Me: Wait . . . cocaine??? And pic please.

The picture came first, a side-by-side shot of a man sitting on her couch juxtaposed with the real Jack from the movie. *They were identical,* as if the cartoon creation had climbed right out of the screen and into her living room.

Another text came while I was still staring at the picture.

Deanna: And I'm pretty sure he does drugs. William insists he's just European and doesn't do drugs . . . anymore. William is naive.

Me: He. Looks. Exactly. Like. That. Skeleton.

Deanna: Seriously, it's Halloween over here . . . or Christmas. Have you had dinner? You should come over if you can stomach eating with a skeleton. Okay, I'm being mean. He's not that bad. Will you come??? Saaaaaave me!

There was no way, and I was too tired to even try to come up with an excuse.

Me: No.

She didn't even pause.

Deanna: Then I'm coming over. I'll see you in fifteen.

Me: What? You have company!

Nothing.

Me: Deanna?

Nothing.

Me: Are you really coming?

Five silent minutes passed, during which I bit my nails, made a mental note to file and paint them later so no one suspected I bit my nails, and then attempted to remove my shoe again until my phone pinged beside me.

Deanna: I'm in the car. Told them I had to go to the bathroom, where I briefly contemplated cocaine. Don't eat. I'm bringing dinner.

I scrambled to my feet and hobbled around my house, trying to decide what to clean first. How was it possible for one person to make this big of a mess? I barely owned anything!

I'd just finished shoving the last armload of crap into the pantry, my faux cleaning method, when Deanna knocked on the door.

She breezed in, bringing life into my living room along with two white bakery boxes and a bottle of something pink and, I hoped, alcoholic.

I peered inside the top box. "What is this?" I asked.

"A charcuterie."

The box was filled with sliced cheese, rolled meats, different fruits, nuts, and artfully arranged vegetables. "Did you just have this lying around?"

"I made this one earlier today. It was *supposed* to be for book club, but I was already exhausted. I spent the day with Mere, going over why we can't afford our own space right now. Yeah, I'm starting to wonder why I'm still her friend. Then the bachelorette party I was supposed to cater canceled after I'd already made food. And then King showed up. I knew he was coming, but . . . it's always a shock to see him at the door. When I opened the fridge, those little meats and cheeses sang, 'Take us!' So *I* said, 'Screw it,' grabbed the box and this." She held up what was indeed a bottle of pink champagne. "And I brought dessert in this box. Impromptu girls' night." Her face melted into slight insecurity. "I hope you're not too mad at me for barging in."

Excitement flashed through my body. Grant had texted me yesterday, telling me that he'd talked to Mere. Operation Sabotage was in motion. Deanna might be sad now, but she had no idea what awaited her. "You brought dinner, dessert, and champagne. You're forgiven." I stretched toward the dessert box, but she held it out of reach.

"Later. Why are you only wearing one shoe?"

I had completely forgotten about my shoe predicament.

"I can't get it off. I'm going to have to coordinate all my outfits with this one, final pair of shoes."

"At least they look nice. This *one* does at least." She placed the champagne on the cardboard box serving as my coffee table. "I'll get it off."

After pulling some magical hand potion from her purse, she slathered my foot and finally released me from the designer footwear.

I rubbed the ham pulsing at the end of my leg. "You think I could sue Jimmy Choo?"

"These are Jimmy Choos? What size are you? Can I borrow them?"

"Obviously I'm one size bigger than whatever these are, but my mom gave them to me, so they're probably two sizes too small." *Did my mom give me everything I have in my closet?*

My stomach growled loudly, interrupting whatever she'd been about to say next. I opened the charcuterie box and drooled.

"I forgot flutes," she said. "Do you have anything we can drink this out of?"

I went to the kitchen and came back with two coffee cups. "I'm afraid this is it."

She rolled her eyes but took both heavy, off-white mugs and filled them.

The bubbles tickled my nose. "Why was this King guy over at your house if you hate him so much?"

"I don't hate him. I just . . ." She sighed, then crunched a sliced red pepper. "He's trying to get William to go to Bonnaroo for his thirty-eighth birthday in a couple weeks. Apparently, Grant already said yes, so William wants to go, and he wants me to come because Elaine's going with Grant. And King's girlfriend Halo is going with him."

Elaine.

"Bonna-what? And Halo? Are you serious? You're making these names up."

Her laughter filled the room.

"I keep forgetting you're not from here. It's a big festival held in mid-June every year. Music, food, arts, crafts, yoga, you name it. Everyone sleeps in a tent or their car." Her smile was exaggerated. "We'd only be going Saturday and Sunday. One night. But still. Frankly, the fact that William is considering it makes me question our entire relationship."

I googled it as I nibbled a piece of cheese wrapped in salami. "It actually looks like it could be fun." I scrolled through some pictures of carefree, smiling people, all of which Deanna scowled at. "Ooh, look." I turned my phone back to her. "You can rent a fancy RV that's already set up there so you're not crammed together with a bunch of sweaty people. It's technically referred to as 'glamping.'"

She poured more champagne into her coffee mug. "I don't know. Glamping?"

"Glamorous camping. Like camping, but with all the amenities of home," I said, forcing cheer into my voice.

It was kind of nice being the encouraging one. Then I took it a step too far by saying, "What if I go with you?"

She sat straight up. "You would go?"

"If we got one of those RV things. Yeah, I'd go." *Who am I?*

"You could bring Chad," she exclaimed, apparently warming to the whole idea a lot faster than expected.

The smile faltered on my face. Right. Chad. "I'll ask him," I said, extra cheery.

My phone jingled. I'd planned to ignore it until I caught a glimpse of who it was from, Erin. She'd sent a picture of a letter. I apologized to Deanna and read it.

June 5, 2023

Erin Westerly,

This letter is to inform you that your employment with Twin Cities Financial (TCF) has been terminated, effective today, June 5, 2023.

You will receive your final paycheck, as well as any payout for leave you have accrued while working for TCF, in the coming days by the same method(s) in which you were previously receiving them.

Your healthcare benefits will remain in effect for 120 days post-termination.

Please return all company property and vacate your desk of all personal belongings by end of day today.

Please keep in mind you have signed multiple confidentiality agreements. Please review the attached documents. Should you violate any of these agreements upon termination, legal action may be taken against you.

Expect a call by next week from a TCF human resources representative for your exit interview. If you have questions regarding your compensation, benefits, signed policies or how to return company property, please contact your representative: Al Starks.

Sincerely,

Human Resources, Twin Cities Financial

A GIF of a bedazzled Catherine O'Hara as Moira Rose from *Schitt's Creek* followed the letter, with her saying, *I can't say I didn't see this coming.*

"What is it?" Deanna asked.

I handed her my phone. Erin had been fired because of me.

"Marketing master Erin?"

I nodded.

"There's no reason on here."

I leaned back against the chaouch cushions. "Minnesota's an 'at will' state. As long as the reason isn't discrimination, an employer can fire any employee without giving cause."

"This isn't fair."

"No, but she defied Houston." *Because of me.* I dropped my head into my hands.

"You're blaming yourself, aren't you?"

"Of course I am. If not for me, Erin would still have a job. I hate Houston."

"I hate him, too, and I've never even met him. The situation isn't fair, but you didn't make her do anything. You didn't even know about it. It's not your fault."

"But I feel responsible. I told her she'd be fine."

"She's probably better off not working for that guy."

"I need to call her."

I touched her initials at the top of the text, then pressed call. It went straight to voicemail, but I got a text back: On phone with mom. Will call as soon as I'm off! Told you, didn't I? 💀

I told her to call anytime and apologized twice. Like Deanna, she said it wasn't my fault.

"I have to make this right. I need to find her a job. She has a degree. I'm gonna call Chad and my mom. They'll know someone."

Deanna put her hand on my arm. "Wait. I have an idea."

I eyed her with skepticism as she nodded and looked at the ceiling, a plan percolating under her hair.

"Okay, bear in mind, I haven't completely thought this through." She uncrossed her legs and leaned forward. "Let's do this over dessert. Do you have anything?"

"I thought you brought dessert."

She shook her head and put her hand on top of the unopened box. "These aren't any good. I shouldn't have brought them." Her face flushed hot pink.

"What's in the box?"

She shook her head again, held the package against her. Now I had to know.

I pried the cardboard out of her fingers and opened the lid, stared.

"Deanna, this is a box of penises."

Deadpan, she said, "They're penisbutter cockies."

I looked back down at the dozen penises in my lap and started laughing.

"You know that bachelorette party that canceled? Well, the bride gave me a picture of exactly what she wanted them to look like. She seemed normal when she hired me! And I took the job because I need the money for this B and B. But you wanna know the worst part?"

I was still laughing. "This isn't it?"

"I also made cockolate-dipped strawberries." She was now laughing so hard I barely understood her. "And I . . . repurposed them . . .

for . . . the ladies' Bible luncheon today. A bunch . . . gray-haired ladies . . . penis-dipped fruit. Going to . . . burn . . . in . . . hell."

"That"—I gasped for air—"really blows."

After five solid minutes of laughing so hard we cried, we composed ourselves and each grabbed a dick.

Holding the cockie millimeters away from her lips, Deanna said, "I can't do this."

"Why, because they're freakishly huge and way too realistic?"

"I can't help it that I'm good."

"Exactly what is your talent here?"

She took the penis out of my hand and returned both X-rated desserts to the box. "I'll save these for book club, but that does mean we don't have a dessert."

"Wait." I got to my feet. "I have the perfect thing." I ran back to the kitchen and then returned to the living room holding a box featuring our mutual boyfriend.

"I love you," she said, and my heart flipped as she got off the couch and headed toward me. I didn't know what to say, how to feel. No friend had ever told me they loved me, but no one had ever invited themselves over, eaten stolen charcuterie platters, drunk borrowed champagne, made glamping plans, or tried to feed me anatomically correct pastry either.

Instead of hugging me, she did something even better. She took the box out of my hands and kissed the Cap'n square on the lips.

I relaxed and realized that somehow, without meaning to (and in some cases actively trying not to), I had developed a real friendship with this woman. Ridiculously, warmth moved across my body.

A red "berry" tumbled onto the floor as Deanna shoved a fistful of cereal into her mouth and crossed her legs under her on the chaouch. (I was never gonna stop calling it that.) "You hate marketing, right?"

"That's an understatement."

"Erin is good at marketing, right?"

"I haven't implemented her idea, but she's not shy about marketing."

"It is a *good* idea." She rolled her eyes. "You made bold moves in your life. You picked up and moved, you rented an office, you signed two clients from a coffee shop because you took advantage of the situation. And now, you act like you want to throw your hands up because you've hit a couple bumps. You've barely begun!"

"Hey, that's not fair. I—"

She shook her head. "No. I'm not letting you give up because you feel sorry for yourself. You're the reason I'm pursuing my dream now when, for so long, I didn't think I could. But I saw you *doing* it, and that changed everything for me."

I was speechless, opposing thoughts hitting my mind at once. I wanted to be fired up by her pep talk, but she also didn't have all the facts.

"Erin has a good marketing plan," Deanna went on. "She just got fired. She needs a job."

Her eyebrows bobbed.

I stared at her.

"Hire her! Hire Erin." She'd had too much champagne.

"But, she's in Minnesota. And my WeWork contract is up in twenty-two days. And maybe it would be easier if I just started looking for a job within an established company. It would be less stressful." I wanted to impress and inspire, but my energy was tapped.

She closed her eyes, her lips flattening to a line. "Okay, let's work through this. First, Erin used to live here. Maybe she'd consider coming back, but even if not, there's remote work. I'm almost positive she'd be interested. Why else would she spend all that time practically planning your marketing event by email? Second, you need to renew your lease. You can't end this at three months. And we are nowhere near considering that last thing. Don't you remember Houston? You don't need to go through something like that again. This is *your* business." She stopped, her eyes glassy.

I held my face in my hands, letting her words wash over me. Deanna made it sound simple. But I thought about all the money I could lose. WeWork wanted longer-term commitments if they could get them. I couldn't afford long term anymore. And Deanna was probably right about Erin, but if she was interested, would I be pulling her into a sinking ship? I couldn't keep living by what might potentially happen. I needed a sure thing. And to top it off, I was not sure I could do this.

"I'll think about it," I said, wanting to please Deanna, wanting to be what she thought I was.

CHAPTER 20
THREE FEET BETWEEN US

I don't like Grant. I don't like Grant. I don't like Grant.

Those were the seventh, eighth, and ninth times I had repeated that under my breath in response to him saying two words to me: "Hi, Penelope."

I sat next to Grant in a large white van roughly two weeks later and picked at my seat belt in the row behind the front, counting off the nine reasons why I'd probably regret my decision to go to Bonnaroo.

1. Van roster: Me, Grant, William, Chuck, King, Halo. No Deanna. Deanna wasn't going to Bonnaroo. She, Mere, and Keyondra had procured a huge catering gig (without penises). *Deanna wasn't going to Bonnaroo.*
2. A skeleton was driving the van: Jack the Pumpkin King, to be exact.
3. My feelings for Grant were getting more muddled. He'd encouraged me to ride when I'd been hesitant after my accident. He'd talked—about trivial things: organic toothpaste and the best lighting for property photography— while riding by my side, far behind the rest of the pack. This weird connection we had made me comfortable and uncomfortable.

4. Grant smelled good, always the same, with slight variations: fresh-cut grass or pine or maple, always something
   from nature, always mixed with the faint hint of trail
   mix. Smelling your friends is acceptable, right? That's
   allowed and doesn't have to mean anything.

5. Grant's girlfriend. He was off limits. A friend. The nov-
   elty of his attention would wear off, eventually. It had to
   because if it didn't—

6. King's crystal-wearing, zen-goddess girlfriend Halo, who
   didn't believe in shaving her armpits, and incidentally,
   the only other woman in the van.

7. Elaine wasn't in the van for some work reason. I couldn't
   decide if that was a good or bad thing. Elaine and the rest
   of this birthday party were meeting us there. Grant and I
   were friends.

8. No Chad. He'd accused me of taking time away from
   us, forbade me to go, then retracted his order when he
   saw my face and assured me I wasn't the kind of girl who
   enjoyed camping and told me I'd be miserable. He probably wasn't wrong, but I hadn't wanted to back down,
   so I'd told him I was going whether he went or not. He
   decided not to come, and we'd had our first official fight
   as a couple.

9. *Deanna wasn't going to Bonnaroo.*

Life crawled with complication, and Deanna's idea hadn't made
things any clearer.

I'd taken small steps forward during the past couple of weeks. I'd
met a little man named Myra at the coffee station outside my office after
he'd had a massage to help with his sciatica. He was cute and cozy and
the best part of that day, and our conversation—where I didn't need
to turn him into a number—traveled from coffee flavors to discussing
what I did for a living.

"I'm a financial planner," I told him. "I've been trying to start my business, but I'm afraid it's not going so well."

"You don't say?" He sipped his coffee, and his wild eyebrows made me smile. "Do you know your stuff? Make people money?"

"I do. I know what to do once I have someone's account. The problem is getting there in the first place."

"Would an old man like me benefit from your services?"

I took him to my office, and after an hour of answering questions and repeating my usual presentation, I added his modest accounts to my book.

Then I met with Piper as scheduled earlier this week. She'd been in a hurry and had essentially thrown her money at me. Girl had bread (gluten-free bread, but still). She didn't want to take the time to understand all the details. She said that's what she had me for. I'd even managed to avoid the massage she'd threatened me with.

But I couldn't get excited because as soon as I'd added them, Chad's parents had pulled their business. Chad had tried to tell me that it wouldn't last, that they'd had to do it to show Vicki support, but it was another blow. And I knew they wouldn't be back. I didn't want them back.

But I couldn't stop second-guessing myself. I'd entered a cycle of doubt that I couldn't seem to escape from, which had started after losing the Fletchers and having my character questioned and had snowballed from there.

So, I'd spent most of my time perusing job listings at various companies around Nashville. My WeWork contract was up in a little over a week, and the leasing office warned me that if someone else came along who needed a longer commitment, they wouldn't be able to hold my place.

I loved Nashville. I had a friend. *Friends*. But what if I'd simply acted too rashly?

People made the kinds of life-altering decisions I had after careful months of thought and planning. I hadn't thought any of it through when I'd left TCF in March; I'd acted on impulse, out of desperation. My plans now seemed to be written on a ticking clock, which made action almost impossible. Faced with all the potential choices and pathways, I felt paralyzed.

So, Deanna or not, I was taking this trip to get away from all the pressure, and hopefully acquire some sort of clarity. I promised my answer about a longer commitment by Monday, June 26, a day before my lease was up, *if* no one wanted the space by then. I'd face that if I had to. But I should've biked to Bonnaroo.

When we stepped out of the van, a woman, covered in gold paint with strategically placed jewels serving as her only clothing, sashayed past us on stilettos as she winked, slowly licked her lips, and blew a kiss at Chuck.

"What kinda hell is this?" Chuck said.

I legit giggled, then pointed to a stand loaded with cotton candy in clear bags. "At least they have cotton candy. I'll be getting some of that."

William threw his arms out. "Embrace it, Chuck. This is our new home. At least for the night."

Chuck grimaced. Everything about him was rugged: thick beard, sun-worn face, hands pocked with calluses. His lost-cowboy drawl was right at home in his plaid mountain man shirt, and when he spoke, his voice—no matter the words coming out of his mouth—said, *It'll all work out fine.* A number six, rolling through life like he was on a wheel.

King laughed and squeezed Halo's butt as his eyes followed the nearly naked Amazon woman. "You'd rock an outfit like that, babe."

She whipped around, putting hands on hips. "Do you know what kind of chemicals are in that paint?" Halo kept talking, something about the environment, as she followed King, who was making a beeline for a vendor selling beer.

William gestured to the retreating couple. "How long do you think they're gonna last?"

"I give 'em less than a week," Chuck said.

"I say they don't even make it through this trip," I added, surprising myself. They'd argued about the stupidest things on the way down here. How to properly fray a garment. Women's fashion in the 1800s. The exact cause of the impending honeybee extinction. I didn't see how they'd made it this far.

"I'll take that bet." Chuck extended his hand. "'Cause I'm guessin' there are enough mind-altering substances around here that their differences won't matter."

"You guys are horrible," Grant said in all his Grantiness. "Leave them alone."

"Don't you wonder how they got together in the first place?" I asked.

"Sex," Chuck said. "Speakin' a sex, here comes your girlfriend, Grant." Chuck nodded to the group walking toward them.

Every ounce of excitement washed down to my toes as flawless Elaine walked over to us. Her soft waves somehow defied the summer humidity as she wrapped her arms around Grant and said, "We've been waiting for you guys!" Then she planted her coquettish red lips right on his.

"Where's Deanna, Will?" Someone else, a man this time.

After William explained Deanna's absence, I was introduced to the rest of their party, three other people whose names I forgot three seconds after hearing them.

I tried to concentrate on what this athletic blonde woman was saying, but my eyes kept wandering to Grant and the woman who wasn't leaving his side. And how she kept finding excuses to touch him. A charming laugh with a sweep down his forearm. An absentminded caress on his back as the group batted around conversation.

It didn't bother me. Of course it didn't. And it didn't bother me that she continued to cling to Grant's arm like a fungus. A gorgeous, intelligent little fungus.

I looked away. Wasn't that what a happy couple *should* look like? I hated public displays of affection, though. That was it: the only reason

I'd started fantasizing about shaving the woman's head in her sleep was that open affection freaked me out.

William walked up to my left. "You okay? You . . . look like you want to strangle someone."

I counted to five, stopped gritting my teeth, and forced a laugh.

"A fly won't stop bothering me." I waved a hand in front of my face, swatting at the nonexistent insect. "Super annoying. Anyway, I'm gonna get a drink."

He looked as if he'd bought my fly story. "Get me one, too, would ya?"

"Sure, what do you want?"

"Surprise me."

As I stood in a short line, I twisted the band around my wrist and focused on the large stage. The dreadlocks on the drummer's head flew up and down like animated breadsticks, keeping time with hands that moved like pieces of a machine. It was loud, the music, the laughter, the chatter; the whole place was alive. I tried to soak it in as I stood amid the colors of "Roo"—shirts, tents, banners, and skin tones.

Chuck, who'd joined William when I returned, screwed up his nose. "Wine?"

"What's wrong with wine?"

Chuck looked at William, then back at me. "I'll be right back with a real drink."

As Chuck walked off, William said, "Guess how many times Deanna has texted asking if you're okay?"

"Three?" Deanna had tasked, threatened really, William, Grant, and Chuck with making sure I had a good time.

"Five."

"She's an amazing person, your wife."

"I don't know what I'd do without her." He looked lost without Deanna by his side.

I patted his shoulder. It was sweet.

I stared at Grant and perfect Elaine because my defiant eyes wouldn't stop floating over there no matter how many times I told them not to. Grant was talking to a small group. From this distance, I couldn't hear what he was saying, but everyone had smiles on their faces. Grant belonged with someone like Elaine, someone without baggage. Grant was someone to get invested in, to get lost in, to get lost with. Which made him the exact kind of person I needed to avoid.

Why was I thinking about this?

I shoved up and told them I was going to take a tour of the vendors, hoping my "Oh really" and "That's great" were appropriate responses to whatever they'd been saying.

I bought a lavender lip balm and a handmade quilt that looked like it'd been pulled from a mermaid's undersea dwelling, my souvenirs.

The sun slid across the sky, and morning faded into afternoon. When my legs no longer wanted to support me, I found the group again and sipped more wine out of a red Solo cup as I listened to Chuck's stories while music hummed in the background. Someone suggested getting closer to the stage as shades of evening began to bloom in the sky.

The noise and the wine dislodged the unhealthy thoughts that wanted to nestle in my brain. I'd been sure I was going to short-circuit in a crowd this size, but there was something to this carefree atmosphere, like everyone had left their troubles back home. I liked it. I needed it because I knew reality would soon rip this moment of peace away from me.

The wristband turned me into a superhero, immune to the past, living only in the present, where grown men wore onesies and glow bracelets were the only necessary evening uniform. I wasn't even looking at Grant, whom I knew was only a person or two away from me, when our group stood as close to the stage as the crowd would allow. This evening was for me. I declared it so. The wine agreed.

A new band was introduced, took the stage, wound up the crowd. The roar finally calmed as guitar strums reverberated from the platform.

Arms pumped. Feet jumped. Hair moved in the wind. And the lyrics of a band I'd never heard of before swirled around me, then climbed inside my body. The earth spun under my soles. I felt like I was somewhere else entirely, like the hundreds of people suddenly didn't exist around me. The woman's voice somersaulted over the crowd, singing only for me.

"It's in my mind. I can't outrun . . ."

My eyes scanned the crowd, trying to judge whether anyone else could hear what I was hearing or if I was imagining the words summing up my life.

"Peering over the edge . . ."

Flutters in my stomach.

"All the memories are tied up."

Someone bumped into me, and I looked around. Caught myself on nothing, held up by the words, as if they were a cane.

"I'll keep riding, riding, riding . . ."

The notes beat against my skin.

"And all I need is love."

My eyes traveled to Grant. I couldn't help it, not after the wine had dulled my perfect pretense. And he was looking right back. We stood still, our gaze steady over the vibration of the crowd.

"Can you give me some?"

The rays of the setting sun reached between us, burning the moment into history.

"It's there in your eyes."

Eyes sparkled, spoke in time with the music, focus unbroken.

"I'll pull down my disguise."

Something more than friends.

"But will you stay or disappear?"

Music slowed. Life suspended.

"I was alone, but somehow you've stayed right by my side . . ."

And then, Grant was moving toward me. This was it.

Things were about to change.

CHAPTER 21
LIFE REALIZATION #10: NEVER EAT THE MARSHMALLOWS

Change they did.

The sun shifted. The light moved away. A skinny, shirtless guy ran between us and knocked three-fourths of his beer into my face, reality spitting in my eyes. William bounced back and forth on his feet before pulling off his shirt and handing it to me. Chuck moved to confront the half-naked punk who'd showered me.

The crowd swallowed Grant. The last note of the song faded in the heat of June's setting sun, and I wondered if I'd imagined it all. The lyrics, the music, the man, likely all some buzzed daydream.

I wiped my eyes with William's shirt and nodded when asked if I was all right. I wasn't all right, but it had nothing to do with spilled brew and everything to do with the beautiful woman tucking her arm into Grant's as she smiled up at him and said something that was surely charming. His eyes sparkled when he looked down at her and laughed.

They were perfect.

I pushed my way through the crowd, through a plume of smoke I recognized as marijuana, until I made it to the on-site RV that Deanna had rented for us before she'd abandoned me.

Halo and a slender woman with purple hair were grinding against each other beside the door. They didn't even acknowledge my presence as I passed, tears blurring my vision. I lay on the couch-thing, closing my eyes so tightly I saw stars.

Then I pulled my mermaid quilt to my face and let the gnawing ache around my heart rock me to sleep.

∽

The next day, I shoved my bag into the back of the van and looked up at the three single clouds in the sky, letting the early-afternoon sun fall on my face.

"Where's Halo?" I asked.

Once Chuck got back from the bathroom and we located Halo, we could leave. I wanted to go home, but I dreaded the ride back because I didn't want to be near Grant right now or ever. And why hadn't he ridden with Elaine?

King shrugged his stick arms. "Don't care. We broke up."

William elbowed me, and I tried not to smile. But inside, I gloated, which kept me from noticing Grant until he was right beside me.

"Did you have a good time?" he asked.

"Oh, it was great." I blinked too many times and licked my lips twice, two times too many. It was like the features of my face were malfunctioning.

"I got you something." He leaned into the van and pulled out some fluffy pink cotton candy.

I hate you, Grant. I really hate you.

His eyebrows scrunched when I didn't take the spun sugar. "Didn't you say you wanted cotton candy earlier?"

"Yes! Thank you!" Too loud. Wrong inflection.

I *had* said that, but I hadn't thought anyone was paying attention. If we were going to be friends, he needed to stop being so damned thoughtful.

"William, what are you eating?" King shouted as he ran toward William, who'd been digging in the trunk. King grabbed an empty

Tupperware container from William's hand. "That was my spare! I already promised it to a guy."

William swallowed, looked annoyed. "It's one marshmallow. I'll buy you some more."

Chuck returned from the bathroom. "He ate one of them LSD marshmallows? Deanna's gonna be pissed."

William whipped toward King, who was laughing so hard I was sure he was going to snap in half. "You put LSD in those marshmallows?"

"It's fairly standard, newbie. Where have you been this whole time?"

"Not on an LSD trip!" William was now pacing. "What do I do?" He looked at each of us—all laughing nervously—in plea.

Grant sobered and looked at me. "You should call Deanna."

"Me? Why me?"

"She's your friend."

I shoved him. "She's *your* sister."

He nudged me back. "I'm scared of her, okay?"

Chuck leaned in. "You two need to stop flirting and call Deanna."

"We're not flirting!" My face reddened as I protested, again too loud and too quickly.

Grant blew air out his nose. He was irritatingly un-red as he reached for the van door. "Let's see what happens."

ᮒ

As we were nearing Nashville, William put his hand in the air and swayed, an imaginary rainbow coming out of his fingertips. "The coloooors!" He unbuckled himself and attempted to climb over the seat to catch the musical notes he swore were physically coming out of the radio.

A long belch trailed out of William's mouth as Chuck pulled him back into his seat. "I can actually seeeee my burp! This. Is. *Excellent!*"

"Nobody sees your foul-smelling mouth fart," Chuck growled.

"Mouth faaaaart!" William grabbed Chuck's face and got way too close. "Did you make that up?" Then he felt around for a pen in his pocket. "I'm writing that one down."

King howled.

"Wouldn't be laughing if I were you," Chuck warned. "Deanna's gonna rip you apart."

King stopped laughing.

I texted Deanna a video of William to make sure she still wanted him at home. She did.

Grant's hand brushed mine when he reached for the cell phone in his pocket after a text notification came in, and a little electrical impulse skittered across my insides.

As William insisted the rainbow trees outside were wearing top hats and performing a musical number, I leaned toward Grant, inhaled. "Deanna?"

"Elaine."

I looked out the window, wishing the trees really were wearing top hats and that one of them would reach into the car and sweep Grant's phone right out of his hand. And then I looked at my phone, checking my email as a distraction.

My stomach dropped as I opened the one titled *WeWork Following Up—New renter for your office space*. Someone else wanted to rent my office for the next three months, and I'd been asked to vacate as soon as my contract was over.

My head whapped into the side of the window as King curved into Deanna's driveway.

Grant leaned over and whispered, "This isn't going to go well, is it?"

It took me a second to pull myself out of the email and realize he was talking about William and Deanna.

Deanna waited on the sidewalk, arms crossed.

"See? Pissed," Chuck said as he maneuvered William out of the vehicle.

King took one look at Deanna, threw our bags onto the driveway, and peeled out.

As soon as William's feet hit the aggregate driveway, he ran toward Deanna, then past her, and disappeared through the neighbors' back gate.

Deanna threw her arms up. "Where's he going?"

"The better question is probably how'd he get his clothes off so fast." Chuck nodded toward the elegant swimming pool in the neighbors' backyard.

Grant took off.

"Freeeeee!" William yelled as he belly flopped right into the sparkling water, completely naked.

"No, William! They just came back from a funeral!" Deanna screamed as she, Chuck, and I filed through the gate and ran right into an older woman holding a tomato; her mouth was still open as she gawked at the very naked man leaping up and down in her swimming pool screaming that she should join him and be free.

Grant was bent low over the pool, gesturing for William to get out.

A teenage boy in an ill-fitting black suit materialized from inside the house, pulled out his phone, and pointed it at William and Grant.

I sighed. This was probably going to be the next viral TikTok.

Deanna picked up her husband's pants lying in a heap by her neighbors' tomato plants and held them to her chest. "Mrs. Collin, I'm so sorry for your loss and for William interrupting the wake," she explained. "William has always adored your pool, and he had drugs." She shook her head. "He's . . . he's not a drug addict. It was an accident. He ate marshmallows. He likes to snack, you know, loves your buns."

When Mrs. Collin pulled back in horror, Deanna screamed, "Cinnamon buns! He likes the ones you make. I don't know why I said that. Please don't call the police."

I put my arm around Deanna and spoke for her. "It's a long story, Mrs. Collin, and we are so, so sorry. We'll get William and get out of your hair as soon as we can."

This was going to require a gift-basket apology and years of space.

"Take those fabric shackles off, people, and get in here!" William, from the pool. He was dodging Grant and Chuck.

"It sounds great, buddy, it does," Grant cooed, "but you're in your neighbors' pool, and you don't have clothes on. We need to get ya home."

"You're not making sense." He backstroked away, and every part of him, *every*, glinted in the sun.

"William, get out of there!" Deanna screamed, but William carried on as if she'd told him she'd be joining him in a minute.

"Grant, do something. This is . . ." Deanna glanced back at the wake attendees in black, who were lined up, watching.

"That's it." Grant slipped off his shoes and socks, then his shirt. I had this wild idea that Embrace-Life Grant was giving in, stripping down, and joining William. But his jeans remained as he dove into the pool.

Chuck bent at the edge of the water. "Get 'im to the edge, Grant, and I'll pull his naked ass out."

Silence. Deanna and I covered our mouths. After three failed attempts, Grant finally managed to grip William's waist and pulled. William spun in Grant's arms.

"No pets in the ocean! That little guy's gonna drown!" William screamed as he went after Grant's facial hair.

Nothing deterred Grant, not even his jeans when they rode low on his surprisingly cut waist as he stepped out of the water, carrying his large friend. I tried not to notice, but I couldn't look away, especially after I spotted the small patch of ink on the right side of his lower torso.

Grant has a tattoo.

Hot.

"Get the gate," Grant ordered and then carried William across the neighbors' lawn, to a backdrop of whistles, claps, and cheers from what now seemed like *all* the mourners. When William protested, Grant growled, "Don't even think about it," a husky demand that made my belly flutter. Miraculously, William obeyed.

I wasn't sure which it was—Grant's immediate action, his naked torso, his authoritative strength, rippling back muscles, or the tattoo— but my body ached. I wanted to be William because he was wet and naked and in Grant's arms.

This was *not* how you were supposed to feel about your friends.

I pulled my cell from my pocket, replied to the workspace email, releasing my old office space, and booked a ticket to Minnesota because my feelings for Grant were the last straw. I was not going to be a cheater—again.

CHAPTER 22
FIVE-STAR CHOCOLATE TORTE

A few days after Bonnaroo, on my mother's doorstep, I'd kissed Chad hard on his mouth. A pang of guilt had weaseled its way under my skin as I looked into his face and told him how much I'd missed him. Really, I'd missed my old comfortable bubble that kept the feelings out. Then I told him he'd been right; I'd been miserable at Bonnaroo.

I was mad at myself because I couldn't make life in Nashville work, and I'd developed feelings for Grant, *feelings*, which ruined everything. How could I be friends with Deanna now? How could I act normal around Grant now that every time I looked at him, I'd think of his muscled, wet torso and how much I wanted to rub myself against it?

Chad had smiled, patted my hair, and pulled me to my old bedroom, where I shoved, scratched, nibbled, and pounded him into me because I needed proof that my body belonged in his bed.

This morning, Friday morning, after days of me wallowing at Aurora's house, Chad told me he had a surprise he'd tell me about over dinner.

I spent the day as I had the previous three, alone in my mother's house, reading *Jane Eyre* and mostly ignoring life and the texts from Deanna, Grant, Erin, and even William. Deanna's was the hardest to ignore.

Deanna, Sunday, 4:27 p.m.: **Where are you?**

Deanna, Sunday, 5:32 p.m.: William is such a doofus. I'm mortified. Did you get home okay? You wanna get dinner? I can't even look at William. Grant and Chuck are babysitting.

Deanna, Sunday, 7:49 p.m.: Did something happen at Bonnaroo?

Deanna, Sunday, 9:17 p.m.: Pen, please call. I'm really worried. I need to know you're okay.

After writing and erasing a bunch of words: Me, Sunday, 9:25 p.m.: I'm fine, going to Minnesota for a few days.

Deanna, Sunday, 9:25 p.m.: Thank God you're okay, but did something happen? Aside from William?

Me, Sunday, 9:46 p.m.: I just need some time.

Deanna, Sunday, 9:48 p.m.: Understood. Please call/text if you need anything. Miss you.

Me (after sucking up tears to avoid looks from other travelers), Sunday, 10:05 p.m.: Thanks.

Deanna, Monday, 7:00 a.m.: I need to talk to you. I have something to tell you.

Deanna, Tuesday, 9:23 a.m.: I'm trying to give you space, but when are you coming back? What about work?

Deanna, Wednesday, 10:34 a.m.: You are coming back, right?

Deanna, Thursday, 8:17 p.m.: Okay, I know something's wrong, and I know you don't want to talk about it. I'm here when you're ready. (But if that's not by next week, I'm coming to MN. Consider this fair warning.)

She hadn't sent anything today. A part of me was relieved, while another part wanted her to. Deanna deserved a better friend, but I hadn't known what to say, still didn't. Not talking to her, not responding, was tearing me up. But if I texted, I was afraid I'd blurt it all out, tell her about my feelings for Grant, and I couldn't do that. Sometimes it was better to say nothing, right?

I still had the house and my car was there, so I'd have to go back to Nashville eventually, but right now, all the questions I'd been avoiding were piling together to form a monster I wanted to hide from. I wasn't even looking at open positions anymore because even what state I needed to be in was up for grabs.

I slumped downstairs, wrapped in a black robe and indecision. Aurora poured me a cup of coffee, elegantly leaned one hip against her sparkling countertop, and gave me a pathetic smile.

"He's taking you to W. A. Frost tonight. Your favorite." She'd always told me never to lean on anyone or anything, but a time like this was an exception, when leaning gave the illusion of comfort and self-assuredness.

I had the sudden urge to ask her why she hadn't moved away after everything that had happened here. But I couldn't. One, *I* was back here. And two, we didn't talk like normal people did.

She stepped forward. I thought she was going to reach out for me, but instead, she swept an invisible dust bunny off the counter. "I laid out the perfect dress for you to wear tonight. It's in the guest room. I knew you weren't up to picking anything out."

She would've laid one out no matter how I felt. But she was trying to cheer me.

I swallowed, swiveled off the barstool, and walked to the guest room down the hall, past the baby grand piano on which my mother had forced me to learn.

The dark-navy dress waited on top of the pristine light-jade duvet. The hanger swung in my hand as I stepped back into the hallway.

"W. A. Frost isn't *this* fancy." The silk, the subtle lace and rhinestone detail screamed class rather than suggested it.

"It can be." She winked.

"But, I—"

"This is the kind of dress a woman wears on special occasions," she said, cutting me off, all business now. "Chad's divorce was final today."

Barbie.

I am Barbie.

Her Barbie.

Financial Planner Barbie from the Barbie Career Playset.

"Chad and I think we found the perfect place for you two. He's going to surprise you with it tonight."

The dream house.

"And he's got a job prospect. I'll leave it to him to explain, but it's all lining up. You have no reason to be sad."

Of course not. But I was glad she'd ruined the surprise. At least I knew what he was going to say, even if I didn't know what to say back.

∽

The Fireside Room was an intimate brick-walled space for parties no larger than twenty people. Tonight, there was a single round table in the center of the room, draped with a white tablecloth and finished with a flickering candle in a glass jar that looked like it was about to go out. Fairy lights were hung in sweeps across the white and red rose wallpapered ceiling.

The large fireplace with its vintage brick and its own set of twinkling lights was to my left, and straight ahead, behind Chad, were three wood-framed windows that spanned from ceiling to near the floor and showcased the people-filled outdoor patio.

"You rented the whole room?"

He nodded, a half smile on his lips that was mirrored in his eyes.

I hadn't fastened my bra tight enough. Nothing grounded me. I reached down and fastened the strap of my heels a notch too tight.

Better.

"You look lovely," he said.

"Everyone looks good in candlelight."

He reached across the table for my hand. His hands were solid, manly, capable, the hands of a smooth five.

"I don't like seeing you like this, and I think I can fix it."

"Oh?" I acted surprised, thankful again that Aurora had told me what was coming.

"I golfed with a finance buddy of mine today. He owes me a favor."
He paused for effect. "What would you say if I told you I got you a job
at Hedge International?"

"Hedge International?" I leaned forward. Hedge International was
a dream job. "They're huge." And there were never job postings; positions were filled within hours of becoming available.

Hedge International.

"You're gonna be their newest planner. See what I can do for you?
Did your mom tell you about the house?"

"That the two of you found?" I nodded, still reeling over Hedge
International. "Yeah, she told me."

He pulled up pictures. Posh. Beautiful. Elegant. The perfect living
space to go with the perfect working space.

"I can't wait for you to see it. Everything is falling into place. The
job. The house."

Falling into place.

I studied him . . . his mouth, the slight dimple in his chin, the
husky notes of his laughter. He was a catch and had a life already set
up for me. No more struggle, no more weird, confusing feelings to get
tied up in.

We ate, talked about the house, the job, timelines, but the whole
time, I couldn't shake the feeling that something was wrong. He was
essentially solving all my problems, giving me exactly what I'd been
looking for. So why wasn't I excited?

When dessert arrived, Chad leaned over his chocolate torte with
a single strawberry fanned on top, intense as I'd ever seen him, and
grabbed my hand, lacing our fingers with a look of confidence on his
face, like he was touching something that was already his.

A quiet numbness settled under each stitch of this lovely evening
frock.

"When you find something that's right, you hold on to it. You do
what you have to do to get it. Sometimes you have to go through people

and experiences to figure out what you truly want and need, but when you find it, you know."

His smile crinkled the skin around his eyes, eyes that reflected the room and all the tiny lights around us so they sparkled. He continued to talk about the future, our common interests, aligned goals, practical next steps forward.

His hand slipped from mine, and he slid to the floor, onto one knee between me and the fireplace. I suddenly wished I were on the patio outside, surrounded by plants—anything to give me a little more oxygen because I couldn't breathe, hadn't seen this coming. I searched the room for anything I could fashion into a crude bicycle.

"Penelope Auberge, will you marry me?"

Time stopped.

And my mind ticked off all the reasons to say yes:

1. Chad was handsome.
2. He was taller than me, even in heels.
3. He was intelligent.
4. He didn't want kids.
5. He didn't ask too many questions.
6. A future with him would be oblivious to my past.
7. I could have an instant life, job, house, and husband.
8. I wouldn't have to struggle to find clients.
9. He liked everything about me.
10. He was the Ken to my Barbie.

Everything he'd said was right. Our interests, goals, and logical next steps *had* been the same.

Chad, beaming, lifted my left hand, and pushed a huge diamond onto the fourth finger. It glinted, bursting into a kaleidoscope of colors. He maneuvered back into his chair across from me. "Do you like it?"

"It's gorgeous." I stared at my left hand. The sharp angles and precision cuts pierced into my bubble, popping it and leaving me sitting in a puddle of realization. .

"Do you know what my name would be if I married you, Chad?"

His eyebrows snapped together as if this was the last thing he'd expected. I was as surprised as he was. It was almost as if, like him, I were outside my body, waiting to hear what I had to say.

"I would be Pen Gwinn. Pen Gwinn. *Penguin.*" I started laughing. He shifted uncomfortably and adjusted his jacket, like he might be sweating underneath, but eventually he laughed, too, a little hesitant, awkward chuckle.

Then a new list materialized in my head, but there was only one thing on it:

1. *Take Chad's ring off.*

He liked everything about me because he liked what I'd let him see. But he hadn't seen the real me. *I* hadn't seen the real me, until I'd found myself in Nashville.

His proposal had lifted a veil. He'd laid out all the things I'd told myself I wanted. But when faced with actually having them, I no longer wanted them. I couldn't picture a life with Chad. I loved my new house in Nashville. I loved my new friends. I was still floundering, there was no doubt about it, but the only threads tying me in place at all weren't here in Minnesota. I'd moved on, and I hadn't noticed the changes inside me until this moment.

This wasn't the option I thought it was.

And I wasn't Barbie.

"When you find what's right, you hold on to it," I said, repeating what I remembered of his previous statement, and then I pulled the ring off my finger. "And this isn't right." I held the ring out to him, but he wouldn't take it, so I placed it on the white tablecloth, near his dessert plate.

"I don't know what's next for me." My heart stung. I knew I was hurting him. But this was his life, not mine, not even ours. "But I do know my future isn't with you."

He shook his head, grabbed my hand again, and pushed the ring back onto my finger. "You're confused. Do you know how many women would be thrilled to be in your shoes right now?"

Probably not many. They were way too tight.

He waved his hand between us. "No. I know you better than that. I love you. You need to get away from that ridiculous mustache and those people who aren't like you and me. Hedge International. I can't go back and tell Bryan that you're not interested. No one turns this down. Do you know how that would make me look? My parents already told me I was screwing up by leaving Vicki."

Wow. All this time, I'd just needed someone to lay it all out for me, like a dress. I shoved my sarcasm aside and tried to ignore my rising anger. He didn't know my new friends or the new life that had grown around me, giving me something I'd never had before, something he'd never had.

And I did know how it would make him look, and I was really, really sorry. I knew what kind of person he was. I used to be that person, and I tried to sympathize, especially since this was partly my fault. I could've avoided tonight, spared us both this regret, if I'd been strong enough to know what I needed. But up until that ring was on my finger, I was considering the life he presented, really considering it. Because it was easier than dealing with all the potential failure and all the feelings that I'd opened myself up to. And if we'd had an affair, at least it was because we were meant to spend the rest of our lives together.

But life was going to be hard no matter what I did. The difference was that I had a chance at happiness in Nashville. I did not have one here.

"Houston did what he did," he went on. "It wasn't right, but you had your crisis, and I let you. Now it needs to end. Let's get back to real life. Marry me. Take the job. It's what I know you want."

"I'm so sorry." I took the ring off again. "I can only imagine what my turning down the job will cost you. And how you must feel. But I've been trying to build an empire, when all I really need is a village."

"What are you talking about?"

"When the Fletchers didn't sign with me, I started doubting everything. And then your parents pulled out."

"I told you—"

"I don't blame them, but it was the loss of another really big client. And it felt like the end. I was questioning all the decisions I'd made, but I've been so focused on what I didn't have or what I'd lost that I haven't been focusing on what I *do* have. I think I've been confused about what it is I actually need to start a business on my own."

His mouth was slightly open, as if he couldn't fathom where this was going.

But it was becoming clear. As I spoke, a weight was lifting. "I know you don't understand, but I love Nashville. And I'm just now realizing that I don't have to have a fancy office or huge clients to be happy or even successful." I'd been ignorant, trying to make this transition work in only one way, when I hadn't considered any of the others. I had a house that was paid for, and it might not be as professional as an office with a glass-topped desk, but I could just as easily work from home. And I felt foolish. Deanna was right: if I really put myself into this and stop letting the doubts stand in my way, maybe I could make this work.

"I met a little man named Myra at the coffee station outside my office several days ago," I told him. "He's now my client." I shook my head. "I don't need the big guys; I need Myra." Tears were in my eyes because now I knew where to put all my energy. It wasn't going to be easy, and it was terrifying, and I'd still have to deal with my feelings for Grant, but that was exactly what I'd do. I'd deal with them. Because not even Grant was going to stand in my way. I didn't want to lose what I had in Nashville, so I'd learn to control myself.

"Fuck Myra." His words made me flinch. His jaw tightened as he leaned forward and once again picked up my hand and the ring and slid it back on my finger.

I was too stunned to stop him, too wrapped up in my realizations.

"Dammit, Pen, I thought you were stronger than this. I'm not going to let you ruin this for us. You're going to move back here and take the job because that's what sane Pen would do. Someday, you'll thank me for pushing you through this dark time."

I was done.

He didn't deserve my sympathy. He wasn't the victim here.

He was an ass.

"You know what? I don't need to wait to thank you. Thank you. Thank you for showing me without any doubt that I'm doing the right thing. And in case you're too thick to comprehend what I'm saying, let me lay it out for you." I lifted his hand, took the ring off my finger, and jammed it onto his pinkie as far as it would go. Now, he was too stunned to do anything. "I don't want you. I don't want Hedge International. I don't want the perfect little house you and my *mother* picked out for me." I started to walk away, but I turned back. "You know what I do want?" I picked up my dessert plate and his. "I want this five-star chocolate torte."

I clomped away in my too-tight heels and my mother's silk dress, a little token that would forever be the reminder of the night I took my life back.

As I passed the bar, my phone rang. I set the tortes down on the counter, asked for them to be boxed up, and pulled out my cell. Erin. Impeccable timing.

"Hey, Erin. What's up?"

"Hey. I know it's kind of a weird hour on a Friday night, but I have some news. Am I disturbing?"

"Not at all, just dumping my boyfriend after he proposed to me." I glanced behind me, wishing they'd hurry up with the tortes before Chad came out here.

"Whaaaat? Chad? Where are you?"

"W. A. Frost."

"Like, five minutes from me W. A. Frost?"

"Yep."

"OMG. My ex is on a date. You wanna come over?"

I hesitated; then a waiter handed me the boxed desserts. I certainly wasn't going back to my mother's. And I was going to need an assistant.

"Text me your address. Do you like chocolate torte?"

CHAPTER 23
ONE GIRL + ONE DOG =

"Forgive the furniture," Erin said, waving me into her living room and pointing to a leather chair that would've been nice if it hadn't been completely destroyed by . . . a wild animal? "When Kane broke up with me, I let Hulk tear into his favorite chair. I'm not proud."

"Where is Hulk?" I looked around for her dog.

"With a friend. I took him over when I thought I had plans for tonight so he wouldn't be alone. Funny, I'm the one who ended up alone." She threw a blanket over the chair and curled up in it. "I can't believe you're here! I was sulking. This is perfect."

I handed her one of the to-go containers and a set of plastic utensils from the paper bag they'd given me at W. A. Frost. "Well, my return wasn't planned, and the proposal was a complete surprise."

"And you said *no*? In that dress? That was cruel. You look hot."

I nodded. "Thank you."

"Tell me everything."

I told her some of everything as we ate the torte, and I built up my nerve to ask her to work for me, but oddly, I hadn't felt compelled to view her as a number. I think I was riding the high of my own self-discovery.

I didn't know what the job would look like going forward, especially since I didn't have a workspace for much longer, but I was going for it. If you didn't ask, you didn't receive.

I'd turned my phone off because it had been buzzing furiously in my purse. My mother. I couldn't handle Aurora right now.

"Wow," she said. "I had no idea he was such a jackass. Now I feel bad."

"About what?"

"About accepting the job he just got me."

"He got you a job?"

"I thought you knew."

I shook my head.

"I never spoke to him personally, but at the interview, they told me I came recommended by Chad. It's at the law firm where he works. Not finance like I wanted, but it's a job. And I need money so I can get out of this place. But I can't work there now that . . ."

"Of course you can work there. He's a good lawyer. He works at a good firm." I placed half my torte on her coffee table, suddenly feeling sick to my stomach. Chad had gotten Erin a job. I didn't know what to settle on. Disappointment? Appreciation? Guilt? I was feeling it all. I wanted to leave. My post-proposal confidence was fading.

"Umm, your face is kinda saying it's not okay."

A bitter laugh escaped my lips. I started to lie, but I was so disappointed that I told her the truth. "I was going to ask you to work for me. But now—"

She stood up, knocking the last few bites of the torte onto the floor. "Yes."

"What?"

"Yes, I'll work for you," she said.

"But you just said—"

"Forget what I said. I want to work with you."

I was silent for a few beats.

"I was actually going to suggest it until this job came through, and then I felt like you'd helped get me the job, so I had to take it. I'd much rather work with you. I'm trained in finance, and I want to be a part of what you're doing. Honestly, I moved to Minnesota because of my ex. I grew up in Nashville. My family is there. I'd like to come back. I want to help you. I think I could."

Hope pulled at my muscles until I was smiling. "I think you could, too, but I haven't even worked out the details. I wasn't planning to ask you this now at all."

"If you want me, I'm there, but there's one thing." Her tone went cautious.

"What?"

"Could Hulk and I stay with you? Just temporarily?"

But her family. She said she had family in Nashville. Stay with me? Me? I don't—

"Oh, thank you," she said. "Thank you!"

Why was she thanking me?

Apparently, I'd said yes.

Erin and her ferocious dog were moving into my house in three weeks.

∞

After leaving Erin's in borrowed sweats, I stayed overnight in a hotel but managed a flight home the next day. The Uber drove me straight to Deanna's from the airport. I needed to see her and tell her that she'd been right, that I was going to give this my all, for real this time. More than anything, I needed to apologize.

We picked up right where we'd left off as if I hadn't left without a word. I told her about the whole trip, though not the reason behind it. I couldn't mention Grant. No one needed to know about that; he wasn't an issue anymore. I was over him.

"I'm proud of you," Deanna told me.

"Thanks. But in a few days, I won't have an office space anymore because—"

"Because someone else leased it for three months?"

I stared.

Her eyes twinkled, the light catching the moisture in her eyes. "It was William's idea, actually. We believe in you. If you give up, then *I* might be tempted to give up."

That was why I could make this work. She'd surely taken the money she was saving for her B and B and sacrificed, for me.

I'd lived my life alone, unsupported, pulling myself up from my own bootstraps, when I pulled myself up at all. Now, there was a hand on my back, pushing me forward when I didn't think I could take another step.

"Thank you," I whispered, and threw my arms around her. I'd work twice as hard because I was no longer just working for myself.

CHAPTER 24
ACT CASUAL × THREE

For three weeks, I communicated with Erin long distance while she prepared for her move, and I put everything into my business. Chad was no longer a client, so I had even less wiggle room, but thanks to little, disheveled Myra, I'd met with and signed two members of his mah-jongg group. I was a long way from where I needed to be, but I felt better than I had in a while.

I'd also successfully avoided interacting with Grant. I'd been so busy that my excuses appeared legitimate—until today, when suspicion had gleamed in Deanna's narrowed eyes after I'd told her I didn't want Grant's help moving some new furniture in. So I'd backtracked, and on this mid-July Saturday afternoon, Deanna was assembling the new kitchen table, and Grant and William (back to his fully clothed, sans acid, and not-jumping-in-pools self) were either chatting with The Nose or bringing in the new couch. I'd sold the chaouch for a fraction of what Chad had paid and purchased a new one, along with some older pieces from a thrift store on Twelfth Avenue. I pretended I wasn't avoiding Grant, but he looked alarmingly good moving furniture, so I was definitely avoiding him. Erin was due to arrive any second, and my panic over living with someone was a solid distraction from his Michelangelo-sculpted forearms.

I hadn't lived with anyone since college, and thankfully Silent Selma—a computer science major—had been so shy that we'd only spoken a handful of words during the whole two years. Fate. After that, I got my own apartment.

I ran upstairs and spent seven minutes on my Schwinn, spinning until it hurt, then pushing past the pain until I heard noise below me, people entering, talking.

Downstairs, a group of numbers congregated. The cycling had helped, but if I was going to avoid hyperventilating at the idea of living with someone, they all needed to be numbers.

A squealing three ran across the room and hugged me, physically wrapped her arms around me, and squeezed before I could think.

I'd definitely made a mistake.

"Thank you so much, Pen," she said. "This is going to be great!"

I nodded and said something agreeable, then looked around for the dog, whom I imagined running up shortly, like his owner, and chewing my face off.

"Where's Hulk?" I spied the number ten (Grant) on the new couch, cuddling a teddy bear. Where did he get that stuffed animal, and why was he childishly petting it like it was . . . oh, it *was* alive.

"That's Hulk." Erin pointed toward Grant. "He's actually not that friendly, but for some reason, he likes . . ."

"Grant," Grant said. "It's the mustache."

"He wouldn't let either of us touch him." William indicated himself and Deanna, and I expected to need them to be numbers, but I didn't. They were just William and Deanna.

When I reached my hand out to touch Hulk's brown, curling fur, he growled and showed his teeth, growing in size, like the Hulk.

Everyone except Erin and Grant stayed away from Hulk as we chatted until there was a knock on the front door.

My stomach flipped because I certainly wasn't expecting anyone else. The Nose, holding a pitcher of what appeared to be lemonade, stood at the bottom of the steps.

"Hope I'm not disturbing," she said, and it was the first time I'd ever heard her voice. It was gravelly and cut out in places like a poor radio connection. "Saw those two handsome men lifting that heavy couch and thought you could use some refreshment."

Grant leaped up and took the lemonade from her. "Thanks, Devina. That was really thoughtful of you, wasn't it, Penelope?"

I realized then that I'd just been staring like a spectator. All these weeks, I'd silently sort of communicated with my neighbor from afar, and seeing her up close was throwing off our balance.

"Would you like to come in?" I asked, stepping aside and unintentionally pressing my arm against Grant's, who had stepped onto the porch with me since he and . . . Devina? seemed to be old friends. I didn't pull it back right away, and he didn't move.

"No, thank you. Appreciate it, though. Maybe another time, but Pen, can I speak to you a moment?" Devina motioned me toward her, and I stepped down the front steps. Once Grant had moved back inside and I was close enough, she took my hand in hers, squeezing with intention. I'd originally seen her as a nosy four, but she was definitely an eleven, two lines side by side, neighbors with something invisible connecting them in between. "Wanted to apologize for not being more neighborly. Tend to keep to myself, but glad you moved in, and I'm here for you if you need me. Should've said that before, but saying it now."

She put her hand up to her throat and nodded, which I assumed meant she needed to stop talking.

"Thank you," I said. "That means a lot. And thank you for the lemonade. That was very thoughtful."

"Owed Grant. He makes a divine green tea."

She started to back away and wave, so I quickly said, "Please let me know if *you* need anything."

She nodded, waved again, and headed for her house.

Grant handed me lemonade in a glass I didn't recognize when I stepped back inside. "Where did this glass come from?"

"Umm. I bought them," Deanna said. "You can't drink everything out of mugs."

"I have glasses!"

She rolled her eyes. "This lemonade is magical. That was so sweet of your neighbor."

I nodded. "You know that's my first time actually speaking to her?"

"She's a sweet lady," Grant said. "She's survived throat cancer on her own. She and her family had a falling-out. They don't speak."

"Wow, I didn't know."

"How do *you* know this, Grant?" Deanna asked.

"She talked to me and Grant outside," William chimed in. "Sounds like she's had a rough life." He turned to me. "She's been worried about you, too, a single woman in this area, so she's been keeping an eye out. Apparently the neighborhood's nice, but occasionally there's an incident, especially during Titans season."

"Proximity to downtown," Grant said, nodding.

Erin started talking about her grandparents and some gunshot incident, and I probably should've been listening, but I was thinking about Devina and how I'd inadvertently misjudged her. She'd been looking out for me, and I'd assumed she was being nosy.

The conversation bounced from neighborhood safety to something called the Color Wheel, an upcoming cycling event, and then William, Deanna, and Grant stood to leave.

"They're really nice people," Erin said after I'd closed the door. "So you and Grant are a thing?"

"What? Why would you ask that?" I threw my hand out in an effort to appear casual and slapped it into the wall.

Her smile was devious. "Oh."

"What?" I attempted to cross my arms but, forgetting how to configure them, gave up and let them flop by my sides like an ape.

"Nothing. It's just that—"

"Grant has a girlfriend!" My voice had gone too high. I toned it down, brought it back to casual. "We're friends. He's that way with everyone."

"He wasn't with Deanna."

What was wrong with her? "Deanna is his sister."

"I see." She was smiling again, like she knew something I didn't. "I probably shouldn't say anything, but I know when someone likes someone else. It's a gift. And, he may not know it yet, but Grant likes you. He looks at you like he can't get enough. So!" She clasped her hands together and looked around as if she hadn't just ruined my life. "I can't wait to see what you've done with the place."

She scooped Hulk into her arms, and we moved in and out of rooms that had embarrassingly not changed all that much, while I tried not to freak out.

CHAPTER 25
LIFE REALIZATION #11: SERENITY CANDLES ARE LEGIT

Roughly two weeks later, fatigue gripped my shoulders, turning me into Quasimodo as I juggled my bag, a handful of papers, my house keys, and my cell phone—massage therapist Piper had told me not to carry it in my pocket. Well, she'd bent over and told my ovaries not to allow it, but they'd passed the message along.

Erin had found an all-female entrepreneurial group online that held weekly accountability meetings in Nashville. She'd approached the group and, working her marketing magic, arranged meetings for me with four of the women. They were invigorating interactions because each woman was looking to start her own business, and two of them had signed with me on the spot. But being "on" for that long had drained the life out of me, so I was hoping to sneak into the house and head up to my room.

Soft music was playing when I opened the door, and very pleasant smells swirled in the air, awakening my stomach.

"Pen, is that you?" Erin called from the kitchen.

"Yep. Headed your way."

Living with someone had its challenges. I had to think about where I threw my clothes. I had to wash my few dishes every day instead of letting them sit and be my excuse for getting takeout. I had to find a home for all the stuff stashed in the pantry because an avalanche had almost buried Hulk. And tonight was another challenge. I'd been prepared for cereal alone in front of the TV, but I was going to have to force myself to be polite.

"Are you hungry? I made dinner," Erin said, motioning toward the kitchen table, set with bohemian napkins reminiscent of her apartment, silverware with wooden handles, and pink short-stemmed glasses filled with iced lemon water. The flame inside an amber glass jar in the middle of the table seemed to be dancing to the instrumental jazz. Everything was lovely, except that candle, which reminded me of my dinner with Chad.

I was taken aback by the display. "This is beautiful."

"Arugula salad with sautéed chicken, shaved parmesan, and a homemade raspberry vinaigrette. A thank-you. We should get to know each other better." She smiled and placed the plates on opposite ends of the table. "The candle's from Piper. I chatted with her today. It's supposed to inspire serenity and aid in digestion." She shrugged. "I can't say I buy into all her practices, but I'm willing to try nearly anything. And we both deserve a good meal." She laughed. "We've got a lot of work to do."

"You've already done a lot of work," I said, scooting into the chair opposite her. The atmosphere she'd created had a calming effect, and I didn't miss my Cap'n Crunch as much as I thought I would. "Two of the ladies signed." Hulk's ears perked up from where he was curled on his mat in the kitchen.

She clapped. "I knew it! They were the perfect team to approach. You have two more meetings tomorrow with other ladies from the same group."

"I don't know how you're able to do this so fast. I'm glad, don't get me wrong, but it kind of makes me feel . . . inadequate. I couldn't seem to get it done."

"Here's how I see it," she said, slicing into her chicken breast with a knife. "We have different talents, right? That's why you hired me. Marketing isn't your strong suit, but I'm pretty good at it." She put a bite into her mouth, then started waving her fork around. "*You* know how to seal the deal, but I don't know enough to do that yet. It's the perfect partnership. We each focus on what we're good at and create a thriving business. There's an art to knowing what to focus on and what to leave to someone else. You'll wear yourself out if you try to do it all alone. So you're not inadequate, you're a savvy businesswoman. Divide and conquer, right?"

"Well said."

"Eh. I've been reading a lot of nonfiction, and it's seeping in. I love this business, though. And seriously, you inspired me at TCF. I don't think you quite realize how amazing you are. You outperformed all the guys, and dimwitted Houston was too egocentric to let you do your thing. TCF could've shined."

"Thank you," I whispered, my chest swelling. It felt good for someone to acknowledge my hard work, which was happening a lot lately.

This evening wasn't going as planned, but I was thankful I hadn't missed this conversation. I was thankful for her—just Erin and not a number, which surprised me. And this meal was fantastic. "I'm really glad this has worked out. But I have to admit: hiring you was Deanna's idea. I was ready to give up."

"I think the right people come into our lives at the times we need them most. I mean, think of our situations. We were both struggling, dealing with some pretty ugly stuff, but if we hadn't been struggling, we might've missed this." She waved her fork between us. "We've found our people."

I chewed, taking in her words and thinking that she was too young to be enlightening. "You're exactly right."

"Okay, enough sappy stuff. If you thought today was busy, just wait." Her pointer finger jabbed the table. "I want to talk about this big dinner. We're gonna fill your book!"

She had no doubts, and I smiled, a big one.

She put her palms in the air. "Okay, I know you aren't wild about Piper, but hear me out . . ."

With elbows propped on the table, she proceeded to talk for the next twenty-five minutes, and I forgot how tired I was.

CHAPTER 26
A MILLION RAINDROPS

"How did I let you guys talk me into this?" My eyes cut to Grant, William, and Deanna.

All around us, dozens of bicyclists were clustered together on a hill behind a starting line, all wearing white, like an impending avalanche.

Someone in a tie-dye shirt near the start rope yelled into a microphone, thanking the riders for joining in this year's color ride. Based on the famous Color Run, this cycling event—the Color Wheel—showered each rider with colored, food-grade cornstarch as they made their way down a stationed path. All raised funds went to Venture Miles, an organization bent on ending human trafficking.

"You'll love it! I promise," Deanna answered, raising her voice against a warm August gust.

William scooted up to my left. "I love riding, D. *This* is silly."

She shrugged. "It's for a good cause!"

Elaine leaned over Grant to join our conversation, which made it harder to pretend she wasn't there. "I agree with you, Deanna. I'm riding more and more because of this guy, and I love it." Her eyes literally sparkled as she glanced at Grant, whose smile in response made me feel itchy.

Why did the woman always have to touch him? And why did she look like she was about to pose for *Cycling Weekly*? You didn't wear a brand-new, hot-pink-and-black, skintight tramp suit when you were about to have colored powder thrown at you, especially when everyone was explicitly told to wear white. I made myself stop. Elaine was anything but a tramp, and I hated admitting her positive qualities, her many, many positive qualities.

It was all fine. Totally fine. Grant and Elaine were still dating. Grant and I were friends.

It was totally fine.

I was totally fine.

It was totally fine.

Erin and I had lived together for a little over a month at this point, and for the past several weeks, we'd both kept our heads down, making plans and growing our business. She cooked most nights she was home but had spent several with her family—I wasn't sure how she worked so hard and managed to interact with so many people—leaving me either alone or with Hulk, whom I'd bonded with over late-night movies when I was too wired to sleep. *He* liked Cap'n Crunch.

I hadn't spent much time with Deanna, though, except to discuss the catering menu for the upcoming marketing dinner, which had now turned into a client appreciation event as well. I also hadn't been on any bike rides with William and Grant. This particular ride meant a lot: precious time with all my new people—and Elaine.

"It's like you people have a code that I'm not programmed to interpret," Deanna pouted.

"Aww," Elaine cooed. "Don't worry, Deanna. We can stick together if these guys get ahead of us." Another sparkling grin. A playful pat to Grant's arm.

"Nah, we'd never leave Deanna behind," I assured her with a smile I hoped held no disgust.

Elaine might have Grant, but she *wasn't* getting Deanna.

"If this is what gets you to ride, I'll take it." William pointed past me and Deanna to the clunker Grant was on. "Where's Gaia?"

"She doesn't like these rides." He shook his head and grimaced. "Colored powder in every crevice . . ."

"That's something we have in common," William said, which earned him a stern look from Deanna. "Isn't she jealous?"

I started to protest—*out loud*—but managed to stop myself, realizing William had been talking about Gaia, not me.

"She takes care of me; I take care of her. We agreed that her staying home was best for both of us."

"Oh, Grant," Elaine said, butting in. "What does 'Gaia' mean?"

"Gaia was a Greek goddess."

"The personification of the earth," I finished. I'd researched it.

Grant smelled like the earth, like the dirt rose up one day and spit out a man. The name was perfect. But I wished I'd kept my mouth shut because I was being petty, trying to show Elaine up.

Normally, my body automatically knew what to do on a bicycle, but now, I was overly aware of how each limb was positioned and how each piece of lint on each limb was positioned in case Grant looked my way because I-know-when-someone-likes-someone Erin had told me Grant liked me *weeks* ago. And even though I knew he *didn't* like me like that, the thought had been rolling around in my head like a wheel that wanted to run over Elaine.

"Everybody ready?" Grant glanced from left to right.

"As I'll ever be," I said under my breath. At least I didn't have to worry about seeing them as numbers; I was riding, which was my other coping mechanism.

The brightly adorned man with the microphone started counting down, and a sea of helmets bobbed on the road as the riders prepared for takeoff.

"Three . . . two . . ."

"Don't forget to keep your mouth closed!" William shouted.

"One!"

A shot was fired into the air, and along with it, a rainbow rained down on all the riders as if a leprechaun had leaped across the road to his pot of gold.

The loud cheers and giddy laughter momentarily stunned me, and I was nearly run over as wheels started moving forward.

"You okay?" Grant's voice strained over the crowd's excitement.

"I think so. Just wish I'd listened to William and hadn't opened my mouth." My tongue flicked against my palate as I tasted the slightly bitter powder that had been thrown in my face.

A gust of laughter shot out of him. "Rookie mistake. Yellow suits you, though."

I puffed a small cloud of yellow powder in Grant's direction as he and Elaine rode off. I hated the way his compliment slowed me down and made me want to wear yellow every day from now on.

I didn't see them again until the green station, where lime-colored powder was caked on top of our already red, orange, and yellow forms.

Deanna caught me watching Grant and Elaine throw fistfuls of powder at each other. "She's nice, isn't she?"

"Very. They make a cute couple."

"You hate her, don't you?"

I choked, my arms flopping by my sides. "How can I possibly hate her? She's one of the nicest people I've ever met. She's beautiful. She's funny."

"And you actively avoid her."

My hands went to my face. "Is it that obvious?"

"Nah. Probably just to me. To everyone else, you're Prickly Pen." She winced when my head whipped toward her.

"Is that what people call me?"

She shrugged. "Don't get me wrong, I adore you, but you don't always give off the friendliest vibe. If I hadn't caught you with your guard down at the store that day, we probably wouldn't be friends now."

My mouth dropped open, which was ridiculous because I knew this about myself.

"I'm kidding. Mostly. But you *could* stand to lighten up. It's okay to live. It's also okay to like Grant."

"I don't like Grant." The words shot out of my mouth like a cannon; then I picked up a pile of powder and catapulted it into Deanna's face. Playfully, I hoped. All fun and games here. No repressed feelings.

She huffed, rubbed her eyes, and spit powder out. "I know you went to the restaurant to meet Grant when you found out I couldn't make it."

Fire. My face was on fire. "So? I felt sorry for him, and we're friends."

"If you were friends, you wouldn't have pretended it was a coincidence."

I blinked. "How do you—did you tell him?"

"Of course not. What kind of friend do you think I am?" She spit again. "There's no denying Elaine's a good fit for Grant, but that doesn't mean there isn't someone better. They haven't been dating that long. He started dating her about six weeks before you moved here."

That made over six months. That wasn't a long time? "Grant deserves someone like Elaine."

"Grant deserves someone who loves him as much as he loves her." Deanna shrugged and put her feet on her pedals. "Maybe that's Elaine, maybe it isn't." Her hand moved, and before I could react, I was covered from head to toe in green powder.

Ol' Prickly Pen had that one coming.

On our way to the next station, the sun vanished, and rain poured in sheets. Nearly drowned out by the sound, a man shouted into his cupped hands and directed all the riders to a large rec center a short distance away.

Bikers pushed toward shelter, through the puddles rapidly forming in the grass. William, Deanna, Elaine, and I were moving in the same direction until I realized Grant wasn't with us.

I looked back toward the path. And there he was, alone on the paved trail, legs straddling not-Gaia, arms outstretched, face to the sky as rain danced around him, completely uninhibited. Like nothing else mattered.

"What's he doing out there?" Deanna asked.

William hunched his shoulders against a gust of wind. "Being Grant. He does this kind of thing all the time." He turned back in the direction of the pavilion. "Come on, ladies. He'll meet up with us when he comes to his senses."

Deanna followed. Elaine hesitated. I turned back toward the path.

"You aren't seriously thinking of staying out here with him," William half asked.

"I'm beginning to question whether we need to start building an ark here; someone needs to get him."

"Maybe I should come with you," Elaine offered, staring down at her hands.

Elaine was the last person I wanted with me.

"Oh my goodness, your hands are white!" Deanna shouted, gesturing to Elaine's hands now too.

"I have Raynaud's." Responding to our blank looks, she went on, "My fingers turn white or blue when I get too cold. Blood vessel problem." The August heat had significantly cooled in the rain.

Deanna steered Elaine toward the shelter. "Come on. Pen can try to talk some sense into Grant and join us if she can't."

"Once he's set, he's set," William said, but I leaned my bicycle against the thick trunk of a maple tree and moved toward Grant before anyone said anything else and silently praised whatever that Raynaud's thing was.

"You're as absurd as he is!" William shouted.

"More so!" I returned, sloshing my way back to the main path. They didn't know what this was going to do to my hair.

The rain beat down like percussion. Grant was barely visible through the curtain of water, but I moved forward anyway. Even though the day had been approaching hot, the lack of sun and the stream of water cooled my skin. This was a mistake. William was right. I knew that. Why was I still outside?

When Grant saw me, his mouth curled. He unstraddled his bike and met me just as my foot hit the pavement. "I thought you were taking cover."

"I was until I saw you out here like a madman."

"Aren't you just as mad if you're out here with me?"

"That's what William said." I linked my arm in his, tried pulling him forward. Heat spread from the spot where our slick skin connected and spiraled throughout the rest of my body until I nearly forgot it was raining. "Come on." My voice was charred by the increasing heat of his contact, so the words came out husky and too sensual.

"You know what I think?"

That we should stop touching?

"Apparently I have no idea because we're actively drowning, and you don't seem to care."

"Again, you're right here beside me."

"I came after you!"

"Look around, Penelope. What do you see?"

"Rain. Lots of it." My arm was still in his, so I tried pulling him forward again. I shouldn't have been out there alone with him. It was dangerous. I might do something I'd regret, because this heat actively building inside me was scrambling my brain cells.

He spun me around, held my shoulders so I faced away from him. He whispered in my ear, "Stop thinking of this as the thing that ruined the ride. Stop looking at the water as something you need to escape. It's a *dance*. Each and every cold drop on your skin is refreshing, like the best spa you could ever visit, and the smell . . . oh, the smell. That smell is summer. An entire season summed up in one downpour. And everyone else is missing it."

His breath swirled against my ear, eliciting more heat, like a flare in steadily burning fire. For several seconds, time was suspended in the drops falling all around us.

"So," he went on, "I'm thinking you didn't follow the others, because you wanted this. Right here, where you don't know what to expect next, but you don't care because you're free."

What was he saying?

I watched the red, orange, yellow, and green powder that covered us both cascade down our bodies like a discarded sunset.

We couldn't stay like this. I moved out of his grip, turned, and smiled back at him, pulling off my helmet. And then I reached down to unlace my expensive running shoes—shoes I never should've worn to a color ride. I pulled them off and tossed them on the pavement beside me.

His eyebrows arched, amusement tucked into his half smile. Then I ran, my socked feet leaving the trail and heading into the wooded area just on the other side of the road.

Water splashed into my face. *A spa,* he'd said. And that was how it felt. Arms outstretched, head held high, I brought my feet down in the oversaturated mud, brown water flying up on either side of my legs, my white leggings a human canvas. I'd needed to be away from Grant, but also, I *was* free.

It felt *good*—until my foot slid on a patch of bare dirt that had turned into a mini mudslide, and I coasted to the ground, laughing like a maniac in my own personal mud bath, surrounded by tall deciduous trees whose leaves were fighting the weather to stay attached.

He dropped down beside me. When I finally stopped laughing, I let my head fall back into the mud, but it wasn't the ground. It was Grant's lap.

Our eyes snapped together. A large raindrop fell from his mustache and hit my cheek.

"I don't know what came over me." I also didn't know how I was able to speak with my head in his lap.

"That's the best way to live. Not knowing what comes next."

"Isn't that the scariest way?"

"Not if you're living in the moment, enjoying what's right in front of you. The future can't touch right now. Neither can the past."

I shouldn't have done what I did next, but I wasn't thinking, which was the problem. I pushed up, threw my arms around his neck, and pulled his face to mine. I kissed him like the next moment didn't matter. I kissed him now. Not was. Not will be. Now.

The cold droplets sizzled wildly when they hit the heat of my skin. I barely registered the rough prickle of his mustache against my face, because my focus was on the softness of his lips as they moved against my own. My pulse beat with the thud of the rain still popping around us.

When he pulled away, our eyes remained locked. His fingertips adjusted the hank of hair about to land in my left eye.

Then he swallowed, his eyes breaking from mine. He guided me up until I was sitting. I crossed my feet at my ankles and wrapped my arms around my legs.

Our moment was over, and I didn't like the one that followed, the one where I had to pay for what I'd done.

"I'm sorry. I shouldn't have—"

"Done exactly what I asked you to do?"

An awkward laugh fell out of my mouth. "You didn't ask me to kiss you."

He shifted in the mud, propping himself up on his arms.

"I like you—"

I stopped him before he could say "but." "Why do you like me?" Like the kiss, I shouldn't have asked it. But I wasn't ready for this to be over. The cover of rain and mud made the whole scenario surreal, like I could do anything without consequence.

"You want a list? Okay." His head rolled on his shoulders as if he was warming up for a sprint. Another man would've laughed the question off. Grant met it head on. "You're funny. You're easy, and not in the bad way. Being with you is like being alone, if that makes sense. You're a little tough to crack, but I've found it's been worth the effort. You're kind, considerate . . ." He stuck his neck out. "Shall I keep going?"

I hoped the rain hid how much he'd affected me.

"You don't really know me."

"Don't I? I know you like honey on your waffles instead of syrup, but not so much that it pools on your plate. I know you count the ice cubes in your glass even if you're deep in conversation, and condensation seems to fascinate you beyond logical explanation. I know you love animals, even though you don't want the responsibility of taking care of one yourself. I know you love Hulk, even though you pretend he's annoying. I know you're self-conscious about your hair. And you think you're unlovable."

I'd been watching him with rapt attention, but this last thing made me inhale sharply.

"How do I know all those things?" He read my face. "When you care about something, you pay attention. It's impossible not to."

His words knocked all the air out of my lungs.

On either side of me, I squished mud through my fingers. Was this just a Grant thing? It had to be. He probably knew these things about the lunch lady behind the counter at the meat 'n' three. I said as much to him, and he chuckled, a low rumble that said, *Of course I do.*

"I don't think I'm unlovable." I felt more than saw the skepticism nestled into Grant's brow as he looked at me. I shrugged. "Okay, maybe a little, but it's mostly the other way around."

"Explain."

I wasn't sure he'd understand. My eyes closed. "I don't think I'm capable of loving, at least not how I'm supposed to."

"Same thing."

I opened my eyes and looked at him, uncomprehending. "How is that the same thing?"

"Sometimes, when you find the *right* person to love you, reciprocation is automatic." Grant rocked forward and, in a surprisingly smooth maneuver, propped himself up on his knees, bringing his face closer to mine.

It irritated me that he was minimizing my major life flaw. I always picked the wrong person, the married person, the person I could never truly love because it was easier. If I didn't really love someone, then I couldn't be hurt when the relationship ended, could I?

"It's not that simple," I said.

"Have you heard of Holi?"

I shook my head.

"It's a festival they have every year in India. It's why I like this color ride. They do this sort of thing, throw color around. People come together and forget all the wrong done to them, all the bad things, all the negativity. They celebrate unification. I've been. And every single person there was smiling because they'd let it all go.

"It's okay to let yourself feel grief and sorrow, but it's also okay to let it go, to let people in, to let all kinds of people love you and be loved in return. A lot of people will hurt you, but when you find love, friendship, a good hairstylist, whatever, it's worth it. And life isn't worth living if you don't take risks."

"How do you—"

He touched my cheek like he could distinguish tears from raindrops. "I've been thinking about this stuff ever since you told me about your brother. I won't pretend to completely understand, but I've been where you are, that headspace where life seems impossible. I think these are the things I would've wanted to hear, that I eventually learned."

I collected the thoughts scattered around my head as I held my hand up. I watched each swell of water hit my palm and scatter the dirt clinging to my skin as I wondered . . . wondered about Grant and what made him unlike anyone I'd ever known.

I'd been with good men. I'd stayed with them because they made me feel safe and comfortable, but they were safe because I knew I'd never love them. They were comfortable because I wasn't completely alone. As soon as they wanted more, I got out. I'd tried to change that with Chad, convince myself I was capable of commitment, only to discover that I wasn't actually changing. I was trying to put a puzzle together with missing pieces, or rather, the wrong pieces entirely.

The rain stopped, and as suddenly as it had left, the sun returned. The loss of privacy stung. Now our conversation seemed spotlighted by the sun, something I couldn't hide from.

In the distance, riders filed out of the shelter. I wondered how we would explain our mud-caked appearances.

I nodded, and Grant helped me to my feet, our conversation over just like that. I wanted to pull him back, stop him from leading me forward, back to the others, back to Elaine. I wanted the rain to start again. I wanted to kiss him again. I needed more time right here.

My heart ached because I knew what he'd said was true. Wasn't that why I'd moved in the first place? A reckoning. I hadn't been sure what all I needed to change, just that I couldn't keep going the way I'd been, repeating the same grayscale pattern, a stagnant life, devoid of color and vibrancy. And here I was doing the same thing over again, kissing a man who belonged to someone else. But this time, I was certain of this man's relationship status.

Even though I was sick with guilt—because I didn't regret kissing him as much as I should've—I shoved the corners of my mouth upward when Deanna ran up. As she asked questions and scanned our clothes, inside I told myself the only reason I'd wanted to kiss Grant was because he was off limits. I told myself he was like every other relationship I'd had: a safeguard against real hurt, someone I couldn't ever truly love.

What I wouldn't let myself focus on was the thought that came on the heels of the first, one much scarier than the idea that he was like everyone else.

The one that told me he wasn't.

CHAPTER 27
LIFE REALIZATION #12: BREATHING ISN'T ALWAYS AUTOMATIC

"No, I think we should leave your money right where it is," I said into the six little holes on my office phone as I clicked my nails against the glass of my desk. "Your investments are more than safe, Myra. They're expanding at a healthy rate. Let your friend take the gamble if he wants, but I'd advise him against it too. I don't think it'll turn out the way he hopes."

That was all my client needed to hear.

I *loved* this. *My* business. *My* clients. *My* expertise. Finally happening. I'd come to Nashville around five months ago with a rough sketch, and I'd drawn and erased a frenzy of lines on repeat, but over the past several weeks, Erin had been helping me fill in the scene, until we'd nearly drawn something recognizable.

It never got old, that feeling of faith, people putting their hard-earned cash in my hands and trusting I'd make it grow. I always made it grow.

No one could take that feeling away from me now that I owned it personally.

I turned back to my desk, my muscles prepared for an inelegant victory dance, but when my eyes landed on the doorway, it was my heart that performed a rather enthusiastic gymnastic routine. Grant was holding a bouquet of flowers just inside my door, with Erin grinning behind him.

"Hi. I hope I'm not disturbing."

Disturbing what? My day? My life? My sense of reason?

For five days, *five days*, I'd been agonizing over that rain-drenched, amazingly romantic, incredibly foolish color-ride kiss. I was also working very hard to get Grant back into the "friend" category inside my mind. I certainly wasn't ready for him to be this close, in my office, holding a bouquet wrapped in white tissue and making me want to run over to him and do it all again.

Erin's eyebrows bobbed up and down behind Grant's back. We were sharing my office—she had a desk in the corner—until we could figure out something more permanent, and if she hadn't been awesome at her job, I would've fired her for the smugness perched on her face.

"Grant, what are you doing in my office?" And why was Erin shutting the door? For Elaine's sake, I couldn't be alone with this man. Hell, for my own sake. For Grant's sake! I couldn't be trusted. "Do you want me to take a look at your investments?"

I calmed a fraction, even as I felt my face darken. Because of course that was it. He was here for my expertise, not me.

"Yes," he said.

I'd just told myself that was why he was here, but even so, disappointment sidled up next to me.

"Well, great. I wish I'd known you were coming. I would've put something together. I have generic packets here." I patted the tidy, metal and vintage wood letter tray on the right side of my desk. My life and home weren't organized, but my desk always was. Numbers demanded organization. Papers with numbers on them demanded organization. "But if I'd known . . ."

"That's okay. It was a spontaneous decision. These are for you, by the way."

I took the extended flowers, held them stiffly like a delivery boy.

"You don't strike me as the kind of guy to leave your finances up to chance."

Something smelled amazing. Sure, Grant, but this was something more. I looked at the flowers, which on closer inspection . . . "Are these . . . cookies?" They were definitely cookies, little, flat heavenly disks wrapped at the bottom with tissue paper so the baked goods looked like they were blooming. He'd brought me a bouquet of cookies.

Damn this man.

He nodded. "I thought I remembered you saying your two favorites were chocolate chip and snickerdoodles. The snickerdoodles are on the bottom."

He'd cozied himself into one of the chairs across from me. He was enclosed in my office—even if the doors were glass and Erin was unabashedly spying with googly eyes. He filled the space with the smell of the outdoors and chocolate chip cookies. It made me want to ride and eat, but not eat now because my stomach was doing the Macarena. "You're perfect. I mean . . . *they're* perfect." *Just stop talking, Pen.* "Thank you," I concluded, then surprised myself by adding, "I should probably put these in some milk."

He laughed, and I was stunned that I'd made an applicable joke during such duress.

"So, tell me why you're here. My investing expertise, obviously, but what's your goal? How much are we investing, and do you have a preconceived direction for these funds?" I was comfortable again. I grabbed a new-client folder and walked my fingers along the pages until I got to my favorite, the one with all the colorful lines, the one that said, *Do you understand this complicated graph? I do.*

"I was thinking more about a time investment."

The sheet of paper fluttered back and forth as I pulled it into the air. It was as confused as I was.

"A time investment?"

"Yeah. And less a question of where to place my time, and more of where I'd like you to."

I put the colorful graph face down on my desk. A black-and-white chart stared up at me. I crossed my hands over the graph and stared at him.

"I don't understand."

"I'm not a subtle guy. I know there's a way to do these things, but I don't care. I've learned it's important to go after what I want, conventions aside."

My mouth had gone dry. He wasn't saying . . . "And you want . . ."

"You. I want you."

I blinked. I stared. I counted to seven.

"But . . . but. Elaine." Had I misheard him? Was this one of those times when words had come out of his mouth, but I'd heard what I wanted to hear instead of what he'd actually said? Maybe he'd said he wanted two of something. Or he wanted to chew something. I needed to breathe.

"Do you remember the color ride, when we were out in the rain?"

Did I remember? As if I hadn't thought of that moment three times today already. I nodded.

"I told Elaine about the kiss. I had to. I felt horrible about it."

The kiss. *Horrible.*

I'd misheard him for sure. I plucked one of the cookies out of the bouquet and started eating it. Chocolate chip or snickerdoodle, I didn't know because . . . food? Now? I was *far* from hungry. But I needed something to do with my hands and my mouth. For all I knew, I had accidentally picked up the new-client file and was snacking on a color-coded chart. This was so unexpected.

"She *wasn't* happy. But she's trained to help people work through relationships, so that's what she wanted to do, work past it."

"Oh, well, that's great. And you don't have to worry about me doing anything like that—"

"*She* was willing to work past it, but that kiss . . . Penelope." My name came out on a sigh that entered my body like the breath I needed to take. "I don't want to move past it. I want to live in it. I want to do it again."

I sat there, speechless, a doofus with crumbs falling out of my mouth.

He scooted to the edge of his seat, his smile huge under his stupid mustache, his adorable mustache. His hand rose to my face, where he dusted off the corner of my mouth.

"Will you go out with me?"

Unable to speak, I bit my lower lip and nodded.

How the eff was I going to date this man?

CHAPTER 28
FIRST OFFICIAL DATE

"Where are you taking me?" I fingered the blindfold across my eyes as I sat in Grant's passenger seat on our first official date, Sunday, September 10. Grant had wanted to wait two weeks to show Elaine respect, which had been fine with me because I'd needed to adjust to the idea. But I hadn't really adjusted, I'd just panicked, and barely functioned, having to turn clients into numbers even though we were discussing finance, and even that hadn't worked. "I'm taking this thing off."

"Eh." He pulled my hand away from my face. "Not yet."

"Grant, this thing is itchy. What's it made out of anyway? Horsehair?" I didn't want to tell him, but I liked the itchy blindfold. It was oddly soothing, the uncomfortable thing to focus on instead of my anxiety over this date.

"Wool. And we're here." He shifted the car into park and turned off the engine. "Keep it on. I'm coming around to get you."

He opened my door, bent down, and lifted the blindfold. His proximity flipped my stomach.

I stretched and surveyed our surroundings.

Like a diving board waiting for a diver, so was the rock before us, a jumping-off point for the eyes as they scanned the world below. The carpet of trees gave way to a city turning on at dusk. High up on this mountainside, it was as if a basin had scooped up the setting sun,

serving it when it was the most awe inducing, something you wanted
to be suspended in.

I thought back to our seconds in the rain, where sunset-colored
powder pooled at our feet. This was another occasion I'd tuck away, but
now, Grant and I were together, and were I to kiss him—

"This is my version of Chattanooga's Sunset Rock," he said. "We
can hike to the actual Sunset Rock tomorrow if you want to, but there's
something about *this* spot."

"We're in Chattanooga? Isn't this two hours away from Nashville?"
I lost time when I was with Grant. Two whole hours had melted away.
"Wow. This is the most spectacular sunset I've ever seen."

"You know that generic 'happy place' people talk about? This is
mine. It feeds the soul."

We stood in silence, transfixed by the energetic colors fading into
one another. Once the majority of the sun had nestled into the trees,
leaving a generalized glow behind, Grant pulled a blanket from the bag
at his feet and then lined his hands up, looking from the ground back to
the sun like he wanted to make sure the blanket was in the perfect spot.

Under his spontaneity, a sense of order defined his life. To look at
me or my office, you'd think we had the same values. But step into my
home or look under my skin, anything below the surface, and I was
a mess. What if he was only attracted to the superficial me? He'd seen
some of my cracks, but he hadn't glimpsed the faults that waited to
swallow us both.

Suddenly the peace of the sunset was being stretched tight like the
corners of Grant's blanket.

But as he patted the ground beside him, his smile gave me a piece
of myself I wasn't sure had ever existed before. That single possibility
that this was the person I'd needed but had been afraid to find filled
a hole in my heart, despite all my reservations. But my heart was still
like swiss cheese, and the other holes mocked me, reminding me that
if I continued down this path with Grant, I'd have a lot more to lose.

I took a deep breath and fought the fear that clung to the future moments, a fear that all this could end.

"Are you hungry?" he asked.

"Starving. What did you bring?" I reached for the cooler, but he stopped me.

"The best thing is already here."

Aww, Grant. But seriously, where was the food? I envisioned wineglasses, a pinot noir, sliced cheese, olives, and dried figs.

He reached into the bag beside the cooler again, and instead of bringing out the spiral ham I'd hoped for, he pulled out a handheld shovel.

He winked, moved off the blanket, and started digging in the ground beside us.

Digging.

"What are you doing?" My voice was singsong, like I was talking to someone who'd lost it.

"Give me three minutes."

"What are you doing?" I repeated in the same tone.

He *had* asked me to a picnic, hadn't he? Surely I hadn't missed the part about eating wild grubs or being buried in the woods because he was a psychopath. And if he planned to kill and bury me, couldn't he feed me first? Or at least have the decency to get a bigger shovel so this wouldn't take so long?

As I contemplated whether to get up and head back to the car or embrace that my date had pulled out a garden implement and was hacking at the ground, Grant said, "Here it is."

I blinked as he pulled a small piece of pottery from the ground.

"What are you doing?" I asked a third time.

He dusted the dirt from the little brown ceramic pot and held it up. "Feeding you. Do you know what this is?"

Do I look like I know what it is?

He opened the lid and exhibited an array of green, white, and red material that floated in a liquid. "Is that what's left of the last date you brought out here?"

"Kimchi! It's kimchi." Grant held the container up like the dish was worthy of praise. "Beautifully fermented cabbage. You've had it before, haven't you?"

My eyes widened. "This is our dinner?"

"Well, not *just* this, but I told you the best thing was already here. I buried this onggi about twenty days ago."

"I thought you said it was kimchi, and you *buried . . . food.*" The man I thought I was falling for had unearthed our picnic dinner from. *The. Ground.*

"Where's the romantic picnic food? The brie, the—"

"We can have those things any old time. This"—he inhaled deeply—"this takes time to develop flavor and depth. Taste it. I made this one myself."

"You made it yourself," I repeated.

I should've known Grant's idea of the perfect accompaniment to a beautiful setting sun was fermented cabbage. I should've known because it was the last thing I would've expected.

"When I was first starting out, I helped a Korean couple design their first home. They were extremely pleased and invited me over for a traditional Korean meal."

He rummaged around in the cooler and brought out two plastic wineglasses and a bottle of sauvignon blanc.

He twisted a corkscrew into the soft cork and slid it out, then filled the cup he handed me halfway with the pale, straw-colored liquid. After filling his own, he leaned back, propping up on his elbow and crossing his outstretched legs at the ankles. "It was a large party. Extravagant decorations. Lavish food. I barely understood a word anyone said, but the food . . ." Grant shook his head, then held up his gathered fingers and kissed them. "I fell in love with the spices, the flavor variations, the smells. But you wanna know the best thing there?"

"The kimchi?" I guessed.

"The grandma. She was dressed like royalty. As I was leaving the party, she had her granddaughter translate a message for me." He looked out into the last rays of the sun, which was melting away behind the trees like the slow disappearance of ice cream in a cone. "'It doesn't matter what's in here.'" He pointed to his head. "'It matters what's in here.'" Then his hand moved over his heart. "'You chase this, Grant. This truth. Do you understand?' I nodded. Her daughter was speaking English, but it was like I could understand her Korean without help."

I took another sip and smiled over the rim of the glass. This is what contentment felt like.

"I probably shouldn't admit this, but I thought of kimchi as an allegory for our relationship." Then, like he'd just said something romantic, he reached up and touched my face, a slow caress down my cheek. "Because it takes time to develop and is really healthy, and . . . are you ready to try this so I'll stop talking? I learned how to make it from that little Korean grandma."

I didn't want him to stop talking. I wanted him to go on forever. I wanted to keep listening forever.

He lifted the spoon to my lips.

There was no way I wasn't trying it now. I nodded without fuss and opened my mouth.

I chewed, picturing the tiny Korean woman and a twentysomething Grant making kimchi together. I wasn't sure whether it was that mental image or the food, but to my surprise, it was . . .

"Good," I said, shocking myself.

An *I told you so* perched on his lifted eyebrow. He put the spoon down and handed me his glass of wine.

"She also gave me this." He pulled out a second little pot from the cooler. This one was more rustic; the deep–sea blue pot had three tiny flowers carved into it and looked like it held not only rotting cabbage, but stories, pulled from the past and secured in that vessel. "This is a fermentation pot, an onggi. She made this one herself. I ordered the other one from Amazon. It's tradition to bury the kimchi during the winter to keep it from freezing, but why not now, right?" He took the pot and placed it in the hole left by the other onggi in the ground, and then he covered it up again.

"For next time. Fermented foods are good for the gut."

"How romantic—you worried about the state of my intestines."

"How else would you know I cared?"

"Ummmm, chocolate."

"Look in the cooler."

Inside, beside the tiny vase of miniature pink roses, were little petit fours, small, dark chocolate cakes with white chocolate dollar signs on the top of them. My eyes floated to Grant's, misty. "Did you make *these?*"

"Hell no. Deanna made them. I told her what I wanted them to look like. She also made the chicken salad cups and those bite-size quiches." He pointed back inside the cooler. "She must've thought we'd turned into gnomes or something because everything is small. Is that—"

I cut him off, my lips pressing into his. It was too perfect. He was too perfect. I didn't deserve him, or at least, he deserved someone who would think of desserts shaped like little houses to surprise him with. I bet Elaine would think of that. But that didn't stop me from letting my lips roam his, letting our tongues get tangled like brambles on a perfect summer day, when the sun's warmth heated your skin but the cool breeze balanced it out.

"You like the picnic?" he asked, pulling away with a smile. I didn't want to stop kissing him.

I nodded.

As the city lights beamed from windows and streetlamps, the trees and rocks folded in like a nest around us. The lanterns Grant had retrieved from the car danced like tiny fireflies, and we munched on sumptuous chicken and smooth bites of egg in pastry.

"You grew up in Nashville?" I asked. "Did you always want to be an architect?"

Up to this point, I knew a lot about Grant—that he liked healthy, "gut-protective" foods, that he was impulsive yet grounded, how he made me feel when I was with him—but I knew little about where he came from.

"The city and I kind of grew up together. After my parents died, I spent a lot of time walking around downtown, looking at decades-old buildings right next to the new ones going up. And it all kind of fell into place for me. They called out to me, told me what to do."

"I like that. Your parents would've been proud."

I wanted him to talk about his parents, to tell me what had happened to them, but I couldn't ask because I knew what it felt like when people asked about mine.

"How much has Deanna told you about our childhood?"

I shook my head. "Nothing really. I've heard you both talk about your parents fondly, but I know very little."

He half smiled. "You want to know about me?"

I swallowed, nodded. "As much as you'll tell." I picked a piece of phyllo dough off the side of a quiche, let it melt on my tongue. "You already know a good bit about my past. I know nothing about yours."

"Fair enough." He took a sip of his wine. "My dad, Davis, was an actuary. My mom, everyone called her Clemmie, was an ICU nurse."

His eyes narrowed to slits, and a line materialized between his eyebrows, a tiny number one. "Are you sure you want to do this?" he asked.

My stomach tensed as if ready to flee, but I wanted to do this, to know more about Grant. And I wasn't going to let my past rule me. "You can tell me." It was what he'd said to me when I'd spoken the hardest words about my past.

"They were killed in a car accident when I was seventeen. Deanna was twelve."

I closed my eyes. My grandparents had been killed in a car accident. I never knew them. Every time I thought of that, I wondered if life would've been better if they'd lived.

When I opened my eyes, he was watching me. "Was it hard when they died?" It was a ridiculous question, but I wanted him to go on.

He nodded. "Very hard. But I'd grown up around death. My dad figured out when people would likely die and how much their lives were worth, and my mom worked to prove him wrong. It was like their professions were in exact opposition to each other, but I couldn't imagine a better team. They both taught me death wasn't to be feared, that life held balance, a purposeful coupling of fragility and resilience. Is this too philosophical?"

"It's powerful."

"It's almost like they knew they weren't meant to live long. My dad even had me read an essay by this guy who lived in the fifteen hundreds, Montaigne. If I remember correctly, it was titled 'That to Study Philosophy Is to Learn to Die.' He thought if we could understand death, we could understand life, and thereby live life to its fullest."

I rubbed my hand over the blanket until my palm was hot. "That sounds like you. Living life to its fullest."

"Yeah, well, it took me a while to get there. I didn't exactly fall back on that premise when they died. I was devastated, too old to live with anyone else, too young to know what to do next."

"So what did you do? Did you end up living with family?"

I thought about twelve-year-old Deanna. She'd lost both her parents at the same age I'd lost Brandon. I couldn't stop my mind from wondering what life would've been for me if I'd lost both my parents instead of my brother. I wished it had been them instead of him.

"This is probably going to sound silly, but . . ." He shrugged.

I reached for his hand, surprised by how easy it was for me to just be here with him, open.

"I was crying one night after I'd tucked Deanna in. My aunt and uncle were staying with us, helping us decide what to pack so we could go live with them for a while. I'd been tough up to that point, put on a brave face. I wasn't quite a man, but enough of one to feel like I should leave the crying to my little sister, so I closed myself in my parents' study."

I squeezed his hand in mine. This was how he knew. He'd felt what it was to lose someone he loved beyond life. I tried not to cry for seventeen-year-old Grant, but tears moved down my face anyway.

"I was sitting at my dad's desk, soaking some actuarial table he had expected to look at again. And then somehow, I was standing beside the wall opposite their desks. It was covered in pictures of family, friends, and even some of my mom's patients. Then there were old newspaper articles and framed quotes. I must've walked past that wall a million times, but that day, my face rested on a quote I'd watched my dad frame years before."

He looked out over the rock, quoted: "'Everything we hear is an opinion, not a fact. Everything we see is a perspective, not the truth. You have power over your mind—not outside events. Realize this, and you will find strength. Very little is needed to make a happy life; it is all within yourself, in your way of thinking. When you arise in the morning, think of what a precious privilege it is to be alive—to breathe, to think, to enjoy, to love.'"

As he spoke, the words itched with familiarity. "Marcus Aurelius," I said, finally placing it.

His head snapped toward me. "You know it?"

A wave of something I could only describe as magical passed over my arms, cooling my skin, which was weird because I didn't believe in magic; I didn't believe in anything, not after Brandon.

"One of my college professors read that quote in a history class when we were studying the fall of the Roman Empire. I remember because I wanted to live those words. I wrote them down, kept it as a bookmark for the whole semester."

He smiled, nodded. "I've since learned that most people attribute it to Marcus Aurelius, but he might not have actually said it."

"You're kidding?"

He shook his head. "I'm not exactly sure who did, but it doesn't matter. The sentiment stands. Anyway, I copied it that night, onto the back of a printed table that told people when they were gonna die, and put it in my pocket. The next day, I told my aunt and uncle I wanted to stay at home, in Nashville. They thought I was foolish. They reminded me that my little sister was *twelve*, but it was the first time I'd seen Deanna smile since my parents died. I knew it was the right decision."

He pulled a piece of paper out of his pocket. It was soft and yellow with age. I opened it carefully to reveal the handwriting of a grieving seventeen-year-old boy with more grit and determination at that age than most people had in a lifetime, a whole lot more than I'd ever had. Losing Brandon had destroyed my family, had crippled me. I never could've done what Grant had done.

"I carry it everywhere I go."

I wanted to carry it everywhere I went, but I handed it back to him. "You stayed home alone with Deanna? You took care of her?"

He nodded. "I raised her, and she raised me. We made it work. I think I got a little lost along the way, a little anal. I made sure everything was clean and in order and we ate our vegetables, because no one thought I could do it. Everyone told me what a mistake I was making. Maybe it would've been easier another way. I don't know. But I set out to make my parents proud and to prove everyone else wrong. I think that's why I'm the way I am now: overprotective of D because I had to be in the beginning. And some people don't understand me because of it. They see me as arrogant, too confident, a know-it-all. But I've worked like hell to make sure everything fit together. The greatest thing I've learned through it all is that you can't please everyone, and it changes your world when you stop living for them and you start living for you."

"Grant, I want to be like you."

"I want you to be like *you*. Despite what William might tell you, I don't want to date myself." The last word caught in his throat, and he put a hand to his back, obvious pain shooting into his face.

"What's wrong?"

"I tweaked my back a few days ago at the B and B worksite." Another grimace crossed his face.

"You're really hurting, aren't you?" I scooted close, slipped my hands under his shirt, and dug into the tight muscles of his back. "You're tense." *I* was tense. Touching him had turned my whole body on, a Lite-Bright with all the pegs pushed in.

He tilted his head back. "I'm better now." His deepened tone oozed into my core, softened my rigidity, and liquified my insides until I was a jellyfish. I felt his low moans in my palms as they permeated his back and shimmied into me, through my hands, to my wrist, then arms, shoulders, then my breasts. I wanted him.

"I like you, Penelope."

The words were almost too bright, as if my eyes and heart needed to adjust to the light of them after being kept in the dark for so long.

"I do have a talent for back rubs," I said, trying to pull up back to the surface before I got completely lost in it.

He turned, faced me, caught my hands in his. "Not because of the back rub."

His eyes, like his words, bored into me, made my pulse clang like one of those windup monkeys smashing cymbals. "I've never felt like this. I think you're it."

I stopped breathing entirely, air lost in the maze of my lungs, as I tried to make sense of what he'd just said.

The silence was so filled with possibility I shook. "Is this because of the Marcus Aurelius thing, because—"

"It's not because of the Marcus Aurelius thing." His head tilted up to the sky. "Okay, maybe a little. That's definitely something I'm not going to ignore, but I liked you before we ever set foot on this mountain." He reached up and ran a thumb over my cheek, making my body shiver. "But I said it tonight because of the Marcus Aurelius thing."

This thing between us was moving too fast. What we'd shared tonight was deeper than anything I'd ever had, anything I'd allowed myself to have, and I'd already been more intimate with him than I'd been with any other man in my life, and he'd barely touched me. This was different.

We stared into each other's eyes in the dusky light, next to a little pot of fermented vegetables.

He leaned into me, and his lips gently caressed mine, not a kiss, but a whisper that dipped all the way to my toes.

"How's your back?" I asked, breathy because I knew what was coming next. I needed it to so I would stop thinking and could focus on all the physical sensations that pulled my body like taffy.

"What back?"

He pulled away, bit his lower lip as his eyes devoured me, then swept my hair aside and bent to my neck. A warm tingle fanned out from the spot where his breath met my skin. I closed my eyes and waited for his lips, waited to see where he'd touch me next. The moment stretched, him maddeningly out of reach, until he began his trail of tiny, succulent kisses up to my ear, where he half sighed, half groaned, and I came half undone. My body arched toward him, and then he whispered the most peculiar thing: "I'm not going to make love with you, Penelope."

I blinked, my body prepared to hear a completely different combination of syllables. Surely he was joking, and this was some twisted bout of foreplay.

"How do you know I want you to?" I teased, letting my hand move across the spot where I'd seen his tattoo, allowing my fingers to trace the waistband of his jeans.

"That look on your face tells me you want me to."

"So what if I do?"

"I won't do it."

Were we playing, or was this about to get religious?

If we were playing, I was going to give as good as I got. If this was religious, well . . .

I leaned down to his ear and huskily asked, "Are you sure?" And then my teeth softly scraped against his earlobe.

His moan told me he wanted this as much as I did, so I was surprised when he leaned away from me.

"Please don't tell me you're a virgin."

His half smile was tortured. "I'm not a virgin, but I *am* serious about sex and you. Taking that step means neither of us will go anywhere."

This was rapidly changing course. We'd gone deep, mentally deep, and I was proud of myself, but now I needed to stop being deep, except for the kind of depth where one part of him sank deep into one part of me. And now, I was saying "deep" too much in my head. "You think you might go somewhere?" I asked, because maybe he was still on the fence about us working out. Maybe he'd realized I was damaged and could never be like put-together Elaine.

"Oh, I'm not going anywhere. Except maybe here." He kissed my cheek. "And here." His lips flitted across my jaw. Then moved behind my ear. "And definitely here." This was confusing while simultaneously lighting me on fire.

"Grant." I managed to pull away from him. I needed to know what he meant, even more than I wanted him to touch me. "What are you saying?"

"I'm not going anywhere, but I think we should wait until you're convinced I'm not going anywhere. You're new at vulnerability. You've admitted that you've never really opened up to anyone. I want to get to know you. I want you to trust me. I want an emotional connection before a physical one."

What?

"And what if I said that was now?" How was he logical when the heat inside my body was burning away thought? I wanted his hands on me. We'd already had an emotional connection. The physical would help balance out all the emotional, so I wouldn't turn into a puddle of doubt and self-consciousness. I knew how to be physical, and now, he was stripping me of some of my best attributes.

"You really believe I'm not going anywhere? Because if . . ." He swallowed hard. His eyes searched my face as if waiting for me to unexpectedly prove him wrong so he could pull me back into his arms.

"The truth?" I asked.

"This isn't going to work any other way."

I shook my head. "No. I don't believe you're here to stay. I want to, but I don't." Everyone left. That was my entire life's experience. It was going to take a lot to convince me that our relationship wasn't more of the same. Grant was different. He'd broken barriers no one else had even chipped, which gave way to this: my openness to try. But trying didn't come with guarantees.

He pulled his lips into his mouth and nodded gravely. I'd confirmed his concerns. "Then we'll wait. No sex . . . for now."

What man refused sex? I should've lied, told him I was all in. But he would've seen through it.

His hand pushed up my thigh and around to my back. "But that doesn't mean I can't do this in the meantime." Then, he pulled me into a kiss that made the sunset seem like a kindergartener's painting . . .

CHAPTER 29
SEXY AT 7:58 A.M.

"Why don't you come inside?" I pulled at Grant's heather-blue long-sleeved shirt as he shook his head, refusing to budge because he knew what I was trying to do. It was the following Saturday—way too early—and he was here, at my house, to pick me up. But I had other ideas. Erin wasn't here, and I wanted to convince him that over the past week—since he'd told me we weren't going to sleep together—I'd become the picture of emotional stability.

But he was wise to my games—having nearly broken his "rule" last night when I slipped my hand somewhere it probably shouldn't have been—and now, he wouldn't even step past the threshold. I'd also told him how my relationship with Chad had been more of a physical connection rather than an emotional one, which hadn't helped my case.

I slipped on my most alluring smile in the doorway, but Grant crossed his arms and looked away.

I dropped the smile. "Fine! But do we really have to go this early?"

"I forgot you've never been to a farmers market. Everything will be picked over if we don't get there right as it opens."

"I *told* you I'd never been, which is why you insisted I go."

"I told *you* it was a sexy place to go, and then *you* insisted on going."

"Oh yeah, right. Well, I think I was desperate when I said that because in the morning light, I just don't see how vegetables are going to be sexy." Seriously, broccoli wasn't a turn-on.

"That's why we're going. I'll prove it to you."

"Why don't you come into my kitchen and prove it to me there. I'm pretty sure I have a few veggies in the crisper drawer."

"I'm almost certain that's not the case, unless it's a shriveled potato with eyes."

"Not sexy?"

"Not sexy. Now come on."

"Let me get my shoes."

As I headed down my sidewalk, the cool, fall-ish air lifting my mood, Devina walked across her lawn and up to my driveway, where Grant's car was parked. "Where are you two heading so early?"

"The sexiest place on earth, apparently." Then I reddened. I didn't know my neighbor well enough for such sarcasm.

"The farmers market," Grant explained, his lips curling the way they did when I amused him.

Devina clasped her hands together. "Oh, I love the farmers market. Haven't been in years, though."

"Would you like to come?" Grant asked, and I instantly deflated. I liked Devina. We'd talked about her antiques collection when I'd returned her pitcher, and it was a pleasant conversation, but I could only imagine the farmers market becoming less sexy if she joined us. And I already didn't have high hopes.

"Wouldn't dream of it. But take some pictures of those heirloom pumpkins for me. Always wanted to decorate my porch with them. Nothing prettier than those and chrysanthemums for fall decor."

"Definitely," Grant said as he hopped into the driver's seat of his Jeep and immediately started the engine. He was serious about getting there early.

"You two have fun," Devina called as I hustled to the passenger seat before he left me.

"So what makes the farmers market so sexy?" I asked, pulling my seat belt on and feeling like we'd said the word "sexy" far too many times. "Shirtless farmers on tractors?"

"Let's hope not. And you'll see."

⌒๑

We pulled into the Franklin Farmers Market at 7:58 a.m., two minutes before it opened. It was a massive congregation of food trucks, tents, and tables behind a series of large buildings that apparently housed more goods. People were already swarming around like bees.

I reached over the car's console and grabbed Grant's arm as he was trying to exit. "You didn't tell me there would be this many people."

"What are you talking about?" He looked into the rearview mirror at the market, illuminated by the morning sun behind us. "This is a light crowd."

"Maybe we were hasty in starting a relationship," I said, meeting him at the back of his vehicle. "We are definitely not on the same page. Have you even met me?"

"Too late. You should've thought of that before you kissed me." He slid his arm around my waist, gave me a quick kiss that made my stomach fizz with delight, and led me forward. "It'll be crowded, but I picked this place because one, I love it here, and two, I do know you, and no one will be paying attention to you or asking you personal information. We'll blend in and have fun. Plus, I think you'll change your mind when I show you where we're eating breakfast."

The fizz from the kiss turned into full-blown carbonation. He did understand me. I hadn't told him about my numbers thing. But he knew it wasn't people in general that made me uncomfortable, but rather nonbusiness interactions.

"Please don't tell me it's one of those health smoothie trucks," I said as we approached a truck with colorful drawings of leafy greens and beets on the side of it. Grant drank kale smoothies with alarming regularity.

"It *is* a truck, but no smoothies." He pulled me by the hand through the thick crowd, stopping in a line so long that I wasn't sure where it led.

I narrowed my eyes. "Well, you're in charge. I have no idea how to navigate this circus."

He squeezed my side and pointed toward a white-and-red sign that read **ELLIE'S OLD FASHIONED DOUGHNUTS**.

$$\sim\!\!9$$

"I take it all back," I announced, licking my fingers at one of the gray picnic tables on a raised platform in the center of the market. "This doughnut is worth being trampled for."

He laughed and bit into cinnamon sugar–covered dough. "I knew you'd like it. Okay, here's the plan. We're only eating what we buy here today. You'll get everything for lunch. I'll get everything for dinner."

I froze, the last bite of my strawberry doughnut halfway to my mouth. "You want me to cook?"

"Absolutely not. I said you *pick out* what looks good. We'll cook together."

"Smart man." I shoved the last bit of doughnut into my mouth— way larger than a bite—and dusted my hands off. "Okay, I'm in. Where do we start?"

"That stand right over there." He pointed. "Do you see the glass drink containers? We're going to share a lavender hibiscus basil tea."

As we maneuvered through the crowd, I tucked into him. "Do you buy your cologne here? Because this place smells like you."

"I don't wear cologne. Oh, the pumpkins Devina was talking about." He pointed to a large tent that had stacks of multicolored pumpkins—a mix of greens, whites, and oranges—arranged in front of flowers. A flatbed truck parked nearby had hundreds of similar pumpkins in the back.

"We need to remember to get Devina a picture."

"Absolutely. We'll pass right by there on the way out."

We'd inched to the front of the line at the tea place, and Grant paused our conversation to order. "One lavender tea, and I haven't seen this one before." He pointed to the middle container.

"It's our seasonal special, cinnamon sage," a gray-headed woman told us.

Grant glanced at me, smiled, then said, "We'll take one of those too."

"I thought we were sharing."

"We'll share both."

The tea lady handed us each a cup and wished us a good day.

Grant put two straws in the clear, plastic drink cup filled with the lavender tea. I'd assumed we'd take turns sipping, but Grant shook his head, insisting that we drink at the same time. "But don't close your eyes. You'll be tempted to because it's so good."

The cool, sweet liquid hit my tongue, and he was right: my initial reaction was to close my eyes, but, as instructed, I kept them open, locking gazes with him as we both took a drink, groaning at the same time. An electric sensation shot through my body as a silent, almost-too-intense conversation passed between our eyes.

When we pulled back from the cup, I took a deep breath. "Grant, I was wrong. The farmers market *is* sexy."

His look went from intense to pleased. "Good thing we've only just begun."

From there, we went to a fish place, where Grant purchased wild Alaskan salmon for our dinner, and then to a stand where fresh, colorful vegetables spilled out from wooden baskets that were turned on their sides.

"Ooh, dip." But then I looked at the label. Kale pesto. "No thanks."

"Well, I'm trying it." He popped one of the sample-size, kale-covered bread squares into his mouth. "You're missing out." He lifted another to my lips, and I hesitated, looking around to see if anyone was watching, because I didn't want to draw "cute couple" attention. "It's just the two of us," he whispered.

It so wasn't just the two of us. But everyone else seemed preoccupied. I reluctantly opened my mouth and snapped the bread from his fingertips, like a wild dog who hadn't eaten in a few days.

"Ow, I think you bit me," Grant said.

"Well . . . we're in public!"

"Okay, let's back it up a notch. It's clear you're not ready for that level of intimacy."

I squinted at him. "I just . . . I don't want to be one of those couples."

"That like each other?"

"Grant!"

"I'm kidding. I knew it was a stretch. I was just thinking it could be hot, if you licked something off my finger." He winked at me.

I stared back, my eyes dropping to his lips, partially hidden by his mustache. "Maybe later, in the car," I said and then started walking toward a table piled with homemade sourdough.

His low chuckle caressed the side of my face as we walked to the bread, where the scent was intoxicating. We bought two loaves and a pan of sourdough cinnamon rolls from a woman who knew Grant by name.

Next we visited a candle booth, FLORA + MOON, which sold handcrafted, small-batch candles in little glass jars. I was planning to pass it by, but Grant suggested we pick one and have dinner by candlelight.

"Close your eyes," he said, lifting one of the jars and covering its label.

I studied him through my eyelashes, my skepticism making him and the woman behind the stand laugh. "This isn't going to be like the kale dip incident, is it?"

"Oh, this sounds like a good story," the woman said.

I shook my head. "Trust me, it isn't."

He smirked. "Just close your eyes and guess what scent this is."

I obeyed because this sounded much more fun than him feeding me in public.

I inhaled when he told me he was ready, and my nostrils delighted in a tantalizing mix of warm vanilla, pumpkin, and spices. "Are you sure this is a candle? Is it pumpkin pie?"

"Heirloom Pumpkin," Grant said as I opened my eyes.

"I want to eat it," I said.

"Well, I don't suggest you do that," the owner said with a laugh, "but it is one of my most popular, along with this one." She handed me a jar, and I told Grant to close his eyes.

"Okay, what do you smell?" I asked, trying to hold in my amusement because he was never getting this one.

"Why are you laughing?"

"No reason. But this should be an easy guess." I smiled at the owner conspiratorially.

"It smells like . . . citrus, maybe something floral, almost like hair spray, but that can't be right."

"What's your guess?"

"Hmm, this is a tough one, but I'm going to have to go with Dolly Parton."

My mouth dropped open. "How did you—"

"I saw it before I closed my eyes." He flashed me a sheepish smile as I slapped his arm.

I set the candle down and pulled out my credit card. "Well, I'm getting Smells Like Dolly Parton because, really, how can I not?"

"I'll get the pumpkin one."

"You get ten dollars off if you buy three," the woman said.

We settled on Autumn Moon because the hint of cedar reminded me of Grant.

From there we picked up a bag of brussels sprouts, a jar of maple syrup, and pasture-raised bacon because when I'd turned my nose up at the thought of brussels sprouts for dinner, he'd promised to make them yummy by adding bacon and syrup to his recipe.

We sucked on orange blossom honey sticks while I finished purchasing my lunch items: homemade tortilla chips, something called Tailgating Salsa, smoked trout dip, guacamole, and the kale pesto, which was shockingly good. All for a chip or bread and dip fiesta. We grabbed a bag of sweet potatoes to finish off Grant's meal and then ran back to get a jar of honey—the sticks were amazing—before we headed back toward the pumpkins.

I pulled out my phone to snap a picture, focusing on a particularly tall stack with a round white pumpkin perched jauntily on top. "You know what?" I dropped my hand to my side. "Forget the picture: we should take one to Devina."

"Brilliant. But what if we took her a whole stack?"

I clapped, surprised at my own excitement. "What if we took her *two* stacks for each side of her entryway?"

His eyes sparkled as he pulled me toward him until we were inches away from each other. "What if . . . we decorated her entire porch."

I nodded, the idea warming me. "Do you think we'd be overstepping?"

"I think she'd love it. It was a great idea you had."

As we carried armloads of pumpkins and mums, I wished the morning didn't have to end. This was the absolute best day I'd had in a very long time. Grant made everything special. Even a tomato held a story as he had me sniff one and then imagine the hand that had picked it and the journey it had made from ground to plate, something I never would've done.

In the car, we drove toward my house surrounded by the scent of dirt and flowers, our surprise for Devina piled into the back. I pulled out one of the cinnamon rolls, unable to wait, and munched while Grant drove.

"I'm going to have to sign a lot more clients if we do this again. We spent a fortune."

"Did you have fun?"

"This has been one of the best days of my life."

He beamed in the driver's seat. "Mine too."

"Do you want some of this cinnamon roll? Like everything else, it's amazing."

"I do but can't take my hands off the wheel."

I tore off a piece and slipped the pastry into his mouth, but as I pulled my hand away, he grabbed it and licked my finger, applying just enough sucking pressure that sparklers went off in my lower regions. "I thought you said you didn't want to take your hands off the wheel."

"I thought *you* said 'in the car.'"

Sexual tension stretched taut on the rest of the ride home, but it was mostly dispelled when we unloaded Devina's pumpkins and flowers onto her porch, laughing like we were high school pranksters the entire time we stacked pumpkins and arranged the bushy flowers.

Once done, we rang her doorbell, surprised she hadn't already heard us laughing and come out to investigate.

We stepped back when she opened the door and threw our arms out at the scene we'd created.

Her surprise at seeing us there morphed into shock and then tears.

"You didn't have to do this. I just wanted a picture." She wiped her cheeks and beamed.

Grant smiled. "Well, we can take one for you."

"I can't believe you two did this for me. Come in. I will feed you cookies."

"Actually, have you had lunch? We bought a bunch of dips, chips, and bread. Why don't we all share it." The words had been surprisingly automatic on my tongue.

Grant took my hand and squeezed it, that solid pressure against my palm more real than anything I'd ever had.

"That would be lovely," Devina said, a look of pure joy spreading across her wrinkled face.

"Careful," Grant said, pulling me against him as we followed Devina into her house. "This one bites."

CHAPTER 30
LIFE REALIZATION #13: GETTING RID OF A SINGLE MAN IS HARDER THAN YOU THINK

September faded into October, and over the next several weeks, Grant and I had what I assumed was a fairly normal relationship (minus the sex). Business was improving as well. It was the first time in my life where I felt like I belonged, like I fit here in this place, in this moment.

Tonight—the Saturday night we'd been working toward—the early-October evening breeze bustled around festive tables at the Grove, the production space we'd rented for the big country music client dinner, where we hoped to ratchet up our success.

Erin was a wizard. She'd coordinated with Deanna, Mere, and Keyondra and tucked new and potential future clients together around raw-wood tables scattered on a bed of fallen pine needles, below the strings of incandescent bulbs that swung from pine to pine. A huge buffet table, laid out like a cornucopia, was several feet to the left of an elevated stage, where musicians were putting on a free show in hopes of capturing the attention of one of the scouts—a group of people I'd never met before. The scouts had been invited by the country music husband-and-wife team from my coworking space, who were trying to get their clients gigs.

Piper, the massage therapist, was on the premises, running her hands all over people in a large white tent at the back of the gathering. Michelle exhibited her graphic design skills with strategically placed signs and decor, and I'd given a lecture about money, showing, with larger-than-life tables and graphs (courtesy of Michelle), how I could make it grow.

The chatter was loud, and people were coming up to me, asking questions or setting up meeting times either online or at my office so we could talk more. I was positively giddy. This was working. If we signed a fraction of those who seemed to be interested, then we'd be well on our way to being a real, competitive business.

Beau, one of the performers hoping to catch the eye of a talent scout, came up to my table. "I've thought about what you said." His eyes broke from mine to glance at Erin. A wide-mouth grin lit up his face and hers. He was cute and maybe young enough for her, and she'd spent a lot of the evening with him.

"Beau," Erin said, batting her eyelashes like a true southern belle. "Can I set up an appointment for you to come into the office and talk more?"

"I'd like that, Miss Erin." His voice was like the chords of a country music song.

I'd found that a lot of people in Nashville didn't have that stereotypical southern accent. Most who lived here weren't from here, but when I heard it, there was something comforting about that lengthening of vowels. Erin certainly enjoyed it.

"I look forward to speaking with you soon, Beau," I added.

I glanced at one of the tables and freaked out, slapping Grant's arm, my focus ripped from whatever was happening between Erin and Beau.

"It's Fred and Doris!" From the meat 'n' three Fred and Doris. This elderly couple had become my ideal life picture. I was fascinated by them. "How are they here?" They were sitting next to Black Coat and Beige.

He pursed his lips. "I invited them when I went to pick up the banana pudding."

Deanna had been deep in conversation with Mere, bordering on an argument, about their ability to buy a physical location for their catering business, but her ears were always attuned to food, and she threw her head back to say, "I'm still mad about that pudding."

"Deanna," Grant said, "I love you and your food, but my girl needs clients, and this stuff will clinch the deal." He pointed to the barely touched pudding in front of him, and I tried to hide my serving by tossing a pastry on top of it.

Her mouth dropped open. "How dare—"

"And give the B and B thing a rest. Invest with Pen, and it'll come." Grant winked at me.

"When Pen will *let* me invest with her!" Deanna tossed her hair— she was becoming irritatingly persistent about the B and B—and turned back to her conversation.

She and I had discussed investing, but I'd been hesitant. I didn't want money to ruin our friendship, something I valued more each day, but I also knew what I could do. I had a binder with her name on it already. I just needed to make it official.

I squeezed Grant's arm and leaned into him. "I keep meaning to tell you: I have access to Deanna's Pinterest page. She has a board called 'Future B and B.'"

"I don't know what that means."

"It means I have pictures of exactly what Deanna wants her B and B to look like."

His eyes sparkled in the moonlight. "You're amazing, you know that?"

I nodded—I didn't feel amazing—and looked back at Fred and Doris. "What do you think they're talking about?"

"You can ask them when they come by your office to discuss their fortune."

Hand to chest, I gasped. "They're coming to my office?"

"Yeah, baby! See what I can do for you?" He winked. I'd told him Chad had said this during his disastrous proposal dinner, and we'd been dropping the phrase, a little guiltily, into conversation whenever it fit.

Chad had called, several times, but I'd made a clean break. I also hadn't answered my mother's calls since my last trip to Minnesota. I was compelled to listen to her voicemails, though. They held accusation along with sadness that made me feel unsteady, like my stomach was in an unending cycle at the laundromat.

"Should I walk away with both our puddings?" I laughed and reached for his serving, but he didn't try to stop me. "What's wrong?"

He arched his back. "My back. It's bothering me again."

I started to suggest he should see a doctor, but this was back pain, which likely would resolve on its own, and doctors were full of bad news. He didn't need to see a doctor. He needed rest, a relaxed schedule. He needed me to be the girlfriend I'd never been and care for him.

"Maybe you should go home." I wanted him to feel better more than I wanted him here. "I need you in tip-top shape for game night tomorrow night, so we can beat the pants off William and Deanna."

"Oh, I'll be ready," he assured me.

I leaned in closer, sliding my hand up his thigh, just shy of his crotch. "Maybe before they arrive, I can take *your* pants off."

"If you move your hand any higher, I'm going to take you on this table in front of all your new clients."

"Promise?"

"So you won't let me feed you in public, but you'll let me take you on a table?" He reached for me, but I pulled away, determined to torture him, and he winced.

"Your back?"

He waved my concern off. "Shh. Don't let Will and D hear you. It keeps getting better, but that monster ride the other day set it off again."

I rolled my eyes. "Show-off."

Erin and Beau walked up.

"You should go see Piper," she said, having apparently overheard our conversation.

"No!" I said. "She does things."

Erin rolled her eyes. "Umm, yeah. That's her job, and she's amazing. She worked on my neck, and it was orgasmic."

"No massage should be orgasmic," I said, still concerned with Piper's lack of concern for any kind of boundaries.

Erin's fingers entwined with Beau's—fast—as she walked toward Piper's tent and motioned for Grant to follow her.

"I think I need one of those massages," Grant said, winking at me.

I put my lips to his ear before he could stand to follow. "If you want an—"

He held his hand up. "Not changing my mind. Unless you can honestly tell me—"

I threw my arms up, cutting him off. "Just go, Grant!"

He walked off with Erin, Beau, and William, who'd decided he wanted in.

If he'd been another man, I would've ignored his grimace of pain and carried on. Grant was different. I wanted him to do what was best for him, even if that was an orgasmic massage from Piper. That was what a normal, caring person would do when their significant other was under the weather.

Significant other.

Significant.

It felt good to care, to really *care* about another human's welfare. I winced at the thought of who I'd been. Now that I was invested, my body wasn't quite sure how to move, like my limbs weren't comfortable with anything this real. How does a robot become a human? What does one do with the nuts and bolts previously holding one together?

When Brandon was still alive and when our mother hadn't yet morphed into a machine and Dad hadn't started drinking, our parents would read to us. *The Velveteen Rabbit* floated in and out of my stack. A stuffed bunny became real because of a little boy's love. After Brandon died, I ripped that book to confetti and flushed the scraps of paper down the toilet because the little boy got sick in the story, but *he* had been okay. *He* had gone on to live his life. Brandon hadn't.

The sentiment of the book held true. Love—Grant's, Deanna's, William's, and even Erin's—was slowly but steadily softening my hard edges. I'd lived with a dull ache in my belly, a distant longing for what I didn't have, and now that I was getting it, the ache was fading. As country music filled the air alongside the smell of barbecue and freshly cut grass, I was happy.

Happiness came from having all the right ingredients, like a cake. Leave out one item, baking powder for instance—Deanna was rubbing off on me—and the dessert fails.

As I breathed in the night air, satisfaction and fatigue warmed my chest, until I looked across the courtyard and saw—

Chad.

He strode toward me, his golden hair highlighted at each incandescent bulb. White T-shirt. Fitted black blazer. Jeans.

I couldn't move.

Someone said something beside me, but I couldn't make out the words. And then I watched Deanna head straight toward Chad like a linebacker.

He stopped because Deanna didn't give him a choice. He opened his mouth, but Deanna put a stop to that too. She was facing away from me, but Chad appeared to be listening, his unshaven jaw and shaded undereyes becoming more pained the longer she went on.

They stood like that for a while, Chad occasionally saying something I couldn't hear. At one point he called out my name and tried to move around her, but Deanna wasn't having it.

It was a warm evening, but at the sight of Chad, that chill had taken residence inside me. An arm came around my shoulders, led me several steps in the opposite direction until I couldn't see Chad or Deanna. It was Keyondra. She was warm, smelled like vanilla, and somehow felt like home, which was probably because her scent came from the black vanilla leave-in conditioner from the Carol's Daughter line. We'd talked about it, and I'd tried it. I'd tried every curly-hair product out there.

She pulled me close. "What is *he* doin' here?"

"I don't know."

I was shaking, and Keyondra held me against her until Deanna walked up to us and exhaled. "He's gone. Tenacious, though. He did not want to leave without talking to you."

"What did he say?" Seeing him again was like a slash of paint across a delightful portrait, a reminder of my past and who I'd been.

"He said he wanted to apologize, to let you know he still had feelings for you. I told him that you'd moved on, and it would be best for everyone if he did the same."

I nodded. "Thank you."

"Well, it didn't end there. He was pretty insistent, said he knew the two of you were meant to be together. That's when he tried to get around me. So, I told him Grant probably wouldn't agree because you and Grant were now dating. He took that one hard. He left after I told him if he really cared about you, he'd leave you alone, because you are happy."

The air was heavier and more difficult to breathe. And then, I wanted Grant, even if I had to go through Piper to see him.

"I can't thank you enough, Deanna. It really shook me seeing him there. It was just so unexpected."

"I saw that." She wrapped her arms around me and squeezed.

Then I told her I needed to see Grant.

"Ahh, you're finally ready?" Piper said. My resistance to her massages seemed to make her want me to have one even more.

Grant's smile faded when he saw my face. He maneuvered off the massage table. William replaced him.

"Piper, you're a magician," Grant said; then all his focus was on me. "What's wrong?"

"Chad." My voice was barely above a whisper. "He showed up here."

He looked over my shoulder. "Chad's here? Now?"

"I kicked him out," Deanna answered, but Grant was already running out of the tent.

"Pen." I turned at the sound of Piper's voice but glanced back out the tent doors to where Grant had vanished.

William let out an awkward moan as Piper's hands kneaded his back.

Orgrossmic.

"I'll go after Grant," Deanna said, and then she disappeared too.

"I don't want a massage," I started. "I really appreciate it, but—"

"Fine. You're the one missing out because I know I could help you, but that's not why I called you back."

I moved from one foot to the other. "What is it then?"

"Keep an eye on your man. Have him come back and see me soon. There's something off about his aura. He needs a cleansing."

This is what she'd called me back for? I would do no such thing, but I said, "Sure."

"Please, Pen. It's needed."

"Right. I'll tell him. Thank you." Then I ran out of the tent, smack into Beau's broad chest.

"We were just coming to find you," Erin said, her hand permanently fused to Beau's. "There's a crew set to clean up. We're going to watch Netflix and chill, at Beau's." She winked at me. "It was an amazing evening. We have so many scheduled appointments. I knew this was a good idea. You need anything else?"

"It definitely was, and I don't need anything." I gave her a look that hopefully conveyed my pride, even though I was preoccupied. "I'll see you tomorrow?"

She walked off, beaming. I didn't think she even heard me.

I crossed the lawn, finally spotting Grant and Deanna talking . . . alone. Thank God.

"Don't worry. He's gone," Deanna said as I came up to them. "Where's William?"

"Having an affair with Piper in the tent." I forced levity I didn't feel.

"I'll go get him," she said. "Wonder if Piper does threesomes," she added as she walked off.

"I don't think she realized what she said because that doesn't even make sense." I casually tucked my arm into Grant's, but his body was rigid.

"I can't believe he showed up here." I'd never seen Grant so agitated.

"I don't want to talk about it. He's gone. Will you take me home?"

His exhale was long and rough, but he nodded. "Let's go."

When we pulled into my driveway twenty-five minutes later, I pushed my palms into my eye sockets. "I don't know why this is affecting me so much. It's just that things finally feel like they're coming together, and then he shows up."

Grant's hand spiraled around my back. "That's the way life is. Bittersweet. The bad always comes with the good."

I raised to meet his eyes. "I don't like that."

"I don't either."

We were silent for several seconds until he turned toward the windshield and put his hands on the steering wheel, his knuckles blanching. "I didn't like how jealous he was when we first met; then, when you told me how he proposed to you, I was furious. But I'm glad he was gone before I got out there because my instant reaction was to confront him, and I didn't have nice things running through my head." Grant turned toward me. "But he cared about you, in his own broken way, and he's trying to fix his mistake. He can't fix it. I won't let him, but I understand it. It's what I'd do. If I'd done something to hurt you—and I'm going to try like hell not to—I'd work to get you back."

My head fell against the headrest, unsure what to do with the compliment. "I don't want to be alone tonight." An electric current ran through my muscles, giving me a jittery, unsettled feeling that I didn't want to face in the silence of my house, especially since Erin wouldn't be there.

Without asking me where I wanted to go, he backed out of my driveway.

CHAPTER 31
TWO SECONDS OF JASON STATHAM

After we'd spent a couple of hours talking—likely Grant's effort to calm me down—I tossed and turned all night, my mind moving from the marketing event, to Grant, to Chad, each subject fracturing in my mind like shoots on a tree branch as old feelings wanted to resurface.

When I woke up the next morning in Grant's guest room, it was late, and the day felt sticky with cobwebs from the night before. There was a tap on my door, then Grant asking me if I was ready for lunch.

"Thanks for letting me sleep in," I said after freshening myself and joining him in the kitchen, wearing the T-shirt he'd given me to sleep in and my dress pants from the night before.

"You needed it." He placed a sandwich in front of me, some sort of sprouts peeking out from under grainy bread. "Should we cancel game night with D and W?"

"I'd nearly forgotten," I said, picking up the sandwich. I wanted to scrape the sprouts off but didn't want to hurt his feelings—he'd sweetly made me lunch. "I'm still game if you are. And where's your sandwich?" I took a bite of mine. The sprouts tasted like hay, but the turkey and avocado mostly covered it up.

"I snacked a little while making yours and decided I wasn't all that hungry."

It was probably the sprouts.

Despite being freshly showered, he looked a bit like I felt. He bent backward, hands on his lower back.

"Are you still hurting?" I asked.

"A little bit."

"I have an idea. Why don't we snuggle up on the couch with popcorn and watch a movie before William and Deanna arrive?"

"I like that idea."

"I should have some spare clothes in my work satchel, which I think is still in your car. I'll go get it and change."

I indeed had spare clothes—a tunic top and leggings—but I liked being in Grant's shirt, so when I came out, I explained that I'd "only" found pants; then I forgot about my little fib entirely when I saw that he was wearing a button-down and slacks.

"It's game night, not the opera, Grant. Are you seriously going to wear that for us to cuddle on the couch?"

He looked down at his clothes like he couldn't fathom why I'd suggested such a thing.

"You do own sweats, don't you?"

"That's the black-and-white number with the tails, right?"

I opened my mouth, but he stopped me. "All right, all right. My old-man wear it is."

Minutes later, he walked into his living room in a white T-shirt and gray tapered jogging pants.

Aye. That man knew how to wear a T-shirt. Just the right amount of fitted.

I held out my arms and wiggled my fingers. "Get over here."

When he sat down, I snuggled against his side, sinking onto his caramel-colored vegan leather sofa, and pulled a creamy L.L.Bean blanket—one side soft fleece, the other a cabled pattern that resembled a fisherman's sweater—over us. Grant's condo was small and efficient, a two-bedroom defined by clean lines but somehow still managing to be comfortable and alive. Which was probably due to the many plants scattered in each room that felt like they were always watching.

He kissed my temple, squeezing me gently with the arm he'd wrapped around my middle. Then he pointed the remote at the small TV across from us. "Now, how do you work this thing?"

"Give me that." I swiped the remote, pointed it at the screen, and moved my thumb over the buttons. "I can't believe you don't know how to work your own TV."

"Why would I want to watch people doing things I could be doing if I wasn't sitting on the couch?"

"Because it's fun, and every other normal person on the planet does it."

He started to speak, but my finger jerked to his mouth, stopping the "If everyone on the planet jumped . . ." speech I knew was poised on his lips, his full lips.

I let my finger linger on those lips and imagined them kissing down my body. Our kisses thus far had been passionate, our hands groping, our bodies pressed impossibly close, but we'd always stopped. His genteel supervision of my virtue was sweet, refreshing even, but it kept my lower half preparing for a party that wasn't going to take place anytime soon.

And he was wrong when he'd called his clothes "old-man wear." I'd never lusted after an "old man" in a T-shirt and fleece-lined cargo sweats. He looked incredibly hot, vegging out on a movie where the actor was doing all the things Grant wanted to do.

When he leaned over, his tattoo peeked out from under his shirt. I couldn't resist, so I lifted the fabric, exposing the blueprint of a house I now knew I would find. How could it have been anything else? I ran my fingers along the thin lines and smiled. I'd thought about getting my first big, seven-figure return tattooed across my ankle, but a tattoo was a commitment.

"It was the first building I designed entirely on my own," he'd told me the first time I'd seen it up close, when I'd been trying to coax him out of his clothes.

I tried to focus on the movie, tried not to think of how many ways that tattoo could be pressed against me or of all the things I wanted him to do to me when he wasn't in pain.

∽

William pointed a finger at Grant. "You're a cheat! There's no way Pen got *The Transporter* from that dinky performance. *Planet of the Apes*, maybe, but not—" William turned to confront me. "There's no way! He had to have mouthed the answer to you."

Game night was in full swing, and my reply came in gasps as I horse-laughed. "No . . . promise."

Grant blew on his knuckles, brushed them against his shoulder, and sauntered back to his seat beside me.

I lost it, full-on this-can't-be-cute guffawing.

A smile tugged at the corners of William's mouth. "Pen, cheating isn't this funny."

"Didn't . . . cheat," I answered, normal fluid sentences eluding me.

"He looked at you!" William shouted.

I jabbed my finger in Grant's direction.

"What Penelope's trying to say is," Grant started, "we're simply superior human beings on all counts, with a particular competency for charades."

Deanna threw a small, house-shaped pillow at Grant.

William stood. "We're leaving!"

"Don't leave!" I screamed, finally composing myself. "We watched *The Transporter* this afternoon by complete coincidence. I made a comment about Jason Statham's sex appeal, and Grant insisted it was all in the look on his face, and if he mastered that same look, he'd be just as sexy."

Grant twirled the corner of his mustache as he tried another look that only made him look like he needed a suppository.

I cut my eyes over to Grant, suppressed a smile, and then went on, "Well, he paused the movie, and for far longer than you'd think possible, he tried out every look he could think of on me. And finally settled on the one you just saw. *That's* how I knew."

"Pathetic," Deanna said.

"No, it's genius," William said. "It has to be the look because Statham's balding, for goodness' sake!"

"See!" Grant looked at me as he pointed at William. "Finally, another reasonable human being."

William dipped his head in agreement. "We could both be that sexy if we wanted to."

Deanna put her hands on her hips. "You mean, I could've been married to Jason Statham all these years if you had simply been looking at me the right way?"

William stuck out his lower lip. "Pretty much."

"Then by all means!" She gestured to the men. "Commence with the Statham look, and Pen and I will melt all over the carpet."

William lowered one eyebrow while simultaneously raising the other.

Grant nodded his approval. "Not bad! Get a load of this." He pointed to his face.

William's head bobbed. "I think *I'm* falling in love with you."

"And who could blame you?" Grant wiggled his shoulders with provocative flair. "What's Jason Statham got on this?"

The two men went back and forth. They were so absorbed in congratulating themselves on being so handsome that they didn't notice Deanna and I retreating to Grant's kitchen.

Deanna pulled the lid off a small aluminum container on the black granite countertop. "After the whole Chad thing, I didn't ask: How many people made appointments with you at the event last night?" Her excitement made me feel special.

"Fifteen. I don't know how many will actually sign with me, but I have fifteen appointments, and Erin's working on some social media event with Lady Mama, who promises more. I might have to start turning people away."

Deanna clapped. "She's awesome!"

"Lady Mama? She's intense."

"Lady Mama *is* lit AF, but I was talking about Erin."

"Yes, Erin is amazing. I'm thinking of asking her to be my business partner. Please don't ever say 'lit AF' again. Do you even know what that means?"

"As fuck I do. Okay, you're right. I will never say that again. But did you say you were going to ask Erin to be your business partner?"

"I think so. She does way more than a secretary. What do you think?"

"I think it's a great idea! You and—"

"Why is it we always end up in the kitchen?" Grant interrupted and peered over Deanna's shoulder as she sliced through homemade brownies, revealing a gooey marshmallow center.

"D! Marshmallows? This soon?" Grant cut his eyes to William, then pointed to the pan. "You okay, buddy? The last time you saw a marsh—"

"Not funny, Grant. Not funny." William glared.

Deanna covered her smile with her hand and said, "I didn't even think about the marshmallows!"

I wanted to laugh, but I was too busy salivating, literally salivating. Grant in his sweats, Statham single-handedly taking on the bad guys, Grant's hand absentmindedly caressing my back—I was about to explode or at least need to change my panties. These brownies—marshmallows or no—were going to help me release the built-up tension. If sex wasn't on the menu, I'd eat away my lust.

Deanna patted her brother's face. "Shall I cut you an extra large?"

She waved the knife above the pan, the chocolate-draped marshmallow clinging to it every bit as seductive as Jason Statham's clenched jaw and an acceptable substitute for biting into Grant's fleece-covered ass.

Grant sucked air through his teeth. "D, I can't believe I'm about to say this, but can I save that extra-large piece for tomorrow? Indigestion."

Deanna's face fell. "But . . . but . . ."

"Hand me the brownie," he responded.

"It's all that junk Pen makes him eat," William said. "His delicate, grass-fed stomach can't handle it."

"Be quiet, Marshmallow Center. I'm not that bad!" I defended. When had this become about me? "The other night, I made him Tater Tot hotdish."

"You mean 'casserole,'" Deanna said. "And Marshmallow Center has a point: that casserole hardly counts."

"I mean 'hotdish.' And it has vegetables!" I knew this was a stretch, since the vegetables were either in the title of the canned soup or diced and fried from a freezer bag, but I *had* chopped a real, live onion on Erin's cutting board. "I may not eat as well as Grant, but—" I turned to Grant for reassurance. He had the gall to look away, suddenly fascinated by a fleck in the granite countertop.

"It's my fault then?" I said when everyone was silent, and then I threw Grant under the bus. "I think it has more to do with the back pain than the indigestion anyway." I turned to Deanna. "He tweaked it that day we did William's monster ride."

"Penelope!" Grant exclaimed.

My nose shot in the air. "Well, it's not because of my apparent horrible food choices."

William stood and pointed a chocolate-stained finger at Deanna and me. "First, let's put this 'Marshmallow Center' business to rest." Then he turned to Grant. "And I knew it! I knew you couldn't handle my ride!"

Grant turned to me and threw his hands up. "Well, let's tell them the details of my latest colonoscopy while we're at it!"

"You got a colonoscopy?" William was in full hazing mode, likely overcompensating because of the marshmallow comments.

"Wow. I wish I hadn't said that. Given our extended family's cancer history, my doc suggested one."

This silenced William and completely arrested me. I didn't know any of this. What did it say about our relationship? Should he have told me? I forced an inhale and counted to ten to stop my mind from racing long enough to realize why Grant wouldn't have told me.

Cancer. He knew about Brandon. He'd seen my freak-out session at the hospital. He was probably worried about what I'd do if he did tell me. And I couldn't blame him, because even at the sudden shift in the conversation, I was shaking inside.

His eyes met mine for a few seconds, and then he looked back at Deanna, who was actively frowning.

"You're still having back pain?" Deanna looked at her brother much like she would a suspicious science experiment.

William walked between us and Grant.

"Ladies, my handsome friend here simply hurt his back and has a little indigestion. Let's cut the old man some slack. He's ancient, but he's not dying, for goodness' sake."

"Just when I was struggling to remember why we were friends." Grant patted William's shoulder.

A sly smile slid onto William's mouth. "Can't take my pick, though, huh?"

"Here we go!" Grant wagged a finger. "Oh, I can take it, it's you that—"

"Have you seen a doctor?" Deanna asked, as if the men hadn't been talking. "It could be a bulging disc, herniated even. A friend of mine had to have surgery because—"

He closed his eyes. "I'll call tomorrow."

Deanna nodded, relief softening her features.

"Now can we drop this for the evening?" he asked. "I love attention, but this isn't the kind I want."

We returned to the living room, and as we played games I no longer felt like playing and ate brownies I no longer felt like eating, Deanna's words played over and over in my head.

Have you seen a doctor? Seen a doctor? A doctor?

We'd been messing around until Deanna had gone serious, which I didn't like because it reminded me of orgasmic Piper saying Grant's aura was off.

CHAPTER 32
LIFE REALIZATION #14: SOMETIMES YOU *CAN'T* DO IT BY YOURSELF. WELL, NOT *IT*. JUST . . . UGH.

"Grant! Please open the door!" The neighbors would likely be calling the police at any minute, but it was ten in the morning, and I hadn't heard from Grant since game night the previous evening. I'd let his slightly awkward goodbye and Deanna's doctor comment and everything else get under my skin.

Nothing was wrong.

He was fine.

So why did I rush through my meeting with the Whitsons? And why isn't he opening the door?

I raised my hand again, but the door opened, relief flooding me as I fell into Grant. I'd neurotically imagined all kinds of horrible scenarios: Grant unconscious on the floor, or his back seizing and him falling down the stairs he didn't even have.

But, he was fine. He was . . . I stepped back and looked at his face. He was *not* fine.

"I thought this was indigestion, but I threw up last night, and I feel worse than I have in years. It's a bug, not indigestion, and you don't want to catch this. You should go."

My mouth moved up and down, but I didn't think I was saying anything.

"No, this isn't ER-level stuff," he said. "If you insist, take me to an urgent care."

"What?" My hearing tunneled.

"You told me to get dressed, that you were taking me to the ER." He eyed me suspiciously.

So I had been saying something. At least some part of me knew what to do, whether or not I was conscious of it.

"Right. Let's go."

⌒୨

There were fourteen cars in the urgent care parking lot. I'd been distracted by the hollowness around Grant's eyes, and I didn't think, not fully, about what taking him to a medical center would mean.

But when we pulled into the parking lot and I saw the words on the door, my head went fuzzy. I tried to tell myself this wasn't a hospital; it was next to a Chinese restaurant, for goodness' sake. But my fingers shook. I couldn't unfasten my seat belt.

I couldn't do this. He needed me, and I couldn't freaking go inside.

He saw my ludicrous struggle to extricate myself from my vehicle. "I knew this was a bad idea. There's no need for you to come in. In fact, you should go. I'll call Deanna to get me when I'm done."

I shook my head. "No. I'll wait for you."

I disgusted myself. *He* was the sick one, and *he* was consoling me instead of the other way around.

"I'll wait," I said firmly, giving in to crippling anxiety. I at least had the wherewithal to know that the longer we argued about my certain inabilities, the longer he'd stand in the parking lot, not being treated.

Hesitation flashed on and off his face. "It doesn't look like there are many people here. Hopefully I won't be long."

I nodded. "I'll be here."

I sat in the car, wrapped in shame and self-disappointment as he walked in alone. This was ridiculous. I needed help.

I wanted to be the right kind of partner for Grant. I wanted to trust him. I wanted to have sex. And unless I had help, I didn't think I was ever going to get there. Not sex help, though. I pictured someone standing in our bedroom, directing us on position and form, maybe even holding up a card with a score on it. Was this some sort of sick coping mechanism to distract me from my gigantic flaws? If so, it was weird—much weirder than my numbers or my cycling—but it was kind of working.

Someone came out of the Chinese place carrying a sack with a big, yellow smiley face on the side of it. I wanted to be happy like that, like a damned smiley face on the side of a Chinese take-out bag.

I closed my eyes.

I inhaled.

I exhaled.

I thought of Aunt Tif all those years ago and our few minutes in a therapist's waiting room. I missed Aunt Tif. Where was Aunt Tif? Why hadn't my mother let me go to therapy then, so I wouldn't have to do it now?

I pulled out my phone.

I glanced at the door to the clinic, pictured Grant going through it.

I decided to make the appointment before I changed my mind.

CHAPTER 33
THESE ARE A FEW OF MY FAVORITE THINGS

The next morning before work, I was sipping a green tea in Grant's living room. I'd spent another night in his guest room, to make sure he was steadily mending after the trip to urgent care. They'd confirmed a stomach bug, which was a relief. Deanna's and Piper's concern had been real, but over something temporary. I could handle this.

"I guess I'll see you at three o'clock," he said into his phone and then hung up.

"Three o'clock today?" I asked.

"Yeah. The urgent care clinic sent my information over to Dr. Remke, my primary care doc. They want to see me today. Good thing my schedule's light."

"But you're fine."

He shrugged. "They're thorough."

"If it's just a stomach bug—"

"I haven't been for my annual checkup." Mild annoyance laced his voice as he cut me off. "They're probably just trying to get me in there."

I wondered if, only after a month of officially being a couple, he was getting tired of my phobias.

But why go to the doctor if you were fine? Irrationally, I didn't want him to go, but after his near-snap at me, I certainly wasn't going to say that.

I tried to appear casual. "Do you want me to drive you?"

Please say no so we can both avoid another scene.

And I could avoid telling him that I had an appointment with Dr. Schultz, a therapist, during my lunch today, one I'd snagged due to a cancellation, giving me less time to stew and back out. I was dreading it, but I needed this person to help me, so the next time Grant got a cold or cut his finger or—God forbid—went to one of these silly "annual checkups," I wouldn't lock myself in my vehicle and gaze longingly at a smiling grocery sack.

"No, I'm feeling better," he said. "Not a hundred percent, but I can drive. Plus, I'm meeting with my team today. They're finished with the venue hall addition, and the ovens are going in thanks to that Interest clipboard."

I smiled. "Pinterest." But I couldn't be excited over Deanna's surprise because the question *Everything's okay, right?* popped in and out of my head. Of course it was. Normal people followed up with their doctors all the time. *I* was the abnormal one for not ever going to the doctor.

I scratched my face. It wasn't itchy, but my anxiety was kicking up. It was going to be a bicycle day. *Let's change the subject, shall we?*

He reached out and touched the lock of hair that had fallen into my eye; one hank had escaped my silk wrapping during the night and was doing this flippy thing. He looked at me with a strange pensiveness that made me squirm a little on his couch, like I was a painting in an art gallery that had to be pondered over to be understood.

"I'll get this doctor's appointment out of the way; then we can have a nice evening. Dinner out?"

"Sounds perfect." I tapped a finger on my lips. "What's that soup-and-sandwich place called off Twenty-First? Ben's?"

"Hal's, and it's a date."

Still staring.

"Grant?"

"Hmm?"

"Is everything okay?"

"What?"

"You've been staring." I gave him a pathetic smile, then in a sing-song voice added, "It's freaking me out a little."

"You're one of my favorite things in life, you know that?"

A grounded feeling washed over me, coupled with one light as air. "I can honestly say you're one of mine too."

The hair flipped back in my face, and this time when he leaned in to tuck it behind my ear, his lips moved in too.

His kiss bordered on urgent, and I fell into it, swimming in its depth, awash from head to toe in a connectivity that made me lose my orientation in space. When his lips were pressed into mine, a promise solidified, a promise to never let go.

When we pulled apart, our chests rose and fell in tandem as we both recovered our breath. My lips tingled, and I licked them, looking into his eyes.

He was Grant. Not a number. My glorious, mustached Grant. Maybe I didn't need to see the therapist.

"I'd better get to work," he said, struggle tightening his stance. Control. I loved that it took that much effort for him to keep distance from me.

I needed to go, too, as I—thankfully—had another full day of new-client meetings. But this whole no-sex-until-Penelope's-sure thing was his idea, and I didn't want it to be easy.

"Meet you at Hal's?" I asked, shoving my feet into violet heels that popped at the bottom of my all-black power outfit. Then I went to him, ran a hand up his chest, and put my lips teasingly close to his. "Maybe tonight we'll come back here, and you can give me another kiss like . . ." My hot breath slid over his mouth as my finger traced

248

the vein at his neck. His eyes rolled back in his head, and his jaw tightened.

"You'd better go." His swallow was visible. Control. I wanted to break it.

I flicked my tongue over his mouth, pulled back, and winked at him. Then I slowly walked out the door, his gaze heating my backside.

CHAPTER 34
I'LL TAKE "MORE THINGS TRYING TO RUIN MY LIFE" FOR $1,000, ALEX

I stood outside the therapist's office, reading the number 1-0-0 over and over again until the zeros turned into eyes that started boring into me.

I'd picked a therapist at random. Well, not completely random. When I'd opened my eyes, my finger was pointing to a Chandler Taylor. Chandler sounded too much like Chad. I fudged a little and went with Dr. E. Schultz, a few names above, because the name Schultz sounded vaguely familiar, like the universe was giving me a sign.

My arm shook as I pulled the door open and walked up to the white wood reception desk with a tiny succulent in a marbled pot, comforting myself with the idea of a ride after I left. (Grant had insisted I take Gaia. And I melted a little that he trusted me with his prized possession.)

"I'm here to see Dr. Schultz. My name is Penvelope." I shook my head. "Penelope Auberge." I needed to breathe, to calm down. I needed to picture this woman as a number. I concentrated. Her tortoiseshell glasses said she was an eight. She morphed from scary receptionist to a delightful number eight with turtle essence.

"Yes, of course." The eight's smile reflected in her eyes. "I see you've already filled out our new-client forms online. Thank you. Let me grab today's intake paperwork. You can bring it back to the room with you."

She disappeared for a few seconds, and I looked around the empty waiting room.

Thankfully, this place looked nothing like a medical facility. The chairs were like ones you'd find in a posh living room, in varying pastels, sitting atop abstract rugs of the same shades. Despite the room's attempt to make people feel like they were visiting a friend rather than seeking psychological guidance, I was pulled into the past. Aunt Tif. The little girl. The numbers. My mother. That memory sharpened. My limbs turned to gelatin, and my eyes cut to the door as I waited for my mother to walk in and pull me out again, to tell me I didn't need to see a therapist. Therapists asked questions.

But my past wasn't going away, no matter how much better my life became. Loss had made my existence a colander; everything fluid had been drained away, leaving a hard shell of a person behind. I'd been this way for too long to change what was now a fundamental part of me, at least on my own.

I recognized my need to be here. That had to mean something. I *knew* I was a number-obsessed, emotionally crippled disaster. I also knew, even after just one month together, that I wanted a life with Grant. And he deserved someone who didn't have—

The eight returned, smiled like she completely understood the plight of everyone who walked through the door, then led me to Dr. Schultz's office and instructed me to sit in one of the two chairs across from a slim desk and fill out the paperwork. Dr. Schulz would be right in.

The room was spartan, efficient, so free of clutter that I could only focus on my thoughts. That smell, I'd smelled it before, but I couldn't place it.

Maybe this wouldn't be so bad.

I tried to focus on the words on the intake form.

"Pen?" The voice came from behind me, and like the smell, I recognized it instantly. Dread circled from my head to my toes. Of all places, what was *she* doing here?

I stood, whirled around. "Elaine?" Grant's Elaine.

No, not Grant's anymore. Someone else's Elaine now.

Beautiful, sophisticated, therapist Elaine . . . *therapist.*

Chunks of information fell into place. The familiarity of the last name. The perfume.

This couldn't be happening.

Why hadn't I put this together? How could I possibly be standing here in front of the woman Grant had dumped for *me*?

Blood drained from my face. Dr. E. Schultz. *Dr. Elaine Schultz.* Why hadn't her name been spelled out anywhere?

Humiliation stung the back of my throat. I'd come here wanting help with overcoming my problems. Dr. *E. Schultz* had, up until about a month ago, been one of them.

The utter absurdity of the whole mistake burrowed into my abdomen and up my throat, emerging first as a cough, then projecting across the room as laughter. I stood in Dr. E. Schultz's office, laughing my ass off because what else was I going to do? Cry? I felt like crying, felt more like crying than laughing, really, but laughter was what my confused body had decided to produce.

"I don't think this is funny." Elaine stood still, a scowl on her prim face.

I waved my arms, then blew out a breath, desperate to agree. There was nothing funny about any of this. I picked up my purse and started toward the door, but Elaine blocked my path.

"What did you hope to accomplish by coming here?"

I shook my head. "I picked you at random. I needed to talk to someone." A harsh breath escaped my mouth. "I can't believe it's you." I didn't know if any of this made sense to her ears, but I hardly cared.

"You didn't know who I was when you made the appointment?" Her delicate eyebrows came together as she kept her arms across her doorway. "Genuinely didn't know?"

I moved my head from side to side. It was hard to believe. Even I wasn't sure this hadn't been some kind of subconscious weird act of . . . weird act of what?

I shrugged, angry at the universe. This was what happened when I reached out for help. I ended up in the one person's office who couldn't possibly help me.

I'll take "More Things Trying to Ruin My Life" for $1,000, Alex.

Alex wasn't the host anymore, but it would always be Alex to me.

"I didn't recognize your last name. And everywhere I looked, there was only your first initial. I wouldn't be standing here right now if . . ." I was getting teary. I tried to breathe. I tried to get angry, anything to burn away the moisture threatening to come out of my eyes.

Dr. Schultz blew a breath through her perfectly formed lips. "I go by my first initial so it's ambiguous if I'm a man or a woman. It's more for conferences and such, and it shouldn't matter, but it does." She gestured toward the pair of light-pink chairs. "Would you like to sit down?"

My stare was blank, and nothing on my body moved except for the bastard droplet rolling down my face. Did this woman honestly think I would sit back down?

"I should go."

"Please. Obviously, I can't act as your therapist. While I'd like to think I could remain objective and put my feelings aside, it would be sticky, a conflict of interest. But I'd like to think your coming here was, perhaps, divine intervention. Maybe we could both have a bit of closure, work out unresolved feelings. And the hour's already booked."

The line between her brows as she gestured toward the two chairs again was near-pleading. And to my utter surprise, my feet moved back toward the seat instead of away from it. If I guessed, I'd sat down out of curiosity, to learn more about the woman Grant had left behind for me.

"Thank you," she whispered, as if my being here was a favor to her. "And once I have a better understanding of why you're seeking a therapist, I can refer you to the best one I know. That I can do. Deal?" She sat in the chair beside me and stuck out her hand.

"I *guess* that's fair." And we shook.

And then we spent the next thirty-two minutes not as patient and therapist, but as two wounded women who wanted to understand why life was the way it was. By the time I left her office, an appointment for later that same day already made with Hannah Hardiman, a therapist who specialized in grief therapy and traumatic pasts, I think Elaine and I both felt lighter.

She'd spent the past several weeks wondering what she'd done wrong and admitted to thinking Grant was the man she was going to spend the rest of her life with, even though they'd been dating for less than a year. In the end, she'd been just as intimidated by me as I was by her, twin inferiority complexes settling in both our chests. After we talked, and she realized that mine and Grant's connection was as strong as it was and that both Grant and I had tried to fight what was happening between us, Elaine said she felt like she'd finally be able to move on, which made me feel better. But it also made everything sharper because—it was easier to get hurt.

Elaine made *me* realize that what Grant and I had was even more special than I'd originally thought.

Later that day, I walked into Dr. Hardiman's office, prepared to do what needed doing.

"Tell me a little about yourself," she'd started, her quiet confidence immediately reassuring.

I started out with the small things, the general things—where I was from, my profession, *most* of my hobbies—and the more I talked, the easier it became.

"Tell me about your family," Dr. Hardiman said next.

There it was, the *f* word. Hadn't I known it would come up this soon? Wasn't that why I'd come here in the first place?

Fatigue settled over me, reached into my mouth, and pulled the words out.

"My father died thirteen months ago." Over a year. I hadn't registered time passing. "He became a cheating alcoholic who drank himself to death. My mother became a control freak, a coldhearted woman who didn't even care her husband cheated or her daughter was crumbling inside. We don't have the greatest relationship." The words marched out of my mouth in a solid line, without emotion, like I was talking about someone else.

Hannah—she insisted I call her by her first name—nodded as if I'd told her that I had the most wonderful mother and father in the world. "'Became'? Did something happen?"

I thought about the box of Brandon's things in my storage closet. The room wanted to spin. From somewhere in the distance, I heard my voice say, "Brandon, my brother Brandon."

CHAPTER 35
LIFE REALIZATION #15: CARAMEL AND PUMPKIN BELONG TOGETHER

"What are you doing?" I asked as I came into Grant's kitchen the next morning, dressed and ready for work. I'd spent a third night in his guest bedroom because after dinner at Hal's, I'd fallen asleep on his couch. I woke up to him carrying me down the hallway sometime in the night. I didn't let him know I was awake; I just enjoyed being in his arms. Then, he'd tucked covers under my chin, stood beside the bed for several seconds, pulled the covers back like he was going to join me—*hooray*— then groaned and retucked the sheets around my shoulders. He'd leaned down and kissed me softly on the forehead, then quietly walked out and closed the door, leaving me alone in the dark.

He ran his hands over the large map in front of him on the circular table. He looked better, and after talking to Hannah, I felt much better. I had a list of books she'd recommended, which she'd said would supplement our treatment plan (one to two office visits a week) and help me better understand my issues. Life was looking up.

"The true question is, What will *we* be doing?" he replied to my earlier question. His finger traced the wriggly-edged semicircle he'd drawn that extended from the southern part of Tennessee and dipped into the northern part of Alabama.

"You're planning a ride?" My finger followed his along the route, ending with a slow caress down the side of his hand. His finger automatically curled around mine. "When?"

"Ten days from now. Deanna and William are both free. I've already cleared it with them."

I ignored the fact that he'd already talked to William and Deanna about this. While the illness shouldn't be an issue in ten days, his back issues might be. "I don't know. Do you think—"

"I'm tired of thinking. I need to be back on Gaia. She cried last night when I put her back in the garage. Okay, maybe that was me. But life is short. All we have is today. All we have is . . ." He waited for me to finish.

"Right now," I said, pulling my hand out of his and curling my leg under me as I sat in a chair beside him that looked like it had been spit out from a tree in the forest.

"It's only a weekend, so it shouldn't interfere with your business." His finger brushed my chin, pride shining in his eyes. Somewhere inside me, a cup was filling, one that had been empty for so long. This man was on my side.

"If anything, it'll enhance the business," I said cheerily, loving this moment, the two of us planning a trip together, like a real couple. "You know what riding does for me." The map crinkled when I scooted it toward me. "It's overnight?"

He beamed as he nodded. His skin was still a little yellow, and I wondered how I hadn't caught the bug. Something that turns your skin yellow must be vicious.

"We'll ride all day," he went on. "About eighty miles in, we'll make camp in Franklin State Forest on the Cumberland Plateau." He pointed to the area on the map. "Then we'll ride back the next day." His finger trailed the return trip back to the Walmart parking lot in Manchester, where we would start and end the ride. I smiled because this wasn't far from our campsite at Bonnaroo.

This was going to be good. This was going to be great.

⁓

"Okay, we've got a ton to talk about," Erin said as soon as I walked into the office building an hour later. "I'm set up in the conference room again today, as I need more space. Your first meeting rescheduled for two o'clock this afternoon, which was when we were supposed to be having our weekly meeting, but I moved it up to now."

Weekly meeting?

"Can I get a coffee first?" I'd had a sex dream last night that involved Grant and the caramel pumpkin crumble coffee they serve right outside my office doors. I hadn't remembered the dream until I smelled coffee, and now I needed it before anything else happened.

"There's already a coffee on your desk, and we need to talk about this whole monkey circus extravaganza."

"Do those words belong together?"

"The Lady Mama event is on for next weekend. I totally thought she was bananas when she said her monkey was going to be reading palms at this Halloween thing, but since it's an exotic-pet adoption for wealthier-than-sin people, it kinda works. I made a few Canva posters, she tweeted them, did a TikTok video, and an Insta feature, and we have a *ton* of wealthy exotics on your schedule. We need to show face. These people are nuts and loaded and might be in costume, which means we'll need costumes."

I'd forgotten all about this. "Next weekend? I can't." Bless Grant and his overnight ride.

"The twenty-eighth?"

I nodded.

Her face said it couldn't fathom my response; her mouth said, "You have to." *Well hello, bossy.*

I almost wanted to give in to her for showing such gumption. "Grant's got this whole weekend ride thing planned. He's really excited." And we'd *just* done a marketing event.

"Can't you do it another time?" She looked irritated. I'd never seen her irritated. "There's a lot of potential here."

I shuffled through my bag, pulled out paperwork. "Here." I handed the papers to her. "I need a partner. And you can go to the thing this weekend." It was a *her* event, not a *me* event. *And we've just done an event.*

Her eyebrows kissed as she read over the paperwork. "What . . . are . . . you . . . saying?"

I smiled. "I'm saying I know you'd love to have your own clients, and I want you to be my business partner. You slayed the event last weekend, your organization rivals mine, and clients love you. I would still be struggling if it wasn't for you. You're the most overqualified assistant, and it feels weird calling you one when you work as hard as I do. This business is rightfully yours. Now, let's make it official."

She moved the hand that had been clasped over her mouth and wiped at the tears on her cheeks. "I don't know what to say. It's a dream come true, but . . . I can't afford the classes, the tests. I've looked into it and—"

"I'll cover everything. It's a good investment. I know. I'm a financial planner."

She laughed through tears. I wanted her to stop crying.

Then she lunged at me, wrapped me in another tight squeeze, and said, "We do make a good team, don't we? But are you sure?"

"You trust my business expertise, right?"

"Of course. I—"

"I'm sure. Now, you catch them, and I'll reel them in. And use those social media skills to find us a new assistant."

She squeezed me again and let out a noise that hurt my ears. "I won't let you down." She jumped up and down and headed out the door, but then immediately returned. "I totally forgot about the rest of our meeting!"

I gestured to the chair across from my desk. "By all means, update me."

"Okay. First, your mother called again. We've got a WeWork gathering with everyone next week to meet the new lawyer moving into the last office space on the floor. I got married. You need to look at the brochures Michelle created and decide on our name, which might change since I'm going to be your partner!" She squealed again. "I'm moving out this Sunday. And we already talked about the palm-reading monkey, which I'll handle while you go bike riding, so I think we're all set."

She got up to leave.

Back that thing up. "Erin! Did you say you got married?"

"Shh." She flopped back down, a torn expression on her face. "I haven't told anyone. My mom would flip if she knew, which is why we're telling everyone else that we plan to get married in six months."

"Married?" I was stuck on that word. "Beau? Or another guy you've known longer than . . ." I counted back to the party. "Four—"

"Four days. I know. It's outrageous, right? It is." She was pacing, throwing her hands up as she walked back and forth. "I'm kind of freaking out, but we have this connection, and he's so stinkin' cute and he jokingly asked me to marry him after we had the hottest sex ever, and then we started talking about values and goals and hopes and dreams, and the next day . . . we did it."

Her rapid-fire speech, coupled with the content of said speech, left me stunned silent for a full ninety seconds. Spend four days in Grant's guest room and a lot happens, except sex in Grant's guest room. Didn't she know the divorce statistics? The US divorce rate was somewhere north of 50 percent: 750,000 divorces each year, and that number was probably significantly higher for people who'd only known each other for *four days.*

"I don't know whether to be happy for you or smack you or question my decision to partner with you."

She pointed at me. "I won't let you go back on that. We're committed." She put her hands in her hair. "Like me and Beau." Then she spun back into the chair. "We probably should've waited, but why? I mean, when you know, you know, right? It feels right. Even when I'm panicking as I say it all out loud, it still feels right. We know each other better after four days than a lot of people do when they get married. We've talked about the hard stuff. And you wanna know the best part?"

I raised my eyebrows. *The sex?*

"I'm really, really happy. And you've made me happier. Houston firing me and my moving back to Nashville were two of the best things to ever happen to me. And you get your house back!"

That little tidbit didn't make me as happy as I thought it would. I liked living with Erin. And my heart hurt thinking about losing Hulk and that tiny little paw that found its way to my leg while we watched TV together.

We finished up the details of the meeting, hugged again, and, as soon as she closed the door to my office, her words echoed in my mind.

When you know, you know, right?

CHAPTER 36
84.49 MILES TO GO BEFORE I SLEEP

Grant and I sat silently in his Jeep in Manchester, waiting for William and Deanna to show up for our overnight ride. Caught up in thoughts, I watched a little girl, still in her Halloween Minnie Mouse pajamas, tug on her father's arm as they and the girl's three other siblings shuffled into Walmart.

When you know, you know.

After I'd seen Hannah several times, my anxiety and fear of the future were slowly improving. Until I thought about Erin and Beau.

And then I wanted all the answers all at once, an overnight fix to my problems.

I looked down at the notes I'd typed into my phone, tried to concentrate. Grant had divided up a series of interesting spots along the ride and had tasked each of us with being tour guide for a portion of the trip. A large, unspoiled area called May Prairie was one of the first locations we would encounter, and it was my responsibility.

I found myself texting Hannah, who'd told me to text her if I needed her. I never intended to, but my finger pressed send, cuing a pit to sprout in my stomach.

Me: Erin got married.

She texted back right away. I glanced at Grant, who was staring out the window, deep in thought. I looked back at my phone.

Hannah: How does that make you feel?

Me: Inadequate.

Hannah: Why?

I glanced at Grant again. Then started typing, erasing, typing again. Should I pay her for this text exchange?

Me: ~~I don't know.~~

Me: ~~She's making a mistake and I should've~~

Me: Shouldn't I be sure about Grant by now?

I went there, to the question that had been eating at me ever since Erin had spilled her big news.

"They're here." He opened his car door. I jumped and dropped my phone onto the floorboard.

William, wearing a skintight Spider-Man one-piece, headed straight for the trunk, where Grant helped remove bicycles and equipment.

Deanna met me halfway between the cars. She was adorable in a black suit with a single spider on the left shoulder and her hair in a ponytail.

"Are you supposed to be the Black Widow?" I asked.

She rolled her eyes and pulled at the fabric. "William's idea, since we're close to Halloween. I think I'm too curvy for all this spandex."

"There's no such thing as too curvy."

"Breakfast." She handed me a large paper sack.

I unfolded the bag and peeked in. *Muffins.*

"Sorry we're late." She pointed back to the bag in my hands. "Pumpkin muffins, packed full of yummy things that'll keep us going."

Grant materialized beside us. "We're almost set. The gear is evenly distributed, and we have everything we need."

We scarfed the muffins.

"You're not going to eat the rest?" Deanna asked Grant, who was wrapping half of his up.

"Just pacing myself," he said.

"You didn't like them?"

He sighed. "Deanna, they were lovely. I don't eat much at the start of a ride. Ask them." He tipped his head toward William and me.

I nodded.

Deanna put her arm through her brother's. "Are you sure you feel up to doing this ride?"

I'd asked him the same question more than once, but hearing Deanna ask it and seeing the look on Grant's face made me determined to stop badgering him.

"The real question is . . . ," he started, bending toward Deanna. "Are *you* going to be able to handle it? This ain't your color ride."

Her mouth dropped open in outrage. "I do Pilates!"

He looked unconvinced, but instead of replying, he turned and started jogging toward the automatic Walmart doors. He called over his shoulder, "I hope those muffins don't slow you all down! One brief stop, and then I'm going to ride!" Finger in the air, he attempted a halfway successful midair heel kick.

I watched him until the doors slid open and closed again.

Before joining a cycling group, I'd thought people riding on the side of the road in their spandex looked ridiculous. But watching Grant now, I understood. He was pulling off the cycling suit, which made *me* want to pull it off *him*.

I pictured his face flushed, his mustache waving in a gentle breeze, like Fabio's hair, as he dripped sweat after riding twenty miles. With his natural outdoor scent concentrated on his hot skin, he'd stand close, whisper something breathless in my ear, teasing me. The no-sex thing made *everything* erotic, and while I wanted it to end, I had to admit I was kind of enjoying the excruciating weeks-long bout of foreplay.

Pass the salt, a normally innocent table request, turned into prolonged hand touching as the saltshaker changed users. *I love salt*, I'd say, pushing out my chest like a salt vixen. *It's the saltiest*, he'd reply, letting the words rumble in his chest as he eyed me suggestively. I'd dash a little on the back of my hand and slowly lick it off, and he'd watch me, swallowing hard and then flicking his tongue over his lips. And then I'd—

Deanna snapped her fingers in front of my face. "You in there?"

My cheeks went hot when I realized the three of us were still standing in the Walmart parking lot, nine inches away from a used piece of bubble gum.

"I'm worried about him." Her hands were on her hips as she stared at the Walmart doors. "Something's off."

"Grant? He had a stomach bug. He's recovering, but he's fine." Hadn't she seen him *run* into Walmart? He was healthier than I was. He was—

"It's just that—"

"Are we going to the bathroom or what, ladies?" William interrupted, rubbing his hands together. "I'm ready to ride."

The three of us consolidated our trash and followed Grant as I shook off Deanna's unsettling words. I soothed myself by remembering that she was his sister. She was worried about her brother, and that was sweet, normal even. I was reading too much into everything, I decided.

In the bathroom, I pulled out my phone again and saw Hannah's text reply. I would likely lose service when we started riding. I was glad she'd replied so quickly, and then I felt horrible because I'd texted her on the weekend, when she was supposed to be taking a break from psychos like me.

Hannah: The surest way to set yourself up for personal failure is to compare yourself to someone else. We all progress at different rates. Instead, compare your past self to your present self. Are you improving? (We both know the answer is yes.) Enjoy your unique journey. Let Erin enjoy hers. You've been through a lot. I'd worry if you were ready to marry Grant tomorrow. You aren't there yet, and that's okay. It doesn't mean you won't get there when your time is right.

I inhaled her words, then sent a final text.

Me: I'm sorry to bother you on the weekend. Thank you.

Hannah: Anytime, Pen. See you next week.

Back in the parking lot, we were packed and ready to go.

As we put feet to pedals, I didn't look back.

CHAPTER 37
TWENTY-FOUR SERVINGS OF SEX IN THE WOODS

A few minutes later, we turned right onto Asbury Road, a short stretch with uninspiring houses on one side and May Prairie on the other. I spouted my memorized trivia like a proper travel guide: 492 acres, mixed swamp, tall grass, short grass, three hundred plant species, et cetera, et cetera.

Grant smiled. I'd done my homework, and the professor was proud.

From there, we rode into the little town of Viola, where the light-blue face of the tiny town hall greeted us.

Grant stopped as the sun struck a waterfall rushing from the rock of one of the hills. I watched him watch it. Colors echoed back with the sound of the water as they disappeared into a white froth and then were carried away to a depth the sun hadn't reached yet. The surrounding trees stood like a chorus ready to sing, dressed in vibrant fall garb.

This was why we'd come . . . untouched nature. It was part of our relationship. Nature was always herself, never pretending to be something she wasn't and never apologizing for the various moods she found herself in. I took a deep breath, hungry for a reset, until the ride made us all hungry for lunch.

We stopped at a place called Mountain Goat Market, a large brick and painted-cement building featuring a mural with mountain goats atop bicycles.

As we walked in and joined the line at the reception desk, Grant looped his arm around my waist and kissed my helmet hair. I smiled at him, unable to resist running my hand over his chest. We were a couple, a real couple, moving at our own pace.

My heart flipped in my rib cage.

William grabbed menus from the counter and passed them out.

I loved this place. This half-suburban, half-rural route with its sloping, tree-lined landscapes and small eateries that were famous for homemade cinnamon rolls or cycling mountain goats possessed the southern charm I was growing to love.

"And what are we stuffing our faces with today?" a young, heavily bearded man asked as we approached the front of the line.

William pointed to two items on the menu. "I'm going to kick a TreeHugger in the face with a Flying Pig."

The beard on the other side of the counter nodded slowly. "I'm writing that down just as you said it."

Deanna ordered next; then The Beard looked at Grant and me. He turned the menu toward me and pointed to the Kale Yeah pizza.

"Uhh, Kale No."

"But you loved the dip at the farmers market."

"But this is pizza."

He rolled his eyes, then pointed to the Goat BLAT. *Bingo.* He knew me better than I liked. Or maybe I liked how well he knew me. Or maybe I was still confused about how I wanted him to feel about me. No, I wanted him to know me. This was ridiculous. I needed to stop and order my sandwich.

The Beard wrote down our orders, but before we left the counter, Grant pointed to the felt letter board sitting beside the cash register. "Ladies."

The letters spelled out the message for the day: JUST IN CASE NO ONE TOLD YOU TODAY: HELLO. GOOD MORNING. I BELIEVE IN YOU. NICE BUTT.

"You should pay special attention to the last line," Grant whispered in my ear.

I resisted the urge to grab his butt, and we each took one of the red stools around one of the large industrial spool tables that sat in the middle of the room.

Before long, a woman in a cow costume brought us our food.

"Once we get to the campsite," Grant started, nibbling some kale, "we'll pitch the tent and have enough time to explore the trails on foot before sundown."

"You'll feel like exploring on foot after this?" Concern crept into Deanna's voice.

"Well, we may want to stick around the camp, because we're in for a treat."

"What kind of treat?" I asked. "Did you bury fermented vegetables there too?"

He exhaled a laugh. "I've told you we're staying at the Franklin State Forest campgrounds, right? Well, when I was researching the area, I came across a mountain biking group that planned to have their semiannual gathering this weekend. I messaged them to see if we could join in, and as luck would have it"—he shimmied his shoulders—"they're a pretty friendly folk. Locals. They know the ropes and the terrain. Tonight, they'll be grilling steaks and telling ghost stories around a fire."

"That sounds like fun!" Deanna said with enthusiasm. Probably because being around a fire meant sitting down.

"I've got to hand it to you, Grant," William said; "this trip hasn't disappointed."

Grant nodded, his mustache splaying in delight.

William was right: we all needed this.

After we'd set up camp and met the mountain biking locals, Grant grabbed my hand and pulled me away from everyone else. We walked slowly, listening to the sounds of scurrying animals in the brush and the soft call of birds overhead until we'd made it to the base of an unadorned deck overlooking rolling hills that reached into the heavens, touched the clouds, and then dipped back down to the earth and dove into the water like an eagle morphing into a mermaid.

I wondered how many had stood on this very spot—suspended over a fiery tapestry of nature—and proposed. I thought of Erin and Beau and wondered if that would ever be me, us. It seemed impossible. Then I reminded myself not to compare my relationship with Grant to anyone else's.

A large bird caught my eye, soaring across my field of vision, a paintbrush on canvas. "Do you ever wish you could fly?"

"All the time," he replied.

"Not just fly." I pointed into the distance, where dark-gray wings caught the wind. "She can see everything. The big picture. If we could fly, we could see it all at once. We could know outcomes, be sure we were taking the best path because we wouldn't be limited to only a few feet in front of us."

I sounded like Philosophical Grant, which I wasn't sure worked on me. "You make me this way," I said, responding to his smile. "Somehow, I see life differently because of you. A year or two ago, I would've looked at this same view and appreciated it, but not in the way I do now."

I couldn't quite meet his eye when I said this, but I reached for his hand, squeezed, then grabbed the other one. Our joined hands were continuous, like a Möbius strip, with the inability to tell where one ended and the other began.

"You saying that makes me feel like I can do anything, like I *will* do anything." His voice was low, rolling in his throat, overcome by an emotion I couldn't quite read.

"I want to be as free as that bird." I unlocked our hands and threw my arms into the air. "Living life like she does, like you do."

"Then do it."

"Then do it," I repeated, inhaled, and then looked up at the sky and let the breath go.

"Penelope." I rode on the way he said my name.

Slowly, I let my head drift back down from the sky.

He pulled my arms around his back, bringing us closer, and then he bent to my mouth, letting his lips move in a tantalizing caress. I pushed into his body, each curve of mine pressed into each curve of his.

Somewhere in the distance, our bird friend let out a congratulatory screech. Consent. It was okay to let go, and from all appearances, that was exactly what we were going to do. This was what we'd been waiting for.

He brought his hands down to my thighs and lifted me, pushing my back against a tree trunk. I wrapped my legs around him, feeling his outline so hard against me my body ached.

He pulled back, looked into my face, and whispered, "I love you."

My breath came faster; my head got lighter, like it was disconnected from my body for several seconds.

And my mouth clamped shut.

I couldn't say it. I physically couldn't get the words out. I couldn't tell him that I loved him back. I didn't want to be in my head then, surrounded by uncertainty and apprehension. I wanted to keep doing what we'd been doing before he'd said the thing. He'd simultaneously ruined the moment and made it perfection.

I put my mouth back on his and slipped my tongue past his teeth, not to ignore the words, but to thank him for loving me. I didn't hide the urgency in my tongue. I let the feeling course through us both. Maybe it wouldn't matter that I couldn't speak.

He shoved his hands into my loose ponytail and cradled my head. I massaged the back of his neck, wanting to pull him through me. We were caught up. Neither one of us noticed we were falling until we hit the ground in a tangle of entwined body parts, landing hard on the twigs, leaves, and dirt below us.

On our backs beside each other, staring past the kaleidoscope of hues on a web of branches and into a sky that was beginning to darken, I giggled. Before long, Grant joined in, and we laughed so hard we couldn't get up.

He reached over to brush something out of my hair. "Are you all right?"

I let out a satisfied breath. "I'm more than all right. Life with you is always an adventure."

"Not all adventures are fun." He brought my hand up to his lips. He'd gone pensive again, like he was falling inside himself. It was a shift, anyway, and it changed the mood. I wondered if he was upset that I hadn't told him I loved him.

I let out a groan as I crunched up to a sitting position. "They don't all have to be, as long as they teach you something."

His forehead rippled. "And what did you learn from this fall?"

I stood, dusted my hands off, and looked down at Grant, who was still sitting on the ground. "To stop kissing you in the woods."

He threw his head back. "It's one data point! You need more than two to draw any sort of conclusion!"

"Well, I have at least two." I held up my pointer and middle fingers. "Two months ago, the first time you kissed me in the woods, we both were drenched to the bone and nearly caught our death of pneumonia."

He stood, inched closer, as if prepared to defend his ability to kiss me anywhere and everywhere.

"If I recall correctly, *you* kissed *me*. How was that *my* fault?"

"Because you insisted on being a wackadoodle in a torrential downpour, while every other sane individual had run for cover." My voice elevated until the last word was punctuated with a tone he could never hope to reach.

"Are you calling me absurd . . . again?"

"If the shoe fits."

"You're not going to let me kiss you in the woods?" he asked. "There's doggone romance coming out of these flowers and setting with that sun, but you're not going to let me kiss you in the woods?"

I crossed my arms in front of me and shook my head. I wasn't sure why I was doing this.

He looked away and then back at me. "Ever?"

"Never."

Don't believe me, Grant. Come and kiss me again.

He took a large stride toward me. When his hand started toward my face, I reached out to push him away. "What are you doing?"

He stopped, opened his mouth to let the exasperated sigh escape. "There's something in your hair. I was trying to get it out for you."

"Oh."

His face was inches from mine as he reached up and then, in a seductive whisper, said, "And I also wanted to tell you that you can't catch pneumonia from the rain."

"What?"

I was totally caught off guard as he dropped his arm to the back of my shoulders, the other encircling my waist as he expertly tilted me toward the ground and kissed me like a ballroom dancer dipping his partner in a sultry Latin tango.

I pretended to resist, but I wanted this, him and the "doggone romance," whatever that was.

Just when we'd recovered what we'd lost in the fall, just when I was about to shove him to the ground and mount him, we heard William's voice call out.

"Pen? Grant? Where are you guys?"

I hated William.

Grant growled as he set me upright. "Shameless! I thought you said you weren't going to kiss me in the woods anymore."

He left me gawking at his back.

William came into view as we passed a large maple. "Did you guys hear me calling? Why didn't you—" He stopped talking when he saw us, my disheveled hair and red face, Grant's dirt-streaked clothes.

"Oh," he said. "Didn't mean to—"

Grant stepped forward. "We were about to head your way but couldn't tear ourselves away from that." He directed William's attention to the deep orange of the nearly set sun, amplified by the golden trees.

William's mouth formed an O as he stared into the distance. "No wonder you guys didn't come back."

"That and we fell in the brush." I needed to explain our appearances.

Grant leaned down. "Fell . . . or tumbled in a hot—"

I squeezed his arm. "Shhh!"

"The mountain crew is all set up," William said, "and they're taking dinner orders. You can choose from steak, chicken, shrimp, or be totally insane and go vegetarian. I seriously think these people are somehow related to D because they didn't say 'steak'; they asked if we wanted 'rib eye with shishito pepper salsa.'"

"Ooo. What's shishito pepper salsa?" I asked.

"I don't know, but it made D squeal. I'm getting that." William started walking again.

"Maybe later we can finish what you started," Grant whispered.

"What *I* started?"

The curl to his lips was devious. "I was innocently trying to get that flower out of your hair."

"I bet there wasn't even a flower."

"Oh, there was a flower."

His half smile made me want to shove William into a bush and have my way with Grant. Instead, we walked hand in hand as I wondered what the locals had in store for us.

CHAPTER 38
LIFE REALIZATION #16: ALWAYS DRINK THE MOONSHINE

The fire roared, as did everyone around it. Dinner was over, and the crew had congregated in a loose circle, telling regular stories, roasting marshmallows for s'mores, and drinking . . . a lot.

"And I had no idea!" one of the mountain guys said for the fourth time. "Her phone had been ringing the *whole* time!"

Unprecedented (and unwarranted) laughter shook the forest.

I exchanged a look with Deanna as one guy recounted the tale about how he'd accidentally ridden off with his wife's cell phone. It rang and rang, but he didn't notice because her ringtone had been set to bird calls. "She's an ornithologist!"

I'd only been able to stomach a couple of timid sips of their moonshine concoction—frustratingly called Sex in the Woods—so the stories weren't that funny, but I manufactured a few guffaws to suit the atmosphere and turned everyone into various digits when I needed to, which wasn't often because of the alcohol or because I was too preoccupied or because the attention wasn't on me. It was nice to lean back and watch them all without expectation or pressure to contribute.

"This is good," William said, a little too loudly, lifting a paper cup to his lips.

Grant peeked into William's cup. "Slow down, buddy. We've got a long way to go tomorrow, and we're not slowing down because you can't hold your sex."

"Oh, I can hold my sex," William assured him, then told the group a story about a guy who'd accidentally ingested psychedelic drugs and ended up naked in his neighbors' swimming pool. He definitely couldn't hold his sex.

As everyone laughed and William embellished, my mind drifted.

Grant *loved* me.

The three words were on repeat, a reverberating whisper in my ear, reminding me of how much I had and how much I had to lose.

In his arms, the moment's intensity magnified. The rough bark against my back, the prickle of his mustache, the subtle texture of his tongue, all three contrasting significantly to the softness of his lips on mine and the pressure of his hands on my body, a touch that was both firm and gentle.

I love you.

This was real, more real than anything else in my life, which meant it could hurt more than anything else in my life, which was why I'd kissed him in response.

It had been years, *years*, since I'd said those words to someone else. After Brandon, my family had stopped saying "I love you." It'd become a jinx. If you said it, bad things might happen.

Now I was in a nest of emotions I didn't understand, a part of me near-jubilant, the other part simply terrified. Did I love Grant? Was this what love felt like? I think I did love him. But I wasn't completely ready for this.

I didn't know how unready I was until what happened next.

I could've sat there all night with his hand in mine under an inky sky scattered with stars that didn't have to compete with artificial light. And perhaps I would've stayed right there and tucked my head into his shoulder if Kellan hadn't started talking. Her words yanked me back around the fire.

"I hate my brother," drunk, twentysomething Kellan said. "I wish he was dead. Like seriously, dead."

Everyone laughed, assuming she was joking.

But for me, all noises in the forest paused. All the laughing faces went silent, like a black-and-white film with subtitles. Kellan hated her brother because he'd ruined her relationship with a *really hot* guy, who, according to her "overprotective" brother, had been planning to cheat on her.

I wanted to grab the girl's face and tell her that she should be thanking her brother. Because at least her brother cared. At least she *had* a brother.

I was forced to bend at the waist and hold my face, the beginning of a panic attack.

I contemplated getting up and taking a moonlit ride, but blood wasn't reaching my head. I wasn't sure my head was still attached to my shoulders, and I didn't trust myself to stand up, let alone get on my bicycle.

Grant's hand was on my back. I thought his hand was on my back.

"Penelope?" His voice was far away as I shrank inside my skin, all moisture in my mouth evaporating into the night.

I tried to force myself upright, but my body wouldn't move. I couldn't control it. My tight lips, of their own accord, managed to whisper, "Sick. Drink. Give me . . . minute." He must've heard because his hand was moving in slow circles on my back, returning me to my body, and he didn't ask any more questions.

I was so hot, yet shivering, as I focused on Grant's hand and its repetitive arc—right side, bottom, left side, top—as I tried to steady my breathing and pull up the concepts I'd read in *Unwinding Anxiety*, one of the books Hannah had recommended.

This is science. Defuse the trigger. Distract the mind.

This was a panic attack, and it would pass.

Right side, bottom, left side, top, I repeated in my head as I kept time with his hand.

The laughter somehow gained momentum, relentlessly beating against my eardrums.

This is a panic attack.

I'm not dying.

I'm not dying.

This will end.

I was breathing again. It was passing.

The laughter settled into a hum in the background. I lifted my head, made eye contact with Grant.

His jaw was tight.

"I'm sorry," he whispered, his eyes boring into mine.

He knew. He knew where I was, in my head, in the past. With Brandon. And he wanted to protect me, but he didn't know what to do. That was what that look was, *pain*. I was hurting him.

The story, Grant's stomach bug, his understanding, the declaration of love. It was suddenly all too much. A little demon inside me chanted: *Escape, retreat, bury.* I rubbed my sweaty palms on my pants so fast they burned and then pushed to standing.

"I'm going to the bathroom. Then to bed." I didn't wait for a response but moved as fast as my unsteady legs would propel me.

Escape, retreat, bury.

Another roar of laughter made me jump, and I nearly sprinted the remaining twenty feet to the door, where two painted figures told me I'd made it to the camping facilities.

It took me nearly twenty minutes to compose myself enough to emerge from the bathroom, and I headed straight for our tent, which was large enough to accommodate the four of us. Inside, Deanna was already tucked into the sleeping bag to the right of mine, and Grant was sitting with his legs stretched out in front of him on top of his bag to the left.

Deanna propped up on her left arm. "Grant and I were giving you five more minutes before I came to make sure a bear hadn't pulled you out of the bathroom and run off. They started the ghost stories out there, which was my cue to say adios."

I couldn't laugh. I managed a pathetic smile, but my face was numb; I wasn't even sure the corners of my mouth had lifted. At least it was dark, and if I was lucky, they wouldn't be able to see what my splotchy face was doing.

"Can't hold my liquor, I guess." It was far from the truth—I'd held my liquor better than I'd like to admit on a few too many nights—but the thought of telling them the real reason I'd had to rush to the bathroom risked me having to do it all over again.

"Pen, are you all right?" Deanna asked. Curse her empathy.

Grant covered for me. "She needs rest."

Deanna opened her mouth, but as my eyes adjusted, I saw him give her a slight headshake. She didn't ask any more questions. And I was very, very grateful.

Some part of me registered that I was overreacting, but how do you stop doing something you've always done?

I'd been wrong and naive. This wasn't easy. I wasn't the new person I'd told Chad I was. That Old Pen had remained lurking under the surface, waiting for the trouble, the *I love you*, the *I want my brother to die*. I wanted to crawl out of my body; I was sick of myself. Because I knew Grant loving me was a good thing. But I didn't deserve his love, and even if I could convince myself I did, he didn't deserve to be tied to all my emotional issues, the ones ready to spring forward at the worst moments. And I knew Kellan was joking, but her words had been a knife, barely having to touch my old wounds before they ripped open and everything poured out.

William came in, and there was hushed discussion I only half paid attention to. When the interior of the tent fell silent—the outside still annoyingly loud—Grant whispered, "Good night."

His hand squeezed mine.

I squeezed his back, words wedged in my mouth like a shoe that wouldn't come off.

His breath on the side of my face was warm and as soothing as anything could be for me in that moment. And I wondered if I should let him go, free him from all this, from everything inside me that would put that look of pain back on his face. He'd been through just as much as I had. He didn't need anything else. He didn't need me.

On my back, I tucked the edge of the sleeping bag under my chin and stared at the top of the tent. A warm tear tickled my face as it slid down my cheek. I resisted the urge to wipe it away.

The cackles and gasps of the others outside the thin fabric were far away. Kellan's drunken, thoughtless comments had taken me back to my childhood home, when my mom had sat down on the edge of my bed and told me my big brother had gone to heaven. Just before, I'd put away my toys, loaded the dishwasher, eaten my vegetables—even the ones I didn't like—because I'd told God that's what I'd do if only Brandon could come home. But he didn't come home; he was never coming home.

I swallowed the ball of bitterness that had crawled up my throat and turned onto my side, wishing I'd had more of that moonshine.

CHAPTER 39
LIFE REALIZATION #17: LIFE ALWAYS LOOKS BETTER IN THE MORNING

The next morning, Stealth, the man in charge of this trip, stood with a spatula hovered over a cast-iron skillet in the outdoor kitchen he'd created. "The pig's a-flyin'. And coffee's over there." He pointed Grant and me to the metal container dispensing piping-hot life juice.

I cradled a cup of coffee in both my hands. I wasn't sure when my memories had faded into sleep, but it wasn't early. I shook my head, trying to loosen the remnants of the dream clinging to the inside of my skull like spiderwebs. My brother, tubes up his nose and, at one point, stuffed into his mouth, a plastic octopus trying to claim him.

In the light of day, my problems looked smaller, and my destructive thoughts faded ever so slightly.

"Did you sleep okay?" Grant asked me. "The red lines on your eyeballs suggest you didn't."

I nodded, touching my fingertips to the puffy skin under my eyes. I'd tried to hide them, but I hadn't brought my eyedrops, and concealer shouldn't be used on eyeballs.

My mouth opened, closed, opened again, then blew out a sigh. "I was too wired to sleep, and when I finally did, I had a nightmare."

He rubbed my arm, but my whole body responded to the touch.

"You feel like the trip back? We can call it off, call a car."

"You'd end your meticulously planned trip just for me, wouldn't you?"

"You know I would."

"How is everyone so chipper?" Deanna rubbed her eyes with one hand, massaged her hip with the other as she joined us. "I can barely move." She pointed to our cups. "Where did you get that glorious substance?"

We pointed to the coffee, and when she turned, she ran straight into Stealth and the light-blue, moisture-wicking muscle shirt stretched across his admirable pecs.

"Well, aren't you gorgeous?" Deanna turned back toward us, her face red, her mouth open in horror, like she couldn't believe she'd said that.

She mumbled an apology and ran off in the opposite direction of the coffee.

The laugh helped bring me further back to life. I lived in the present, not the past. I was trying to, anyway.

Keep trying.

"She's cute," Stealth said. "She seeing anyone?"

Grant and I covertly exchanged elbow jabs. "I'm afraid my sister's happily married."

"Too bad. Well, I've gotta grab my crate of eggs. This place is about to swarm. Hope you all are hungry. My pumpkin french toast is to die for." His spooky laugh faded.

"So we have to tell Deanna that Stealth has the hots for her," I said when Stealth was out of range.

"Sure we should ruin a marriage?"

"Positive, I'd want to know if—"

My thoughts came to a screeching halt because Kellan walked over. I immediately started to shake.

"You guys with us all day today?" she asked.

I felt silly for wanting to avoid her, but she was like a walking grenade in my mind, and I was scared that if she said the wrong thing, I'd break again.

So I was thankful when Grant spoke. "I'm afraid not." He stood. "We've got the second half of our ride back home, and we need to get an early start if we're going to enjoy everything on the list." He held his arm out to me. "If you'll excuse us, Kellan, we need to grab a quick bite before we head out."

When William and Deanna returned, Grant hurried us through breakfast, despite William wanting to savor the food and Deanna wanting to rest.

They didn't understand his rush.

But I did.

He'd studied my face, and I knew he was registering my paleness, the deer-in-headlights gleam in my eyes. He watched my hands shake so badly I could barely eat. He made small talk to distract me. He pressed the side of his body into mine to steady me, to let me know he was there. And I saw it, all without words; his actions were clear.

Last night, staring at the top of the tent, I'd contemplated breaking things off with him, resigned to being alone with a past I couldn't seem to let go of. Because just when I'd thought I was moving forward, a handful of drunken words had so easily pulled me back.

But as he herded William, Deanna, and me toward our bikes, even as they were midconversation, midbite, something clicked for me.

There was no way I was letting him go. I might be neurotic, but I wanted him, and I was going to keep him. I had to keep taking steps *forward*, no matter how small. Had Hannah said that, or was it in one of the books? Didn't matter. Deep inside, I knew he was what I wanted. I just needed to figure out how to be what he needed.

As our group said our goodbyes, I thought about what I knew Hannah had said. I needed to let Brandon go. His illness and death had been the start of everything else.

I could do this.

I focused on the road, the wheels under me, and the wind on my face. As soon as I got home, I'd open Brandon's box.

CHAPTER 40
HALF-WHITE, HALF-BLACK

"Listen, I've got a really busy day tomorrow, and I'm scheduled for a test at my doctor's office," Grant said as we neared my house on the way back to Nashville. "We might not see much of each other this week."

I straightened in the passenger seat, put the bite of trail mix that was on its way to my mouth back in the bag.

I didn't know how to take his words and the cautious way in which he'd said them. But the possibility of him not wanting to see me was what loomed largest. Then I reheard the word "test."

I stared out the window into the dark. "What kind of test?"

He swallowed. "It's nothing, just a CT scan, maybe something else. Routine."

"Okay." The acid in my stomach bubbled like a cauldron.

We pulled into my driveway. Erin wasn't here, and I remembered that she was moving out, probably already gone.

I opened the car door to get out, but Grant grabbed my arm. "I shouldn't have told you I loved you."

Tears instantly burned my eyes. He was taking it back.

"No, no." He pulled me closer, kissed my head. "I'm handling this all wrong. I *do* love you." He closed his eyes and inhaled. "I'm freaking not sleeping with you until you're sure; then I go and tell you I love you.

I'm an idiot because I know you're not ready. It just slipped out, and it's not fair." He put his head on his steering wheel. "None of this is fair."

"Grant, I—"

He held up a hand to stop me, then gently cupped my chin as he looked directly into my eyes. "I meant every word, but I don't want to pressure you. I'm not sorry I said the words. I'm just sorry I said them now. It's not the right time. Am I making sense?"

I nodded. If I spoke, I'd cry, so I held on to his hand and squeezed.

Then, he gutted me. "I think we should take some time apart. I need time to digest some things, okay?"

The words bumbled around my body, bruising every organ they hit up against.

We'd barely had *any* time together, and now—

I knew I needed to say something. But I didn't. Because I couldn't.

He saw me to my door and kissed my cheek, all without looking into my eyes. Then he walked back to his car and drove away. And I'd said nothing. I hadn't fought for him. Hadn't fought for us.

I dropped to my knees in my partially filled living room, my heart shattering to bits and scattering like confetti all over the old carpet that still needed to be replaced. I should've known this was how it would end.

But then Grant's face materialized in the darkness as I pressed my palms against my eyes, his bright face in the woods. *Earnest.* No one could hold that much intensity in their eyes and not mean what they said. Then, in his car, he'd apologized for loving me. He *hadn't* taken it back. He still loved me. If the tables had been turned, and I'd told him I loved him and he hadn't been able to say it back to me, wouldn't I be crushed? More than crushed?

He was only human.

And while a part of me—a large part—was still scared of that love, I didn't want to be someone he had to apologize to for loving.

Which meant facing my biggest fear: the possibility that I could lose the person I loved. I'd done all the work to let him in, and for what?

To let him go again? Because I was scared? Grant was there, waiting—for me. All I had to do was meet him halfway, not even halfway. He was simply asking me to take a step forward.

I smiled, hope thrumming through my veins because I'd just realized something. I was the cause of my own misery. I stood, shaking but filled with determination, and went to the downstairs closet, where I'd stashed the box of Brandon's keepsakes, a small container that held way too much power.

I pulled it out of the darkness, into the dim light of the living room. My heart was already racing, but when I saw the box, it was ready to leap out of my body. What if, instead of helping me move forward, this pulled me back even more? What if Hannah was wrong? I was about to open a box filled with memories that only made me think of all that had become impossible when Brandon took his last breath.

The past is only as big as you allow it to be.

I'd allowed my past to grow without restraint until it had overshadowed my whole life, which was what it was doing now with Grant, letting it threaten what was starting for us.

I'd unfairly tacked my life's ruination on my brother's death. I had to let him go, had to let go of the fear of losing someone I loved. Grant wasn't going anywhere. I had to stop my past from being an excuse to remain stagnant. It didn't own me; I owned it.

Hannah had put a lot in perspective in a short time. I wanted a new life; I wanted freedom. And I wanted it so badly that it was like lighting a pile of kindling with a match.

She'd also said something about forgiving my parents, but one step at a time, right? I didn't even know what that would look like, especially since my dad was dead and my mother was a humaniform droid who didn't think she'd done anything that warranted forgiveness.

I went to the kitchen for a knife, then returned and folded my legs under me right in front of the box. I took a deep breath, then sliced into the tape around the lid, slowly lifting one corner to peer inside, as if my whole childhood might leap out and laugh in the face of my progress.

A weathered paperback copy of *Old Yeller* was on top. I pulled it out, thumbed through the pages, and let the memory overtake me.

⌒⑨

My brother, framed in his upstairs bedroom window, carefully folded a page of *Old Yeller* down to hold his place as he looked out to see what the commotion was in our front yard, where my twelve-year-old friends and I were no longer playing.

A group of Black girls, the ones who hadn't taken well to my new haircut, shoved the group around until I was standing in the middle of their circle of four. I'd never forget the look on their faces, like by existing, I was ruining their lives. It scared me. I looked up at Brandon, so far away, yet the cover of *Old Yeller* was crystal clear, a blond Lab with the saddest look on his face, like the dog sympathized with me.

"Why don't you put grease in your hair?" one of the girls said, Tameka. She'd picked on me before, pulled my braid, when my hair was long enough to have a braid, and pretended she hadn't when I confronted her.

"Because I don't want to," I said, trying to be brave, trying to stand up for myself. I didn't know what they were talking about, why they were so angry over a hair product, or why they were surrounding me.

"Your hair looks stupid," the larger one, Vee, said—her name was Virginia, but everyone called her Vee. She came toward me, broke the circle so she bumped my arm with her belly, hard. I fell. And they laughed, except for one girl in the four. A look of regret passed over her face. I'd talked to her, thought we were, if not friends, friendly acquaintances. But the look passed, and she joined in, especially when some of the other kids around started laughing too. My friends, the ones I'd thought of as friends at least, looked embarrassed, backing away like they'd just realized they should probably question their association with me too.

Mr. Goff, the gigantic White art teacher with hands like tennis rackets, walked down the sidewalk with his one-eyed shih tzu that always appeared in desperate need of a bath. He looked at me, and for a few precious seconds, I thought he was coming to help. I think Brandon did, too, because he stayed in the window. But when Mr. Goff saw me, he leaned down, picked up his dog, and hurried back to his house three doors down.

Tameka came up to me on the ground, and I braced myself, wrapping my arms around my middle, sure she was going to kick me, but she didn't. Instead, she reached down and grabbed one of the many colorful clips in my hair, what I used to keep my too-short style from flying all around my face. It was the first time I'd thought my hair was kind of pretty, like artwork on my head. I'd even received a few compliments at school earlier that day. My mother had told me that morning, as she and I placed one clip after another in my hair, to embrace my curls. They were different, she'd said, but they were beautiful, and everyone was going to love my new style.

My mother had been wrong. These girls did *not* love my new style. Tameka's hand came away with one of the clips and a hunk of my hair. I screamed. Someone else pulled out another clip, more hair. They laughed, and I tried to crawl away, but someone was holding me down. I realized it was the girl who had looked regretful for those few seconds, her sympathy evaporated.

As suddenly as I'd been attacked, it stopped, and all the kids were gone, except for one who held my shoulders as I cried on the ground, my new shoes scuffed with dirt, my pants the same.

Brandon.

He held me in his arms, apologizing over and over again, apologizing for taking so long to get downstairs, apologizing for my hair, apologizing for what those girls had done and for what everyone else hadn't.

I couldn't stop crying. I blubbered at him, telling him, between rasping sobs, that I wished I was White and that my hair was straight and that my lips weren't as full, so I'd stop getting picked on, so I'd stop feeling like I was always waiting to be picked for one of the teams. Because which side did we belong on, he and I? We weren't Black. We weren't White. And neither side knew what to do with us.

He let me cry until it was all out. When I'd fallen silent and the yard glowed as the sun transformed from its afternoon sharpness to the subtle golden gleam of early evening, he pushed me up and told me it would be okay, that we had each other. We were the same. As long as I had him, I'd have someone who knew what it was like to be in the middle, to belong between two big groups.

We were the mixed kids, the ones who had light skin but coarse, curly hair that our parents didn't know what to do with. He told me I had it harder because I was a girl, and girls were meaner than boys at my age. He held my hand as we walked inside and up to my bathroom, where I cried some more when I saw my hair.

My brother told me I was beautiful, that I'd be beautiful even if I shaved my head, because what I looked like on the outside didn't matter. I didn't believe him, of course, because it did matter. The hesitation on the White kids' faces told me it mattered. The open disgust on the Black girls' faces told me it mattered. But he'd been trying to calm me down, and it had partially worked. It got me to stop crying, at least.

He tried to fix my hair, to repair the matted, torn bits sticking out all over the place, but in the end, he'd called a friend of his, and his friend's mother came to our house with a bag full of hair products, a gorgeous Black woman whose curls were defined, big, and unapologetic. Her kindness as she washed my hair, layered in products, and gently combed out my curls didn't change what had happened to me in our front yard, but it changed how I saw people. Black, White, Hispanic, mixed: it wasn't the color of your skin that made you who you were; it was how you lived and how you treated other people.

She told me the girls who'd bullied me were angry because I had Black in me but had light skin and could get away with things they couldn't. She told me that they probably didn't even understand why they'd done it. She told me it would get easier.

Later that night, after dinner, Brandon asked me if I was okay.

I nodded. I wasn't, but I was tired of talking about it. "Thanks, B. I love you."

He sprang one of my temporarily defined curls. "I love you too, little sis."

⟡

A large tear fell onto the faded cover of *Old Yeller* in my lap. In the first years of my life, my brother was always there. The two of us had been a team. When our mom was out climbing the corporate ladder and our dad was busy building his medical practice, it was Brandon who had been there. Every. Single. Time.

And nothing else mattered because together, we could get through anything.

I sat for a long time, pulling at the feelings woven around my heart like loose threads. It was more than losing my brother and friend; it was losing someone who understood what it was like to be me.

I placed the book beside me, then riffled through the rest of the box. The lump in my throat was nearly unbearable when I palmed the scrappy little monkey wearing a red bow tie. My brother had kept it under his pillow for good luck.

The monkey got a special place in my lap as I moved from a gnawed, stubby pencil Brandon had used to do his last sheet of math homework, to the mint-condition baseball card he had kept on his bedroom shelf. It wasn't until I saw the leather-bound notebook that my hand stopped moving.

Instead of picking up the journal—Brandon would never let anyone call it a "diary"—the one he'd started writing in after his diagnosis, I returned the contents to the box, everything but the monkey.

That was enough for tonight; I wasn't as brave as Brandon had been. Brave even on his last day, when he'd folded the journal into my hand and told me to read it whenever I missed him.

I had never opened it.

I looked up at the ceiling. "I miss you, brother. It's been twenty years, and I miss you like I lost you yesterday."

I closed my eyes and slowly inhaled, holding the breath for as long as I could. Then I pushed upright, carried the box back to my bedroom, and, as I placed Brandon's monkey next to the purple Beanie Baby on my bed, I told them both I'd read the journal within a week.

Before I did, I needed another session with Hannah.

CHAPTER 41
LIFE REALIZATION #18: I NEED A FRIEND WHO LIKES TO WALK IN OTHER PEOPLE'S SHOES

I'd tried to move my Wednesday appointment up, but Hannah wasn't in the office. A family emergency. By Tuesday night, I couldn't wait any longer. Deanna became my stand-in therapist. I hadn't spoken to Grant because I wanted to do it right. I needed someone to tell me I'd analyzed this appropriately, because even though I was beginning to trust myself, I was new at it. And now, I had people in my life to talk things out with. I wasn't entirely alone.

So, in her warm kitchen, late in the evening, when she was still recovering from the long ride two days before and needed sleep for the long workday ahead, Deanna listened.

The first time the doorbell rang, Deanna had to remind me that it was Halloween, but William was taking care of the trick-or-treaters as we hid in the kitchen.

My phone buzzed with a text. My mother. If you don't call me, I'm coming to you, it said. Empty threat. I would not call her. The last time we'd talked, she'd told me how horrible I was for not seeing Chad.

I confessed everything to Deanna. My brother, my parents, Chad, my own denial of it all. When I told her about making an accidental appointment with Elaine, she spit her tea out onto the table. She smiled as I told her how therapeutic our final conversation had been and then silently let me babble on and on, refilling cups, nodding, and hugging me about a dozen times.

I waited for condemnation, judgment, but none came.

"Why aren't you telling me to stay away from your brother?"

She held on to my hand and squeezed, empathy and tears in her eyes. "You act like you want me to."

I swallowed.

"Do you know why I wanted us to be friends?" she asked.

"Because . . . I was building a business and you wanted the B and B and—"

She shook her head. "That was part of it. You inspired me to do things I hadn't done before, but it was more than that. I haven't been through exactly what you have, but I know what it's like to push people away while actively needing them. I lost my parents, and that was hard, but I also . . ." She dropped my hand and repeatedly smoothed the tabletop as if trying to flatten a wrinkle in the wood. "Ten years ago, William and I lost our twin babies."

My gut seized and then sank like I'd swallowed lead. I'd never even wondered why William and Deanna didn't have kids. I didn't have them, didn't want them, so it had never occurred to me to question why these amazing people weren't parents.

"I was five months pregnant when we went to my OB, and she could only find one heartbeat." She inhaled. "And then . . ." She looked away from me, the past clinging to the lines of her face, making her frown, but it was so much more than a frown. It was the embodiment of pain, a transformation of her whole body, like she was someone else. "And then there were no heartbeats," she whispered.

That tiny, tear-filled whisper shattered my heart. Tore at my expectations. Shredded my walls.

I didn't pat her. I didn't reach for her hand. I grabbed her—and held on.

She, like me, was broken. I wasn't the only one with a past.

I would be a better friend.

She pulled back. "I haven't told you because I don't talk about it." She looked me full in my face. "I *can't* talk about it. But I know what it's like to lose something you want so badly it tears you apart. I know what it's like to put the pieces of yourself back together and try to move on. But you're never the same. The cracks show. The glue shows. That experience taught me that you have to wallow in someone's dark places to fully understand why they make the decisions they do. Life isn't black and white. It's all mixed." She smiled and then grabbed my hand. "I think my hurt saw yours."

I stared at her for several seconds, our eyes traversing the common ground that connected us. And I realized how selfish I'd been. Even when I thought I wasn't being selfish, even when I actively tried not to be, I'd missed something. I'd missed this.

It wasn't about me.

It was about us, all of us.

We held out our arms at the same time. We walked into an embrace, two women with common pain. The bond we had stabilized our glued pieces.

"Pen, you are good enough," she whispered.

The black tar that had been holding me down, keeping me from flying, dissolved. Deanna and everything that made Deanna who she was gave me strength. I, too, would find my strength in weakness.

"I'm going to tell him," I said. "How I feel."

She shook her head. "When you're ready."

"There *is* one thing I need to do first." Now wasn't the time to tell her about Brandon's journal. "And I need to convince Grant to take time away from work and stop going to the doctor for these routine RT scans."

She straightened, and her voice rose. "RT scan? You mean CT scan? Grant got a CT scan? Why?"

"It's a routine part of his physical," I reassured her. It felt nice to tell someone else that everything was fine, that something medical was not the worst thing to ever happen to a person.

She stood, glanced around the room as if looking for something. "A CT scan isn't routine. They do a CT scan when something is wrong." Her tone caused a murmur of dread in my stomach.

"Then I must be misremembering. Maybe he said something else because he told me it was routine." I was holding on to that word, saying it over and over again: "routine." Nothing special, nothing out of the ordinary. Everything was fine, and I wasn't going to let Deanna's understandable concern for her brother get me worked up.

I closed my eyes and breathed. Those feelings of anxiety were my old fears flaring up again. Everything was fine.

When I opened my eyes, Deanna was looking at me. "I'm sure you're right," she said, calmer. "I'll call him later."

I left Deanna's, and as soon as I got back home, I raced upstairs. It hadn't been a week, but I pulled my little box away from the corner and tossed the lid onto my bedroom floor.

My fingertips traced the leather binding of Brandon's journal.

So many years had gone by, and I was going to hear his voice again. A part of me didn't want to do it, afraid I'd find something that would shatter my brother's memory, but I had to, needed to. If this was even part of what was holding me back, I was *going* to. Emboldened by Deanna's friendship and Grant's "I love you," I loosened the leather binding and opened the first page.

My name was at the top, followed by a comma. I fanned the pages. The journal was completely empty, several pages having been ripped out at the beginning, leaving little jagged paper triangles in the crease of the book. Brandon's diary wasn't a diary, at least not anymore. It was a note to me. I flipped back to the first page and read the four lines.

Sister,

YOU WILL BE OKAY. I WANT YOU TO BE
OKAY. IT'S OKAY TO BE OKAY.

   I love you,
   Brandon

I touched the letters, each one written in all caps by a fifteen-year-old boy who was wiser than his years and who loved his sister, a little girl who had flopped across his legs and cried about how nothing was okay and never would be again.

I was on a proverbial cliff made up of my past and all the decisions I'd made along the way. I'd spent my life afraid to jump, scared to live without Brandon, like being happy would be betraying him somehow. But all this time, I'd been betraying him by not living.

I held my breath, then let it go.

For the first time in a very, very long time, I was ready to tell someone else I loved him. I was ready to jump, and I prayed I would fly.

CHAPTER 42
"I LOVE YOU" OVER A TRIO OF SCOOPS, MINUS THE THREE SCOOPS, MINUS THE "I LOVE YOU"

I think we should take some time apart.

I tried not to let the words become bigger than they were, but I hadn't seen Grant since he'd dropped me off after the ride four days ago. We hadn't spoken. Now, work was suffering—I'd called a client by the wrong name earlier in the day.

I needed to see him, so I'd texted, asking him to dinner on Wednesday night because I couldn't let another day pass without putting myself out there. All the way.

He'd told me to pick the place, but he requested Thursday night instead, which worked just as well for me, except for how excruciating it was to suddenly know what to say and be forced to wait.

But Wednesday had slowly faded to Thursday, and tonight, if all went according to plan, life would be as close to perfect as it could get.

I'd taken special pains with my appearance, a black sheath, elevated by a simple strand of exactly fifty-eight pearls and matching bracelet with twenty-three. I'd reserved a table at Old Hickory Steakhouse inside the Opryland Hotel, a Nashville resort with indoor gardens and waterfalls. Locals went there to have dinner, walk around the tall, glass-ceilinged atrium, eat waterside, or ride in the Delta Riverboat along the indoor river. It was a Nashville must-see, and I had never been. I wouldn't tell Grant about the room I'd reserved with the internal atrium view until after dinner, after me and my eighty-one sea jewels had told him I loved him.

This evening as I'd spritzed on my special-occasion perfume, a subtle floral scent, I'd practiced in front of the mirror, trying different combinations of the three words to accentuate.

I love you.

I love *you*.

I *love* you.

Three words, Grant. I. Love. You.

Definitely not that last one.

My skin vibrated with the thought of speaking the words, however I ended up saying them.

⌒〇

"Hi." I bit my lower lip, almost shy at seeing Grant again, at my front door, after what had felt like months.

"Hi." His smile was as big as mine, and his navy suit made his eyes pierce even more deeply into me.

I wanted to run to him, wrap my hand around his royal blue tie and use it to pull him to me, but seeing him also knotted my stomach.

"I've missed you," I managed as we headed down the sidewalk to my car. I told him I'd drive because I needed to focus on the road so I wouldn't self-destruct in the passenger seat.

His smile faded slightly, not a lot, but I noticed, which only made me more nervous, and determined at the same time. But I didn't want to tell him I loved him while we were in the car. Then, I didn't want to do it while we parked and near-silently walked into the hotel, padding across the carpeted halls like friends instead of people in a committed relationship, then onto the concrete pathways where there were too many people to have an I-love-you declaration.

I decided to wait until we were settled across the table from each other, beside a waterfall, surrounded by real, live foliage, with comforting, rich smells wafting up from the plates in front of us.

But now, as I sat and picked at a Cowboy Rib Eye Steak, the anticipation had amplified my nerves and made my tongue as thick as the Lobster Mashed Potatoes I'd ordered. I was afraid that if I tried to speak, it would all come out as one unintelligible blob, conveying a brain abnormality instead of the sentiments of my heart.

But the lights were perfectly dim, a combination of flickering gas lampposts and curtains of twinkling lights raining down all the way from the glass ceiling that appeared to be miles above us. I needed to do it now. I inhaled and counted to three under my breath.

"Grant?"

"Hmmm?"

"I—"

Something was off. His body sat across from me, but his mind was somewhere else. He glanced at the water cascading over the rock, snaking between elephant ears and ferns and all other manner of vegetation that I didn't have names for. He wasn't looking at me.

I was competing with *water* for his attention, and so I stopped, waiting for a better moment.

He didn't notice that I'd cut myself off. Another bad sign.

Now, the meal was over, and we were walking along the water's edge, past people taking pictures with their phones, my arm in his, slowly heading for Bravo Gelato.

I'd do it there. "I love you" over a trio of scoops. Two spoons. One bowl. Zero waterfalls.

And I'd tell Grant what I hadn't told anyone in years. His face would widen into a grin that would make his absurd, beautiful mustache stand away from his lip in delight. He'd sweep me into his arms and loudly proclaim "Finally!" as he spun me in the air, carried me to our room, and threw me on the king-size bed, where we'd make love all night. Then, the next morning, after we were blissfully sore, we'd eat croissants on the balcony overlooking the atrium, like we were lovers in Paris, sipping green tea in plush, white bathrobes.

Yes, I would tell him over gelato. I smiled at my impending triumph. His detachment would fade when he knew I was all in. We would be happy.

But on the way, he stopped on the indoor sidewalk, next to the ridged trunk of a palm tree.

He hesitated.

Grant never hesitated.

He took my hand.

His eyes burrowed into mine.

He swallowed.

His face was *not* the face of a Parisian lover. His face held regret. "I wanted to tell you something over dinner, but I couldn't bring myself to do it."

He looked back at the damn waterfall.

I had no idea how hard I'd been holding on to this romantic fantasy until the look on his face and the tone in his voice threatened it.

The edges of his mouth were pulled down in a deep frown, like each corner was just barely holding on to the weight of what he had to say.

Blood rushed through my ears, or maybe that was the sound of the waterfall.

Why'd they keep it so hot in here?

And how had I missed the signs? I'd been so preoccupied with plans to tell him how much he meant to me, and *his* plans were to tell me that things were over between us. Why else would he have that look on his face? But it didn't make sense. Just days ago, he'd told me he loved me.

I could fix this. I had to fix this. I hadn't been open enough with him. He didn't know how I felt. I hadn't said "I love you," but I was ready. Ready to scream it loud enough for anyone and everyone passing by to hear, for all the people in the rooms with interior atrium views to look down on us and witness.

We needed to get to the gelato, the cool, creamy gelato. Everything would look different over ice cream. I pulled at his arm, tried to move toward the—which way was it?

"Penelope." The way he said my name made me think there was a part of him that didn't want to say it. And it was the first time I didn't want to hear him say it.

And then my mind caught up with my body; this was more than a breakup.

My ears struggled to parse the words as the tone behind them deafened me.

How could I stop this from happening? It was so damned hot in this place. The water looked cool. If we weren't going for gelato, maybe I could go for a swim, a quick one. Then I could get out and tell Grant—

He took my other hand, but I couldn't feel his hands on mine. I looked down, saw the line where his skin met mine, but it could've been a drawing. I tried to wiggle my fi . . .

"I have cancer."

Cancer.

Cancer.

Cancer.

The word echoed in my head, rolled down the indoor sidewalk, slammed the balcony doors of all the rooms with an interior atrium view.

"Penelope, did you hear me?" he asked.

"Cancer," someone said, maybe me.

"Yes. Pancreatic cancer. That CT scan suggested it; a biopsy confirmed it. My doc's sending me to a surgical oncologist. I see him tomorrow."

I think he paused, but all my senses were so dull I couldn't be sure.

"I suspected, but I was trying to be optimistic. Penelope, pancreatic cancer is . . ."

Routine. What the hell happened to routine?

His words faded in and out.

Poor.

Prognosis.

Surgery.

Stent.

Chemo.

Radiation.

The words didn't make sense, at least not in the sporadic way I was hearing them.

"I'm sorry." Then I heard my mother's voice say the same thing to a little girl who also didn't want to hear an apology. "Given everything you've been through, I can't imagine telling you anything worse than telling you I have cancer."

Please, God.

Cancer.

The word became a tangible thing that stepped outside of Grant's body and punched me in the stomach. The word grew in size, towering over the trees, the greenery, covering all the lights on its way up to the glass ceiling, where jagged shards rained down as the word burst through the panes and reached all the way up to the moon, turning everything pitch black, darker than pitch. This was nothing, the blackness of nothing, and my whole body vanished into it, completely lost.

CHAPTER 43
ZERO JIMMY CHOOS

There was a three-inch circle of drool on my pillow when I woke to pounding. My room was dim. Out the window, the early-morning sun stretched in the sky, or was that the afternoon sun? I didn't know what time it was, what day it was. How long had I been asleep? I didn't even remember getting in bed.

I thought back. Grant had come to my house. I drove us both to—I looked down at my crumpled black dress, the pearls on my wrist, and reality slammed into my chest, knocking me back on the bed.

Grant.

Pulling at the skin on my forehead, I tried to dislodge events. Had he taken me home? I didn't remember driving. The last thing I remembered was standing beside a palm tree, him telling me he had . . .

No.

More knocking. Someone was at the door.

Please let it be Grant. I started to move downstairs but stopped. What did I say when he told me? I needed to remember before I faced him.

It couldn't be true.

Why wasn't he here now?

I looked around for my phone, threw back the bedspread, the sheets, tossed the pillows, scanned the nightstand and the dresser.

I needed to get to the door.

I ran down the stairs and raced to the front entrance. My fingers slipped on the knob because my palms were so sweaty.

I needed to see Grant.

Why didn't I remember coming home?

The lock finally relinquished under my fumbling fingers, and when the door was thrown back, my mother stood on the other side of it, wearing a linen suit the color of straw. I looked past her, caring about her only if Grant was tucked into one of her pockets, but they were likely faux pockets anyway.

He wasn't in her pockets, and I couldn't do this now.

His car was gone.

"Penelope." My mother stepped back, my appearance no doubt unacceptable.

Why did she call me Penelope? Didn't she know that's what Grant called me, *only* Grant?

Where is Grant?

I left Aurora standing in my doorway and turned back inside, trying to find my phone. Surely he'd called. If nothing else, I needed the phone to call him. I needed to see him.

I searched everywhere, my mother chasing after me until I finally gave up and faced her. She'd asked me fifteen times what I was looking for, and when I'd finally answered, instead of helping me look for it, she asked how I'd lost my phone in the first place.

Then, she pulled us into the kitchen and over to the table. I sat in the chair she'd shoved me into, vaguely aware of my mother moving around in my kitchen. I didn't care. I pressed my hands into my eyes.

Think. Think. Think.

I was replaying the events from last night for the fifth time when my mother set a cup of tea in front of me. I stared into the steaming darkness; a few bubbles floated on the surface, popped.

Pop. Pop. Pop.

My mother sat across from me, ruler straight, her hands wrapped around her mug. "What's going on?"

As my mind fell into my standard background criticism of her primness, I realized I was sitting the exact same way.

"What are you doing here? What day is it?"

She looked horrified. "Day? It's Friday evening. How can you not know that?"

Friday evening? My date with Grant was Thursday. I'd lost a whole day.

"Why are you wearing that dress?" My mother stood and walked back and forth across my kitchen, concern on her face as she decided what to do with me, her heels clicking like a sophisticated metronome. "I'm glad I came."

"Why are you here?" I asked again, wanting this over with so I could find Grant or at least my phone.

"I want you to come back home." She sat, folded her hands on the table, used her business posture, her professional tone, the tone she used to make things happen, control her environment, bend the world to her will.

"I am home."

She shook her head. "This isn't your home. Look at this place. Look at you. You're confused. You need to be grounded, with solid people like Chad."

I stared at her. This was a repeat of the proposal. Instead of getting angry, I felt sorry for her. After Brandon, she'd decided who I'd needed to be, and she ignored what didn't fit her mold, tucking it out of her mind so she could go on pretending. Like I had.

But I couldn't pretend anymore. I didn't have the energy for it or her.

I snapped. "Last night, the greatest man I've ever known, the greatest human I've ever known, told me he had cancer, and I don't know what I said to him! I need to call him. I need to make sure he's okay, that we're okay."

For several seconds, my mother looked like a scared, paralyzed animal, not the statuesque woman she'd made herself into. In those seconds, I thought she might understand; for those brief ticks of the clock, I thought we'd reached some kind of breakthrough.

She closed her eyes, and when she opened them again, there was Aurora Auberge, cold, withdrawn, determined.

"I will not let you make this mistake. Cancer? God knows you don't need that. You shouldn't do this. I won't let you do this."

I stood.

"You owe him nothing," she went on. "Chad is healthy, strong, willing to—"

"I can't go back there."

"You don't have to worry about Houston anymore. He's discredited. He's been seducing wealthy women, drugging them, and then threatening exposure if they didn't heavily invest in TCF."

"Extortion?" I looked into my mother's face. Then, she pulled a folded newspaper seemingly out of nowhere and spread it on the table in front of me. Houston's picture was on the front, in handcuffs.

Houston McGregor is an extortionist.

Then it hit me: he was also a *rapist.*

"They want you to take his place at TCF." A look of utter pride brightened my mother's face.

"What? Who wants me to take his place?"

"The higher-ups. They didn't agree with what Houston did to you. They didn't realize it until I made them aware."

I stared at her.

"We're both trying to make this right." Was she, too, admitting some kind of wrong? Had I entered an alternate reality where people realize their flaws and actually try to fix them?

They want me to take Houston McGregor's place. Me.

I reveled in the thought. I saw the newspaper headline, the hypothetical one that would be placed right across from Houston in an orange jumpsuit.

Penelope Auberge saves Twin Cities Financial from corrupt extortionist and rapist, Houston McGregor, the same man who, months ago, tried to slander her.

A woman. A mixed woman. In charge. I saw my picture, a smiling, confident portrait. I saw justice. I saw hope in my mother's face.

Aurora took my hand in hers. *She's holding my hand.* It was weird, but also, kind of nice. "Come home. Start over. You don't have to do this. Moving back would be the right thing to do, for your career and future. There's no question."

She was giving me a way out.

As the clock ticked from one number to the next, I let the past and present wash over me: what had happened, what hadn't happened, what was happening now, what would happen. Everything converged.

"Thank you for coming here." I knew it hadn't been easy. "Thank you for all you've done to help clear my name. But I *am* home, and I—"

I grabbed my purse. I couldn't afford to say anything else. I needed to find Grant. I walked out my back door, leaving my mother standing in my kitchen.

But Aurora followed me. "You don't owe him anything!"

I whirled back around. "I owe him *everything*!" And as I opened my mouth to say something else, the need to be telling this to Grant, not my mother, sliced through me.

I moved past the garage to my car, praying my keys were in my purse.

"Penelope! Come back here." My mother caught up to me, talking louder and more desperately outside than I'd ever heard her. *This* was shaking her world hard enough that yelling in my driveway seemed reasonable to her.

She beat me to my car door, stood in front of it. "Where are you going?" she demanded.

"To find Grant."

"You can't go out like this. Your hair. Your makeup. You don't have any shoes on."

Funny, I hadn't noticed my feet were bare until she'd pointed it out. No wonder she'd outrun me.

I started to go back inside; she lifted her hand to lead me.

Then I stopped. I didn't need shoes. Of course I needed shoes, but now it was the principle of the thing.

"Get out of my way, Mother."

She protested. I repeated. And we went back and forth until I contemplated physically picking her up to move her out of my way.

She must've finally recognized the unchangeable force inside me because she stepped aside, a rigid step.

"You're making a mistake. This is *beyond* foolish."

"No, you're the one *living* a mistake. I'm thankful I finally woke up from this sleep we've both been under."

I ignored my mother and her high-heeled logic. As I wrenched open my car door and praised whatever entity had allowed my keys to remain nestled in my purse, my eye caught movement.

Devina was running across her lawn toward me, her features scrunched in concern, so I stopped, halfway between sitting and standing.

"Are you going to Grant?" she rasped, coming to a stop by my open car door.

I looked at her, bewildered. She knew about Grant? "Yes, I'm headed to his house right now."

She shook her head. "Didn't you get his message? He's not home."

"No. I can't find my phone. What message?"

"He came here last night with his sister to make sure you were all right, said he told you about his diagnosis and that you didn't take it well. Said he was going to give you some space to wrap your head around it because he didn't want to burden you because you'd been through too much. Went to his friend's cabin in the mountains. Chuck?" Her words tumbled over one another, like the thoughts in my head.

"Chuck's cabin? He's there now? Do you know where it is?" Desperation stung my chest. Grant felt impossibly far away, and I needed to close the distance.

"Don't know when he was leaving, but that's what he said. Want to use my phone to call him?"

Three times I called, and it went straight to voicemail. I felt panicky. The sky seemed to commiserate as it darkened, with thunder rumbling in the distance. Rain was coming.

"What about his sister? Can you call her? She'd surely know the address."

I held Devina's phone in my hand, willing myself to remember Deanna's phone number, but it was useless. I'd relied on my phone to store that information and had never committed her number to memory.

"I'll go to her house," I said, needing to make progress. A single raindrop landed on my forearm, but I barely registered it.

She nodded. "Yes, go. And, it's worth it. He's worth it. A short time with a good man is far superior to none at all. I know."

Her words touched places in me I didn't even know existed, but she didn't need to tell me that. That was why I would move hell and earth to find him. I knew I wanted Grant no matter the surrounding circumstances, and now I needed him to know it.

"Penelope."

My head jerked toward my mother, whose existence I'd forgotten until she said my name.

She folded her lips into her mouth as her eyes filled, but she said nothing else. And I didn't waste any more time.

Phoneless and shoeless, I drove to Deanna's.

CHAPTER 44
LIFE REALIZATION #19: COLD CHERRY PIE IS THE BEST DINNER EVER

Rain threatened to plant me in William and Deanna's lawn as I ran down their sidewalk barefooted to their front door. My fist banged on the wood. Just when I'd started climbing into the bushes to peer into a window, the door opened. William. His eyes took in my appearance, the rumpled, half-soaked dress, my hair—oh, my hair. My makeup was likely still clinging to my face, but for the first time in my life, I didn't care what I looked like. I didn't care that people knew I was a mess inside and out. Something else mattered more.

Grant mattered more.

I peeked around William. "Is Grant here?"

"No, he—"

"Pen." Deanna pushed around William with her arms out, but as soon as we embraced, she stiffened.

I pulled back and scanned her wide-eyed expression, her features tense, a mix of hurt and incomprehension.

"You . . . you left him. I just don't understand."

"I'll go get a towel," William said and then exited the room.

As Deanna's eyes filled, so did mine. I hadn't been thinking about her and what she must've been feeling. She had to know.

I couldn't stop my lips from quivering. "You picked him up?"

"How could you leave him stranded like that? He kept trying to tell me that it was a lot for you to take in, given all you'd been through, but what about what all he's been through, Pen?" She stomped away from me. "It's not always about you!"

Her elevation in tone made me jump.

She spun toward me. "Your reaction hurt him, but he won't admit it because he loves you. Last night when I picked him up from Opryland, he wouldn't tell me what was going on until he made sure you were okay. Then he told me he needed to go to Chuck's cabin to sort through all that was happening to him, but I know he was doing it for you, to give *you* space to decide whether you wanted to be with someone who was *dying*." The last word was bitter and broke her. She flopped down on her couch and cradled her head in her hands. "And I had to hold it all in because I didn't want my feelings to be one more thing he had to worry about. But I can't—" She broke off on a squeak.

The silence that lingered after Deanna had stopped talking squeezed in, like a corset laced too tight. The pressure kept me from moving right away, but when air finally reentered my lungs, I slid forward and onto the couch next to Deanna, fully expecting her to shove me away.

I inched my arms around her, waited, and when she didn't stop me, I fully embraced her, and she collapsed against me.

Then, we cried together.

I'd done a permanent thing, an unforgivable thing. I'd done the worst thing I could imagine doing. *I'd left him.* And I wanted to wallow in my own self-deprecation, but I shoved it aside, my current mission overshadowing everything else.

We clung to each other on Deanna's couch as William draped a towel over me. Once I'd collected myself enough to speak, my voice sounded odd, like I was in a tunnel.

"He told me, and then I didn't remember what happened after that. I . . . I think I must've blacked out."

She pulled away from me, wiping her face as she caught her breath. "He said he told you and that you stood there, staring into the distance; then you took off, ran out of the hotel. When he realized he couldn't catch you because he was in pain, he called me." Her anger had drained away, and her voice sounded small.

And that was when it hit me, full in the face: Deanna was me. She'd been given horrible news about her brother, and she was trying her best to process it on her own.

I grabbed her hand and squeezed too hard. She had no reason to forgive me, but I was going to try. "I need you to know that I'm in love with your brother. I don't know how to explain last night. Telling you I'm sorry doesn't even begin to explain what I am, and there's no excuse but that I wasn't fully in control. But, if he'll have me, *if you'll have me*, I want to be there for him. And for you."

Her eyes filled again. "He needs you." She paused, her body shaking slightly as she pointed to herself. "I need you."

William stepped up to us. "We need each other."

Deanna and I craned our heads up to William's sad smile, and then the three of us held hands, a silent pact passing on contact.

"Grant needs to come home," Deanna said, moving beside me on the couch like a bird. "He needs to know that you—"

"Can I use your phone? I can't find mine," I said, interrupting. She was right. Grant needed to know that he wasn't alone, and he'd waited long enough.

"The cabin doesn't have good service," William said. "I'll be shocked if you can get through."

"Then I'm going to Chuck's cabin," I said, after he'd been proved right by several calls going straight to Grant's voicemail.

He shook his head. "It's pouring. You shouldn't even go home, and you *definitely* shouldn't try driving two hundred miles on back roads you aren't familiar with." I'd never seen him this insistent. It was incredibly annoying. "We'll try again tomorrow or wait for him to come back. He's working on a big project; he won't stay gone long."

"Just give me the address," I demanded. A storm wasn't going to stand in my way.

"It's a cabin in the woods. Winding, narrow roads," he explained. "You can't go tonight."

"904 Raven Branch Pointe." This came from Deanna. William and I turned toward her in surprise. "Grant needs to know, William."

His jaw tightened. "It's not safe."

But I knew the risks, and I didn't care. Maybe I should've, but I didn't care about the danger because I'd already faced the worst; nothing could compare to that.

"I'm going. I have to."

Deanna slid her arm under mine and lifted me to my feet. "Come to the kitchen. Have coffee. It'll keep you awake. When did you eat last?"

I winced. I didn't deserve her kindness, but every muscle in my body filled with gratitude. "Yesterday's dinner with Grant."

"Then we'll have pie too."

I stopped our forward progress and put my hand on her arm. "You forgive me?"

"I'm sorry you reacted the way you did. I'm sorry Grant had to experience that pain. I'm sorry for yelling at you. I'm sorry for everything that was, for everything that is, for everything that will be. I'm so much more than sorry that my brother has . . ." She choked, unable to say the word. "But I'm not sorry my brother met you. So yes, I forgive you."

I nodded, raw emotion keeping my voice low. "Do you think Grant will?"

"If I know my brother, he'd respond to that by saying, 'For what?'"

While William made coffee, Deanna pulled a cold pie from the fridge, stopped to grab forks from a drawer, and placed three-fourths of the pie and the forks on the kitchen table. "Let's eat this before you go see Grant."

Tears were still coming, off and on, with a will of their own. "That sounds wonderful."

We ate the rest of the pie, and then I headed into the downpour, darkness and despair blurring the trip to Chuck's cabin.

CHAPTER 45
THREE WORDS

Hours later, my spirits lifted when I saw a light on in a cabin. This had to be the one. There was nothing else out here, but the numbers on the mailbox at the end of the endless driveway were smudged, and I couldn't be sure.

I knocked frantically on the cabin door, and I nearly cried when I saw Chuck's rugged face.

"Please tell me Grant's here."

"Pen? What are you . . . you made it all the way out here in that?" He pointed to the storm. "At this hour?"

"Grant's asleep in the guest room." A gorgeous woman with flawless dark skin pulled me into the neat but rustic room, where a fire roared and a golden retriever excitedly wagged its tail. "Come in, come in."

"Pen, this is Celia, my wife," Chuck said.

"I'm going to get you some dry clothes," Celia said, and she left the room before I could tell her that I didn't need dry clothes.

"Where's the guest room? I need to talk to him."

A door opened in the hallway fifteen feet away from me.

That face.

That was what I'd driven two hundred miles in the rain to see. *That* face. *Home.*

My chest rose and fell, but that was all the time I let pass. I didn't wait for him to move.

I ran.

I threw my wet arms around him, and he lifted me off my feet. Then I pulled back and kissed his mouth, a deep kiss that served as the preamble to the next thing I planned to do.

When he set me back down, I didn't let go. I was never letting go. I grabbed that face between my hands. "Are you listening?"

He tipped his head forward.

"I love you. I love you. I love you. I love you. I love you." My voice trailed off in a whisper. "*I* love you. I *love* you. I love *you*. I love you. I love you."

CHAPTER 46
LIFE REALIZATION #20: MAKEUP IS NOT WHAT MAKES YOU BEAUTIFUL

For three seconds, after his smile had faded and we'd finally pulled apart, when his eyes searched my face, I regretted not taking the time to change and make myself presentable. Not in the usual way I'd needed to maintain a flawless face, but when he looked back at this moment, I didn't want him to remember dark smears under my eyes and hair so big it could knock someone over.

Grant, in his black T-shirt and flannel pj pants, ushered me into a bathroom that looked like a spa you'd find in the wilderness. The candle-like lamps flickered, casting a golden glow across the rough-hewn stones that lined the walls. The sink was a metal bucket and sat atop a whiskey barrel. In the back left of the room, a distressed copper claw-foot tub beckoned guests to shut themselves away behind the burlap shower curtain. Stepping into the detached shower, which had the same natural rock as on the walls, would be like tucking into a cave, another world, protection from everything outside this bathroom. I wanted to pull Grant inside and never come out.

He grabbed a fluffy white towel hanging from an antler sticking out of one of the rocks and wrapped it around my shoulders.

Our silence mingled with the heavy drops beating down on Chuck's metal roof, a peaceful melody for our reunion as he gently patted me dry.

Then his fingers intertwined with mine, and he lifted my hand to his lips, kissing each finger on my right hand. "I can't believe you drove here in weather like this. It was too dangerous. I could've lost you."

I wondered if he'd thought he'd already lost me. "Grant, I am so sorry." Words were inadequate, so I pushed everything I didn't know how to say into my eyes, hoping they would somehow convey the depth of my regret.

His finger moved to my lips. "Shhh. We're together right now, and that's what matters."

Of course that's what he would say. That's who he is. He wasn't about to let the past stand in the way of his future. And I'd work to make sure he'd never regret his decision to let me back in.

He was the type of man many didn't understand, but he kept being Grant no matter what.

"And you're sure you want this?" I gestured to the mess in the round hanging mirror as I held my rapidly frizzing hair in a ponytail with my hand. But what I really meant was the whole mess: me, my life, my hang-ups, my emotional basketcase-ness.

"Yes, Penelope, I am quite sure you are exactly what I want."

I pointed back toward the mirror. Probably because it kept me from asking if he was sure, really sure, because I still didn't understand it. "Well, maybe not just like this," I offered.

"Maybe not just like this." He moved around me.

For a few seconds I thought he might find me so repulsive that he'd need to leave and let me get myself together, but he grabbed a whiter-than-white washcloth on one of the carved shelves on either side of the whisky barrel. He turned the hot tap on at the sink in front of me and let it run as he moved the cloth back and forth under the water.

I was mesmerized by his hands as they wrung out the cloth and then moved to my face.

"You are beautiful." He ran the fabric across my forehead with a gentle sweep of his hand. "But you try to hide, behind this." The cloth swept under my eyes. "You don't need it."

He was taking off my makeup, what was left of it at least. I closed my eyes, and he moved over my eyelids, hardly pressing at all. The tenderness of his hand, as it skimmed across every inch of my face, soaked into the pores of my skin all the way to my core.

"That's better." He placed the washcloth on the edge of the sink and pulled my hand out of my hair so it fluffed out. Then he took my clean face in his palms. "I knew I'd like this face best, and where have you been hiding this hair?"

He turned me until I was facing the mirror. He wrapped his arms around me and positioned his face close to mine. And there I was, my naked face pressed next to his, my natural hair nearly suffocating him. No cover. No perfection. Just me.

"You have always been beautiful," he said to my stripped reflection. "But you are more beautiful now than I have ever seen you." I knew his words had nothing to do with my reflection.

My heart filled with an indescribable sensation that gathered me up and somehow, even with the future uncertain, gave me security.

We stood in silence, staring at each other's reflections. In that time of quiet, I thought about all Grant had, all the people in his life who were there for him without question, all those who loved and cherished and appreciated him. I thought about how, as much as he did have, he still wanted me.

"I like you," I said. "I didn't think I liked you when we first met."

"I'm pretty sure you hated me from that first night."

"'Hate' is a strong word."

He lifted his eyebrows.

"Okay, maybe I hated your mustache, but I think a part of me was irritated because you were the person I was trying to be."

"You were trying to be a man with a freaking awesome mustache?"

I hip-bumped him, and we both laughed. But I wasn't done. My feelings for him had remained tucked away, even from myself, until now, until this instant, when there was nothing left between us. The fear was still there, nipping at the edges of my brain, making the words somewhat halting, but it was now something I could overcome—because of him.

"You changed my life. You saved me. I owe you—"

He was shaking his head, hard and with purpose. And then he turned toward me, looked into my unlined eyes.

"Me?" He shook his head again. "No. Don't you ever attribute such amazing feats of strength to me. You didn't need me; I didn't save you. All this"—he pointed to my chest—"was right here. Always. *You* did this. *You* are the hero. You are *my* hero. All you needed was someone to show you it was possible, that you could. And maybe I can take some credit for that, but everything else, Penelope, is on you. 'Very little is needed to make a happy life; it is all within yourself, in your way of thinking.'" I squeezed his hand. "Anything is possible, to anyone at any time, but you decide if and when you believe that and what to make of it when you do. I didn't do that for you. You did."

"Grant."

"That first night we met, when you hated me, you know?" I rolled my eyes, and he smiled. "You'd just left everything and started over when you realized you needed to. You were doing it all. *All.* And I'd been focused on doing it one way. There is more than one way to live and be happy. You taught me that. That's why I bought Deanna's property. *You* changed *me.*"

His words wrapped around me and lifted me off the floor, suspended above my body, immune from time and place.

I didn't know how to respond, so I responded with an unburied truth: "I want to marry you."

"I want to marry you too."

I shook my head. "I'm serious. I want to marry you right now. I've been so afraid my entire life, so afraid to lose, that I've missed out on everything. And I've just now realized life isn't about holding back. It's about holding on."

I looked around the room, a bathroom, but I was going to do it anyway. I went over to the shower curtain, unhooked one of the rings holding the fabric across the tub. I turned back to him, got on my knees, and held out . . . a shower curtain ring. I felt incredibly silly and second-guessed myself when my knees hit the *bathroom* rug. But I thought about him bringing me that green tea and dropping to his knees all those months ago, even though he barely knew me, even though Chad was half-naked and staring him down, just to get what he wanted, no matter how he looked.

We'd been dating for approximately two months, but we'd known each other for near eight, and it felt like so much longer. But no matter how long it had been, it was enough.

"Grant, will you marry me?"

He joined me on the floor. "Penelope, yes, I will marry you." He wrapped his arms around me, holding on as our breathing synchronized.

He didn't ask me if I was sure. We didn't talk about what came next or the sorrow at the periphery of our happiness. We didn't discuss diagnoses or treatments. We didn't look with longing at the future we might or might not have.

Instead, I inhaled his scent, the essence of nature.

My fingers ran across his skin.

I gasped when his hands moved against mine, across my shoulders, to my upper back, to the clasp of my dress. The heat from the zipper moving down my back made me shiver.

As the dress parted, he peeled the damp fabric from my body and moaned as his eyes scanned me from head to knees—makeup-less, in the black matching bra and panty set I'd put on over twenty-four hours ago, still wearing exactly eighty-one pearls.

Then he kissed me, a slow, steady kiss that lingered on my lips even as his mouth trailed down my neck and chest. He groaned when he made it to the top of my bra, his hands replacing his mouth as he gently ran a finger over the lacy black fabric. My heart stretched in my chest, underneath his touch. I didn't need anything to hold me together, but I wanted those hands on me, on every part of me, as I let every part go. His palms followed the curve of my sides until his thumbs rested on the barely there waistband across my hips. My whole body warmed when the tips of his fingers circled my waist and then dropped to graze my inner thigh.

He moved to my eyes, his gaze so heated the whole room caught flame. And then he pulled me to my feet, and as he lifted me off the ground and into his arms, he whispered, "I've wanted to do this for a very long time."

I flicked my tongue against his earlobe as he carried me across the hall to his bedroom, unconcerned that we might run into the owners of this house.

And behind that solid, wooden door, under a flannel comforter and beside rustic cabin decor, we lived in the only moment we had, the only one we were promised, the only one anyone can ever be promised.

Twice.

CHAPTER 47
LIFE REALIZATION #21: I MIGHT BE CAPABLE OF HOMICIDE

Over the next couple of weeks, I tried hard not to think about losing the one thing I so desperately did not want to lose, which took constant redirecting as Grant underwent a flurry of tests, lab work, and minor surgical procedures to improve his chances of chemotherapy success. We found out that his cancer wasn't "resectable." In other words, it couldn't be cut out because the tumor involved his liver's artery and vein. We were told to prepare ourselves for a long and potentially ugly battle. Though, according to the doctors, he was doing surprisingly well. I hated the word "surprisingly." It meant they hadn't expected him to do well.

But if anyone was going to kick cancer's butt, it was Grant.

"I need you to prepare yourself, Penelope." Grant had turned to me, crinkling the thin white paper on the exam table we were both sitting on, with an expression so severe my stomach flipped. "It's possible I'll lose the one thing that defines our relationship." He leaned over as my chest vibrated with worried anticipation, and then he whispered, "The stache."

I let out an exasperated sigh and nearly shoved him off the table.

The oncologist had laughed. "Some people lose their hair on FOLFIRINOX, some don't." Like so many medical terms we'd been forced to learn over the past few weeks, this was yet another horrid acronym.

Grant had grabbed my hand and squeezed. We were getting through it one step at a time, and with Devina's help; she understood what it was like to go through cancer treatment. She'd beaten the odds, and she constantly encouraged us both.

I wouldn't say I was doing well, but I coped in the ways that suited me particularly: riding my bicycle religiously and using numbers in two ways. First, I'd turned most of the hospital staff into various digits; then, as Devina had suggested, I made spreadsheets and lists, documenting Grant's treatment schedule with precision and accuracy, and learning about pancreatic cancer.

"There will be times you'll feel helpless," Devina had told me, "but education and organization are your friends. You're a businesswoman. Lean into your strengths."

I'd done exactly that, and she'd been right. It had helped. Unfortunately, that meant learning statistics, things like only 20 to 30 percent of stage-one pancreatic cancer patients will be alive in five years.

I scared myself with the numbers. I soothed myself with the numbers. I was up and down like ocean waves. One minute, I was a confident mermaid swimming in Grant's optimism; the next, I was a drowning diver, ready to be eaten by the sharks, the facts that defied the optimism.

When someone's time has a known end, you tend to cling tighter than before, which was what we were all doing today, preparing for a Saturday-morning group ride together.

The November air had a bite to it, chilling us until we'd started moving. Erin, Beau, and Deanna had joined our regular riding group. I'd tried to cancel this particular ride because of the dark circles painting the skin under Grant's eyes, but he'd wanted to go. And I wouldn't deny him what he wanted, not now, because I didn't know when he would stop asking. I'd tasked myself with watching him in such a way that he didn't know I was watching him. So here we were, in the cold, staring at a long, flat road ahead, surrounded by trees and patches of grass and relative quiet.

"Let's talk wedding plans as we ride." Deanna rubbed her hands together.

"Yes, let's!" Erin said.

Beau rode back toward William and Grant, and I wanted to follow.

"I don't want a big wedding, you guys."

Deanna's plans had grown in size and number ever since she'd heard about my proposal.

Her eyes glittered. "But—"

"No. Grant and I agreed. A simple ceremony back at Chuck's cabin the week before Christmas. Only family, except Chuck and Celia because it's their cabin and Chuck's ordained." I was apparently weird for thinking a wedding was a private thing, love shared between two people. I didn't understand why everyone wanted to make a public spectacle of it.

The road was mostly deserted, so we were able to fan out a bit and keep a conversation going.

"There are so many other people who are going to want to be there. What about Erin, Mere, Key—"

"Don't make Pen feel bad about not inviting me," Erin said. "If they invite one person, they have to invite them all. To spare feelings, they have to do it this way."

"Thank you for understanding, *Erin*," I said, hoping it would prompt Deanna to do the same, but she only huffed.

I covertly glanced back at Grant, hopefully making it look like I was only talking to Erin and not watching him. He'd moved slightly behind us to make room for a passing car. He was at the back of the pack. I slowed.

Deanna continued, "Wouldn't you be hurt if you weren't invited to Erin's real, fake wedding?"

"Pen will be at my wedding," Erin said before I responded. "Not the same thing. Have you told your mom, Pen?"

I sighed. "No."

"You should tell her," Deanna said.

"After." We'd had this conversation before, so I hoped my tone would encourage dropping the subject of Aurora. I was afraid of what she'd do if she knew. It was a risk I wasn't willing to take.

"Flowers?" Deanna questioned, and I wondered if she'd already picked out oversize bouquets.

"Nature. Chuck's cabin will have trees on a carpet of fallen leaves. Done."

"*Bare* trees towering above a carpet of old, slimy, trampled sludge. How about ivory roses and dusty miller with sprigs of berries? You know who could put together a beautiful arrangement?"

"Keyondra? She's helping me with something else."

Deanna was relentless. "She can still do flowers."

Keyondra was helping me with Grant's third wedding gift. Grant thought our first dance at the reception was going to be to Etta James's "At Last." Little did he know I was planning to surprise him with three solid minutes of complete and utter embarrassment; I was going to shuffle.

While Erin and Deanna talked about my dress, two riders passed us. Grant was now behind William and Beau, and I couldn't make out the expression on his face. I slowed again.

"Okay, what about music?" Deanna continued.

I inhaled. Too many things to think about. I had Grant and my clients. End of story. "The soft chirp of birds?"

"You mean the screech of vultures ripping up the flesh of a dead deer in the woods?"

"Deanna!" Erin shouted.

"I'll bring a Bluetooth speaker," Deanna decided, unfazed. "Actually, I think Celia plays the violin. And then there's the reception. You *are* going to let me throw you a party afterward, right? Grant already said yes, so there's really no stopping me. We'll have it at my house."

"And you wouldn't have thrown a party if he'd said no?" She had no idea that the party was going to be in the venue hall in her new B and B, and I loved that she didn't know.

"Of course not, but I have to at least pretend to care about your feelings on my big day—I mean *your* big day."

I rolled my eyes. I wanted to be married to Grant. We didn't know how much time we had together, and I didn't want to waste any of it planning a wedding. But then it hit me, why this wedding was so important to Deanna. It was a distraction and a thing she could do for her brother, the only thing she could do.

"Tell you what," I said, looking out at the trees just feet away from us. "Do whatever you want. As long as I don't have to make any decisions." *This* was something I could do for her.

"Wedding guests?"

I shrugged. "Whatever."

Her excited squeal scared me a little. I'd regret this.

She huffed. "Why is this ride so hard? It looked easy when we started."

"This is a false flat," I told her, which I'd learned from Grant the last time we'd done this route. "It looks flat and unthreatening, but there's an imperceptible gradient that gives you a real workout."

A sardonic laugh fell out of my mouth. Life was like a false flat. It looked smooth and easy and straightforward, but it was a steady, arduous climb to the finish, leaving you haggard and out of breath.

A white Honda flew past, going too fast beside a group of cyclists on the narrow-shouldered road.

"That's why I don't ride!" Deanna shouted from behind me.

I looked back, stopped.

"Where's Grant?" I asked.

No answer.

Several seconds passed.

William and Beau came up beside us.

No Grant.

A chill tightened my skin "Where's Grant?" I asked, louder this time.

"He told us to go on," William said. "I listened because you remember what happened the last time I didn't."

Grant had given us all a lecture about not treating him like he was an invalid.

My heart pounded in my chest. My legs pedaled back. Sweat trickled down my neck.

I saw Gaia first, mangled in a heap on the gravel shoulder. And then I saw him, lying in the grass a yard away from the road.

Still.

A scream curled in the back of my throat. I threw my bicycle and ran.

CHAPTER 48
LIFE REALIZATION #22: IT'S ALWAYS SOMETHING

The cold, white tiles.

The muffled voices.

The smell of rubbing alcohol and floor cleaner and dinner trays.

The slight squeak of a passing bed, someone else going for imaging.

The laughter that didn't belong.

The silent sobs coming from the person crouched against the wall because she just couldn't stand up anymore: me.

Grant hadn't been killed by the white Honda that had ripped his bicycle out from under him, but while he was getting his fourteen stitches, I tried to find life inside this hospital, our life. Because this accident was *one more thing*, and I felt like I was dying inside. How could we live within the confines of this diagnosis, chemo and radiation interrupting what little life we had left?

I went into the bathroom, where an onslaught of anxiety left no room for the food inside my stomach. When I was done, but still sunken inside, I stepped back into the hall.

A young girl wearing a beanie was being pushed past me in a wheelchair. Her gown fell off one bony shoulder, and before her mom could pull it back up again, I saw the bandage on her upper-right chest. It was a port. I knew because Grant had one in the exact same place. A little implanted reservoir, just under the skin, that connected to a vein so a chemo patient wouldn't have to continually get stuck by needles. The nurses could "access the port" instead.

I started to turn back into the bathroom, hit by another wave of nausea, but the pale girl looked up at me with her watery blue eyes and smiled. Then she went back to talking to her mother, a casual discussion about a dance next month.

They were living, laughing. They were here at this hospital, merging outside life with hospital life, but they weren't making a distinction. They were just living wherever they were. I wanted to follow them, to observe. I wanted to take notes, make a spreadsheet. I wanted to know how to do it when everything fell apart.

⁓

Later, when I carried thoughts of that mother and daughter into Grant's room on the fourth floor, where he'd been transferred so they could watch him for the night, he was crying. I'd never seen him cry over his illness, and it scared me.

I ran to his bed.

But he wasn't crying over his injuries or illness. He was crying because he'd lost his best friend. Gaia was gone, totaled. In the middle of Grant telling me about his plan to put her in storage because he couldn't bear the thought of scrapping her, there was a knock on the door.

Dr. Killjoy, Grant's oncologist, breezed in, smelling of hand sanitizer and leather, and told Grant he shouldn't ride anymore.

"It's not safe or wise," he said, his tone matter-of-fact, like he wasn't crushing Grant's heart in his oversize fist.

I hated Dr. Killjoy. What kind of oncologist has a name like that anyway? That was his *real* name. But I'd researched it. He was the best in Nashville.

"I'm not going to ride either," I told Grant once the intelligent jerk had closed the door.

"Umm. That's not a good idea."

I shrugged. He was right. I would probably live to regret the promise. Riding was like breathing for me. Could I promise to stop breathing?

"I don't care. I'm doing it." I meant it. I'd stop breathing for him.

As darkness crept through the small hospital window and the halls quieted, Grant motioned me over to his narrow hospital bed. Hip to hip, we could almost pretend we were home, all but for the occasional interruption of the nurses, who checked his grip strength and asked him the date and who the president was—apparently concussion protocol. It made me think back to my own concussion, when I hadn't been able to remain in the hospital for even five seconds. I wasn't the same person, though I did have to regularly suppress the urge to ask him if he really needed to be here. I was going to attempt to live where we were, wherever that took us.

"I want to go to a dark-sky park," Grant said.

I shifted from lying on a patch of uninjured shoulder so I could see his face.

"Then we'll go. Isn't there a whole community dedicated to keeping the sky dark in California?"

He smiled and nodded. "There is. We'll go there if you prefer. I don't care where, as long as I have you and the open sky."

He reached over, let his finger move down the side of my face. I grabbed his hand and held it in mine.

"Some July, we'll go to Spain. There's a lavender festival in Brihuega every year, midmonth. One of my friends arranges his visits to his parents' house in Spain around the festival; it's *that* good." He moved his free hand in front of us as we pictured the fragrant, budding lavender fields and the warm sun on our skin. "They celebrate the blooming of the lavender with all kinds of activities: painting exhibits, hot-air balloon rides, paragliding, tours through the fields, cooking master classes. We have to go."

"Then we'll go there too."

"While we're in Spain, we'll visit the Puente Nuevo, New Bridge, in Ronda. I've always wanted to see the city separated by a gorge. From what I hear, it's a magnificent view." He closed one eye. "Though they're also known for bullfighting, so we probably won't want to stay too long."

"That sounds wonderful. The lavender and the cooking classes. Not the bulls."

"Not a fan of bulls?"

"Oh, I'm a huge fan of bulls, and bullfighting for that matter. I thought you wouldn't be interested. But if you are, by all means, let's—"

He laid his head back against the pillow. "We aren't going to see the bulls."

My fingertips played over his forearm. "Suit yourself."

"But maybe we'll go to Cappadocia, Turkey, instead. A city cut into the hills." He paused, picturing it. "I hear they're planning to start a new tradition of hot-air balloon rides with champagne breakfasts."

"Mmmm. Then we must go there."

"Then we'll of course have to hit all the most talked-about bike routes. Maybe we'll start three hours southwest of London. Isle of Wight, Great Britain? Huh? Huh?" He wiggled his eyebrows. "Rolling hills beside dramatic seas and long curvy roads that'll take us past both cliffs and lush green valleys."

I suppressed a smile. "Were you a travel agent in your former life?"

"I'd be a good one, don't you think?"

"Only if the next thing you were going to suggest is the Route des Vins."

"Mmmm. I like the way you say that." My accent was horrible, and we both knew it. "Tell me more."

I arranged words in my head. "Vineyards grace the landscape, known not only for their luscious wine selection but for their stunning, jaw-dropping scenery as you pedal through the multimile route from France into Germany."

He nodded, an impressed flare to his mustache. "A little over the top with the whole 'jaw-dropping' bit, but I definitely want to go."

"You knew about that one before I told you, didn't you?"

"Can you reach my laptop?" He pointed toward the rolling table near my side of the bed. Deanna had dropped his computer off.

I retrieved his laptop, pulled it onto the bed, opened it, and entered his password. The first thing that popped up was a spreadsheet where Grant had started a list numbered one to twenty-three.

"Check out number seven."

I scanned until I reached number seven, where he'd typed the words "Route des Vins."

I looked at him. "You have this all listed. You're serious." When had he done this? My eyes moved back to the screen, where Grant's imagination took us on bike rides that spanned the globe.

No.	Location	Notes
7	Route des Vins	Vineyards. Wine tasting.
8	Sun Moon Lake, Taiwan	Low-key, easy terrain.
9	Route 10 in Holland	One of the best bike trails in the world.
10	The Udaipur trail in India	Immersed in the people and villages of India.
11	Easter Island, Chile	Plan a bunch of touristy things to do in addition to riding.

"These sound amazing," I said, my voice shaking. Reality reached all the way down until it gripped my bones and squeezed. All of these places *did* sound amazing, but we would never go. He hadn't made this list for *us*; he'd made it for me. Here I was, trying to find a way for us both to live together, and he was making plans for my life without him. My body shook.

He put a hand over mine.

"But you know where I'd like to go most of all?" he asked.

I couldn't speak. If I spoke, I'd start screaming, cursing cancer and God.

"Let's go to our place. Close your eyes, Penelope, and think about our Sunset Rock in Chattanooga." His voice was low and comforting. "A romantic picnic. We're looking out at the trees and the city lights."

"And we won't dig our food out of the ground because no one in their right mind digs up a romantic picnic dinner." I was trying—so hard I was trying.

"And we won't dig our . . . hey!"

We closed our eyes on the mountain, breathing in the cool, evening air under the open sky that trailed down to a city waking at dusk, and we fell asleep, the two of us curled together in each other's arms, the wind gently sweeping over us.

CHAPTER 49
LIFE REALIZATION #23: COLD CHERRY PIE IS STILL THE BEST DINNER EVER

Two weeks before the wedding, my body was covered in a layer of cold sweat. Butch, a large muscled number five, reached for my hand, helped me to a sitting position. I'd been with him for twelve hours. It felt like twelve hours, but it was actually about forty-five minutes. Forty-five minutes of complete torture, but wedding present one of three for Grant was complete, and I still had two weeks to find the right lingerie, the second gift.

Butch asked me if I wanted to see—he looked pleased—and I looked down at my lower abdomen. I'd walked into this tattoo parlor, only able to handle the thought of needles because Grant was at a chemo infusion, accompanied by Devina, the only one I'd let in on my secret tattoo gift.

As Butch instructed me on bandaging and keeping the area clean, I thought about the evening to come. Grant and I were scheduled to have a night in with a movie, popcorn, candy, pie, and ice cream, the works. Then we'd celebrate his good lab results the way we celebrated all his little medical victories these days—after good food, *really* good sex.

The man was hot in bed, or maybe *we* were hot in bed. Anyway . . . *hot*, and not just in bed, all over. *All over.* He might not have been able to ride Gaia, but he could definitely ride other things.

I'd pictured Grant pulling my shirt up to reveal the inky masterpiece on my abdomen and going wild. Now, I realized he'd lift my shirt up and see—a bandage. Much less sexy. Oh well, maybe it could work to my advantage. I could tease him with what was underneath, drive him wild with anticipation.

I'd worked myself up on the way to the condo. (We'd been jumping back and forth between our two places, trying to decide where to live as a married couple.) But as soon as I walked into the living room, what I saw sitting on Grant's couch completely extinguished the fire smoldering in my lower regions.

My mother.

As I stood there, my mouth hanging open like a cartoon character's, Grant told me that the business trip he'd gone on had actually been a trip to my mother's house. He'd wanted to go alone; now I knew why. He told me that life was too short not to try. He told me if he'd had another chance with *his* mother, nothing would've kept him from it. And then he walked out the door, leaving me alone *with my mother.*

How dare he! *His* mother was not *my* mother . . . but the pain in Aurora's eyes bent my knees until we were face to face on the couch.

"I'm sorry," she started right away, as if she'd been rehearsing the words and needed to get them out before they left her mind. Tears fell into her expensive, cranberry-colored sweater. I'd never seen that happen before; I was transfixed. "I thought I was doing the right thing." She shook her head, squared her shoulders, and blinked away the tears.

"I need to tell you this without blubbering. When Grant told me that you were getting married, and I didn't know . . ." She put her hand over her mouth. "I knew I had to do something. I knew it that day I watched you pull out of your driveway without shoes, when I was trying to hold everything together. But I didn't know what to do or how to do it."

Was she here to talk me out of marrying Grant?

She reached for my hand, but shock had numbed me, and I couldn't grip hers back. She pulled her hand into her lap and held her own.

"When Grant came to the Cities, he told me I needed to stop holding it all in, that I needed to talk about whatever was inside me."

Grant went to talk to my icy mother, the mother who'd told me to leave him.

"But that's how I've managed, by holding it all in." She was speaking in her usual analytical tone, softened slightly, and it didn't fit with the words she was saying. "And I couldn't understand *how* he knew. I'd spent my whole life making sure everyone thought I was fine. And then I wondered if *you* knew, and then I wondered who *else* knew."

She paused.

"What happens when I let it all go?" Her voice went shaky, but she wasn't crying.

I'd asked that same question over and over again the past months. I couldn't believe she was asking it now.

You can't know, I wanted to tell her.

"But that's all there is left, isn't there?" she went on. "That's what I've decided, at least. I might lose you if I tell you, but I'll definitely lose you if I don't. That's how I lost Tif, but I never tried to get her back."

Her voice cracked, like her throat had been stripped. I knew that feeling too.

"Do you want some water?" I spoke for the first time.

She nodded, and I went to Grant's kitchen, filled a glass, wished he were here, then returned to his living room and handed my mother the water. She downed half of it, and her hand shook as she placed it on the table beside the couch.

I wanted to reach out to this very real version of my mother, but I was scared she'd fall back into herself, and I wanted more time with the softened person who lived behind the hard shell.

"There's no excuse; there is only explanation. It might not make a difference."

Tell me.

I still couldn't speak, but I wanted her to go on.

Tell me.

She inhaled, closed her eyes, and when she opened them again, her face was firm. "Tif and I had a brother, Samuel. Sam."

Sam? No, that was wrong. My mother had one sister, Tif, the only family she had until she didn't.

She nodded, like the disbelief on my face was something she had to answer.

Tell me.

"When I was fifteen, I snuck out to a party my parents had explicitly forbidden. But I was infatuated with this guy Ryan, one of Sam's friends. He was cocky and disgusting, and he wanted me at that party, so I went. At some point, I wanted to go home as badly as I'd wanted to get there, but Ryan and I had both been drinking, so I called Sam, who was seventeen. He could drive, and I begged him to come get me. He'd told me to stay away from Ryan, so he was furious and wouldn't come." She paused long enough to reach for her water glass, and a quarter of it splashed onto her jeans, but neither of us acknowledged it.

Maybe I was wrong when I'd said my mother was on Grant's couch. My mother didn't have a past, didn't have a brother named Sam, would never talk like this.

"What did you do?" I asked, suspended in this moment.

She curled her fingers around the glass.

"I took Ryan's keys." She was looking past me as if at a screen that was playing out her memories. "And I drove his car. I couldn't stop crying because I felt so guilty. I'd done all the things I never should've done. And then, the tears kept me from seeing the other car on the road." My mother started crying then, crying with her past, fifteen-year-old self. Crying for the first time—ever.

A cold sweat broke out on my body because suddenly I knew where this was going. One thing she *had* told me when I was a kid was that my grandparents had been killed in a car accident when my mother was fifteen, by a drunk driver.

"The alcohol kept me from reacting," she went on, her voice robotic now. "I slammed into that car. I was fine. Not a scratch. Nothing. But I killed the person in the other vehicle, the old, teal BMW Sam had been given on his sixteenth birthday." A long pause. "I killed Sam," she whispered. "He'd decided to come get me after all. I killed my brother."

No. I held my face in my hands as the words crashed into me, as if I'd been there to feel the impact. The sight was vivid behind my eyes. A flash of teal caught in headlights. The crunch of metal on metal. The thud of a chest hitting a steering wheel. The silence of life extinguished. And then the screams that surely followed and likely lived in my mother's head.

"I told you your grandparents had died in a car accident," she somehow went on. "They didn't die *in* it. But I killed them, too, when I killed Sam. Technically speaking, my mother killed herself four months later. And I didn't know how to navigate a relationship with my father after he stopped speaking to me, and now he's passed. If I hadn't . . ."

The glass cracked in my mother's hands, and we both stared down at her lap, where blood dripped from her palm. I grabbed a wad of tissues and encouraged her to get up to tend to her injury, but she shook her head.

She held the tissues against the cut. "If I don't finish now, I might lose my nerve." Her eyes clung to my face, devoid of expectation. "If I hadn't done all the things I shouldn't have done, we would've stayed a family. You don't get over that, Penelope. Brandon was taken from me, from us, because *I* had taken my brother. Tif tried, God love her, she tried to tell me it wasn't my fault, but I didn't want forgiveness. I didn't deserve it." She glanced at me, looked away, looked back like she was forcing herself to keep eye contact.

"And I ruined a good man. Your father. He loved us, but he couldn't cope, especially after I convinced him it was my fault. He, too, tried to tell me it wasn't, but he was broken, and I was convincing. I stayed. I cared for him as he drank himself into oblivion and cheated because I deserved it. It was my punishment. When he was with someone else or drinking, he wasn't with me, and he could forget. I could *never* forget. And after he died . . . *he died.*"

Her head bent forward until I couldn't see her face. Her body shook, and I wasn't sure I could keep looking at her. I didn't know how to digest this new information. It weighed me down, kept me in place, but something was moving inside, a slide puzzle righting itself, the picture that had been distorted for so long finally clearing.

"Nearly everyone I love is gone, and it's all my fault," she whispered.

Before I reacted, she slid to her knees, narrowly avoiding a shard of the glass she'd crushed in her hands.

"You're the only one left, Penelope. Pretending it's all fine isn't working anymore. I'm pretending harder than ever, and I'm losing you anyway. How do I stop losing you?" Her last words were louder than the rest, so full of anguish that a piece of me ripped in two. I'd come near hating my mother, resenting her and wishing she were someone else. She *was* someone else. I just never knew it; maybe she never knew it.

Her head remained bowed. Her question hung in the air.

How do I stop losing you?

This was something else I'd been asking. About Brandon, about Grant, about myself.

How do I stop losing you?

I didn't know the answer to that question. But without a word, I reached down and lifted her up. I led her to Grant's kitchen, where I ran her hands under cold water and helped her bandage them.

Then I opened the refrigerator and pulled out the cold cherry pie that I was supposed to be eating with the man I would marry in two weeks.

In the silence of Grant's clean kitchen, my mother and I ate pie.

CHAPTER 50
LIFE REALIZATION #24: ALWAYS PUT PANTS ON BEFORE YOU CRY

"This is it," Grant said. "Tomorrow we get married. You're really going to go through with this?"

"*You're* really going to go through with this?"

We were back at Chuck's cabin in a room with a large, carved canopy bed and a bathroom attached, settling in before Grant and I became husband and wife. Deanna, William, Chuck, and Celia were here, but everyone else was scheduled to show up tomorrow evening. Aurora was staying in the nearest hotel. I wanted to forgive her, but I needed time.

I'd asked Hannah to tell me what to do because wanting my mother in my life, after everything, seemed wrong. She told me the following:

1.   There's nothing wrong with me wanting my mother in my life.
2.   Sometimes people are too damaged to react logically; the past obscures the present, so what you think you're doing isn't what you're doing at all.
3.   A child never stops loving their parents, not fully, and you can love through hate.
4.   Love is stronger than hate.
5.   Love is stronger than anything, can overcome anything.

6. It's *my* life, *my* decision.

7. I need boundaries.

Grant pulled me over to him and kissed me, his slightly scraggly mustache tickling my nose. How could I ever live without that mustache tickling my nose?

Is love stronger than death?

"I'm going to shave it," he said.

"Your mustache?" I immediately shook my head. How had he known I was thinking about his mustache? "No."

"She's not the same." He held out a razor. "Henrietta leaves on her own terms."

I tried to smile but frowned instead.

He shook his head. "I don't want you crying on my wedding eve."

"Can I cry tomorrow at your wedding?"

He wrapped his arms around me. "We'll both cry tomorrow. But tonight, after we shave Henrietta, we make love. Show me again."

I lifted my shirt, exposing the onggi, the little kimchi fermentation pot I'd had tattooed in the same spot Grant had his blueprint. I'd only been able to hide it from him for two days, and then he kept asking me to see it. It had turned him on even more than I'd hoped.

He groaned. "Needles? For me?"

"Turns out there's not a lot I wouldn't do for you, Grant Miles."

He licked his lips like I was dinner. "On second thought, you *might* cry from pleasure tonight because I'm going to try something new. New face, new sex—"

Someone knocked lightly on the door.

I looked from the door back to him. "I'm not into threesomes. Unless it's Jason Statham at that door, and then I'll think about it."

He shoved me onto the bed. "No, gross! That's my sister."

"Please forget I said anything."

"Gladly. And for the record, I'm not sharing you with anyone. I texted Deanna, asking her to come in here. I think now's a good time to have that talk. Get it out of the way before the wedding."

I nodded. I couldn't take another "talk," though, especially if I wasn't supposed to cry.

He opened the door, and Deanna breezed in, arms crossed. "I'm kinda busy preparing for tomorrow, since *snow* is forecasted and we're doing this outside and I need to refine my five backup plans. Snow. Flood. Tornado. This is Tennessee weather, fickle as—"

"Deanna," Grant interrupted.

"Just remember that as you keep me in here." Her voice quieted. She knew.

I hurt for her.

"I'll let you two have a few minutes. I'm taking a shower." I gave Grant a soft peck on the lips and shut myself in the bathroom, avoiding eye contact with both of them.

"You feeling okay?" I heard Deanna ask, hesitation in her voice.

I tried not to listen, but the door was thin. I removed my makeup with a tissue as their voices floated through, almost as if I were still in the room.

"Couldn't be better," Grant replied.

"This was the perfect place for the wedding."

I pulled off my leggings and reached for the knob inside the wood-framed glass shower, to warm it up before I removed the rest of my clothes. Then I realized my shower cap was still in my bag, beside the bed. I couldn't shower without it. Tomorrow was my wedding, and humidity was the devil.

I flattened my palms against the slab of wood serving as a vanity and eyed my toothbrush. I'd brush my teeth.

"Deanna," he said. "The end is going to be . . . hard. For me, sure, but for you . . ."

I pulled my hand back from the faucet, waited as a blob of tooth-paste fell onto a knot in the wood.

"I thought you were going to be positive."

I wanted to close my ears, to turn the rain-style shower on, get in and pretend this conversation wasn't happening, but I couldn't. In my oversize sweatshirt and panties, I slid down to the flat rug that was edged with little white trees and wrapped my arms around my legs, my toothbrush forgotten.

"How we deal with death is at least as important as how we deal with life," I heard Grant say. "That's what Captain Kirk says, anyway."

"You know I hate *Star Wars*."

"*Star Trek*. But seriously, there's a difference between positive and realistic. If you're too in the moment, then you might avoid planning for the future, and you should always plan for the future."

"We were supposed to grow old and gray together." Her voice rose. "Me, you, William, and now Pen. That's how it should be. That's how I pictured it." I heard a thud, like she'd slammed her fist against something. "That's what I want. I want your positivity, your advice, your strength. I want my brother!" she nearly yelled as I completely lost it on the floor. Not crying was too tall of a request. "I don't want to lose you, Grant."

"I don't want to lose you either, Deanna."

I silently sobbed, my heart inching out of my chest, tears slipping into the bathroom rug.

I don't want to lose you either, Grant.

How do I tease right now out of all the forever we might not get? How do I stop thinking about what I'm going to lose before I even get it?

How am I going to do this?

Silence pulsed beyond the door as I attempted to slow my tears, until Grant said, "Don't think for a second I didn't need you as much as you needed me. Not long after Mom and Dad died, Aunt Jamie tried to convince me to let you come live with them. Told me you'd be better off. Because she said that kids learn not what you teach them, but what they see, which was too much on my shoulders. She was wrong. I needed you, D, to make me who I am because I knew if I didn't get it right, they'd all be watching, waiting to take you away from me. But most of all, I became who I am because I knew you were watching."

"We needed each other." Deanna's words were muffled but still audible.

"You're going to be okay, sister." His words were adamant. I visualized him looking into his sister's face. "You're going to be okay," he said again. Then he told her to say it.

"I'm going to be okay," she repeated.

"Say it again but mean it this time."

"I'm going to be okay."

"Again."

This time, I silently said it with her.

I'm going to be okay. I didn't believe it for a second.

"Deanna." He paused. "You're going to be okay."

"I'm going to be okay," she repeated again.

I lay down on the rug, my fingernails ripping at the blue loops of fabric.

"And when the time comes you feel like you aren't going to be okay anymore, remember this, when I held your face, and then repeat that phrase for as long as you have to until you are again. And when that's not enough, when you can't do it for yourself, do it for me."

I heard her say she would.

I was jelly.

"This is what Penelope never got to have. There was no one there to keep her going." He paused, then continued: "Promise me you'll be her family too."

"I can't promise something *will be* that already is. Pen has found home, and I'm not letting her go anywhere."

Did Grant know I was listening? The shower had never turned on, and surely they could hear my sobs. Noise traveled both ways.

This was confirmed when he called my name. After I feebly said, "Yes," he opened the door, and he and Deanna bent down to wrap me in their arms. And the three of us held on to each other.

"I shouldn't have been listening." I sucked in breath, my voice too high through tears.

"I told you not to cry on my wedding eve." Grant brushed my hair back from my face, and they both pulled away slightly.

"Life is about balance," he continued. "Without the bad things, we have no idea how good the good things are." He smiled at me, then lifted me to my feet. "Now, help me give Deanna her present."

She put a hand to her chest. "A present? For me?"

Grant grabbed the silver bag with the single piece of tissue I'd talked him into and held it out for his sister. "Merry Christmas."

She eyed him as she glanced into the bag, then pulled out a small, framed picture of a black-and-white building, a picture I'd taken of Grant with his final, finished project several days ago.

She ran her finger around the inscription on the frame.

To: The greatest chef I've ever known. From: The greatest architect who ever lived.

Her eyebrows knit together, and Grant and I waited for Deanna to read the sign on the building above the door: **DEANNA'S B AND B.**

"Is this—" She stopped speaking, looked down at the picture again. "Is this real? This is mine?"

"You know anyone else named Deanna who wanted her own B and B because she's a kick-ass chef, *and* who has a kick-ass brother who would build it for her?"

She threw the picture on the bed and wrapped Grant in a hug. "I don't know what to say." Over her shoulder, he winked at me, then looked pained and mouthed, *Help me.*

"Say you love it." His voice was strained, like she was cutting off his oxygen. "Say you love me. Say whatever you want. Just don't hug me again."

"I thought you didn't want me to waste my time with a B and B. What changed your mind?"

He proceeded to tell her how he'd found the place, how I'd inspired it. Then, he looked at me with admiration in his eyes, and it made me forget, for just a second, that I wasn't wearing pants.

Deanna squealed. "I have this brand-spanking-new B and B because Pen's a kick-ass businesswoman?"

"My fiancée *is* a kick-ass businesswoman, isn't she? And yes, I wouldn't have done all this if not for her."

"This is nuts." She sat on the bed and grabbed her head in disbelief. He shook his head. "This is right."

"I'm forever in debt to you both." She hopped up and headed for the door. "My repayment starts tomorrow evening, by giving you the wedding you both deserve." She moved out of the room and started down the hall, calling out, "I'm going to kill William if he didn't bring my cream-colored satchel with the cloak!"

CHAPTER 51
LIFE REALIZATION #25: CLOAK WEARING IS UNDERRATED

In less than four thousand seconds, I would be Mrs. Penelope Miles. The mirror reflected a tall woman, hair in soft waves—flat iron, followed by a curling wand I'd borrowed from Deanna—gently pulled away from my face in a classy ponytail and accented on the left with a wiry, bejeweled barrette. A swipe of foundation, blush, lip gloss, and my dedicated eye regimen with added sparkle, and I'd transformed into a bride.

A bride.

Outdoors in December, at a friend's wooded cabin, with the sun setting between the bare trees and just beyond a smattering of clouds: it felt right. For the first time in my life, I wasn't scared. Okay, that was a total lie; I was shaking and nauseated, terrified of the future. But even with my stomach fluttering and a light sheen of nervous sweat on my skin, I didn't doubt I was making the exact right decision.

I went back into the bedroom, stepped into a white velvet off-the-shoulder number Deanna had picked for me. The dress was hugging my body in all the right places when the door inched open and Deanna walked in.

She put her hands to her mouth. "You look . . ."

I turned around. "Button me?"

"The buttons are decorative." She zipped the dress and spun me back to face her. "Pen." Tears in her eyes, she threw her arms around me, but then she pulled back and wagged her finger in my face. "Don't you cry. Your eye makeup is flawless. You're perfect."

"I'm not perfect."

"You're right. You need the cloak." She cradled the heavy white floor-length cloak, secured it around my shoulders, and adjusted the sable-fur-trimmed hood.

"Look." She pointed to the full-body mirror.

I scanned from my hair, down the formfitting dress, to the velvet pooled at my feet. I would've felt the same no matter what I was wearing. I was marrying the right man at the right time, even though so many other things were wrong. But I had to admit this dress and this kick-ass cloak made me feel like a woodland princess.

Deanna sniffled beside me. "I've always wanted to have an occasion to wear a cloak."

"I'll let you borrow it after the wedding."

"I bought my own. Now, stay right there, and I'll make sure everyone is in place. And the weather!"

She slipped out of the room. I inhaled deeply, and as I let it all blow out, she returned to the door.

"Come on, sister." She motioned me out of the bedroom, and we walked arm in arm to the living room, stopping only when the outdoor scene was framed in the large floor-to-ceiling windows at the front of Chuck's cabin.

My breath stuttered to a stop. Beyond the panes, the forest was dimly backlit by the golden glow of the nearly set sun. Twinkle lights were everywhere, wrapped around the bare trees, strung between the branches, nestled in tulle.

Chairs had been lined up on either side of a pathway, lit by a million flickering candles and strewn with poinsettia petals.

All the faces in the crowd were looking at me through the paned glass. Fred and Doris. Grant's biking crew. Keyondra and her skinny-ass

White fiancé Conner, Mere and Devon, Erin and Beau, Celia and her violin, everyone from the office (Lady Mama's hair was distractingly shaped into a tree), and Devina.

And then I saw the two people who really made this event surreal. My mother, sitting beside her sister. Grant had tracked Aunt Tif down in Bowling Green, Kentucky, a little over an hour from Nashville. She cried when she'd opened her door and recognized me. I couldn't believe she was here, at my wedding.

My wedding.

I wished my father and Brandon were here, but it was almost as if I sensed them, watching, smiling.

Chuck stood under the arch in his plaid suit, waiting to officiate the ceremony, and next to one of the two enormous bouquets of winter flowers—dusty miller with punches of red berries—stood a smiling William, holding . . . a chicken, a real, live chicken. My hands went to my mouth. William . . . was holding . . . wild Gloria, who had a tiny crown of flowers on her head. My wedding was perfect. How could it not be with a chicken, *the* chicken, as a guest?

The woods, the flowers, the lights, the music, the guests, the chicken—Deanna's vision come to life—it was straight out of a fairy tale, my fairy tale, which wasn't a fairy tale at all, just my life.

Every single bit of it vanished when Grant's eyes met mine. I was vaguely aware of a camera clicking, and I imagined what the picture would show: a beautiful man standing in the forest, looking at his bride just inside a window, everything blurred but the back of her head and the man's smiling, clean-shaven face. (I knew he'd be even more handsome without the mustache!)

I love you, I said into the room.

And he said it back, and I heard him as if he were standing in the room beside me.

This moment was worth everything that would come. This moment would fill my lifetime. This moment shone, overshadowed, guided, reassured. This moment was me and Grant.

"I want to get out there," I told Deanna, still holding Grant's gaze, but she was already gone. I vaguely registered her moving into position opposite William, beside where I would soon stand.

The elongated notes of Celia's violin drifted into the room and led me outside, into the late-evening air, where tiny glitter-like snowflakes danced from the sky and tickled my face as I walked past the candles and into the arms of the man waiting for me.

Chuck's voice rumbled beside us, saying the things you always heard at weddings, even though I'd never been to one.

Grant grabbed my hand, eased a forever band encircled with tiny diamonds onto my finger.

"Penelope, oh, my sweet Penelope." He touched my face. "You are the answer, the answer to every question, the answer to my call, the answer to my prayers. With you as my partner, I have no need for anything else. Not food, not water, not any other person." He looked into the audience. "No offense." Everyone laughed. What was he doing? We'd decided, up until this second, to make everything simple, to repeat after Chuck, *To have and to hold, till* . . .

"I love you with everything inside of me. I love who you are and who you have become. And I will love you forever, uninhibited by life or death, before or after, riding on a bicycle or standing still. And every time I look at you, I will be reminded that nothing is impossible." An icy crystalline snowflake landed on a tear running down his cheek and the two converged, one with nature. Damn him and his humor and his eloquence. We weren't supposed to be speaking heartfelt, heartbreaking, beautiful words, words held in my own tears and soaked up by the fur of my cloak.

"Thank you for being my wife, for rounding out the part of me I didn't know needed softening. Thank you for being you."

In front of everyone, we stared at each other, open, two people looking beyond the surface, diving into each other. The silence was full, full of nature, full of tears, full of promise, full of love, full of life, full of hope.

I smiled. "Jerk. Did you plan that?"

He shook his head. "It just came. When I saw you standing there, I couldn't let Chuck make all those promises for me. I wanted to make them myself."

My tears were no longer elegant but streamed down in a wave that threatened to wash me away. Grant held me in place.

I looked down, desperately wanting to say something beautiful in response. A candle flickered, and I gazed into it. "But I didn't prepare . . . all these people . . ."

He tilted my chin until our eyes met again. "What people?"

I inhaled, and they didn't all vanish, but they dimmed. "Grant, with you as my partner, I don't *want* anything else. I love you with everything inside of me, now and forever, even without your mustache. You are the . . . the spark that lit me. And every time I look at you, I will remember that life is complicated, precious, and worth all the hard work."

It wasn't everything, not even half, but it was true. Like the candles burning all around us, I'd been lit, altered, and I couldn't be unlit. The flame might come and go, but the change was permanent. Together, Grant and I shone, two lights that darkness could not overcome. And I didn't know what might happen next, but the path forward was illuminated because of us.

Why couldn't I have said *that* out loud.

I turned to Chuck. "Say the words."

He cocked a half smile and said the words.

Gloria let out a congratulatory screech as Grant slipped his arms under my cloak, pulled me against his body, and kissed me like no one was watching.

EPILOGUE
"YOU'RE ON YOUR OWN. AND YOU KNOW WHAT YOU KNOW. AND *YOU* ARE THE ONE WHO'LL DECIDE WHERE YOU GO . . ." —DR. SEUSS

Over two years. That's what we got. Grant did better than well, especially after we'd enrolled him into a clinical trial, where he was treated with a novel cancer drug. In the end, it wasn't even the cancer that got him. He developed a "hospital-acquired, antibiotic-resistant" infection after breaking his ankle. The end came swiftly after that. In a way, it was better. We remember him exactly as he was, Grant to the very end.

He didn't suffer; he barely declined. I'm sure the drugs had something to do with that, but I attribute most of his health to Gloria, our daughter. Turns out I was four weeks pregnant with her at our wedding.

Pregnancy equation:

Forty-eight hours with no birth control pills

+

blacking out

+

emotional overload because I'd found out the love of my life had cancer

×

a hot, sexy night when I had frizzy hair and was completely myself

=

a curly-headed, thankfully unmustached, pudgy newborn who'd turned into a spectacular little girl who loved architecture and Barbie dolls.

I was wrong when I'd said life was like a cake with all the right ingredients. Life isn't about having the right ingredients; it's about figuring out what to make when you're missing some.

I'd never wanted kids, never thought I could mother anyone. But Gloria was just the person I'd needed when I didn't think I could open my eyes the day after he died. I opened them for her. And then I kept opening them for her. The two of us had become inseparable.

And now, three months without him, Gloria wrapped her arms around my neck, her little body fitting seamlessly with mine as we walked into Deanna's house, where Deanna was making all of Grant's favorite unhealthy things: sticky cinnamon buns, homemade yeast rolls, pizza crust with cornmeal baked into the bottom. The warmth of her kitchen was like a hug from an old friend. As she kneaded the dough, I almost felt Grant's arm brushing past mine to dip his finger in icing. An ache started in my toes and worked its way to my eyes, climbing out in a single tear that stung.

When Deanna saw us, she dropped to Gloria's level and threw out her arms. Gloria promptly ran to her aunt. Then Deanna reached for me. She'd remained my right hand, before Gloria's birth and thereafter. She'd invested with me, and her business was so prosperous that she was contemplating a second space.

Erin, my dutiful, wildly successful, and very pregnant business partner, walked into the kitchen and whisked Gloria to the backyard, where William and Beau waited on the patio.

Erin and I had our own space now with an additional staff of two, and she was just finishing up her CFP certification. We still kept in touch with everyone from WeWork. I'd taken a month off, but now that I'd gone back, needing the distraction, Gloria came with me, content to sit in the play area Erin had created in the corner of my office. I hoped, by listening to client meetings, Gloria would learn she could do anything, even when everything and everyone told her she couldn't.

Once they were outside, Deanna picked a plain white envelope from the small desk in the corner. "Grant told me to give this to you three months after he died. I don't know what's in it."

My belly tightened, and shaking, I slipped the envelope into my purse.

As Deanna finished preparing the food, I watched William toss Gloria from one side of his lap to the other while Erin and Beau laughed. Profound thankfulness settled over me. I was determined to give Gloria what I hadn't had as a child, what her father had given me as an adult, what I was trying to give myself: presence and family.

We talked about Grant over lunch, but unable to think much past the envelope in my purse, I told them Gloria and I needed to get home. Deanna understood, as she always did, and saw us to the door.

"You're going to read it when you get home?" she asked, tucking her arm into mine as Gloria ran out the front door and immediately bent to look for four-leaf clovers.

I nodded, my eyes already filling.

She turned me toward her. "You're going to be okay."

I nodded again, swallowing past the tears.

She shook her head. "Say it."

"I'm going to be okay."

She smiled, rested her forehead on mine, and whispered, "*We're* going to be okay."

"I don't know what I would do without you," I whispered back.

We separated, but we grabbed each other's hands, needing one more moment of contact.

"Let's not find out."

"Deal."

"I love you, Pen."

"I love you, Deanna."

When other people moved on, went about their routines, and couldn't remember how long it'd been since Grant had passed, Deanna would tuck her hand in mine and squeeze. Like me, she would always know when the world had changed.

∽

At home, I sat in one of the patio chairs Grant had handcrafted as Gloria and our dog, Bran, ran around in the backyard.

My hands shook as I loosened the seal and opened the flap. I had a flash of my brother's journal, the one I'd waited so long to read. I wouldn't make that same mistake again.

The yellowish parchment was thick and heavy, and the faint aroma of trail mix and nature wafted up from the page, what was—or rather had been—Grant.

As I pulled the paper from the security envelope, a key fell from the interior and onto the ground, where I left it, too hungry for the familiar handwriting I glimpsed as I unfolded the letter.

I read the first line and had to put it down again, tears blurring the words. When I was finally able to read on, I laughed out loud at the second sentence. It was so Grant, able to make me laugh even now.

My dearest Penelope,

Hi, my love. It's been a while, hasn't it?

I hope you miss me as much as I'm sure I miss you. Since I wrote this before I left, it's hard to say for certain. Perhaps I'm in a place where I can't miss anyone. But it's impossible for me to imagine a place where I wouldn't be missing you and Gloria.

We didn't have long, but even if we'd known each other our whole lives, from the very start, I'd still say it wasn't enough.

I looked up the definition of "soulmate": a person who is perfectly suited to another in temperament. *You* are perfectly suited to me. And though it might sound cheesy and clichéd . . . you are my soulmate. Maybe it's better said, you are my heart's refuge.

I pushed the letter into my chest, where my own heart expanded and contracted wildly.

I didn't have enough time with either of you. But my life ended at the time it was supposed to, when God intended. And I know you're still shaky on the idea, but my peace is founded in this. I'm where I belong, and you and Gloria are where you belong. And though we're not together in the way we were, *we still are*, my sweet Penelope. There's a piece of me that lives on in you, and I know I took a piece of you with me when I left.

My breath caught in my throat, and I blinked several times to clear my eyes.

I have no right to tell you how to grieve, but don't let the loss of me consume you. If the memory of me can't lift you up, then I fear I have lived in vain. Breathe in the scent of wildflowers in the wind for me. Feel the wind on your face, in your hair, for me. Savor the banana pudding for me. Listen to the early morning's bird call for me. Hold, hug, and kiss our daughter for me. And ride, Penelope, ride with abandon and joy, because I may not feel the burn in my thighs anymore, but I *am* there with you. I am now a part of the wildflower that touches your nose when you inhale its fragrance. My breath is in the wind that caresses your face. The memory of my spoon touches yours as you dip into that decadent pudding. My voice sings alongside the songbird, early in the morning when the earth is still. And my blood flows through the child just feet away from you now.

"Very little is needed to make a happy life; it is all within yourself, in your way of thinking. When you arise in the morning, think of what a precious privilege it is to be alive—to breathe, to think, to enjoy, to love."

Life is for the living. Live, Penelope. You don't need my permission, but you have my blessing. When you move past your grief, don't feel guilt. You cannot erase me, but your happiness enhances my memory. Live again. Love again. And most of all . . . ride again.

I love you. I love you. I love you. I love you. I love you. I love you. I love you. I love you. I love you. I love you.

Yours always,

Grant

P.S. Because I know you'll want to count them, there are ten "I love you's" because that's how many times you said it to me the first time. I counted.

P.P.S. Don't take Gloria when you use the key.

My heart was ripped from my chest and put back again. This letter, *this letter*, was Grant, a reminder that while he enhanced my happiness, he didn't create it, and neither did our child. The rest was on me—what I allowed in, what I allowed out—the little things, because they add up.

It was ironic; I was only able to cope with his death because of *him*.

I palmed the key, turned it over in my hand, and lifted the small tag attached to it. The word **CUBESMART**, in a red, all-caps font, was written at the top of the rectangular attachment with an address underneath. That was it. No instruction or explanation. A key and an address.

Reaching for my phone, I pulled up the map. The place was a storage facility five minutes away, one I'd probably passed a hundred times but familiarity had made invisible. My finger hovered over the figure of a little guy on a bicycle.

Once, and only once, I'd thrown my leg over my bike, in an effort to dispel grief. But the picture of Grant riding beside me had stilled my feet, and in the end, I'd sat crying beside the wheel, my bicycle turned on its side, where I'd thrown it after leaping off. And I'd declined every invitation to join the group rides since, feeling like it would be a betrayal somehow.

His letter made me feel like I could again, like I would again, but not now. I wasn't ready.

Spring was beginning to blossom, and I didn't mind the extra minutes the trip would take on foot. I sent a quick babysitting text, put a leash on Bran, and hoisted Gloria on my hip, ready for the walk across the street.

"Pen!" Devina's gravelly voice came from next door. "Grant's tree came today."

Before Grant died, he'd signed Devina up for a tree and/or flower of the month club to match the corresponding season, the gift that continued to give . . . for his chemo buddy.

I smiled and tamped down the swell of emotion that hovered just under the surface. She told me to bring Gloria over for cookies later as we hurried across the street, where my mother stood in her front yard. Yes, Aurora Auberge lived across the street.

A couple of months after the wedding, my mother had decided she wanted to be close, wanted to really work on our relationship, and had bought the house directly across from mine. She still struggled, fell back into her old ways at times, but she was trying. And to my surprise, I was happy to have her near.

"Morning Glory!" My mother lifted my daughter off the ground as we entered her yard. She was a grandmother, a real one, nothing like the mother I'd had. And she always called Gloria her little Morning Glory, from the earth, like her father.

"I'll be back as soon as I can," I said to my mother. Then I leaned over, kissed my daughter's head, and told her to be good for Grammy.

Gloria kissed my cheek. "Love you, Mommy."

"I love you too, Glory."

Grant's key burned in my hand, and I walked away, my mother holding my heart, a little girl in a pink tutu with a stuffed hammer in her hand, the one Grant had given to her right after she was born.

As soon as I saw the sign that matched the one in my hand, a giddy excitement flooded my abdomen.

I handed the key to the man behind the counter. "I need to find this unit."

He typed something into the computer, then looked up, wide eyed. "You're Penelope! Grant's Penelope!"

He knew Grant.

"I am. How do you . . ."

"Grant told me to be expecting you." Then his face fell. "That means . . ."

My head slowly worked its way up and down. "Grant passed three months ago."

The man exhaled, looked out the window, then turned back to me. "I'm sorry to hear that. He was a good guy."

I appreciated his condolences but, at the same time, didn't know what to do with them. I couldn't be sicker of "sorry" and "was," words people said because they didn't know what else to say.

"I'll take you to the unit."

We walked in silence, and then the man left me alone in front of a red door that rolled up from the bottom.

I whispered, "What do you have for me, Grant?" And I put the key into the lock.

I imagined the units around me, filled with boxes and bags, treasures homes couldn't contain. My foot tapped the pavement as the door finally ratcheted out of my way. And then I gasped.

In the middle of the unit stood the next best thing to finding Grant himself whole and well again.

"Gaia," I whispered as I walked over to the bicycle, my new best friend.

I rubbed my hand across the smooth blue metal, tears coming to my eyes, but these tears didn't hold sadness; they were simply the response of my body being unable to hold all my emotion inside. I recognized the pieces, the salvaged ones from Grant's beloved bicycle, melded with new ones, until it was a seamless masterpiece, old with new, experience with what was yet to come.

All around Gaia were smaller bicycles that graduated in size as you went clockwise around the space as well as a child-size trailer attachment.

I untied the envelope hanging on Gaia's handlebars and pulled out the simple card with a small picture of a bicycle on the front of it. Inside, it read:

> Penelope,
> As my Gloria grows, please give these bicycles and riding toys to her for all the Christmases and birthdays or momentous life events I will miss. When you do, let

her know they're from Daddy, the man who loves her more than she'll ever know.

Oh, and Gaia will ride again.

It just won't be me on the seat.

Ride, Penelope.

Into the future, with my past etched on my heart, I rode.

Author's note

This book wasn't meant to exist. At least, I didn't intend to write it. Its original form was meant to be an experimental short story, a personal challenge to myself to write something new. The characters had other ideas. As we got to know each other on the page, they broke through the confines I'd placed on them and took over. I'd set out to craft a simple love story, to take a set of made-up characters on a predefined journey. Instead, I found myself capturing their unique stories, personalities, and styles, no longer the artist but the scribe. I became the conduit for experiences that were somehow beyond me. I'm thankful to my characters—who I'm convinced are out there somewhere—for their vulnerability and willingness to share, for letting me into their beautiful story. It is my hope that their story touches other readers as much as it's touched me.

Acknowledgments

I almost don't want to include an acknowledgments page, for I am absolutely terrified I'll miss someone. But I'm inspired by Pen and Grant and won't let fear stop me.

First, to my husband, Stephen. For all the words at my fingertips, none are sufficient to convey my appreciation for you, with this book and with life in general. Hopefully you know how I feel.

To Aerie and Amorette, my two little inspirations. I work harder, run faster (figuratively because we all know I don't run), and dig deeper because you two are watching.

To my mother, Athena, a pillar of support. Thank you for always being there and giving me creative freedom. There is hardly a better gift.

To my writing and reader friends and critique partners who read multiple versions of this novel and helped guide it to its final form. To the ones who were there from the beginning, thank you from the bottom of my heart: Cheryl Rieger, Emily Whitson, and Meredith Lyons. An oh-so-special thank-you to Erin Quinn, reader extraordinaire and one of my biggest cheerleaders, Sam McEnhimer, who encouraged me to be true to myself, and Chanel Strandquist, fellow PA who helped inform Pen's Minnesotan roots. To the RPL long-form group: April Bailey, Becky Eagleton, Pam Jones, Dean Rieger, Tom Clouse, Maria Johnson, Michael Sobie, Tariq Lacen, Mark Rice,

Deke Smith, Michelle Thompson, and Daniel Rosas . . . you guys are sexy-and-you-know-it.

To those who helped me navigate the financial and medical worlds, giving this story depth of truth and real-life gravitas: Adam Parsons, master financial planner; Delyanne the Money Coach, whose social media materials I scoured; Hannah Harriman, my kindhearted therapist friend; and Dr. Carl Willis and his wife, Sonya, for being willing to answer my questions on an in-depth cancer case. Lots of information never made it to the book, but all that knowledge helped me craft a real-life scenario.

To my fantastic agent, Ariana Philips, who loved my story enough to want it out there in the world. I am forever grateful for your time, effort, and energy and for your belief in me and my characters.

To my magnificent acquiring editor, Maria Gomez, who fell in love with my words and gave this story wings. You are a dream maker.

To the perfect teammate, my incredible developmental editor, Angela James, who understood my story exactly and helped me refine my work until it shone, and to whom I, incidentally, still owe a box of tissues.

To my heroic copyeditor, Bill Siever, whose command of language, grammar, and attention to detail is not only impressive, but essential. Thank you for seeing the things that had become invisible (and for pointing out all the rules/regulations I didn't even realize were rules/regulations).

To Stephanie Chou, for proofreading and catching all the renegade typos that managed to sneak by everyone else. Thank you!

To Mary Ruth G., who evaluated how I handled emotional and mental health in this book. Your words of approval made my heart swell.

To Karah Nichols, production manager for this book. Thank you for your time, attention, and organization.

To everyone on the Montlake team who worked behind the scenes making this book a reality. I couldn't have been in better hands, and my gratitude is enormous.

Finally, to you, the reader: It is with tears in my eyes that I thank you. Thank you for picking up this book and living with my characters. With you, this story has found the home it began looking for from the very start.

About the Author

Photo © 2023 Christin Suzanne of Christin Suzanne Photography

Before Melissa Collings started writing women's fiction and romantic comedies, she worked as a surgical physician associate in Nashville, where one of her favorite procedures was reconstructing a lower-lumbar tattoo after a back surgery. Her stories, like her, are always a mix: light and dark, laughter and tears, outlandish and grounded, beautiful and ugly, glitter and charcoal smears. Her interests are way too varied; her imagination never fails to get her into trouble; and she lives by her life philosophy: nothing is impossible, and everything is better with glitter—except surgical wounds.